Dancing

The night seemed immense. I couldn't see anything further than three feet away. I could hear only the wind. Then the wind blew a hole in the clouds, and moonlight and starlight shot through, splattering on the upwardly sloping ground before me. I'd drifted more east than I wanted and began to work my way west.

When the wind paused, as though catching its breath, I could hear noises off to my left. Barefooted, Señora Ramirez stepped on a rock and moaned. I covered her mouth with a hand and listened, straining to hear above my own labored breathing.

Sounds grew louder and shadows raced across a patch of open ground, angling across our path. I called Gomez's name, but the wind was rising again and it caught the word and carried it away.

At the edge of vision there was a sudden flash of light. Orange flames were dancing across the roof of the bar. Smoke spiraled thickly upward. I could hear the crack and pops of burning timbers, followed by the higher, sharper report of a rifle. Exposed on the top of the slope, I hurried us down the other side. Señora Ramirez stumbled over vines and cursed under her breath whenever she stepped on something sharp.

Halfway down the slope I saw him. He was running hard, long hair flying out behind him. His gun was in his right hand. Head down, he headed straight for us. I drug the Colt out.

Twenty feet away he must have seen my shadow or smelled my fear. Instincts took over and he veered to his right, raising his head as he ran. Suddenly he stopped and the gun rose in his hand, black, obscene. I stared into the round black eye of his gun and listened to the Leather Man's ragged breathing. The Colt felt like an anvil in my hand, but I kept it still, pointed directly at the Leather Man's chest.

Table of Contents

What They Are Saying About Dancing on the Rim

Chris Helvey's noir novel takes the reader to the underbelly of Mexico, where it's nearly impossible to distinguish the good from the bad. Paul Hampton is a cynical, rich American who stumbles his way in an alcoholic stupor from one pitfall to another in a harsh and deadly environment that seldom shows mercy. He must slip the clutches of evil individuals and his own demons while seeking to find a way to escape across the border to the United States. Helvey's fluid writing will enthrall the reader with tight dialogue, lively characters, and descriptive images in this gritty tale of degradation and redemption.

—Michael Embry, author of John Ross Boomer Lit series

Dancing on the Rim

Chris Helvey

A Wings ePress, Inc.
General Fiction Novel

Wings ePress, Inc.

Edited by: Jeanne Smith
Copy Edited by: Joan C. Powell
Executive Editor: Jeanne Smith
Cover Artist: Trisha FitzGerald-Jung

All rights reserved

Wings ePress Books
www.wingsepress.com

Copyright © 2020 by: Chris Helvey
ISBN 978-1-61309-585-0

Published In the United States Of America

Wings ePress Inc.
3000 N. Rock Road
Newton, KS 67114

Dedication

For Myra Summers, in gratitude for all her amazing help and
unending patience over a literary lifetime.

One

They poured me into my boots and we sloshed across the border at Nogales.

I wobbled as we crossed the parking lot on the Arizona side, the asphalt going squishy and my head swimming in a sweet tequila haze. My companions, however, were annoyingly sober, and we stepped over into Mexico with only a disgusted look from the border guards. Even then the dirty looks came only from the Mexican side. Guards on the American side had given us only cursory glances. They were probably glad to see us go. What was another problem for old Mexico? One more drunk American surely wouldn't hurt.

I was too drunk to care, about that anyway. Worrying thoughts were drifting around in my brain, needling me when they felt like it. They'd been there for months; ignoring them seemed my approach.

Sunlight beat down without mercy on my bare head and I was suddenly very thirsty. I made up my mind to stop at the first bar. Jolene and Stan marched me through a shaded area where certain of the people headed north were pulled from the crossing line and forced to open their bags and packages. No one asked us to do anything.

We stepped out of the shade into a blinding sunlight. My brain throbbed and I tried to block the sun with my hands. Dark-skinned men and women sat behind blankets spread on broad sidewalks, white in the sunlight. Brightly colored trinkets were arrayed on top of the blankets: frogs, bulls, snakes, birds, and turtles. Some were ceramic and some were wooden; the ones I liked were plastic. They had heads and tails that swiveled on coiled springs. Standing behind one of the blankets, a fat man picked up a purple and gold turtle and gently wiggled his hand. The turtle's head bobbed up and down while his tail swiveled from side to side.

"You like, *señor*? Isn't he cute? Only two dollars American."

I gently poked the turtle's head with the tip of my finger. His head bobbed faster.

"Look *señor*, he likes you."

Someone tugged at my arm. "Come on, honey, you don't want to mess with a plastic turtle."

My wife always knows what's best for me. At least she thinks she does. Lately, she'd been getting on my nerves. But then I figured I'd been on hers for some time.

"Just a minute, Jolene. I want to look at the man's turtle. Might just buy it." I smiled at the turtle man.

"*Sí, señor.*"

"No, honey. You don't need any more junk. You've been on a buying binge for weeks."

"Afraid I'll run out of money?"

"Of course she isn't," Stan said. He moved closer and placed a hand against my elbow. I didn't like him standing so close. He was a big man, well over six feet. It was like standing in the shadow of a mountain. I'd liked him better when we first met in Vegas. Had that been only a month ago? Life was slipping away, teasing me from just beyond my reach. I needed a drink more than ever.

Oh yeah, even polluted, old Paul Hampton saw more than most people did sober. I'd seen the way my wife looked at me when she thought I was on the far side, and the way her eyes transformed to frozen marbles when I did something foolish. All those glances that had flashed between her and our fine new friend hadn't gone unnoticed either.

My wife was a difficult woman to please. At least I'd never been able to do it, not fully. She liked her extracurricular pleasures. As long as she kept them out of sight and let me drink in peace, I usually didn't mind. Lately though—

Voices prodded my ears. Sighing, I turned toward the sounds.

"Let's go have a drink," the mountain said. Stan was some guy—he could block the sun and read minds. He also made me nervous. His kind had crossed my path before. Friendly, helpful, eager to please, he was the trained snake that smiled as he sank his fangs into your flesh. Why I put up with him was yet another question I was avoiding. Call me the King of Avoidance. I decided to drown all the unanswerable questions.

I gave the turtle's purple nose a final push and left him bobbing like Jell-O in the fat man's hand. "Okay," I said. "Lead the way."

Pressure increased on the inside of both elbows as Jolene and Stan steered me down a sidewalk that seemed to undulate slightly and gently drift away from my feet.

Just before we reached the first corner, I turned and looked back. Wet black eyes stared at me. They seemed full of sadness and I was suddenly full of anger. To hell with the fat man and his nasty wet eyes. Straightening my back, I whirled around, jerked free and pushed ahead of my wife and our newest friend. Damn the fat man, anyway.

Halfway down the block, a man in a clean white shirt and trousers stood next to a mangy-looking burro hitched to a green and white cart that needed a paint job. Behind the cart a large curving sign read *Nogales, Mexico.* Next to it a small hand-painted sign on a short wooden pole advertised:

Photographic Souvenirs of Nogales
$2.00 American

Jolene and Stan wanted me to have my picture taken. I wanted a drink.

"Oh, go on, honey. That burro is so cute. It will make a great picture for the den."

"That burro looks half dead," I said.

Stan chuckled, the way only men in movies chuckle. "No, no, he's only half asleep."

"Bullshit, or should I say, donkey shit."

Fingernails dug into my left arm. Jolene's lips were curved in a smile, but her eyes were hard. "Oh, come on, Paul. I want a picture of you and the donkey. Just one quick photo and then we'll all have a drink."

"Yes," said Stan, gripping my right arm, "We want a picture of you and the donkey. It will make a nice way for you to remember Mexico."

Yeah, a couple of jackasses preserved forever. I didn't want to have my picture made, period, let alone with a Mexican burro with a skin disease. Why were they so insistent? What the hell good was one more lousy photograph? Dust coated the photo albums at home.

Something was wrong with the whole setup; I just couldn't figure out what. At the moment my head hurt too badly for serious thinking. Promising myself deep meditation on the issue at a more opportune time, I allowed them to lead me down the sidewalk.

The man watched us closely. Lights powered up in his mud brown eyes. "Ah, three amigos who want their picture taken. A souvenir of old Mexico."

"No, no," Jolene said, "*Uno* photo. This man." She pointed at me.

"Ah, I see. The señor, yes. Very good. You will treasure this photograph forever, *señor*. It will always remind you of the wonderful times you had in Nogales."

He gestured at the cart with one hand while he slipped the other under my left elbow. "If you will just step into the cart, *señor*." He gave me a boost and a broad smile that revealed yellow teeth. He smelled of onions, garlic and sweat, tinged with sweet cologne.

Jolene dug in her money belt and gave the man two dollars. He began fussing with his camera. Sitting sullenly on the hard bench, I stared into the sun and smelled burro butt while sweat gathered on my face like liquid pimples.

Finally he snapped the shutter on the dilapidated looking camera and I climbed down and wiped my face. Then we had to stand around broiling while the picture developed. Nothing was going right and my gut said it was only going to get worse.

The finished photo was exactly what I figured—a waste of two dollars. It was unclear from the overexposed image whether the donkey or I was more disgusted.

Giving Stan and Jolene a dirty look, I started walking. They hurried after me with Jolene clutching the photograph in one hand and waving at the photographer with the other. He called after us, but I wasn't listening.

We stepped around the corner and into the deep shade of Hidalgo Street. A white stucco building rose three stories above us. It was cooler in the shade, and for that I was thankful.

My eyes wandered across the storefronts on both sides of the street. A *farmacia*, a bank, a few souvenir shops, and one shell of a building that had been burnt out of business. No bar on the block, but an old yellow and tan dog with ribs showing sprawled in the sun at the next corner.

"Damn, Jolene. What sort of hellhole have you brought us to? I need a drink and there's not a damn bar for miles." I took another look around, but the only thing of interest I saw was an uncultivated cat with green Egyptian eyes crouched on a turquoise window ledge, ignoring me with a certain majesty.

"Oh, come on, Paul," Stan said. "I've been to Nogales many times and never could go more than a block or two before running across a drinking place."

"Well, we had better damn well be running across one soon, before I die of thirst." In the side streets of eternal Mexico, dying seemed a distinct possibility.

"Honey, it's not that bad." Jolene slipped her arm through mine and pulled me close. Her perfume was a mixture of jasmine and honeysuckle. Sweat beaded above her upper lip.

Years of sunlight had faded the street sign to near illegibility. Between the buildings the air had gone dark and quiet.

"Maybe it's not for you," I said. "But it only gets better for me when I get a drink."

"Hush, honey, we'll be there soon."

"Be where soon?"

"Oh, just some place to get a drink. We'll be there before you know it." She mopped at her forehead with a square of white lace.

With the walking and talking and sweating, I was beginning to sober up. My head felt like it was starting to crack open like a melon left too long on the vine. These days it always seemed to hurt when I tried to think, especially when I was sober. Which was why I tried to drink as much and think as little as possible. At times I wondered if I might have a brain tumor, which made me want a drink even more.

A man wearing a sombrero called to us in Spanish from a stall lined with leather belts and wallets and purses. However, I was far more interested in liquor than leather, so I gave him the Mexican shrug and marched on. Jolene's fingers were tracing ancient Mayan symbols on my arm and flies were buzzing around my face. My brain throbbed.

I jerked away and hustled across a patch of sunlight, turned a corner, and came out on another street with no name.

A bouncy brassy blues tune was drifting among the smells of old dogs, aging garbage, grilled onions, crushed peppers, sweat, whiskey and the faint sweet hint of adventure. The concoction smelled like Mexico to me, and it almost quenched my thirst.

The blues were flowing from a bar midway down the block. Above the dark door in red letters were the words EL REVUELO. I didn't know what that meant, but I could hear the clink of glasses and exuberant voices and laughter; I knew a bar when I heard it.

~ * ~

When my eyes had grown accustomed to the dimness, I could see a polished wooden bar fronted by high-legged stools on the left and a dozen tables flung haphazardly across the right side of the room. Each table was ringed by straight-backed chairs and at the far end of the room was a small dance floor. Beyond the dance floor was an oblong stage where a three-piece band played with more passion than precision. Actually, it might have been a four-piece band, as one man kept wandering on and off stage. A couple of times he picked up an instrument, a tambourine, a triangle, but put them down without adding much to the melody.

"He's drunk," I said to nobody in particular as I made my way to the bar and climbed on the leather-covered stool closest to the door, put both elbows on the polished wood and waited for the bartender to find me. He was polishing shot glasses. Once he spotted me he put a smile on and ambled my way.

He sported a black walrus mustache, full lips, unpolished obsidian eyes, and slicked-back hair that glistened like polished jet.

"*Buenas tardes, señor.*"

"I'll have a brandy, double, *por favor.*"

His smile eased wider. "Cognac, *doble - sí.*"

"Quickly."

"*Sí, rápidamente, doble.*" He turned and waddled down the bar. He was quite fat, and with his long black hair, dark clothes, and brown skin he looked like a rather dilapidated bear.

He was quick with his hands, however, and he poured a fine snifter of brandy. I was savoring the first drink when my wife showed up with our fine new friend in tow. Behind the bar, the Mexican brown bear was heading our way. Only a handful of customers were in El Revuelo and they all appeared to be nursing tall glasses of cerveza. Three free-spending gringos promised to be the life of the party.

Soft fingers, like furry spider legs, stroked the back of my neck. I shrugged them off.

"Here you are," she said, as if that meant something.

"Yes, here I sit."

"We've been looking all over for you."

"South of what border?"

"What?"

"Never mind."

"That looks good, Paul," Stan said in a nicely rounded baritone. He was getting to be a real swell fellow, and he was getting on my nerves. We'd known Stan only a few weeks. A stray thought crossed my mind—maybe we didn't know him at all.

I waved my glass at the bear. When he had nodded, I turned toward Stan. "Only my real friends call me Paul."

"Aren't I your real friend?" Stan smiled at me, sharing his mouthful of extraordinarily white teeth. His blue eyes twinkled as he put a hand on my shoulder.

"Sure, you're my good friend since Vegas, since Jolene and I loaned you two thousand to square your markers and bought you steaks and champagne and God knows what else." I let his hand stay where it was; it was too much trouble to shrug it off.

"But I've been driving and making all the hotel arrangements."

"Yeah, you're wonderful." I took another healthy sip and waited for the glow.

"Stan, order me a gin and tonic." Jolene was speaking in her little girl voice, the one that used to make my blood roil. Now it made me half-nauseous.

"And put it on Paul's tab. Oh, and get yourself something cool."

I sat on my stool and stared at the stupid looking son-of-a-bitch in the mirror that ran the full length of the bar, trying to figure out the equation. I didn't like any of the people in the mirror. They looked like people in a painting Edward Hopper might have done on phenobarbital. Too much truth always seemed dangerous to me. Eyeballing my brandy, I listened to Stan order *una gintonic* and whiskey American. His Spanish was fluent. I wished I'd studied harder in school.

The music switched to a slower rhythm and I felt the urge to dance. After one song, Jolene wouldn't dance with me, and neither would any of the other women at the bar. I consoled myself with brandy and told Stan about the time I made two million dollars off a Japanese businessman who thought he wanted something I had. I could have told Mr. Aikido that he didn't really want it, but sometimes it's better to let people find out things on their own.

I went to the bathroom and did my business, washed my hands and face and combed my hair. Between the drink and the wash I felt like I might live. I decided to tell Stan about the high-rise my father had left me in Chicago, but when I returned my new friend was dancing with my wife.

The glow was coming on strong and I smiled at the decadent looking bastard in the mirror. The bear behind the bar was giving me funny looks and I wanted to tell him to go away, but my tongue felt warped. So I sipped brandy and stared at the poor sad fuck in the mirror staring back at me. The glow grew steadily larger and brighter.

After a while the bartender's looks changed to dirty ones, as though he was disgusted with me. When I pointed this out to Jolene and Stan, they agreed with me and we all retired to a table near the dance floor.

People were flowing into the bar. Most were couples who wanted to dance. Blues transitioned to energetic dance rhythms, sliding into a slow song now and then to let the dancers, and the band, catch their breath. It was pleasant to sip good brandy and watch the handsome couples swirl around the floor. Faces shone in the soft light. I started to feel human.

Our waitress came over to check on us. She had long dark hair that rose and fell as she walked, midnight eyes, and a sad soft mouth.

Jolene waggled her fingers at the girl. "We want to switch to champagne."

"We do?"

"Yes, we do. Don't we, Stan?"

"Sure."

"Good," Jolene said. "Now tell us what you have."

The girl named three or four brands. Her Spanish words were soft and sibilant and fell on my ears like soft sweet rain. The glow was growing stronger with each sip and the world was receding, becoming smaller and darker, leaving more room for the fine golden glow. So long as they left me alone, I didn't care if they drank champagne or swamp water.

The girl with the soft sad mouth brought the champagne in a silver bucket brimming with ice. I would never have figured El Revuelo for a champagne sort of place. She poured a little into a fluted glass and Jolene tilted the glass and let golden liquid roll around on her tongue while she did strange things with her eyes. Then she smiled and stroked the girl's arm and told her in Spanish how pretty she was and to pour us all a glass full. I kept my mouth shut. The fact I could understand a little of the language was my business, not my wife's. Keeping a few things to myself seemed to be a good idea.

My wife and our friend were whispering. All I could catch was the word "late." When they thought I wasn't watching they flicked quick glances toward the back of the bar. I was curious, but not enough to do anything about it. They seemed to be waiting for something, but then I'd been waiting my whole life.

Waiting for what? That was a different question altogether. One I'd never quite been able to answer. One that I wasn't sure I wanted to answer.

The waitress smiled at me as she poured my champagne. I smiled back and waited for the glow blossoming in the west to cover the world and consume my mind. The champagne tasted fine and so did the Jefferson Reserve that followed. After the whiskey, the room and the people and the night all began to flow together in a tide of molten gold that carried me beyond the rim.

Somewhere in the bowels of the night a woman came up to me and asked me to dance. She was short and plump and her face was eroded with small craters, like the side of a crumbling mountain. Her eyes were bottomless.

"I'm not much of a dancer," I said.

"What can it hurt?" Her voice was thick, as though her throat were growing together.

"I might fall down, or even hurt you."

"I will catch you falling. You cannot hurt me."

She put out a hand and I slid one of mine in hers. Her skin was smooth, but I could feel bones and sinews working underneath. We crossed the dance floor out of step until we found a dark corner.

The trio had gone into one of their slow numbers and she put her face against my chest. Her black hair reflected the light, and her scent was honeysuckle highlighted with midnight. Her body pressed against me until we were one, swaying like palm trees in a tropical breeze. Tension I hadn't realized was there began to flow out of my body.

"What's your name?"

"I could tell you anything," she said, "and how would you know if it was a lie?"

I buried my face in the black waterfall of her hair. I wondered if Jolene was watching. Glancing up, I saw that she and Stan were dancing at the edge of the light, moving well together, like old dance partners. Watching them, I considered the dancing girl's question.

"I would know. You're not the kind of person who would lie."

"Then you must not ask me true questions."

"Are there other kinds?"

"Oh yes," she said. "There are polite questions and insincere questions and rhetorical questions and questions that have no meaning and questions that have no answer." She spoke soft, modestly accented English that I had to strain to hear above the music.

"And what questions do you ask?" I murmured.

Dancing woman rubbed the softness of her face up and down against my chest. "I ask the sort of questions that men like to answer."

"Do they answer you with the truth?"

"I have known men too well for too long to think of them except as they are."

"And how are they?"

"Because you are one, you know," she whispered as the music downshifted. She pulled me closer in the dark. We danced as one until the music changed again. She kissed me with butterfly lips and disappeared into the smoky dimness. As I walked myself back to my chair, my cheek seemed to burn where her lips had pressed against my flesh.

Minute by minute the glow grew, a hydrogen bomb exploding in slow motion, until the entire world was the color of a sunburned peach, encircled by a thin black rim.

Dancers swirled with a nauseating vigor, and I eased back on my chair, closed my eyes, and focused on the gold, then the rim, then the gold again.

I need the glow. I needed to escape. I needed the glow to escape. Soft breath, tinged with alcohol, caressed my cheek.

"Join me in a rattlesnake, darling?" Jolene pressed one hand on my shoulder.

I shook my head.

"Oh, come on, honey."

"They're too sweet."

"Just one? Stan is going to have one with me."

"Chocolate in liquor doesn't agree with me."

Fingers slid inside my shirt, ruffling the hair on my chest. Once her touch would have excited me.

"You don't want Stan taking your place do you, big boy? Thought you could hold your own when it came to liquor. You're not going to disappoint little old me again, are you?"

"All right, if you'll just shut up." I had the glow now and I didn't need any more alcohol. Just thinking about another drink made me half sick, but it was worse hearing Jolene carry on. All I wanted was to lose myself in the glow. However, I knew she wouldn't shut up about the damn rattlesnake until I drank one or passed out.

She said, "Make it a double."

Fuck you, bitch, I thought. I didn't say it though. Instead, I smiled and kept my eyes closed and focused on the glow.

Smooth coolness caressed my hand and I raised the glass to my lips without opening my eyes. Damn drink was way too sweet, nasty all the way down. I drank it in slow anaconda rhythms. A soft hand cupped my elbow and I opened my eyes and stood. Jolene whispered something to Stan. Her lips moved in slow motion. Stan's left arm slid around my back and we started walking. The room was swirling, so I closed my eyes and watched the molten gold spill over the rim and turn to blue-black silence as deep and dark and cold as glacier ice. My legs turned into rubber. A roaring ocean surged in my ears and I tumbled head first into a chasm of unrelenting blackness.

~ * ~

Somewhere in the cosmos an unseen hand flicked a switch and I floated back from a twilight zone.

My brain was clear the way your brain becomes when you pass out and come to in that brainwave cycle where every image is crystal.

I was sprawled in a wooden chair in the darkest corner of the bar. The band was playing a slow song. People were dancing. It was like watching an old Hollywood film. Time ticked inside my skull, an amplified metronome.

My wife and her friend were missing in action. Moving my head as little as possible, I searched for them. Faces by El Greco flowed in a montage before me. Stan and Jolene were across the dance floor standing in the shadows, talking to a man whose face I couldn't see.

In the hallway of warped mirrors that lined the corridors of my mind, it was clear that I was the odd man out. Surely goodness and mercy were not with me. Promises had been withdrawn. Time to explore new lands, find safer harbors. The scent of my fear swirled through the warm air like the stench of rotting orchids.

The ice that had encased my mind was melting. My brain seemed filled with smoke. Time to pull a Kerouac. Waiting for old Lefty Godot wasn't getting me anywhere.

Moving in rhythm with the languorous dancers, I pushed myself upright. My legs seemed far away. Stilt-walking, I headed for the door that beckoned from the far end of a long, dark, shrinking tunnel. On the far side were the night winds. They were calling my name.

Two

I woke with my face stuffed in a pile of dog shit.

At least it smelled that way.

My eyes were stuck shut.

I tried to raise my head, but the damn thing felt like a cement block. Blind, a scream rose in my throat, but all I produced was an unnatural gurgle. Crying seemed like a viable option, but my eyes were still stuck shut so there was nowhere for the tears to run.

For some small slice of eternity, I lay very still with my face in a stinking slimy pool; I was afraid to guess what it was. I simply lay there, trying to keep my mind still, waiting. I wasn't sure what I was waiting for. Maybe I was waiting for the dawning of a new day, or someone to rescue me, or a miracle.

Sensory data began to seep in. I could hear the buzzing of a fly and feel the warmth of sunlight on my neck. I was pleased I wasn't dead, until I considered the possibility I was dead and eternity was nothing more than face down in a shit-hole.

After a while I began to sweat, and that made me doubt I had crossed over. Sweat in heaven didn't seem appropriate and, though the present was certainly uncomfortable, hell figured to be a lot worse. A gauzy memory of the bluesy bar drifted across my mind and I realized groggily that I needed to get moving.

Behind me I could hear noises, blaring horns, squealing brakes, creaking metal. I told myself to get up. On the fifth try I made it, rolled over and faced the noises.

I rubbed at my eyes with my knuckles and broke them open. A paved street lay before me, wide and white in the morning sun. My head throbbed.

Eyesight was improving now and I could see I was lying in a narrow trough that ran between the street and the concrete sidewalk and served as combination rain drain, garbage repository, and sewer system. A couple inches of brown water lined the trench. Abominations floated in the water: a sun-scalded cat, a dead bird, plus things no longer identifiable, rotting and stinking. In an instant I was sick at my stomach.

After I recovered enough strength, I pushed myself up onto my hands and knees and from there onto my feet. Then I stepped out of the pool of my own vomit that had formed around me like a plaster cast setting up and stumbled up onto the sidewalk.

Like a dying elephant returning to the elephant graveyard, I shuffled uncertainly on legs that felt like they were on loan, sweat running down into my eyes, a burning saline baptism. Half blind, I staggered on until my legs quivered and the sidewalk shimmered. At the end of a block a bench rose like a mirage. Stumbling at the edge, I got one hand on the top slat and pulled myself aboard hand over hand.

The bench was missing two back rails and peeling paint like green dandruff. I sat quietly in the white-hot sunlight and let the world wobble on its axis in its own way and in its own time. Grateful to be alive, I was also confused. Nothing was making any sense. Trying to think only made my head hurt worse.

I must have dozed because the next time I looked up, the sun had crossed the median and shadows were spilling out from the scraggly trees and buildings and telephone poles into the street. The air was so hot it was as if the oxygen were being sucked out by the heat. Baking in the sunlight, I sat watching the shadows grow. It seemed the thing to do. My memory was on vacation.

It came back in stages, notes in a minor key. Sunlight soaked the alcohol out and intelligent thoughts seeped in like water invading porous rock. Nightmares of the day before flickered like old Buster Keaton outtakes. My right eye developed a tic. Dryness coated the inside of my mouth. I closed my eyes.

Voodoo images rose. After a while they swirled into focus, the faces of my wife and Stan. Messages from another dimension. But I couldn't decipher the code.

Brakes squalled down the street. As I looked up into the distorted checkerboard of sun and shadow, a memory escaped. I could see Stan and Jolene, their heads close together, leaning on each other, whispering words beyond my hearing.

A kaleidoscope of memory fragments coalesced in my forebrain, all the wasted years no more than dry locust husks, all the could-have-beens and the might-have-beens and the should-have-beens, all the potential hollowed out from the core. Shame mingled with fears as I stared at the sidewalk, flat and white under an unrelenting sun. Gradually, I became aware of a tremor rocking my body; it was as if the earth itself were quaking. Looking down I could see my right knee rising and falling like a pneumatic jack hammer. Pushing myself off the bench, I stumbled down the sidewalk in search of something to drink. Thirst was consuming me. For once, the contents of the bottle didn't need to be alcoholic.

Sweat washed over me and my hands trembled, but my legs were working better and the nausea had subsided. Seeking shade, I walked along the edge of the sidewalk, keeping one eye out for my wife and our fine new friend. It was obvious my good health wasn't their primary concern. I walked where there were trash cans and benches and telephone poles to grab when my legs went shaky.

Older model cars, replete with rust, broken windows, bald tires, and peeling paint, crouched alongside the curb like metal dinosaurs. Their seats were full of boxes and bags and half-eaten food, dirty clothes, crumpled newspapers, and paperback books with florid covers and titles in Spanish. Crosses were affixed to cracked dashboards, while rosary beads and St. Christophers hung from rearview mirrors. Tires were balding and the car bodies seemed to be hung together with bondo, bumper stickers, and hand-painted block lettering.

Sometimes men and women sold from the trunks of their cars: fruits and vegetables, rabbits in cages, gold-plated jewelry. Sometimes they dozed behind the wheel. Dogs trotted purposefully down the pavement and small dark birds flitted from telephone wires to trees, while large, bottle-green flies buzzed above the open trash cans at the corners.

Before they got a good look at my face, a couple of shop owners called for me to come in and inspect their glorious merchandise. Most of the Mexicans glanced at me with dark eager eyes, then ignored me behind closed, hard faces. Few tourists braved the afternoon heat and those that did were far more interested in bargains and air-conditioned shops than a hung-over *hombre* drifting along the edge of their world. I gave their poochie bellies, varicose veins, and toe-strap sandals plenty of room. At the end of the fourth block I found a small grocery store.

Inside it was nearly dark. High above the wooden floor a brass ceiling fan lazily stirred moist air. There was a nostalgic aura to the place, as if I'd been there before in another life. From behind the counter, a fat man watched me as I worked my way down one of three narrow, crowded aisles.

Amber bottles of beer gleamed in the dull light, but what I needed was water. I came to a cooler filled with bottle water. Sliding the glass door open, I reached as far as I could into the case.

I pulled the plastic top off a bottle and thumbed the black nipple open as I raised the bottle to my lips. Tilting my head back, I let cool liquid run across my lips and over my tongue and down my throat until I had to come up for air. I pulled out two more water bottles from the case, followed by a six-pack of beer in amber bottles, then walked toward the register. The fat man eyeballed me as I reached for my wallet.

It wasn't there, not in my left rear pocket where it was supposed to be. Quickly, I patted myself down. All my Mexican cash was gone, and, worse, so were my credit cards. Then I remembered I'd been carrying three hundred-dollar bills in a special liner in my right rear pocket. Sighing with relief, I reached for them. All my fingers found were lint and air.

With a growing sense of desperation, I began a pocket-by-pocket search, turning each one inside out. Except for a dirty handkerchief and a black plastic comb that was guaranteed not to break, the back two were empty. In the right front pocket there was a key to a Cadillac and two peppermints melted inside plastic wrappers. I wondered who had rolled me. Finally, in the left front pocket, I found some loose change and a couple of crumpled dollar bills.

Pointing at the bottles, I asked "How much?"

Before he named an amount, the man looked me over carefully. He spoke slowly, enunciating each syllable as if he were speaking to a child. His English sounded old and tired, as if he used up most of his supply a long time ago. His dark eyes never left my face.

I counted out the bills and change. Two beers short, I pulled the offending bottles out of the carton and placed them quietly on the counter. Then I put the bills on the counter next to the rest of the beer and the water bottles. The coins I stacked on top of the bills. I was in enough of a hole already; I didn't need more trouble. Fear makes a man act differently.

He counted the money twice, moving his lips slowly, then nodded at me and stuffed the water and four beers into a paper bag without speaking.

I turned and walked down a narrow aisle. Shadows were sliding toward the center of the street, but the heat still rose to greet me as I stepped out the door. Behind me in the dark, little store the fan whirled.

At the edge of the sunlight I paused, uncertain which way to turn. Uncertainty was a condition with which I was on speaking terms.

Like shards of a bad dream, distorted images swirled through my mind, mixed with memories of whispered words and looks I hadn't been supposed to hear or see and odd actions that had seemed merely curious at the time. The fog was lifting. I twisted the cap off an amber bottle and turned left.

The afternoon was strangely silent, as if all life had withdrawn from the heavy air. Nothing was moving on either street or sidewalk and as I walked, my footsteps rang hollowly. Blue shadows spilled silently into the street, reaching for each other with dark, quivering fingertips. Other lonely journeys flashed through my mind like quicksand highways.

At the corner I paused and sipped beer while I waited for inspiration to strike. More memory fragments were rising to the surface and as they coalesced I stayed closer to the shadows and kept an eye out for familiar profiles. I hadn't figured out everything, just enough to be wary.

Without warning, the street lost its sidewalks and turned into an alley. Broken, buckled pavement twisted between three and four story buildings that rose on each side like gray, concrete cliffs. Soon the passage was so narrow that by stretching out my arms I could brush fingertips against rough walls. The world was closing in and I tipped the bottle and drained it.

Little light seeped through the openings between the buildings. I soldiered on, drinking as I moved. Once I stopped and the air was so still I could hear myself breathing. After that it seemed important that I should walk very quietly.

Another walk from another time crept across my mind. I had been young, maybe ten or twelve, a Boy Scout on a camping trip. My father, a sort of an unofficial scout master, had been along and on the second or third day, for some reason I could no longer remember, we'd quarreled. The exact words had faded long ago, but I'd called him names I shouldn't even have known and stomped off into the woods, shouting over my shoulder that I was going to walk back to the road and hitchhike home and that he could go to hell.

I'd heard him call my name and started running. My father had a game leg from the war and there was no way he was going to scramble to his feet and catch me. I distinctly remember laughing as I ran.

For the first couple of hours that afternoon it had been fun. Reasonably sure of my way, I made what I thought was good progress. I expected to see the highway well before dark.

Only as dusk began to fall without my even hearing a car did doubts begin. Night comes early in the woods and long before it was totally dark I was so scared I was trembling. Sounds came from all angles. Some I recognized: birds fluttering in the trees, squirrels moving among fallen leaves, the hoot of an owl. Others, unknown, terrified me.

Sometime in that long night I began to cry. Before daylight I had wet myself. By the time they found me the next day, I was nearly hysterical. My father had only hugged me and said he loved me, but that I had surely worried a lot of people. I hadn't spoken all the way home.

That walk had been almost a lifetime ago. Now I was taking another, one just as full of doubts, only my father wouldn't be there to hug me and dry my tears and tell me everything was going to be all right. Now I knew better. Everything was never going to be all right again. However, as I walked down the empty Nogales alley, I could see things could be better. I could also see that any change was up to me, a sobering thought. In that moment I could almost convince myself that I could do it.

Eventually another street sprinkled with sunlight lay ahead. Across that street was a park. Grass covered the earth after a fashion and a few small trees threw shade. The shade looked soft and cool. I tossed my empty beer bottle in a trash can and crossed the empty street.

There were no benches in the park, but where there was grass it was soft. I found a spot with a good view of the street and sat with my back against a tree. Drinking another beer, I watched the shadows stretch across the pavement from both sides of the street until they caressed each other.

After a few minutes, images of Stan and Jolene began to parade across my mind. When those images faded, I could clearly see the panorama of my stupidity. How could I have been so blind? Drunkenness was only a mirage I had painted for myself to obscure the desert of a life I had created.

Say what you will about Mexico and beer, taken together in moderation they form a serum of honesty. It was disgusting to sit there and peer back over my life. Except for a few business successes, it seemed no more than a never ending montage of cowardice, failure, and drunkenness. The worst thing was I didn't have the usual excuses—a poor childhood, abusive parents, a cleft palate. Business dealings belonged to another realm altogether, and their rewards seemed paltry.

After the shadows touched, the afternoon began to come alive. A truck motor groaned to life. A telephone rang five times before it was answered, or the caller gave up. Just as the phone quit ringing, a brown and yellow dog came trotting around the corner. He crossed the street without looking and came steadily toward me.

His tongue hung out and saliva ran down and dripped on the asphalt. Brown eyes were fixed on me, but he didn't look like a mad dog nor a dangerous one. Ten yards out, he slowed and dropped his nose to the ground, then came on, sniffing the spotty grass and dust ponds.

When he reached me he raised his head with his mouth open as if he wanted a drink of my beer. I told him beer wasn't good for a dog and scratched him behind the ears. He exhaled hot doggy breath in my face and dripped saliva onto my trousers. When he was tired of me, he shook his head and padded across the park with his tail curving into the air.

By then the air was noticeably cooler and the light had begun to fade and I started to wonder where I would spend the night; a grassy bed in the park was better than slumbering in the gutter, but a soft bed in an air-conditioned hotel sounded wonderful. Of course, even the crummiest hotels cost money.

With my wallet missing, I didn't have either credit cards or cash. If I didn't want to spend another night under the stars, I needed to find help. Jolene and alcohol had been my shelters in recent years. Now neither seemed an acceptable choice.

I recognized my weaknesses, even if I failed to voice them. Perhaps I was pathetic; I was not certifiably stupid. Jolene and Stan were both more and less than they appeared. I'd been a fool. Probably still was, only I wasn't quite so blind now. Perhaps I was paranoid, but a voice at the back of my brain kept whispering that my wife wanted me out of the way.

I lined up my two empties in front of the tree and pushed myself off the ground. What to do and where to go were the operative questions. As usual, I had no answers. My head was starting to throb, the hammering pulse reminding me I was alive.

Around me the air was still, as close and hot as the breath of an unseen god. In the gathering dusk one pathway seemed as good or bad as another, so I started walking across the grass, following the path the dog had taken.

Three

Shadows merged until they became one with the gathering dusk. Lights came on in shops and atop tall street lamps. Traffic was heavier; cars and trucks and motorcycles performed a laborious bump-and-grind. Black asphalt glistened under their lights. Shadow creatures formed, grew, vanished abruptly, then grew full again, only to bleed to death against the encompassing dark.

The churning had settled in my stomach and my leg muscles tapped an unknown reservoir and I walked on, past shop doors closing against the night and tired people hurrying into the darkness and streets with no names and dogs with no tails and beggars with no legs and women with no smiles for me. Sounds seemed smothered by the dusk and the smell of rotting fruit encompassed all.

The last of my beer was gone and the water in the final bottle unpleasantly warm in my mouth. I swallowed it anyway and crossed the street against traffic. On the far side of the shining asphalt there were lights and music and raised voices mingling. Perfume, sweeter than the night air, teased me. Scents of alcohol and burning tobacco drifted from open doors. I was a steel ball drawn to a magnet.

Horns blew and men cursed, but I walked on. Traffic parted and I stepped out of the dark edge of the street onto the sidewalk and through the open door into the light. I recognized that a bar was the worst place for me, but in order to think I needed a drink.

23

Loud music and the clinking of glass, mixed with the laughter of women greeted me. Running through the cacophony was the constant, throbbing, guttural, rhythmic sound of people talking. Unable to understand the excited Spanish, I felt the pulse of the words merging with the music. Bottles gleamed in untidy rows behind the high bar and the old familiar urge swept over me. Sidestepping a fat man in a too-tight *gringo* suit, and ignoring the voices of unseen prophets inside my head, I strode toward the bar.

Red glazed pottery bowls were scattered across the dark wood. Nuts and chips and pretzels nestled in them. My stomach reminded me I hadn't eaten all day. I scooped a handful of peanuts in a dirty palm and shoved the load between my lips. Milk and honey they were not, but then I'd been wandering in the wilderness for only one day.

I was munching on the third handful when one of the men working behind the bar strolled over, glanced at the nearly empty bowl, then stared at me. He had a gold incisor you could see when he smiled, and sometimes when he didn't.

"What will you have, *señor*?" His English was accented, but light years ahead of my Spanish.

"Whiskey."

"With soda?"

"Straight, in a tall glass. Water on the side."

He nodded and turned toward the bottles. I grabbed another handful of peanuts. As I popped them into my mouth, I remembered I didn't have any money. I kept on chewing. You never knew when luck might start running again. Besides, I was an American, a rich one. A millionaire who just didn't happen to have any money at the moment. Surely the Mexicans would understand. After all, we were supposed to be good neighbors. A phone call or two should do the trick; it had always worked before.

Finishing the peanuts, I started in on the pretzels. They were thin and salty. By the time the man with the gold tooth returned bearing gifts, I was very thirsty and glad to see him. Gifts had a nice ring to it. Gifts did not have to be paid for. Perhaps this night would work out after all. A little cooperation could smooth out the jagged edges.

Gold Tooth put two white napkins on the counter and set the whiskey and water on top. He showed me his gold as he told me how much I owed. I tried for an expression that showed I didn't understand.

"Two dollars," he said again.

"Just put it on my tab, *por favor*," I said, returning his smile.

He stared at my face hard; he would remember. Then he lowered his unsmiling brown eyes and wrote briefly on a small notepad with the stub of a pencil.

Watching him wander down the bar, I sipped at the whiskey. The iron band around my head began to ease. I took a longer sip and waited for the glow to begin.

After a pair of whiskeys, the bar had grown quite pleasant, with the nuts and pretzels in the red glazed bowls and the bottles gleaming under soft lights in casual rows and the murmur of voices blending with the music. My third whiskey stood at attention before me and the faint scent of lilacs drifted in the night. Nogales seemed quite romantic after dark. I pushed thoughts of Stan and Jolene to a dark empty corner at the back of my mind. I would deal with them tomorrow. Tomorrow always was better for me.

Behind the bar, three bartenders huddled together, speaking too softly for me to hear. Such secretiveness aroused memory fragments of the night before and made me uncomfortable. When their eyes were busy elsewhere, I picked up my whiskey and maneuvered through the crowd, leaving my water behind to confuse them.

All the tables were occupied and bodies filled most of the chairs. I held the whiskey tightly against my chest as I wormed my way through the crowd. A well-dressed couple stood in my way. He had silver hair and ignored me. Tall, with a face like an orchid, she gave me a look that you might give a dog who'd just crapped on your front porch. Ducking my head, I swung around them.

At the far end of the room, I found an empty chair at a small table. Two men with mustaches and mugs of beer sat in the other two chairs. Their faces lifted as I approached. In this corner of the room it was too dark to read them. "May I join you?" Their eyes caught and reflected the little light that found its way to this edge of civilization, glowing in the dimness like a jaguar's. I swept my whiskey hand in the general direction of the empty chair.

"*Sí*," said the man closer to the door.

I sat down and studied their faces. "*Habla Ingles?*"

"*Sí*, a little," answered the same man. He was sitting next to me and I could smell his beer and sweat and aftershave. The silent man sipped his beer as he watched me over the glass with glowing cat eyes.

"Do you speak Spanish?" asked my neighbor.

"*Uno, dos, tres*; that's about it. Oh, and *por favor, gracias, hola, buenos noches, adiós*, and *de nada*. Not bad, huh?"

"What?"

"That's pretty good Spanish for a man who has never been to Mexico."

"Then that is pretty good Spanish."

From where I sat I could see the back wall, the far end of the bar, and the tailbone of the dance floor. For a moment I watched the couples swirl. I hit the whiskey and settled back, waiting for the glow, wondering where Stan and Jolene were. Now that I was inside the bar, their whereabouts seemed less important. One more drink, I figured, and my only worry would be how to pay for my whiskeys.

It was quite pleasant to sit in the near darkness with a gentle stream of strangers flowing by and smell the senoritas' perfumes and listen to the music and watch the glow dawn ever brighter on my far horizon. The man of silence got up from the table and walked across the floor on gimpy legs. He went into the *Gentlemen's* without looking back. I took another sip and studied the talking man.

He sat up straight in his chair, but that didn't make him any taller. His face was the color of leather that had been rubbed a thousand times.

Above the bushy mustache that hid his upper lip, his eyes were dark and flat, almost opaque. His hands were large and I could see calluses on the palms. I couldn't read him at all.

"Are you from here?" I asked.

"*Sí*, from Mexico."

"No. I meant from Nogales?"

He nodded and I watched the lights move in his eyes. "From just beyond."

"You like it?"

My neighbor shrugged his shoulders in the Mexican way. "It is okay."

"Ever lived anywhere else?" I couldn't understand why I was making conversation. Maybe it was the whiskey, or maybe after the night before I simply needed to hear the sound of a friendly voice.

Nodding, he smiled. It was a shy smile, but a pleasant one, revealing surprisingly white teeth. "Twice I have crossed."

"The border?"

"*Sí*."

"Did you like it over there?"

He nodded again, his dark head handsome in the muted lighting. "I liked it very much."

I poured a little whiskey over my tongue and let it sit there for a second before I swallowed. "Why did you come back? Miss Mexico?"

Again he shrugged, saying more with the movement than a page full of single-spaced words. "Without question, I missed Mexico. However, I came back because I had no papers. Your authorities, they sent me back." He lifted his glass, closed his eyes and drained his beer.

I wondered if he was remembering. Memories are important to a man. That I could understand. Sometimes they are all we have. I thought again of my father, remembering when he had been an old man, flesh gone flabby and muscles atrophied. Lines like wrinkled roadmaps etched the years in his face and his voice embarrassed him. Only his eyes remained as I remembered from childhood: clear, hazel, watching me, always watching, always caring, always hoping.

When I was young I'd thought of them as living cameras recording all my sins. Now I wondered. Glass thumped against wood and I came back to the bar in stages, my mind shifting gears slowly. My companion's eyes were open.

"Will you try to cross again?"

The man licked his mustache. "Who can say, *señor*? Perhaps, when the time is right. In Mexico you learn early to never say never."

The air in the bar seemed to have grown warmer. Sweat slid down the back of my neck. I willed the glow to come, but it was hesitating, teasing me. Shadows danced along the walls. I lifted my glass and drank to them, draining the whiskey and running my tongue along the sides of the glass. It occurred to me that such an action was the sign of an alcoholic. Trumpet sounds pierced the night and I twirled my fingers at the waitress. Clearly the glow needed reinforcements.

"*Uno* whiskey," I told the girl with the scar at the left corner of her mouth. "And," I gestured at my drinking *compadre*. He named a Mexican beer even I had heard of and I told the waitress to put it on my tab. She nodded and walked away on slim, well-muscled legs.

"Your women are very beautiful."

"Certainly many are when they are young." He made his smooth face wrinkled. "When they are older, well, who can say? Some remain lovely, others blossom and become even more beautiful, but many others are burdened with too much work and let themselves go; they get fat and wrinkled and no longer care about their appearance."

"Why?"

He looked at me with flat eyes that gave nothing away. "Who knows? As for me, I think it is because they see ahead of them only cooking, cleaning, and caring for the children, and then their husband when he gets old. They feel abandoned by life, therefore, they abandon hope."

"Abandon hope, all ye who enter here," I quoted.

"What?"

"Nothing, just an old saying, and I am full of those."

He nodded as if I had said something meaningful and we sat in silence until the waitress with the scarred mouth and fine legs brought our drinks. I reached to tip her before I remembered, settling for a smile and a promise to myself to make it up to her, although I couldn't see how at the moment. Thinking of such things made my brain ache.

She set our new glasses on the table and took away the old ones. The man picked up his beer and I picked up my whiskey and said, "*Salud.*"

"*Salud* and *gracias, muchas gracias.*"

"*De nada.*"

We drank in silence. The whiskey wasn't bad. The glow, that great, beautiful glorious glow that obscured all my fears and all my failures, was beginning to blossom. Noises seemed to have withdrawn to the corners of the bar. Peaceful, mellow sensations infiltrated my mind and the world spun a little more slowly.

"You are a *Norte Americano*, no?"

I looked across the table at my drinking companion. His beer was half gone, but his face still told me nothing. For all the expression on his face he could be dead.

"Actually, I'm from Kentucky."

"*Sí*, the Kentucky Derby," he said, allowing his lips to part in what I took to be a smile.

"Very good." The glow was closer; mellowing light filtered through me, loosening my tongue.

"This is good whiskey. Is your *cerveza* good?"

"Yes, it is good *cerveza.*"

After another sip, I waved at the waitress. The whiskey became better the more I drank it. She came quickly and we ordered again. I told her to make mine a double.

"My turn to pay," the man said.

"No, no, this is on me." Patting myself on the chest, I smiled at both of them. She smiled back at me with her scar curling across her face like a snake. The man nodded.

When the girl had gone, I asked him his name.

"Pedro Romero. And yours?"

"Paul, Paul Hampton."

The syllables of my name sounded strange on my lips, as though I had been that person a long time ago but had changed and was no longer the same man. My tongue curled around the saying of my name, and I splashed Mexican whiskey on it to straighten it out.

Romero looked at me with his flat black eyes reflecting the light and sipped on his beer.

"You are a businessman?"

"Was. I managed the family firm."

"What did your family make?"

"Mostly trouble; ha, only kidding. We were a dry cleaning establishment, Bluegrass Dry Cleaning. My grandfather started the business back in the fifties and then my father ran it until he died. After he passed I was in charge. Had seven stores across Kentucky. Sold out a couple of years ago. Now I manage my investment portfolio. Manage at it anyway."

Romero leaned forward. "I have never been to Kentucky."

"You haven't missed much, or at least I never saw anything so wonderful that I couldn't stand to leave it behind."

"But your businesses—"

"Yeah, all the stores were successful." I took a careful sip. The glow was growing ever larger and brighter. Soon it would expand beyond the horizon and engulf the world. All my problems seemed small and indistinct, Stan and Jolene nothing more than blurry miniature photographs that had passed through a hundred greasy hands. Reluctantly, I drifted back to Nogales.

"We hired good managers. Listen to me, Pedro; that's the secret to success in the business world—you must hire good managers. You can sit back and oversee the big picture. Then you simply count the money as it rolls in. Actually, my employees did most of the day-to-day work. I chaired the Board and made the key executive decisions. Naturally, I received the highest salary and the most stock options."

"And much money rolled in?"

"Hell yes, thousands a week. Then there is the inheritance. I got half of mine last year. Will get the rest when I turn forty. Millions, Pedro, millions. That is why my wife and I have been on this tour for about three months. Staying in the finest hotels, eating at five-star restaurants, drinking only the good stuff."

My words fluttered around my ears like uncertain moths. They sounded strange, as if another man had spoken them or they had morphed into a foreign tongue. Smoke curled thickly through the room and everyone seemed to be leaning, as though the world had gone lopsided. Closing my eyes, I focused on the glow.

When I opened them again, the room had tilted back to level and the smoke was no more than a fine October mist. Romero was smiling in a vague, unfocused way. I spoke into his smile. "It's been one hell of a trip. Only problem is that at the moment I seemed to have misplaced my wife. Oh well, she'll turn up. She always does. And besides, she has Stan with her."

Saying their names unearthed memories that made me wonder if their showing up would be such a fine thing to happen. Uncertain of what to say, I peered into Pedro's eyes. It was like trying to peer into flat black water.

"Stan is our new good friend. We found him in Las Vegas. He likes to eat and drink and gamble with us." As I spoke, Stan's face swung before me, an unhinged moon, bright and lined with curves and craters. In that moment Stan seemed a more real, substantial figure than he ever had before. Fear curved in a neon arc inside me. I kept talking against the fear.

"For a younger guy he's polite, Pedro, even deferential. But there's something about him I don't trust. Nice looking, if you like the slim-hipped, hairy-chested type."

Pedro Romero nodded and scooted his chair closer to mine. "Then you are on vacation, a *grande* vacation? You have many dollars?"

"Certainly." I drained the whiskey and whistled for the scar-faced night vision who was serving us. "I have millions. Even with what Jolene and Stan and I have spent, I'm sure of it."

"You like this Stan?"

"Don't know him well enough to say that." Memories, dark and haggard, nudged soft brain tissue. I didn't want them. I wanted the glow. "Actually, he's more Jolene's friend. Takes her shopping, to museums, art galleries—that sort of thing. Not my specialty."

Romero leaned forward, elbows on the table. I could smell his breath. "And what do you do, *señor*?"

I didn't like his question. I leaned back, merging into the shadows that crowded together along the wall. The question was one I'd been asking myself for a long time. When a man has money and brains and talents and decent looks handed to him from day one and still manages to waste his life...well, that's when it becomes difficult to explain.

Maybe there was no understanding. Failure would be easier to swallow if you'd been forced to try to overcome some handicap, like being blind or not having any ears. Then maybe a guy could choke down the crap expelled by a wasted life. But when he has no excuses, when the girls liked him and he had friends and a cool car and a starting position on the football team and a free ride to dear old State U, and he still lets it all slip through his fingers...then he has no one to blame but himself. And that's a hard load to swallow. Even alcohol couldn't quite get the taste of that crap out of your mouth. I pivoted back into the light, eyes smarting from the smoke.

"Guess you could say I'm in charge. Just don't ask me what the hell I'm in charge of."

Romero eased back in his chair and nodded as though I had said something profound. "I understand. You are a big man, *señor*; it is only natural that you should be in charge."

"I'm not that big." Romero was starting to get on my nerves, so was Mexico. "Only about two hundred. Being on this trip has played hell with my diet and workout routine. Back in the day I was one hell of an athlete."

I glanced at Romero. He was opening his mouth, probably to ask another fool question. A little companionship in a bar was all right, but Romero asked too damn many questions. "Where is that damn lazy waitress?"

"There she is, *señor*." Pedro pointed toward the far side of the room. All the talk about Stan and Jolene was causing me to lose the glow. Even if only half of what I remembered was accurate I needed to see them before they saw me.

"She is busy with other customers. She will bring our drinks in a few minutes. There is no hurry, is there? You do not have to be someplace at a certain time?"

"No, but I need the glow."

"The glow?"

"Yes, the glow. I drink for the glow, a wonderful warm golden glow that starts like the most incredible sunset you have ever seen and then flows across the world until there is nothing else. It covers everything and I don't have to worry about my business, or what my sister is saying about me, or what my wife is doing, or what her new friend is up to, or my goddamn waistline, or where all my yesterdays went, or even what in the hell I am going to do to get through tomorrow. There is only the glow, and it is enough. And I have to have it, Romero, and I can't get it without another damn drink. So where in the hell is that waitress? Damn her."

"Relax, *señor*. Here she comes now. She will be here soon. I am anxious for another drink, too, but one cannot hurry the waitress. Without her we would not be served."

"Why are you anxious?"

"The zombies, *señor*. I am anxious due to the zombies."

"Damn, Romero, you are drunk. Who in the hell are the zombies? You can't mean that musical group from the sixties?"

"What? I do not understand, *señor*. I am a little drunk, yes. But no more than many other evenings. It is due to your generosity that I am still drinking, for when I came in I had only enough *pesos* to buy *dos cervezas* and the zombies were already out. I could sense them as the sun began to set. They are always there, of course, but some nights they are worse than others. Tonight they were going to be very bad."

The waitress was still three tables away and I wanted to go over and shake her until she produced my drink, but I knew Romero was right, even if he was jabbering like a lunatic. Without her the whiskey might dry up and the glow would surely fade. As if Mexico were tilting on its axis, the room began to spin. I concentrated on the glow. When the revolutions slowed I focused on Romero. "You didn't answer my question. Who are the zombies?"

Like the lens of a camera opening, his eyes widened slowly. His lips came apart. "The zombies? The zombies are devils who torture a man's mind, the terrible guardians of the dark, those who rise up from their graves when the sun goes down. They are horrible, grotesque creatures who crawl into your mind and tell you lies until reality is distorted and you do not know whether it is day or night, or if you are alive or dead."

"You see these zombies, Romero?"

"*Sí*. Everyone sees zombies sometimes. Mexico has many zombies and I have a receptive mind for zombies. I am greatly troubled by zombies."

"And the *cerveza* helps?"

"*Sí*, also the tequila and whiskey and vodka and wine. However, they cost too much for me. I am a poor man."

I thought of my own zombies. I'd never considered them in that way before. They had been merely unnamed shadows moving in my mind.

"Ever tried to fight the zombies? Fight them when you are sober, I mean."

Romero nodded, the oil on his black hair glistening even in the dim light. "Yes, *señor*, many, many times." His head moved again and lines like sad rivers crosshatched his face. "I have always lost though when I was sober. Without the alcohol to help me, there are too many of them and they are far too terrible for me to win. Without the alcohol I know I will lose."

"Goddamn, Romero, we can't let those fucking zombies win again tonight. Let me get that little bitch over here and get us our damn drinks and you and I are going to kick some zombie ass. Yes, my drunken Mexican amigo, we are going to kick all the zombie ass in Nogales, Mexico."

Through the alcoholic haze and the gathering glow, I could see myself standing up and hear myself shouting, "Service, *sevicio, por favor. Sevicio, pronto.* Service! Waitress! *Senorita!* Slut!"

It was like watching and listening to some character in a B movie from 1951 gone out of focus on an aged, wavy screen. Such behavior belonged to an asshole and I knew I was one, yet I kept on. It was an act I'd worked on for years. It seemed to me on that hot night in Nogales I was curving in a choreographed arc toward perfection.

A hand gripped my left arm and a man growled, "Sit down, *señor.*"

Guess it was the whiskey, or the night before, or those memories that had been drifting around my mind all day, but I no longer felt as if I was the man I had been before I crossed the border. It was as though I'd stepped outside my body and was staring at the stranger I'd become. Metamorphosis had begun; I could feel it swimming like a virus through my blood stream.

Normally, I would have simply sat down, or apologized, even offered to buy the man a drink. Not tonight. Rage rose on a whiskey tide and I shrugged off the offending arm and whirled around. I saw only the face of a stranger with a mustache and a white tee-shirt and gold chains encircling his wrists. Uncontrollable emotions gripped me. Knowing full well what I was doing, I swung a right cross toward his face. Out of the corner of one eye I could see Romero dropping under the table.

Gold Chains was a big-shouldered man with quick hands and he blocked my roundhouse with his left arm and smashed his right fist into my gut. I could feel the hard hand drive deep into the soft flesh and the air going out of me with a whoosh and I went stumbling back into the table.

Table legs gave way under my weight and wood and glass smashed against the floor. I tripped over Romero's legs and went staggering back into a crowd. I put my hands up to catch myself and one slapped across a blurry face. A woman screamed. Suddenly, men were shouting and women screaming.

Someone smashed a fist against my nose and I tasted my own blood. It slid down the back of my throat like a sun-soaked worm. I hit the man as hard as I could on the side of his head. He yelped as he staggered back into another man, who shoved him into a tall man in a white suit holding a green glass above his head. The force of the impact sloshed liquid over the rim of the glass. Dark cherry pools splashed onto the front of the white jacket. They looked like misplaced eyes of blood in a great white bird. The figure in white cursed and I saw him fling his glass at the man I'd hit.

That was all I saw for a while because somebody jumped on my back and we waltzed across Nogales in a deranged promenade until my legs gave way under the weight and the whiskey and I fell into a soft body that screamed as we all tumbled to the floor.

The impact flung us apart and I rolled and came up swinging both fists and punched an old man in the ribs and a young man in the eye. I'd never been a fighter and for a second I wondered if Romero's zombies had put a spell on me.

Bodies swirled around me like dust devils. Some people were trying to punch me, others were trying to hit someone else, and some were simply trying to get the hell out of the bar. Someone shouted "*policia*" and a woman cried out in pain. Time for me to be locating the exit.

I took a glancing blow from a chair and went sprawling. Hard boots smashed into my stomach and then the alcohol was coming up and going all warm and nasty down my chin and shirt. A man cursed me for being the son of a female dog and hit me on the forehead with a handful of rings inset with stones. I rolled away from him and caught a glimpse of

Romero going like a wild rabbit on hands and knees. Seemed like the best plan of the night.

Someone else had other ideas. A man with a big gut grabbed me by the hair and jerked me to my feet. Someone I couldn't see grabbed my arms and pinned them behind my back. Jerking and kicking, I got one loose, but Big Gut drove his right fist straight into my chest and all I could think about was trying to breathe and keep my heart beating at the same time.

Big Gut hit me in the face and worked in close and put his hands around my neck. Through blood streaming down from my forehead, I could see the pimple craters that pockmarked his round face. His breath was foul, as though he had been eating carrion.

Then he twisted my neck and the room went dark for a second and all I could hear was a rushing sound like a great ocean receding. From some unknown portal in the universe I caught a surreal whiff of onions and fish and burnt tobacco, and I could see tiny pinpricks of light. Then I was throwing up again, all over Fat Gut's face. He screamed like a woman and pushed me away and I fell against the bar. I sucked in air and tried to clear my mind. To hell with the glow and the zombies; my best bet was to get my ass out of the bar and see if I couldn't get lost in the Mexican night.

Fumbling around the top of the bar, my fingers closed on a reasonably dry bar towel and I swiped away blood. I could see the door now, and the darkness beyond. Some element in the darkness called to me, as though it were alive and welcoming. On rubber band legs I started for the door. A siren shrieked. I tried to move faster, not sure what I was running to or away from.

Halfway across the room I thought I was going to make it, that I'd been granted one more reprieve by a gracious God. Then someone, perhaps one of Romero's zombies, shoved me and I stumbled against a man and a bottle smashed against my head.

The room spun wildly. I was an astronaut floating, lost in deep space. In a pain-fogged vision I thought I saw Jolene. Swaying on my tether, I tried to wave to her. A hatchet-faced woman with dark hair flying around her head stepped forward and slapped me hard on both cheeks. The silver haired man who had blocked my path earlier lifted a cane with a curved silver handle above his head. As though through a fun house mirror I saw the cane descend.

Deep space was no more than a giant wind tunnel, dark and opening to infinity. I could hear the hiss of a stormy galactic sea, and then there was only an enormous black silence.

Four

Floating on a dark ocean I saw only blackness. No light. No meaning. I was content to float in the ebony nada.

Light came first, cautiously, a winter's sun rising against a hard blue morning. Blackness drifted away sluggishly, going in gradients. Still cocooned inside myself, I lay exquisitely still, listening to the rise and fall of the ocean's pulse until realization came that I was hearing my own breathing. Cautiously, I opened my eyes.

Pain colored my world in violent hues: purple and crimson, chartreuse and cobalt. I told myself that if I remained still as stone I could refuse the pain. It seemed like a sound theory, so I closed my eyes and congratulated myself on my cleverness. It wasn't long before I could tell that my theory was preordained to failure. Rather than subsiding, the pain intensified.

For a little while I thought I might die, but gradually, like the ending of an epoch, pain began to subside. A great thirst threatened to consume me and I opened my eyes to search for water. An inverted V of a roof stretched high above me, a tin sky. Bare earth, lightly and sporadically covered with straw, surrounded me. The air was hot and dark with only narrow ingots of light slanting through murky darkness. Dust motes drifted in those slender beams and there was a faint animal odor, as if beasts had been there, but not for some time.

Sweat slid slowly down my face and pooled under my arms and in the small of my back. I decided to try and sit up. I had to work up to it in stages. My head was heavy and a great iron bell tolled inside it. The world whirled, so I shut my eyes and counted to twenty-five, slowly. When I opened my eyes again my head was still throbbing but the world was only wobbling on its axis. I risked a look around.

I was in a barn. The bottom two feet of the structure were stone, with wooden planks above. The roof was galvanized metal and sharply slanted. Gardening tools were stacked along one wall and burlap bags of feed or fertilizer lined another. Stalls near the front would have worked for cattle, horses, or mules. All were empty. Bales of hay were stacked three high against the back wall. Saddles and harnesses hung on curved hooks behind me. The familiar smell of leather was oddly comforting.

My arms ached, so I raised and lowered them to get the blood flowing. Purple and yellow bruises decorated my arms, stomach and chest. Dried blood spotted my torn shirt and when I licked my swollen lips I could feel cracks. My nose hurt and my left eye was swollen half shut.

I couldn't see much future in sitting on the earthen floor of an old barn. Pressing palms against the cool earth, I pushed my body upwards. Closing my eyes, I stood still until the barn quit spinning. When I opened my eyes, an outline of a door was dimly visible. I started toward it.

The first step, with the right leg, went fine.

The second, with the left, was an unmitigated disaster.

An iron force grabbed my leg and pulled it from under me. Pain radiated from my left ankle as I fell to the ground with a thud, banging sore ribs.

Once the pain was under control, I looked down. An iron ring gripped my ankle. A chain of thick metal links trailed from the ring. I tugged on the chain. It rattled in the shadows, but held firm. I assumed the other end must be bolted to the barn wall. Easing into a more comfortable position, I considered my options. They didn't seem numerous.

Thoughts of African slaves cropped up, disturbing what equanimity I still possessed. As far as I knew, there had never been any slave holders among my ancestors, yet I felt a visceral connection to an unknown black man chained to the gunwales of a slave ship. It was an unsettling vision and made me wonder whether I'd encountered a time warp or was losing my mind.

As a child I had experienced visions, the kind where you imagine you are adopted or the offspring of aliens, but when they had started to expand as I entered my teenage years, shifting from exciting to vaguely disturbing, then finally to unnerving, I suppressed them using whatever means was necessary. I managed to keep them under control with girls, or sports, or liquor. After experimentation, I determined that liquor worked best. Over the years the visions had almost become forgotten, surfacing only occasionally, like mysterious air bubbles rippling the smooth surface of a pond. I supposed I had outgrown them.

Somewhere in the middle of the morning I slept without dreams. I woke, drenched in sweat, to the creaking of rusty hinges. I cracked open one eye. One of the tall barn doors was swinging slowly open. Sunlight poured in through the opening and lay in a butter-yellow pool on the earthen floor. A breeze drifted across my face, bringing with it a plethora of odors and the sound of rustling straw. I could smell dirt and manure and aging urine and sweat and my own fear.

I was grateful the light had yet to reach me. Visions from the night before still lingered among the cobwebs of my brain. It occurred to me that I might still be hung-over, or had slipped across an unseen border into insanity.

Shadows fell across the pool of light and I wanted to shut my eyes, as though that alone would prevent the shadows and their creators from advancing. However, a compulsion to see what was coming ran through me, as thick and hot as a living organism. Keeping one eye shut, I fixed the other on the steadily widening yellow pool. I stared at the advancing figures and thought of Stan and Jolene.

A final screech of the hinges and then the sound of wood pressing against wood. Dust rose from the wooden slats in small brown clouds that hovered in the light for a few seconds before disintegrating. Two shadows lengthened and transformed themselves into men.

These men wore hats like crowns and walked across the barn floor as if they owned it. Near enough the same size to be brothers, both were dark and slender and the muscles in their bare forearms stood out like cords of rope. They talked in Spanish as they came toward me.

One of the men hunkered down and cupped my chin in his hand. Unseen worms seemed to be crawling across my face, but I didn't resist as he lifted my head into a sheath of light. It felt strange to be so helpless.

"So, *señor*, you are finally awake. You were asleep for such a long time we were beginning to wonder if you would ever wake up."

"Where am I?" My voice rasped in my raw throat and rattled around in my skull, making my head ache more. I choked back rising bile. The man laughed, a nasty, truncated laugh. He bent closer until I could smell his personal scent.

"You are where you need to be, *señor*. You are here with us. Now tell us your name."

The other man moved out of the light, positioning himself closer to my feet. I felt encircled by the world. The moving man drifted out of sight, but not far away—I could hear the fall of his footsteps. My gut told me they were going to hurt me no matter what I said, but maybe more if I told an obvious lie. I shivered in the dirt like a car-struck dog.

"My name is Hampton, Paul Hampton." Stomach liquids churned. I'd been hung-over enough to know that soon I was going to be sick in a messy way.

"Where are you from, *Señor* Hampton?" There was a lilting to the man's voice as though the interrogation was a tune he knew.

"The United States." I said.

"Where in *Notre America*?"

"Kentucky."

He shrugged and looked beyond me to his partner. Seconds later he peered into my eyes. His dark eyes were constantly moving, searching for something.

"What are you doing here?" His question was sudden and loud.

I tried to think of a diplomatic response. Thinking took too long for the man behind me. He kicked me hard in the small of the back. When I finished coughing, I said, "I'm on vacation."

"With no dollars?"

"I was robbed."

"And no identification?"

"I told you I was robbed."

"Who robbed you?"

"I don't know. I didn't see them. They must have knocked me out from behind."

The man snorted like a thoroughbred at the starting gate. "You mean you got drunk and passed out and can't remember what happened to your money."

"Maybe I was drinking a little."

"A little?"

"Okay, more than a little."

An open palm smacked one side of my face with stinging force. "So, Paul Hampton, you came to Nogales to get drunk without paying for your fun."

"No, no, I have money."

"Give it to me." Quickly, he stretched out his hand. The movement made me think of a snake striking. I was afraid and in need of a drink. Just to steady my nerves, of course.

"I can't," I said, adding hurriedly, "let me explain."

"Where is the money, *amigo*?" His dark eyes had turned dull and hard. The odor of my own sweat was strong.

"My wife has it."

He bent closer until I could smell his sweat, mingled with the scents of aftershave, tobacco, and onions. "Where is your wife?"

My head was hurting worse by the minute and the contents of my stomach kept rolling and tossing like an ocean before a storm. Thoughts of dying crossed my mind. There seemed to me to be a great incongruity to life's little game, for in escaping from Stan and Jolene I'd fallen into a more deadly scene. Seeking small mercies, I smiled up at the man leaning over me. The smile felt sickly on my face.

"I don't know. I was looking for her but it got dark and I got sick and now I'm here. If you'll let me go I'll find her and get the money for you. Now that it's daylight, I'm sure I can find her."

"You mean you got drunk, don't you?"

"I was sick. That's why I started drinking."

"Where is your wife?"

"I told you I don't know."

"Then where is your money?"

"Back in the U.S. I have money there, lots of it. I'm a millionaire."

His laughter reminded me again of the snorts of a horse. He stopped laughing and began kicking me in the stomach. Gasping for breath, I tried to roll away from his boot.

"Where is your wife?"

"I don't know."

Another kick, this one from the rear. The room swung back and forth. "Where is your money?"

A boot slammed into my kidneys, and I wanted to cry. "In the U.S.," I sobbed.

A boot to the stomach and I could feel the tsunami begin.

"Where is your wife?"

"I don't know."

Another kick, this one to the head, and pinpoints of light tap danced across the universe.

"Where is the money?"

"In the—" was as far as I got before the contents of my stomach rose in a sour churning wave and gushed out my mouth and nose.

"Goddamn you, you miserable American son-of-a-bitch, you fucking bastard," was all I heard before the boot smashed into my face. Inside my brain a dam broke and I swirled back into the ebony nada.

Five

I came to with dirt in my mouth, blood on my lips, and vomit drying on my chin. My pants were damp between my legs and the stench of my own feces curled in my nose.

The day had grown old and gone on without me. I could see transformations in the light. Softer, more subtle in its shadings, it highlighted my infantile movements as I eased my face out of the dirt. A surreal beauty permeated that light as it crossed the floor and illuminated the dark, wooden planks that formed the barn walls.

Time passed, like sands ebbing through a Bedouin's fingers. A plate, covered with wax paper, caught my attention. Next to it was a clay bowl with a chipped lip. Aromas of food drifted to me. I scooted closer.

The bowl was full of water that looked clean. For once water was satisfying. After drinking, I felt strong enough to explore what was on the plate.

There was a mound of golden brown rice, a second of beans swimming in a dark sauce, while the third was a plateau of soft tortillas. Scooping up the rice with the tortillas, I ate with my hands. The beans looked deadly and I left them alone. From the distant rumblings in my stomach it was obvious I wasn't up to more.

Savoring the firmness of the rice grains against my tongue, I ate slowly, letting the tortillas go to paste against the roof of my mouth. I couldn't remember when I'd eaten anything more substantial than peanuts.

Strength returned sluggishly. I crawled on all fours, like an old, sick dog, to where dirt met wood and sat with my back against the boards.

From this vantage point I could see the door clearly without having to worry about what lurked behind me. Even though I stunk like a rotting skunk and my entire torso was one big ache, I felt surprisingly good. Granted, I wasn't ready to take on the world, but I was also no longer ready to crawl into a freshly dug grave.

Between the chain on my leg and the feebleness that had invaded my body, I couldn't move much. Instead, I did a lot of wondering in that old barn. Wondered about Jolene and Stan, and how I had been so blind.

Maybe blind drunk was the answer. I wondered if they were still looking for me or if they had left me to the two-legged coyotes south of the border. In the soft, sobering light it seemed clear they had been planning a most unpleasant surprise for me. There wasn't enough evidence to accuse them of plotting my demise, but deep in my gut a nasty intuition told me they wouldn't have been displeased to see a mound of dirt covering me.

I contemplated going to the police. My aching leg reminded me I wasn't going anywhere just yet. Besides, intuition never trumped evidence.

I thought about all the promises I'd made to myself to quit drinking. I began to consider what my lawyer would do when I turned up missing and after that my banker, my broker, and my golf buddies. Finally, I wondered about my auto mechanic. As sunlight started to die and shadows began to bleed across the floor, I decided that my mechanic would be the one who missed me most, and he would actually be missing my Jaguar.

Dreams filled my mind. Not new dreams; not sleep dreams, but dreams from a boyhood so long ago it was if it belonged to another man. Every boy has dreams. Mine returned to me in that cool, dusky, musty old barn, so real in my mind they seemed alive. Yet they had been stillborn. Dreams of athletic glory and unbelievably beautiful women and money to buy everything you wanted, even happiness.

There had been altruistic dreams, too. In my younger days I'd been going to save jungles and oceans, keep old women from starving and rescue young ones from a fate worse than death. It was as though I were being shown an ancient movie jammed in the projector. I wondered if I'd get one more chance to rewrite the script.

Darkness filled the corners of the old barn, spread across the earthen floor and lapped at my feet. Just before the room gave up the light, I heard voices and the dull ring of footsteps against hard ground. Metal rattled.

Scooting tighter against the wall, I squared my face with the doors. One tall door creaked open. Daylight's last feeble slats transfigured the earth in front of the door into a tarnished golden altar. I prayed in silence to the small gods of the gathering darkness.

Three shadowy figures moved toward me. Beyond them was a ring of small hills and beyond the hills the dying sun, hanging low on the horizon, slanting rays of light through gaps in the hills, setting their crests aglow.

The figure in front carried a lamp. Light swung in erratic arcs as he walked. Three paces and the figures revealed themselves men, their boots dragging in the dirt and raising billows of dust. They halted when they saw me, then came on. The door creaked again, followed by the sound of a bolt shooting home. My eyes never left the man with the lantern.

He hung it on a tall pole I hadn't noticed. Lamplight danced as the lantern swung back and forth. Moving out of rhythm with the light, the man walked across the barn and stood over me. From where I sat he looked tall, thin, on the backside of fifty, and bone-tired.

"Name's Wilson," he said in a flat Midwestern voice and stuck out his hand.

I shook it. It was large and full of prominent bones. "Hampton, Paul Hampton."

Wilson jerked his long, narrow head at the other men. They were standing at the edge of the lamplight. "Man with his arm in a sling is Diego, the fat one is Raoul."

"Hello," I said.

They nodded from the shadows without speaking. I couldn't discern their features. Their faces and hair were dark; their eyes so black that only when they moved their heads and caught the light could I swear they had eyes. It was like talking to speechless, eyeless zombies. I thought of my old drinking compadre, Pedro Romero.

"They only speak Mex, and some Mayan." Wilson peered at me through the dimness. "They're basically harmless. Raoul likes to drink too much, and Diego, he likes to snort the white stuff." Wilson's thin shoulders rose and fell. "Other than that they're not too bad. Just don't turn your back on 'em for long. *Comprende*? Under the right circumstances anyone can be dangerous."

"I understand."

"Good." Wilson folded his long legs under him and eased his narrow body to the floor. He sat three feet away from me with his back against the wall. Lantern light played in the curves and shadows of his lined face. I watched the tension drain out of his body, leaving only tiredness. He wasn't an old man, just one aging fast.

Rolling his head on his neck, he glanced at me. His eyes were deeply sunk and dark shadows lurked beneath them. "What are you in for?"

"Don't know why I'm here. By the way, what the heck is this place? You make it sound like a jail."

He snorted. "That's about what it is."

"Then where are the guards and the jailer?"

Wilson spread big, well-formed lips apart and let me see his large, yellowish teeth. He was missing a couple of uppers. "This is a private jail, friend."

"Private! Who runs it?"

"Señora Anita Louisa Maria Ramirez herself ,along with her minions, who are not to be confused with human beings, even though they somewhat resemble them."

"How can anyone have a private jail today? This is the twenty-first century. You make it sound like a dungeon in a medieval castle, complete with a dragon and moat."

"No moats and no dragons. We've evolved to electric fences and armed guards. Otherwise, you hit it on the head."

Wilson rubbed at the tiredness hiding in the lines of his face. "As to how, well this is Mexico, deep in the wilds of Mexico to be exact, and the way I understand the situation, and I'll admit my Spanish is wobbly, Señor Ramirez is a big wheel in Nogales and the only wheel in this patch of god-forsaken country.

"Word is we're somewhere south and east of the border. Guess you could call us unappreciative guests on his ranch. Ramirez owns the best hotel in Nogales, several bars, the only taxi service, and a number of assorted businesses. Sometimes people owe him money and can't pay, or hack him off in other ways, and he has them brought here to serve their sentences."

"But who sets their sentences? I never had any trial."

"Ramirez sets the sentences, along with his wife, and let me warn you, she's the mean one. The señor has lots of other interests: business, travel, hunting, fishing off Baja, bullfights in Mexico City, and, I hear, younger ladies."

He snickered and scratched at a red, puffy place on his arm.

"Señora Ramirez, on the other hand, apparently lives to run this ranch and prison combo." Wilson licked his thick lips and bent his head toward mine. "Don't ever cross her. The guards here are sadists, but she's worse. I've seen her personally horsewhip a man half to death, and a couple of guys who got caught trying to escape last month were pulled out of here one night and never came back."

"When does a man get out of here?"

Wilson shrugged.

"Far as I know, not 'til they're ready to release you. Throw yourself on the senora's mercy for all the good that it will do you. Face it, man, you've got yourself in one hell of a fix." He leaned his head back and sighed. "Damn I'm hungry. Wish they'd bring supper."

More curious than hungry, I asked, "What do they feed you?"

"Usually rice and beans and tortillas. Sometimes there's a little beef, or tacos, or Indian fry bread. Every now and then bananas or melon."

"Pretty unappetizing."

"Beats starving. And believe me, after working a day on this ranch you're damned near starved to death. Breakfast is only some sort of porridge and lunch is usually bread and fruit and, if you're lucky, peanut butter."

Wilson's forearms bulged in the lantern light and I suspected the answer before I asked the question. "What sort of work do they make you do?"

Wilson shut his eyes. "Whatever the queen says. Most days it's working in the fields or building fence. There are one hell of a lot of rocks in this country and they must be planning on using every damn one of them. In the fall we have to help round up the cattle, and once in a while paint some on the house or barn. If we behave we get to clean up the Mercedes." He opened his eyes. "One thing you can count on, buddy, there's plenty of work for everybody."

Wilson turned his head as if he were tired of talking. In the lamplight, it was difficult to judge his age. He had the lines, wrinkles, and aging skin of a middle-aged man, but his eyes still held a semblance of youthful vigor. I wondered what he'd done to get in here.

It grew quiet in the old barn and I began to hear birds outside settling down for the evening. Once, I heard the long, low whistle of a train in the distance and then, much closer, the bellow of a cow. Beyond the pool of lantern light, small animals scurried across the earthen floor of the barn.

My head began to pound again and my body ached like a horse had trampled it. Raoul and Diego spoke softly in Spanish, while Wilson seemed lost in his own thoughts. Tension mounted inside me. Compounded by the quiet darkness, it became too heavy to hold. I asked Wilson how long he'd been at the ranch.

His Adam's apple went up and down, twice. He said, "For fucking ever," and closed his eyes.

We waited in silence, flickering lamplight the only illumination. Raoul and Diego were sitting deep in the shadows. Wilson began to snore softly, like a child.

After what I judged to be about an hour, the door squeaked open and three men stepped inside. Two were carrying trays of food. The third man cradled a shotgun in his arms. Beyond the men pools of light dotted the landscape.

The two men set the trays on the ground and backed out. The man with the shotgun gave up a minute of his life to take a look around. Then he gave us the evil eye and backed out of the barn. The door creaked shut behind him and the bolt slid home with a metallic screech. In a few seconds there was the raspy snick of a lock closing. Raoul and Diego were already pulling the aluminum foil off the plates and Wilson was walking toward me bearing a plate and a plastic bottle.

I stretched out a hand and told Wilson "Thanks." He nodded, turned, and started plodding back to get his own plate.

It hadn't been that long since I'd eaten, but the food was still warm and smelled good. Plus, I figured it would taste better warm now than cold later, so I pulled off the foil.

I ended up eating two tortillas, all of the rice, but none of the beans. After drinking all the water, I tried to find a comfortable position. Diego and Raoul ate quickly, and Raoul eyed my untouched beans, but he never said a word.

Wilson ate slowly and deliberately, as if supper were an assignment he had to finish before he could sleep. I wondered what had happened to his appetite. Maybe he was just making the food last as long as he could. Finally he pushed himself off the floor, walked across the earth and scattered straw to the doors of the barn. For some time he stood there with his face pressed against the boards, staring through the cracks at a slice of the nocturnal landscape. Then he turned and walked to the lamp and blew it out. Darkness settled heavily across the barn.

I'd told Wilson I had no idea why I was chained to the wall. However, when I factored in what he'd told me about the ranch with the jagged remnants of memory, I began to see a little light. Seemed to me that Ramirez must own the bar where the fight had broken out, and in his mind I was responsible for the damage.

Vague memories of drinking whiskey with a Mexican named Pedro Romero kept drifting around and I could remember getting excited about zombies, starting to curse and raise hell. And, of course, there was the fight. Only distorted Fellini memories remained of the rest of the night. Surely they wouldn't keep a man too long for a few hundred dollars in damages and an unpaid bar tab.

Thinking about that unpaid bill reminded me of all my bank accounts, T-bills, mutual funds, and houses and cars back home. All that wealth wasn't doing me a damn bit of good at the moment. With a jolt in my mind like continental plates shifting, I began to wonder if it was doing somebody else some good. Say a certain bottle-blonde named Jolene and an extraordinarily friendly fellow named Stan.

First I wondered where they were, and then what they were doing. I tried to get worked up about it, but the longer I thought about them the more I realized I really didn't give a damn. With every minute that bled to death in the dark it was becoming clearer to me that they were not going to come looking for old Paul. I could see now that it would suit them ever so much better if I stayed lost forever in the wilds of Mexico. My bleached bones were about all that pair was interested in finding. Maybe they wouldn't admit it, and perhaps they wouldn't ever do the deed themselves, but it was obvious, as I reflected on it in my semi-sober state, I suited them dead a whole lot better than alive.

I was starting to need something to drink besides water, and I wasn't considering lemonade or iced tea. If the bastards intended to keep me chained to the wall, they could at least bring me something tall, cool, and laced with alcohol.

As the night wore on and the desire for a drink grew, depression began to slide over me like a cheap blanket. Night sounds began to drift on the wind. An owl hooted at regular intervals and I could hear the scurrying of the small creatures of the barn interspersed with the steady breathing of the men. One of them, it sounded like Raoul, began to snore in a strange, high pitch. Then the wind got up, and all I could hear was it moaning at the cracks and rattling the tall doors in their hinges.

I lay there with the dark pressing down on me and my head aching, listening to the wind, wondering about my wife and my money and how I could get out of this hole, and how I could get my hands on a drink. Escape, for the moment, seemed a remote possibility. If Wilson was right, the ranch sounded like life without parole. For me that was a death sentence.

Slowly the wind seeped inside my brain and carried all the thoughts away. The last thing I remember was hearing the night call of a screech owl. He sounded lonesome.

Six

Daylight came and the big barn door screeched open. Light poured in. Wrapped in the single, thin blanket allotted to each man, I'd been waiting for whatever daylight might bring.

Wilson had said they would feed us. A drink was what I wanted, and it wasn't coffee or orange juice that was on my mind. Ever since I'd come to, my head had been hurting and if I didn't get something with a kick soon it was going to split open at the seams like an old, worn out baseball.

Three guards stepped into the barn armed with rifles and dressed in tan uniforms cut paramilitary style and the flat, long-brimmed hats that Castro had brought to prominence. One of them had a large ring of keys and he walked across the earthen floor and squatted beside me. I kept my eyes on his boots. A key clicked in a lock and the pressure came off my left ankle. I counted to twenty and started massaging aching flesh.

Two other men, unarmed and wearing civilian work clothes, shuffled into the barn carrying trays of food. Three feet inside the door they placed the trays on the ground, turned and retreated. The guards began to back out of the barn. At the door, the tallest of the three said, "Twenty minutes" as he stepped outside.

Wilson and the others were already moving toward the trays. I figured I'd better join them. Hobbling on aching legs, I picked up the last plate.

"Are they always in this much of a hurry?"

"Yeah," Wilson said. "Ramirez runs this place like a factory. Gets us out early. Guess they think it's good for our character. Besides, as hot as it gets here during the day, it's better to work in the morning." He spooned what looked like Malt-O-Meal into his mouth, then swallowed. "Anyway, they let us have a *siesta*, or at least a rest period, after lunch."

Glancing up from his porridge he eyeballed my plate. I hadn't touched the cereal or the slice of yellow melon or the hunk of cornbread. Our morning beverage looked suspiciously like plain water in a Styrofoam cup.

"You'd better get to eating. The lieutenant wasn't kidding about the twenty minutes and it's a long time to lunch."

"All right," I said and dug my spoon into the cereal. I didn't want to eat, but Wilson's words sounded like good advice. Usually, I wasn't big on following advice, but this morning didn't figure to be a picnic.

The best you could say for the cereal was that it was almost warm. It was like swallowing damp sawdust. The melon was overripe, going to mush in my mouth, and the cornbread was dry and stale.

I ate around the edges of my breakfast and watched soft morning light fill the barnyard. One of the guards was sitting on a low stone fence smoking a cigarette. Beyond him a dirt road wound steadily toward hills that occupied the distant ground.

Half of the porridge was all I could choke down. I washed down most of the cornbread and swallowed the melon. I'd just finished drinking my water like a good little boy when the guard tossed his cigarette down and ground it under a boot. Walking toward the barn, he made wide sweeping motions with his free arm and began shouting in Spanish.

Wilson elbowed me. "Come on," he whispered out of one corner of his mouth, "time to go."

We marched single file between two guards. The third guard, the one Wilson had called the lieutenant, walked off to one side. I watched him from my spot at the back of the pack. His eyes were always moving, shifting from one prisoner to another, occasionally flickering to the earth or sky, but never straying far or staying long from the thin ragged line of men.

We marched for what seemed like an hour, but was probably closer to twenty minutes. My head pounded like a brutalized bongo drum, and my legs seemed strangely disconnected from my body, as if they had a mind of their own but weren't certain which way they wanted to go.

Our march led us away from both the barn and the low-slung ranch-style house I could see off to the west. Morning sun glittered off the long windows of glass that lined the front of the house and the chrome of two automobiles standing guard.

Working our way along a wide, dusty path, we walked steadily uphill. Puffs of dust flared around our feet with each step. From the ruts in the trail it was obvious it had rained here recently and heavy equipment had moved along this road.

An orchard ran along one side of the road for some distance, then gave way to open fields. Slowly my legs found a rhythm and it became pleasant to walk with the sun on my face and gaze at crops growing in the fields. Corn grew there and tomatoes, beans, chilies, and melons.

If it hadn't been for my aching head and the intense need for a drink, the walk would have been enjoyable. Morning air was cool and fresh smelling and a willing breeze swirled around remnants of fog that clung to the low places and wafted between narrow strands of scrawny trees. Staring at Wilson's back, the vision of slaves returned. I could imagine myself as an unwilling slave serving a master I'd never seen. I wondered if I was going mad. I stumbled on the jagged edge of a half-buried rock, catching myself with the palms of my hands, and I was back on the trail to nowhere.

We were climbing steadily and my shirt was beginning to stick to my back. Sweat spotted my forehead. Inside my leather loafers my feet were starting to burn. Warmer air kissed our faces as we climbed out of the valley and moved relentlessly toward the sun.

For as far as I could see, the trail wound up the side of the mountain, moving through the tree line and into open meadows, then beyond the meadows to a rock strewn crest. My legs were already aching and the crest looked miles away. I began to pray we wouldn't have to go that far. A wide wet streak ran up the center of the back of Wilson's shirt, but he tramped on with an easy stride.

Raoul and Diego were in front of Wilson. Snatches of their conversation drifted on the thin air. I started craving a drink and thought about that for a while. Then I wondered about Stan and Jolene. After that I only concentrated on walking. Just when I felt my legs could not keep moving, the road forked and the lieutenant shouted, "Halt."

Immediately I dropped to one knee. An instant later the butt of a rifle slammed into the small of my back and I fell forward, moaning in pain.

"Up, up, get up pronto," the guard behind me shouted. His English was heavily accented, but there was no mistaking the meaning. Struggling to my feet, I could hear laughter swirling around me. I concentrated on staying on my feet.

The lieutenant said something in Spanish and the laughter stopped. He gave what sounded like orders in Spanish and Raoul, Diego, and one of the guards turned and started walking up the left fork of the dirt road. The tall man walked toward Wilson and me.

"Today, *amigos,* you will work on the wall. It will be simple but honest work, and it will do you good. Especially you," he said to me, and laughed. "You will benefit from all the good fresh air and the exercise," he said, poking me in the belly with his swagger stick. "Yes, it will do you good, you drunken brawler from across the border. Tonight we will see how ready you are to fight after a day beneath the Mexican sun. If you still want to fight, which I most sincerely doubt, it can be arranged."

He pulled the swagger stick from my gut and tapped it on my left cheek, hard enough to sting the flesh.

"Now get up the trail. Go to where we stopped working last week. Wilson, you know the way?"

"Sure. Let's go, Hampton."

Wilson moved out, heading up the right fork. I struggled to catch up. My breath was loud in my ears. "We'd better move before he thinks of something else," he mouthed. The sun climbed higher in the burnt blue sky. My exposed flesh was turning pink and I longed for shade and a drink.

The road began to curl along the bulging side of the hill. Grass became sparse and finally gave way to rock slides and bare ground. Dust rose around us with every step and hovered in the air like a fine brown curtain. Wilson had sweated through his shirt, and the face of the guard who had come with us shone with perspiration. His uniform was tight across the chest and stomach and he'd lagged behind from the start. His heavy breathing pleased me.

"We ever going to get there?" I panted.

Wilson curled his neck and looked back over his shoulder. "Soon. The wall begins just around the next bend."

"Why are they building it out here in the middle of this godforsaken nowhere?"

"Not real sure. Guess it marks Ramirez's boundary and might keep cattle in, or jeeps out." He grinned at me. "Might be supposed to keep men in, too."

Sweat ran into my eyes. I wiped at it. "Does he have cattle out here?"

"Yeah, runs one hell of a big herd. Sells most of them at the slaughter house in Nogales and uses the rest for meat for his table and to feed his men. Hear he makes good money off his cattle."

"Wilson, my feet are killing me. These loafers aren't worth a damn out here. How can I get some boots?"

"Got any money?"

"Not a damn dime." I thought again about all the money I had back across the border. I would have laughed, only I was trying to keep from crying. I wondered what my father would have thought.

Wilson mopped his forehead with a dirty red bandana. "Then guess you'll have to trade something. What about your watch?'

"Lost it."

"Well, if you can find a guard your size they might want your slacks or shoes. What about a ring?"

"Just a small onyx. Fits so tight I guess nobody could get if off."

"Better than nothing. Should be good for some sort of trade, maybe boots and a hat, or clean socks and shorts. Don't laugh...things get gamey quick out here."

"One more question. What happens when I run out of personal articles to trade?"

Wilson walked on for a minute or two before he responded. "Suppose you'll have to find something else to trade, if you want anything that bad."

Walking was more difficult as we negotiated a rockslide packed with rocks ranging from the size of chicken eggs to Greyhound buses. All seemed to have sharp edges. Sweat ran into my eyes and blinded me. My hamstrings throbbed. I was way too old and out of shape. Only the heavy breathing of the guard gave me comfort.

On the far side of the rockslide the land flattened out. We'd crossed to the rainy side of the mountain and coarse grass, punctuated by thin, scraggly bushes, covered the ground. Mesquite trees threw feeble shade. Higher on the hill, a narrow line of pinion pine formed a jagged green line that ran until the mountain curved out of sight. Rock walls stood like castles before us and outcroppings of rocks dotted the landscape.

Wilson grinned at me with sweat running in twisted lines down his long horse-face. "Well, here we are—the Great Wall of Mexico. Ready to go to work?"

"Not really."

"Good," he said. "Neither am I. Maybe we can talk Jose into a break." Giving me an exaggerated wink, he waved at the guard.

"What about it, Jose, a smoke break, *por favor*?"

Jose caught his breath and said, "*Sí.*"

I sank to the earth. It was already warm, but I didn't mind. Being off my feet was exquisite.

Wilson curled up under a small palo verde tree whose shade was little more than a suggestion. The guard sat on a large rock, pulled a crumpled pack of cigarettes out of his shirt pocket and shook one loose. He stuck it in his mouth and fired up a match. Sharp, acrid smoke smelled foreign in the clear mountain air. The sky was a gigantic blue dome. Clouds looked close enough to touch. A breeze was blowing across the flats and my face. It felt good just to be alive. I swore that once I got out of this mess I'd go straight. I took a deep breath of the clean air and when I let it out I wanted a drink. Sometimes I made myself sick.

No one spoke. Wilson lay still in the sagebrush under the palo verde. Jose smoked his cigarette slowly, blowing smoke through pursed lips, staring south, as if he'd known that territory and was remembering it. I stared up at the sky, stretching huge and blue as far as I could see.

Directly overhead a dark V circled slowly in ever-widening spirals. I watched until the bird was only a black speck moving like a sailboat across a blue ocean that knew no shoreline. Envy filled me and I rolled over and stared at the waving grass. I couldn't bring myself to pretend that I was going to be a better man. It seemed better to exist in the nothingness of the moment. Jamming my brain into neutral, I surrendered to the sun and wind and the vast blueness above.

~ * ~

"Up, up, get up and get to work. Smoke break is over." Jose was ambling toward me. I sat up, stretched, and got slowly to my feet. Wilson was already headed toward the rockslide.

"What we're doing," Wilson said, pointing at the wall, "is stacking rocks to build the wall. They want it higher than a man's head, with the jagged edges pointing up. You lay the flat stones like this," he said, demonstrating with a foot-long reddish stone that was eight or nine inches across. "We'll lay them so, until we get this high. Then we'll turn them on edge and stack them like books on a shelf. Watch the shapes and make sure they fit together. Let gravity do the rest. Understand?"

"Guess so."

"Good. After you do a few you'll get the hang of it." Wilson stopped talking and peered across the landscape. Something in that vast nothingness made him smile.

"Guess we'd better get to it. The lieutenant will come by soon and check on us. He'll want to see progress. If he's not happy, we won't be happy. *Comprende?*"

"Got you."

Wilson turned and walked to the edge of the slide and picked up a large, flat-topped stone. His grunt was audible. Picking up one the size of a loaf of bread, I started toward the wall.

At first the work was invigorating. Muscles I hadn't used in years responded with surprising alacrity. It felt surprisingly good to heft heavy stones and bear the weight to the fence. Even though it took several attempts and a few more demonstrations from Wilson before I began to get the hang of the construction, I found myself actually enjoying the labor.

In twenty minutes I could feel my triceps burning. In thirty minutes my biceps and hamstrings were aching. Gratitude filled me when a cloud strayed between me and the sun. I would have to pace myself or I'd never last out the day.

The breeze began to die. Heat rose. Sweat stained my shirt, and rolled down my face. Judging by the sun, I figured it was about eleven o'clock. Sunlight pressed down without mercy. My legs trembled. I began to watch Jose out of the corners of my eyes and when I could I leaned against the stone fence or fiddled unnecessarily with the placement of a rock.

The sun was directly overhead when I heard a new sound. Wilson's head came up and by the way he cocked it I could tell he was listening too.

At first I couldn't recognize the sound. As it came closer I could pick out the clip-clop of a horse's hooves crossing stony ground. Wilson picked up the pace. That seemed like a good idea. I wasn't sure what was coming and surprises were proving no fun in Mexico. Then, Wilson whistled softly through his teeth…and I turned.

The horse's chestnut hide shone like burnished leather in the sunlight, his tail and mane were black and long. As if he were hearing a drumbeat beyond the range of human ears, his ears pricked and twitched. The lieutenant sat tall and straight in the saddle, looking as if he thought he was the king of the world, and in that moment, with my back aching and the sweat sliding down my face like salty rain, I hated him.

A flat-brimmed hat shaded his eyes and made the top half of his face unreadable. Twin saddlebags bulged over the chestnut's hindquarters. Dropping the reins, the lieutenant slid smoothly out of the saddle.

Jose grabbed the reins and tied them to a branch of a small juniper. He reached up and pulled the saddlebags down. "Lunch time, *señors*."

Lunch was ham and cheese on dark bread, burgundy-colored apples going soft, bananas one day too ripe, semi-stale tortilla chips and a small plastic bowl of salsa. The salsa looked like day old blood with pond scum forming on top. My stomach churned.

For Wilson and me there was lukewarm water to drink. Jose got red wine in a long-necked bottle. The lieutenant passed on everything. I wondered if he had lunch waiting on him back at the ranch.

Hunger had a hold on me and I grabbed two sandwiches, an apple, a banana, and two plastic bottles of water. I ate the apple quickly, but halfway through the first sandwich I began to lose my appetite. Gurglings began in my stomach and a minor tidal wave rose in my intestinal tract. Food was suddenly unappealing. I tossed the sandwich back on the waxed paper and made a dash for the nearest bushes.

Five minutes later I returned, weak and washed out, moving gingerly on wobbly legs. My clothes were soaked through with sweat and my head was pounding. Easing down on the softest patch of grass I could find, I sipped slowly from a water bottle as I silently cursed my wife.

"Look at the tough Americano. One day he is tearing up a bar all by himself and the next day he can't even last through lunch." The lieutenant laughed at his own joke. I lay still and stared at the sky, trying to ignore him.

Jose mumbled something, and then Wilson and the lieutenant were both laughing. Closing my eyes, I sent soothing thoughts to my intestinal tract. When that didn't work I tried to think about something else. For a while I thought about Jolene and Stan, but that made my head hurt, so I quit thinking, and listened to the others.

They were talking about the wall and how hot it was today and how hot it was going to be tomorrow. I began to wonder if diarrhea or boredom would kill me first. The talk turned to a one-legged woman in Nogales who gave the best head south of the border. I never learned her name but did discover that her hair was long and brown and she had worn it parted in the middle since she was a school girl.

Cramps began to subside and were replaced by drowsiness. Lethargy washed over me. I could hear the wind whooshing at the rocks and junipers and sage grass that grew in drunken rows on the hillside. Sunlight pressed against my eyelids and I cracked them open. As if from a great distance, I heard my name being called. For as long as I could, I ignored the call.

Finally, I pushed myself upright and got my legs under me and started walking, feeling somehow liberated and virtuous at the same time.

"Where you been, Hampton? *Siesta's* over."

"Sorry," I said. "My stomach turned over on me and I had to lie down. Guess I dozed off."

Wilson worried with the large rock he was fitting into the line that formed the top of the wall. Giving it a final shove he stepped back and wiped at the sweat line on his forehead.

"Better watch that. Jose's not too bad about extended breaks. Likes them himself, as a matter of fact. The lieutenant, on the other hand, is a real prick. If he thinks you are dogging it he'll take it out on all of us."

"What do you mean?"

Wilson wiped sweat with a hairy forearm. "Who knows? Depends on what sort of mood he is in, and that usually depends on what kind of hell Ramirez or the señora has raised with him. Sometimes it's just an hour's more work, other times he'll make you do pushups until you puke, then there are days when he'll simply beat the living hell out of you."

Wilson gave me a crooked grin that showed off his bad teeth. "All I'm saying, Hampton, is if you value your future, don't cross him. Today you were lucky; he had to get back to the ranch. Mrs. Ramirez wanted to go to town."

"Thanks for the warning."

"Welcome," Wilson said. "Hate to see another reprobate learn the hard way. We losers have to stick together, right?"

"Yeah," I said. "Guess so." Being down on his luck in the wilderness had a way of making a man see things differently.

"What do you mean you guess so? You got any other friends out here?"

Actually, I wasn't sure how much of a friend Wilson was, but at least he hadn't beaten me, or made me do pushups, or stolen my rice and beans. "Nope," I said.

"Then grab a rock. We'd better get back to work before Jose gets through taking a dump."

From our ledge the mountain curved out, then fell away in a long gentle slope to the valley floor. Trees sporadically dotted the landscape, their leaves shimmering in the wind. Sunlight tinted the landscape a ripe gold, and unseen birds sang. It was as if we had stepped into a lost Grant Wood painting. Behind us the mountain rose like a natural battlement, thrusting against a sky beyond comprehension.

"Wilson, why don't we just get the hell out of here while he's behind the bushes?"

Wilson snorted through his nose like a bee-stung moose. "And just where in the name of all that's holy do you think we'd go?"

I jerked my head toward the top of the crest behind us. Surely another valley, one without a prison, lay beyond. "Over the hill."

"Hampton, you're damn near as dumb as you look. On the other side of this mountain is just another godforsaken mountain and beyond that another and another, and if you don't get shot by Jose, or tracked down by the lieutenant, or smashed in a rock slide, or mauled by a cougar, you are going to die of heat exhaustion or thirst.

"Because if you go in that direction there's nothing but two hundred miles of unrelenting desert. Ain't nothing out there but sand, cactus, rattlesnakes, and scorpions. Think you're man enough, then go for it. But this old boy is staying put. It may be a prison, but they feed you and let you sleep at night. You know that if a rattlesnake bites you at least they'll shoot you and put you out of your misery quick. My advice to you, *compadre*, is to get your ass back to work."

As I bent over to pick up a rock I told him silently to fuck himself. The rock was heavy and sharp-edged and I could feel the muscles in my back strain as I lifted it. Desire for a drink began to grow. I could hear Pedro's zombies scrambling around the rock slide. It was going to be a long afternoon. Knowing I wouldn't like the answer, I began considering who I could blame.

Seven

I spent that night massaging aching legs, listening to insects whirling, and wanting a drink, badly. The taste of it was already on my tongue and my body anticipated the burn and then the glow. Lying there in a heavy loneliness I had a vision of my father. The vision was only of his face, and even that was distorted, out of focus the way faces look in a wavy mirror.

Inside me there was a wanting to talk with him, to tell him I was sorry. His name formed on my lips, but I wouldn't allow myself to utter it. Instead, I focused on what I'd like to drink: whiskey, gin, wine, even beer would do. None of them was the solution; I knew that. However, any of them would help me get through one more day.

Somewhere in the night I dozed. When I came awake I was lost. Then I heard Wilson stirring and knew I was on a dirt floor in an old barn in Mexico. Then I remembered I wanted a drink.

Wilson turned over. His face was pointed toward mine. Raoul and Diego snored in the darkness. "Wilson," I whispered, "you awake?"

"What?" His voice was thick with sleep.

"You awake?"

"Am now. What do you want?"

"I need a drink."

"There's water in a bucket by the door," he said as he turned over again.

"Not water. I need a real drink. Know what I mean?"

"Yeah, join the crowd. We could all stand a shot."

"No, you don't understand," I said. "I need one bad."

"So what do want me to do about it? I don't have any damn booze."

In the moonlight that filtered through the cracks in the old barn I could make out the outline of his face. His body was only a dark bulk. The ground was smooth and cool and I could smell the staleness of my sweat and the sweet, moldy scent of old hay. Zombies scratched away in the aphotic corners of my brain.

"Know where I could get some?" I whispered. I wasn't sure how much English my cell-mates understood and didn't know how much I could trust them.

Wilson rolled over his side and groaned. His groan sounded tired. "You might try the guard. Sometimes, if they are in the mood and if you have something they want, they will help you out."

"Who's on duty tonight?"

"Let me think a minute. Oh, yeah, Felipe. Not a bad sort, unless the lieutenant just finished reaming him out. You could give him a try. Just go over to the left door. There's a board with a big crack in it. Just feel down with your fingers and watch for the light. Call to him through the crack. Keep your voice down. We don't want to stir up the lieutenant or the Ramirezes."

"Got you." I was already getting to my feet.

"Hampton."

"What?"

"Be cool. If Felipe doesn't answer, wait a few minutes before you try again. He may be making the rounds or taking a leak or the lieutenant may be close by. Don't fuck things up for all of us. Hear me?"

"Yeah, Wilson, I hear you." Before he could respond I was halfway across the earthen floor. The zombies were coming with me. I could feel their weight on my shoulders. For a moment I thought about the guy from the bar who had first spoken of zombies. I wondered where old Pedro was tonight and sent him a silent blessing.

The sleepers were still snoring gently, like little boys. I stepped over them and fixed my eyes on a sliver of light about three feet to the right of where I figured the door would be.

Kneeling, I put my eye to the crack. Moonlight splashed across the path. Shadows flickered in the wind and in the moonlight the stones were white. Felipe was not in sight.

I scanned the landscape, then pulled my head back and let my eyes rest. I tried again. Still no one there. Perhaps Felipe was just out of sight. As loudly as I dared, I called, "Felipe, Felipe."

Sounds came back to me, soft and indecipherable. Putting my ear to the crack, I listened intently. Decided it had only been the wind murmuring to itself.

I forced myself to count to one hundred. I took another peek. Shadows were more promising. I called the magic name again and returned one eye to the crack. One of the shadows moved across the moonlit ground. In a few seconds I could no longer see the light.

"Felipe?" My voice was more breath than whisper.

"Who is it?" Felipe's whisper was hoarse, the whisper of a smoker.

"Hampton, the American. The new guy. Do you know me?"

"*Sí*, what do you want?"

"I need a drink."

"You have water inside the barn."

"I want something stronger. Know what I mean?"

"Whiskey?"

"Yes, I need whiskey."

"Why do you need whiskey?"

"My legs are sore. I need it for the pain."

The only sound was the wind working its way around the corner of the barn. Finally, Felipe whispered with his hoarse voice, "No, no, you do not need it. Just go to sleep."

"I do need it. Need it badly."

"Whiskey is against the rules."

I considered the situation. Wood was rough against my lips. My legs were trembling and the zombies were hissing. "I can pay for it."

"You have money?"

"I have a very nice ring," I said.

"Money I need. A ring I cannot use."

"This is a very nice ring. I bought it in Las Vegas. You have heard of Las Vegas?"

"*Sí.*"

"Then you know the ring will be very nice. Everything is nice in Las Vegas. Bet you know someone who would like the ring, someone who would buy it."

"Maybe," Felipe admitted.

"Bring me the whiskey and I will give you the ring. When you sell it the money will feel good in your pocket."

No sound came from the other side of the wall. I waited for several minutes then put an eye back to the crack. Every cell in my body seemed to be screaming for a drink. Shadows drifted in the night. Just when I was ready to give up, one of the shadows moved. There was dark, then light, then dark, then the glint of moonlight off glass.

Easing my head back from the wall I stared at the crack and waited. My chest began to hurt. I realized I was holding my breath.

"Give me the ring." Even a whisper is loud in sanctity of the night.

"Hold on." The damn thing stuck for a moment, but I twisted like hell and it slid off. Praying Felipe was honest, I poked it through the crack.

In a few seconds something rubbed against the wood and then the glass was smooth in my hand. I held it very tightly. It was only a half pint. With the zombies chanting in my brain, I made us wait a minute. Then, as if of their own volition, my fingers were busy with the cap. Liquid flowed across my tongue and burned all the way down my throat. Never had I tasted anything finer.

After that first gulp, I made myself sip, with pauses between sips. Now that I had alcohol I could afford a semblance of discipline. I didn't get a glow, but the zombies gradually eased back into the darkness.

When the bottle was empty I licked the rim and pushed it deep into a musty smelling pile of straw. Then I crossed the floor as quietly as I could. No one spoke and I eased my body to the welcoming earth. I lay staring at light crystals sprinkled across the old roof, waiting for morning to come, thinking about my wife and whiskey, and where I'd wandered off the path. Finally, I decided I was in such a mess that it didn't matter when I'd taken the wrong turn. My primary business now had to be finding a way out.

Eight

A week later I got the first glimpse of my hosts. If they'd seen me when I first arrived they might not know me now. I'd traded in some almost new Topsiders for a pair of work boots roughly the right size. The bottoms were worn, but still better for me than the shoes. I had swapped a leather belt from Von Maur for some spare socks and a half full bottle of tequila, and exchanged my Abercrombie and Fitch khakis for a pair of the white cotton pants the locals wore and three bottles of Mexican beer. Even if the oversized legs were two inches too short, the loose fitting pants were comfortable and cooler. My silk shirt had gone for a bottle of Maker's Mark and a tee-shirt that urged people to vote for a grumpy looking man with fat cheeks and a large, misshapen nose.

On one of his rare good days, I had talked the lieutenant out of an old, sweat-stained sombrero I'd found hanging in a tool shed. Except for my relatively pale skin, and that was growing darker by the day, I looked Mexican as hell.

We were hoeing beans in one of the smaller plots that paralleled the house. Diego, Raoul, and the new man were taking a break in the shade of the stone fence. Wilson and I were hoeing hard, trying to finish our rows so we could get lunch, but we both looked up at the sound of a car. Wiping sweat out of my eyes, I watched dust billow as the vehicle rolled down the gravel road. No rain had fallen since my arrival.

We didn't get much traffic out this way, only the lieutenant's jeep and the veterinarian's truck, so I leaned on my hoe and watched them roll. It was better than a parade.

A silver Mercedes with darkened windows and a moon roof braked to a stop in front of the house. Before the dust had settled, the driver had hopped out and hustled around the car and opened the rear passenger door. A woman in a midnight blue suit eased out and gave the house the old once-over. Meanwhile, one of the guards had hurried over to the other side of the car and was holding the front passenger door open. A slender man with hair the color of polished silver stepped out. He wore a light colored suit and dark, wrap-around sunglasses. His thin, sharp-boned face was expressionless.

He said something to the guard in a voice too low for me to understand the words then walked away with a flowing stride. The guard mumbled to the driver and they both went around to the rear of the car.

"Those the Ramirezes?"

Wilson nodded. Sweat slid down his brown face. He was as dark as the natives. "Yeah, that's the royal couple."

I started scratching in the dirt among the beans. No need to aggravate the guards. I kept one eye on the handsome couple. They seemed familiar, though I couldn't be sure from this distance. "Sounds as though you don't like them."

Wilson shrugged. "He mostly ignores us. She, on the other hand, wants things done her way, and the very minute she decides." He looked up from his row, eyes pale and washed out in the morning sunlight.

"Word of warning for you, Hampton. Don't cross her. She can be a bitch, with a capital B, and she runs the place. Mr. R may be the financial genius, but, unfortunately for us, he's often gone and she rules the home front."

I ceased hoeing and gave her a long look. Something about her still struck me as familiar, but I couldn't place where I'd had seen her. Probably in a whiskey dream.

"Yeah, she's a good looking woman. Trust me, though, she's out of your league, and flat out deadly. Don't get me wrong, he can be a vindictive bastard. Saw him make a man who had just stolen one of his prime steaks stick his face in a pile of cow dung. Except for letting him come up for air, he made him keep it there half an hour. Week later that same guy disappeared."

"Let me guess, he never came back."

"That's right," Wilson said. "That's the way people like you and me get out of here. One day we're here, and the next day we're gone." He made a face. "Only thing is, it's a one way trip, one way the wrong way."

I started to say something clever but the guard began hollering for us to come and carry luggage. That beat hoeing beans. Besides, I'd been wanting a look at the inside of the house. Never knew what one might find…whiskey would be fine, a way out of here even better. Dropping the hoe, I tucked my shirttail in.

Leather suitcases, long, flat cardboard boxes, and shiny plastic bags filled the trunk. It looked like an extended family had come to stay a month. I grabbed a gray suitcase and an armful of bags. A guard stacked four boxes across Wilson's outstretched arms and we started for the front door.

After the sunlight, the inside was cool and dark. I stood for a moment on the smooth stones that lined the vestibule, blinking like an owl caught in a spotlight.

"Put them down over there. Lupe can carry them to the rooms later."

Her voice was deep for a woman, confident sounding. Wilson nudged me with an elbow and we started walking toward an archway that separated the first two rooms of the house.

As we went by I glanced at her. Holding herself parade ground erect, she was as tall as I was. In the light from candles that lined the wall, her skin was more bronze than brown. Dark eyes were set deeply in a sharp-boned face. I smiled, but her eyes never wavered from the luggage.

"Set it there. Now go and get the rest, and hurry. It has been a long trip."

"*Si, senora.*" Wilson said. I merely nodded and set the suitcase and bags down.

As we headed toward the front door I let my eyes wander. White adobe walls and dimness broken only by flickering candles set in recessed sconces gave the impression of a chapel. Wilson and I moved across the stone floor like two reluctant, over-aged, dilapidated acolytes.

Watercolors and oils hung low on the walls, splashes of color on a cool white sea. Furniture was heavy and dark. One large piece was wedged into a corner and crystal goblets were arranged in neat rows across the top. There was a brass keyhole in front. I figured it for a liquor cabinet.

When we finished with the luggage, we got lunch then hoed beans until it was too dark to see. Our clothes were soaked with sweat and covered with dust. Smells of dust, beans, horse manure, and stale human sweat hung in the air. All the way to the barn, instead of thinking about how tired I was and the way the days loomed unyielding before me, I reflected on the liquor cabinet.

Nine

Three more men joined us that week. Two of them were dull, forgettable. The third man had long hair as white as Montana snow and black juju bead eyes. More importantly, he had money, or something else someone at the ranch wanted, because he was able to procure an almost inexhaustible supply of alcohol. Often it was wine, but there was beer or vodka or even whiskey on occasion.

One sun-smeared afternoon he and Wilson and I were sitting in the darkest corner of the old barn. Final slivers of daylight were slicing between the slats and striping the earthen floor. We were sipping on a pint bottle of whiskey.

It was pleasant to sit with my back against the worn wood and sip on whiskey while I watched the light change against the darkening earth. All day we'd worked on the fence, and muscles, tendons, and ligaments ached. For the thousandth time I wondered about Stan and Jolene and what I would do if I ever found them.

Wilson and the new man were talking, their conversation drifting in and out like a radio station fading as the miles and mountains got in the way.

"Didn't see you in the fields or at the fence today, Cisneros," Wilson said. He was tired, too, slurring his words as the whiskey worked on his fatigue.

"No, they had me inside today, working on the books."

"How'd you land that cushy job?"

"Guess because I'm an accountant. Matter of fact, I used to work for Ramirez in town. Kept most of his books for over ten years."

Wilson blinked sleepily. "Why did you quit?"

"Didn't quit. Got fired. Expect you can guess why, too, seeing as how we drink like this every evening. For a long time I could handle the liquor and the books. Finally the liquor got control. Screwed up one too many times and Ramirez fired me."

I drifted back into the conversation. "How did you end up here?"

The old man chuckled. "Toward the end, when I was still working for the man, I was drinking way too much, totally out of control. When I drink like that I go crazy, spend money I don't have. Crossed way over the line. Spent it on liquor, women, and horses. Toward the end just gave it away."

"Wish I'd known you then," Wilson said.

"No you don't. I was merely a drunk. Plus, the money wasn't mine. Only Ramirez didn't find out about it until after he had fired me and brought in a new auditor. That's why I'm here now. The new man found the problem in less than a week. Took Ramirez's men two months to find me."

He laughed again. "Turns out I was right under their noses all along, only a few blocks away, staying with the padre at the mission and trying to dry out. Suppose I ought to thank Ramirez for saving me from sobriety. When his men finally located me I'd been dry for the longest thirty-nine days of my life."

"What happened when they found you?" Wilson asked. I was more interested in the contents of the bottle than the old man's story. It was tough to care about someone else when you didn't care much about yourself.

"Before you answer him, take a sip to clear your throat, then pass me the bottle. All this talking is making me awfully dry."

In the dim light I could see the old man's head turning, white hair floating, but I couldn't make out his expression. He took a sip, wiped off the lip of the bottle and passed it to Wilson. Wilson stared at the bottle as if he were trying to analyze the contents, then handed it over to me. I raised the bottle to my lips and let the whiskey flow across my tongue, savoring the burn.

"Hey, you wanna give that back?"

"Sure, old timer. Here's your bottle."

"Now tell us what happened when Ramirez's goons caught up with you," Wilson said.

"Before or after they beat the hell out of me?" The old man laughed and tipped the bottle up and took a swig. He coughed, then fell silent. In the heavy quiet of the old barn it was easy to feel as though we the only men in Mexico, maybe the universe.

"You were saying…" My voice punctured the silence.

The old man gave me a look I couldn't read. "Not a lot to tell. Somebody talked. Maybe they didn't mean to give me up, but they did. One thing you have to learn about life around here is that you have to be damn careful who you talk to. My advice for you gentlemen is to keep anything important to yourself, or maybe tell your one true friend, the one who will stand back to back with you against the crowd. You'll only have one.

"Feed the rest of the world crap and for god's sake don't tell a woman. Not your sister or your mother or your girlfriend, not even your wife. My painful experience is that they will either tell someone else, usually another woman, or hound you about it day and night."

The old man's philosophy bored me. "How about another drink?"

Wilson snorted. "Let him talk."

"That's all right, here's the bottle."

Glass always felt good to me, smooth and cool against my fingers. The glow was starting. The bottle clicked against my teeth and the whiskey flowed. The old man started talking.

"It was raining that night and they dragged me out of the rectory in my shorts. Damn, that rain was cold. Kept asking me question about the money, like how much I took and where was it. When they didn't like my answers they beat me, first with their fists and then with sticks. After a while lights were exploding inside my head and the rain wasn't so cold anymore."

He paused and sniffed, then went silent as though he was remembering that night and all of a sudden it wasn't anything he wanted to talk about. Birds were fussing up in the rafters and a dog barked down by the corral. I could smell the horses and the husky, hollow scent of the old straw. A feather drifted against my cheek, as soft as a baby's lips.

"Hey," the old man said, all loud and sudden against the dark silence, "I need a drink. Where's that bottle?"

I snatched a nip, then stretched out my arm in the darkness.

There was a gurgle and rasping sound as the old man rubbed the back of his hand across his stubble. "That's more like it." The bottle gurgled again, longer this time.

"Now where was I? Oh, yeah. By the time I came to I was hurting bad. Took me a long time to figure out where I was. They had me blindfolded and trussed up and jammed in the back of some open-ended truck. No way in hell for me to escape, so I just tried to survive. Next thing I know I'm here with you birds. Only Ramirez, he's a smart one, figures out he needs a bookkeeper a hell of a lot more than he needs another field hand. So I get to work the numbers magic at day and drink at night. One hell of a deal, huh, *amigos*?"

"Yeah, you're in like a rat down his hole," I said. "Now how about passing that bottle."

"Greedy tonight, aren't you, Hampton?"

"Not really, Wilson, just thirsty. Not in the mood for any preaching either."

"You got a problem, boy?"

"Yeah, Cisneros, lots of them. Right now though, I just need a drink. If that's okay with you two?"

"Sure, that's fine. Here you go, you damn camel."

"Thanks."

The glow was very close now. Anticipation made me quiver. I tilted the bottle back, then tilted it some more. A thin trickle ran down my throat, a drop in a vast desert.

"Damn, damn, damn!"

"What in the hell's the matter with you?"

"It's gone, old man. All the whiskey is gone."

"Sorry."

"Don't sweat it. Hell, it was your bottle anyway. It's just that I was so close." Tremblings ran through my body like minor earthquakes. I wasn't sure they were fueled by desire or anger or fear. I knew it was only imagination, but I swear I could hear Jolene laughing at me. Perhaps I'd slipped over an invisible precipice. Perhaps the devil was playing tricks on me. Perhaps she was the devil. Perhaps I was no longer in Mexico, but in hell.

"Close to what?" Wilson's breath was warm and moist against my face.

"Close to the glow."

"What glow?"

"Never mind. Just be quiet now so I can get some sleep. The lieutenant said we were back on the fence in the morning and that job wears me out."

"Hampton, I don't like to give advice. Never did. But did you ever think about cutting back on the drinking?"

For a moment I didn't respond. Then I said, "Some."

"Maybe you ought to try."

"You think I've got a problem, Wilson?"

"We've all got problems, Hampton."

"Guess we do," I said. I could hear Wilson moving in the dark like a wild animal settling in for the night. The old man didn't say anything and if he moved I didn't hear him. Darkness filled our corner. Only a smattering of moonlight seeped in through the rafters and the cracks in the barn walls. Easing down against the earth, I tried to will the glow but it wouldn't come without the whiskey, and I didn't have the whiskey.

Cursing myself for an alcoholic fool, I closed my eyes, bit my upper lip, then lay there thinking about the moonlight and Mexico, my dad, my cars, Las Vegas, the liquor cabinet inside the house and, finally my wife. Sleep found me wondering where she was and who she was with and what they were doing.

~ * ~

Sometime in the night the old man's voice woke me. He was talking to himself in a low, soft, sad voice. I couldn't catch it all; something along the lines that he'd once had something, but then he'd lost it and now he knew he was never going to get it back again. His was a pathos I could relate to and it generated a certain sympathy for the old fart.

For a long time I lay there and listened to him mumbling and Wilson snoring. Finally, I drifted back to sleep. When I woke the world had gone quiet, the air was cool, and night was dying. Wilson was still snoring gently and the old man had crawled off into the darkness. My head was splitting into a thousand fragments. I needed a drink in the worst way.

Only there wasn't even a little wine for this Apostle Paul's stomach's sake. Funny how that worked, so humorous it made my eyes water. I scooted around and got my back up against the rough wood, watched the light changing in the rafters, and wished I was drunk, or dead.

It was always in moments like these when I saw reality clearly. As clear as I was ever likely to see it anyway. It was in such moments of clarity that I could see I needed to give up my drinking, my anger, my wasted days and wasted nights. But addictions are funny creatures. They start tiny, like a microscopic dot of blue mold, spreading so slowly you hardly notice. And when you did, well, in a strangely satisfying way, they seemed familiar like a dark mole on your chin—ugly and repulsive, but your own. You sort of wished they were gone, but, then again, perhaps they were preferable to the unknown. Sometimes I was so philosophical I made myself sick.

Ten

"You're a lazy son-of-a-bitch, aren't you?"

I opened my eyes slowly, eyelids working like ancient Venetian blinds I'd seen once in a Kansas City hotel. I was supposed to be fixing a leak in the pipe that connected the kitchen sink to the main plumbing and my head was jammed under the nest of curving metal snakes. Off to my left I could hear a faint drip, drip, drip. Under the sink it was quiet and dark and cool, and I'd drifted off.

Mrs. Ramirez swam into focus. She was bent at the waist and her face loomed directly above mine like a newly risen moon. This was the closest I'd been to her and her face was surprisingly large and full of sharp bones. Pinpricks of light burned in her black eyes. Not knowing what to say, I smiled at her.

"You're not lazy, you're drunk," she screeched. Her harsh voice blasted at my ears and made my head hurt.

"No I'm not."

"Maybe you're not drunk, but you have been drinking. Don't lie to me—I can smell it on your breath, you bastard." She kicked my ribs with the sharp points of a black pump. I gasped. She was a big woman with a kick like a soccer wing.

"Who gave it to you? Tell me before I kick the shit out of you."

"I'm not drunk."

"All right, we won't argue. Just tell me who gave you the booze."

"Nobody gave me any booze."

"Oh, so you just helped yourself, you smart-assed son-of-a-bitch." Her shoe found my ribs again and I grunted as the toe rammed home.

"Hey."

"Hey what, you bum?"

"That hurts," I mumbled.

"It was supposed to. You drink my husband's liquor and you lay around all day when you're supposed to be working. He won't like that at all and I won't put up with it. Understand?"

Out of the corner of one eye I could see the shoe swinging again. "I understand, but I haven't been drinking your husband's liquor."

"Liar." She loomed above me, a giant shadow growing darker and closer and larger. "I ought to kick you in the balls, little man. However, since you're here in this condition you don't have any. Now tell me where you got the booze."

Scooting to my left, burrowing deeper under the pipes for protection, I tried to curl up on top of myself. "I haven't been drinking. I've just got bad breath."

"You're an absolute disgrace. Get out from under there."

"The lieutenant told me to work here. I'm supposed to fix the pipes. They're leaking."

"You're bad news, Mr. Hampton. Yes, I know your name. I make it a point to learn all your names. You know mine, so it only seems fair that I should know yours, doesn't it?"

"Guess so."

"What do you mean, you guess so? Either it is or it isn't. Now, which will it be?"

She was close enough that I could smell the jasmine of her perfume and feel the ends of her long hair drifting across my face. Her face was shadow-striped by the pipes, but I could see that it was handsome rather than beautiful.

"Yeah, that would be a fair statement."

"You'll find me a fair woman, Mr. Hampton."

"Good."

"And what did you mean by that?"

"Nothing. Just that it's good that you are fair. Lots of what I say doesn't have much meaning. Most of the time I'm only mouthing. You shouldn't pay any attention to me."

"You're probably right. You're drunk, but you're probably right. I shouldn't pay any attention to you. However, I find it difficult not to pay attention to a drunken man with his dirty boots sticking out from under my kitchen sink. Even your trousers are filthy."

Wrinkling her nose, she inclined her head closer. She had a large, hooked nose with wide, flaring nostrils, the kind of nose that would have looked natural on an Indian chief. It suited her.

"Damn, Hampton, you stink. Don't you ever bathe?"

"Once a week, whether I need it or not. Now hold on," I said as she drew back a hand. It was a large hand with a broad flat palm and I had no desire to feel it against my face. "Just kidding. I wash off in the creek most days and sometimes the lieutenant lets us scrub up in an old washtub behind the barn." I smiled up at her through the pipes. "Actually, I'm pretty clean."

"Actually, you're pretty drunk. Now get your lazy, good-for-nothing ass out from under there right now, before I beat the hell out of you. Do you hear me?"

"Yes, Señora Ramirez."

"Then do it. Faster. Lieutenant," she shouted in a voice drifting towards a scream. "Lieutenant, Jose, Geraldo!"

Footsteps pounded across the floor.

"Geraldo, where is the lieutenant?"

"Gone to Nogales for supplies."

"Damn." She stomped a pointy-toed shoe on the handmade tiles. From my vantage point I could see footprints of the coyotes that had walked across them as they dried in the chilly desert nights. "When will he be back?"

"Maybe tonight," Geraldo said, "or perhaps in the morning. Who can say?"

His pants were thin and faded. They needed washing. I could hear the shrug in his voice.

"Damn! Damn! Damn! Why is no one ever here when I need them?" Shoes scuffed along the tiles and the queen sighed. "All right, you will have to do. Get this man out of here and cleaned up and sobered up. Then get his lazy butt to work, hoeing beans or working on the fence or mucking out the stables. I don't care what he does, just get him sweating and don't let him quit until it's too dark to see. He's a drunken, lazy son-of-a-bitch and I mean to work the shit out of him. Understand?"

"*Sí*."

"Then get him out of here," she said and started kicking again. I rolled to get out of the way, banged my head on a low-slung pipe, and started cussing.

"Both of you get out of here. Now!"

Geraldo bent and got his hands on my clothes and began to drag me out and up at the same time. I took another shoe to the ribs and banged my head on another pipe. Ears ringing, I got to my feet, swaying slightly, waiting for the orbiting to slow.

Hands were rough and active on my arm and then we were walking down a long, cool dark hall. My legs were still unsteady and my feet looked a long way off. Despite the señora's accusations, I wasn't drunk. Granted, I wasn't exactly sober, either.

"Man, you are in deep shit now," Geraldo whispered. "Keep walking until we get out of sight of the house."

"Why am I in trouble?"

"You have hacked off the señora, and no one does that."

Enough alcohol was still in my body to fuel the bravado. "Why not?"

"You will find out. Now keep walking."

Halfway down the hall a short, plump, dark-skinned girl backed from a step-in linen closet into our path. Her name was Juanita and I knew her lips were soft and full and that her nipples had grown hard the night we'd made love in the purple darkness behind the old barn. She smiled at us in pretty confusion, her teeth white and straight and even. I straightened my back and winked at her. Geraldo nudged my arm and we kept walking.

Soon I could see sunshine coating the ground. It was so bright it hurt my eyes. That sunshine triggered childhood memories of sun-soaked afternoons when the world seemed perfect and I never dreamed it would ever change. If the sunshine meant anything to Geraldo he didn't show it. I concentrated on putting one foot in front of the other.

Eleven

"They'll be going soon."

Wilson and I were hoeing beans in the back field, while the old man who could always get booze was sitting in the feeble shade thrown by a pair of mesquite trees looking wryly at the calluses on his hands. The morning breeze had died an hour ago and the sun was beating down. Our faces were awash with sweat. Mopping below my eyes with a dirty red rag, I shaded my face with my hands.

"Who and where?"

The old man looked up from his study of the flesh. "The Ramirezes. They're going to Vera Cruz for the weekend. Business associates are throwing a big party, and the señora loves to party."

Wilson coughed and tried to clear his throat. He was leaning on his hoe, face pale and washed out. For the last week he'd been coughing. "How do you know all this?"

"I have my sources."

"You're a secretive bastard," Wilson said and let the hoe fall from his fingers. He walked between two rows of young beans and sat in the shade beside the old man. "Tell me more."

"What do you want to know?"

"How long they'll be gone? Who'll be left here? And what the chances are we can lay our hands on some booze and women?"

The old man laughed, a high, hollow laugh. "Don't want to know much, do you?"

"I thirst after knowledge."

"You thirst after booze," the old man said and laughed his crazy-bird laugh again.

Carrying my hoe, I walked over to them. "Quit your giggling, you old fool, and answer the man's questions."

"Another thirster after knowledge."

"Fuck knowledge. Tell us about the booze."

"And the women," Wilson added.

"Wish I had a woman right now," the old man said.

I wiped at the sweat traveling down my left cheek. "I'd settle for Juanita and a six-pack to go."

"Yeah," Wilson said, and coughed again.

Shading his eyes, the old man stared across the field. The house was a doll's house at the end of a play road. Stick figures moved around a toy car.

"They're loading up now."

"And?" Wilson rubbed his lips with the back of his hand.

"And they won't be back till late Monday. The lieutenant is going with them, along with two of the guards, Juanita, and Manuel, the chauffeur."

"Why is Juanita going?"

The old man shrugged his bony shoulders. "Who can say for sure? Maybe it's like I've heard, that even away from home the señora likes her comforts."

I glanced at Wilson. His eyes were bright in a face coated with sweat. I turned back to the old man. "What about the booze?"

"Plenty of that and only a couple of ornery guards to watch us. The three of us should have a fine old time."

Wilson hacked and spat. "What about Diego and Raoul, and that young kid with the fancy shirt?"

"Diego went home this morning and Raoul is going to head south tonight. As for the young man..." The old man shrugged and stared off toward the mountains. "A little bird told me he might just be going to Vera Cruz."

Wilson's head swiveled slowly toward the old man. "To Vera Cruz?"

"Perhaps. After all, he is a handsome young man, slim and dark. Cleaned up, he would be most presentable."

I didn't care about the young man. A question had jumped to the top of my brain. I asked it. "You said Raoul was going south tonight? Is he being set free?"

"Not precisely, *amigo*. He is setting himself free, at least for a little while."

"He's going to escape?"

"He's going to try."

"You don't sound like you think he'll make it," I said.

"Oh, he might," said the old man. "He's picking a good time with the lieutenant gone, but he's going alone and that's tough. He's not young or strong, so he will need much luck." Sighing, the old man studied his hands again. "Don't think he has that much luck."

"Why is he going then?"

"He could make it. Get lucky and catch a ride, or steal a car. However, Raoul does not strike me as a lucky man. Instead, he strikes me as a desperate man, and desperate men make foolish mistakes."

"Then why is he going now? Why not wait and find someone to go with him?"

"He is going because Diego is gone, and Diego was his only friend. Now that Diego is gone he will have no one, and some men cannot stand that."

"How's he going?" Wilson asked.

"Across country. At least he has the sense to go south. Walking is easier there and in twenty or thirty miles he will find ranches and beyond them a town."

My nerves were jumping. Freedom was a possibility I hadn't really considered. "Won't they look for him?"

"Of course, and while the ground to the south is flat and good for walking or running, it does not have many arroyos or caves or mountains to hide in. A man would have to be fast, determined, and lucky to get away going that direction, especially as the moon is not full."

Wilson coughed again, deep in his chest, and blinked his eyes against the spasms. "What does the moon have to do with it?"

"Without moonlight a man cannot see the path before him and it is most dangerous to cross this country at night. Without moonlight to guide him a man would have to travel during the day. Obviously, that has its own dangers."

The stick figures were loading up the big Mercedes and the lieutenant's Jeep. Voices carried in the clear air, faint and high like the cries of circling birds.

We watched them until the vehicles began to move and a stick man walked toward us. When he started down the dip in the path we all got up and started hoeing. When he came out of the dip he would be able to see us.

My hoe moved easily among the beans, but my mind was traveling a moonlight trail. For the first time escape seemed more than a daydream. Plans pushed across my mind like clouds before a storm. In the sunlit field it was very quiet. The soft chop of the hoe was clearly audible and I could hear the old man's dry, heavy breathing in the row behind me and, now and then, the nasty wetness of Wilson's cough.

Twelve

It was dark in the old barn, and quiet. Quiet enough to hear rats rustling in corners, the tread of the guard's footsteps outside and the damp heaviness of Wilson's breathing. Staring at moonlight through the cracks, I let the past roll. I'd done that so much lately it had become a nocturnal habit, one I needed to break.

Most nights I thought about Jolene and Stan, or my money hibernating north of the border. Occasionally, I wondered about my friends and whether they were searching for me. When the blues really had hold of my balls I wondered whether they even knew I was missing. What troubled me most was knowing that if the situation were reversed, I wouldn't have even noticed.

When I was in a truth-telling mood, I was forced to admit that most of the people I classified as friends were no more than acquaintances, golfing buddies, or business associates. Jolene had been my only family…Jolene and the red betas, hatchet fish, and neon tetras that occupied the long blue tank in the den. I closed my eyes and saw the water shimmering in the back light and heard the gentle swooshing of the air filter. Jolene and the fish both cared about me for the same reason.

Tonight there was a quality to the moonlight that moved the tides of memory. I sifted back to the family of my childhood. The family I couldn't remember being together for any extended period of time, unless you count a few brief vacations and a couple of months masquerading as years in Pittsburgh.

Often when we had been together it had been less than pleasant. Not that my parents were bad people, more absent than anything else. Absent in spirit, if not body. Only if one of us achieved a success was a fuss made. Problems were worth a stiff lecture, followed by a long cold spell.

My father had made an effort when he was home. However, he'd frequently been away on business trips that lasted for weeks. One, to Japan, lasted almost three months. Mother always seemed to have been going with friends to one meeting or another. In memory, her face was indistinct, as though I were seeing it reflected in a smoky mirror.

My brother had joined the Marines at eighteen after telling our parents how much they disgusted him. Even now I could hear the word 'disgusted' rocketing from between his thin, rigid lips. He spat it more than said it, as if it were a sliver of undercooked liver that had gotten stuck on the tip of his tongue. Andrew Courage I'd called him.

When I'd been sober and he hadn't been on maneuvers, we'd exchanged letters and talked on the phone. Once, I'd gone up to San Francisco when he had garnered a week's leave. I could still remember a certain bar in the Tenderloin where we had pissed off a six-pack of brothers. I'd been sure we were going to die. I'd begged for my life.

After I'd wet my pants they laughed at me and left us alone. In the more than ten years since then I hadn't heard from Andrew Courage. After that rainy San Francisco night, I couldn't imagine hearing his voice again.

Teresa, my sister, was forever fifteen in my memories. She had been skinny, blonde, and dotted with freckles and pimples when I went off for my semester at Dartmouth. Years later, when I was on one of my bar tours across America, a letter had tracked me down in Phoenix. It was from my favorite uncle, George, who had written to tell me that Teresa had been homecoming queen at Rutgers.

That, of course, was before she had been caught dealing, along with several members of the girls basketball team. The last I heard, from a friend of the family, who specialized in knowing things, Teresa had drifted west and settled in L.A. where she'd dyed her hair, added a silver lip ring, and gotten her nose broken in a lesbian biker bar.

Lying on my back, staring at fragmented stars, I understood why my father had turned bitter. He'd worked his ass off all his life and what did he have to show for it? A wife who wandered from organization to organization searching for something even she wasn't sure of, a lesbo-biker daughter, a son who told him to his face that he was disgusting, and another son who *was* disgusting. No wonder his bitterness was palpable.

Rolling over on my side, I whispered to the old man's silent back. "How much longer?"

He curled his scrawny neck and pointed his heavy head at me. "We have to wait until the shift changes. Tonight Felipe will not see or hear us."

Saliva formed in my mouth. "When does he come on duty?"

"Soon. Already it is after midnight. He should come on any minute."

"How will you know?"

"Felipe will check the barn door twice, make the door rattle in its frame. That will be our signal. We will go out the back where the slats are broken. Now be quiet before you spoil it all. Alberto is a prick. He'd like nothing better than to catch us breaking the rules. He's a bad one, Hampton. You can see it in his eyes. Alberto likes to hurt people. And without the lieutenant here, who will stop him? Not that fat sergeant, that's for sure. So hold your tongue." The old man rolled over until all I could see was the curve of his back in the broken moonlight.

Thoughts of the tequila to come helped me lie still. The old man's connections were good, and he had promised. I had no doubts. All I had to do was keep quiet. Moonlight drifted across the earthen floor of the old barn.

Thirteen

"Now," the old man hissed and I rolled up onto my hands and knees and pushed myself off the ground. I must have dozed because I hadn't heard the rattle of the barn door.

Wilson and I followed the old man, hustling across the barn, pausing at the wall, then easing through the loose slats, all sound drowned in the rising wind.

One high-powered security light was affixed to the barn, another to a pole at the far end of the corral, while a third burned against the blackness from the top of a dilapidated windmill. The wind was restless among the clouds and moonlight disappeared often, only to reappear seconds later.

I could hear the moaning of the barn timbers and the whine of the wind in the wires. The landscape was an uncertain mixture of pale light and shadow where the whiteness of the old man's hair bobbed and weaved like a rabbit's tail, while Wilson was nothing more than a long, thin shadow moving erratically in the old man's wake.

The house rose from the earth, massive and darker than the night. Standing in the shadows, I watched the old man pause and cock his head to one side as if he heard voices in the wind. He flexed the stiffness out of his shoulders and rapped twice on the screen door.

Toward the front of the house a light flickered. With our backs against still warm adobe, we waited. The wind was rising and falling, playing guessing games with itself, worrying its way among the small trees and low scrub.

When the wind fell all I could hear was my own breathing and the faint howls of the Mexican coyotes. Then the screen door swung open and a rail of light fell into the yard.

It was darker inside than out. Feeble trickles from flashlights bobbed their uncertain way across an unfamiliar terrain. Tiles were smooth beneath my feet and I could hear the hum of an unseen refrigerator. Smells of garlic, onions, and peppers filled the dark air. The faulty pipe still leaked water onto water, one drop at a time.

We went down a pair of mismatched steps and crossed a breezeway. The wind was cool and I could smell rain. A door screeched open and we stepped into the smoky dimness of a small room made of stones.

"Have a seat against the wall," the old man whispered as he gestured toward a spot near the door. Feeling my way along the wall with my fingertips, I eased down to the cool, earthen floor.

The only light in the room came from a single carbide lantern hanging from a protruding nail and a shelf lined with misshapen, smoldering candles that put out more smoke than light. Most of the candles were no more than stubs, staggering across a flat stone shelf like the broken teeth of an old fighter.

While the old man jabbered with two short dark men, I sat against the stone wall and waited for the poorly lit room to swim into focus. In the smoky dimness, Wilson's face was blurry two feet away. His breathing was audible.

Several wooden shelves were affixed to the walls. A faint mustiness filled the air, tinged with the odor of decaying fruit. Small glass jars, full of unidentifiable dark liquid, sat on the dusty shelves. Broken bottles huddled in the corners. I could read the labels of the closest ones. Once they had held tequila or whiskey.

I wished the old man would hurry with the palaver and get us a bottle. However, there were apparently certain social niceties that first had to be observed, or maybe he was negotiating the deal. I glanced at Wilson but he was staring at the dirt between his feet. I kept my mouth shut and my eyes fixed on the wall before me. Three men stood as still as statues along one wall. All three were thin, dark, and wore their faces like stone masks.

Finally, the old man quit talking and shook hands with the two men who looked like my ideas of Mexicans. Money changed hands. One of the men handed the old man a brown paper sack. The old man smiled and nodded at all the other men before he turned and walked to where Wilson and I were waiting.

"Boys, it's the good stuff," he said as he sank to his knees. His joints cracked and popped as he descended but the smile stayed on his face. He pulled a flat glass bottle out of the sack. The bottle sported a red and gold label with a black bull racing across it. The old man stared at the bull for a moment, then twisted the lid off the bottle. His Adam's apple bobbed. Lowering the bottle he coughed a small, tight cough, and wiped thin lips with the back of a hand.

"Oh, yes, damn good stuff. Here, try a sip."

Wilson stared at the bottle as if it held some long forgotten secret. He hefted the bottle in one hand as if judging the weight, rubbed a shirtsleeve across the lip of the bottle and raised it to his lips. He took a short sip, then a longer one. Then he passed the bottle to me.

The smoothness of a glass bottle always puts me in mind of a woman's breasts. The bottle floated upwards and clanked against my teeth. Liquid fire burned all the way to my gut. The bottle slid away from my mouth, then rose again. The second burn was even more exquisite. The bottle was rising for the third time when the old man's hands clasped my arm.

"Hand it back, Hampton. Every man gets a turn, but we all share equally. If not, I'll just drink it all. Understand?"

"Sure."

"Damn, that's good shit, if I do say so myself. Here, Wilson, ready for another?"

"Righto."

While Wilson took another sip I erected walls in my minds. The zombies were active and I didn't need them swinging over the barricades. Wilson passed the bottle to me. First the burn, then the glow.

Reluctantly, I gave the bottle back to the old man. He held it against his chest like a scared child. Envy rose unbidden. The glow was only a few sips away.

The old man took a hit and passed the bottle to Wilson. Wilson looked at it for a few seconds, but passed it to me without drinking. I had no such compunctions. Camels could have taken lessons from me.

The glow was growing. Stones felt smooth and solid as forever against my back. Strangers across the room were nothing more than dark ghosts. Jolene and Stan were fragmented memories from another life. Even I seemed unreal, a figment of my own imagination.

As if it were being painted on by an unseen god, I felt a smile grow and crawl across my face. I stole another drink before I passed the bottle. Smoke from the candles seemed to have infiltrated my skull. Time seemed to fall slowly, seconds tumbling like small pebbles cast from a great height.

The bottle came back to me and I lifted the bottle until it was smooth and cool and tight against my lips and liquid flowed like an amber river in the desert of my dreams.

Fourteen

They lined us up in front of a low stone wall. The sun was in our eyes. The guards had rifles in their hands. Hungover, I was on the verge of puking my guts out. Even so, I wasn't ready to die.

My legs trembled and a rancid smell filled my nostrils. It wasn't sweat. Wilson was beside me and he couldn't stand, so he leaned one hip against the wall and let his head hang.

I was at the end of the row and couldn't see the others. I didn't want to see them or think about them, or what the morning promised. Instead, I studied the wall.

Here and there a stone had fallen away and a thick green vine snaked through the opening. Yet there was a permanence to that gathering of stones as if they had seen a hundred thousand sunrises before man ever trod across the earth and they would see a hundred thousand more after man had faded to dust and blown to the mountain crests.

Beyond the sagging, curving line of stone were fruit trees: apples, pears, and peaches. Their branches hung over the wall and fruit that had fallen had been raked up in rotting piles against the base of the wall. Bees buzzed around the fruit and crawled across our dirty ankles.

The gang was all here: Wilson and me and the old man, plus five Mexicans whose names were a secret to me, staring at the guards with their rifles and the fat brown sergeant with a black cigar protruding from a corner of his fleshy mouth. His lips were thick and rhubarb red. They looked like cheap rubber. 1 hoped he was sucking in cancer with every puff.

Above the cigar, his eyes were small and bright, with the intelligent appearance that certain wild animals have. I mentally told him to go fuck himself.

Doors slammed and I turned away from the sun. Ramirez walked down the slope. Two steps behind were the lieutenant and Señora Ramirez. She was almost as tall as the lieutenant.

Ramirez marched with the short quick step of a mechanized man. No one spoke. I could hear birds moving restlessly in the fruit trees and the wind moving through their branches. Even the huff and puff of the sergeant as he drew smoke into his lungs and expelled it was audible.

It promised to be a surreal way to die, with birds watching and the wind writing our epitaphs as the smells of burning tobacco and fresh blood merged. My legs shook worse than before.

Ramirez came to parade rest in front of us. Guns moved in the guard's hands. Ramirez stared at us in silence. I tried to remember my life, but all I could do was stare at Ramirez and shiver.

Ramirez turned his narrow head and stared at the sergeant. After a moment the fat man got the drift and plucked the cigar out of his mouth. He tapped it out against the side of his left boot and dropped the butt into a shirt pocket.

Ramirez turned and looked at his wife and the man beside her. The lieutenant stepped forward. Morning grew so quiet that I might have gone deaf. Ramirez walked up and down in front of the ragged line, his long slender fingers clasped behind him. His hair was silver and flowed down his neck like sculpted snow. The crease line in his suit was sharp. Sunshine danced off the polished lizard skin of his shoes.

"I leave for a few hours," he said, as he came to a stop in front of the old man, "and what happens? You assholes turn my hacienda into a bar, a pigsty. You drink my liquor and let candles burn until they flicker out of their own accord. My house could have easily burned down, but it would have taken you scum with it so the loss would not have been without some recompense."

He paused and studied each man. His eyes were bright jet balls and sun shadows played in the curves of his face. I let my line of sight drift. Wilson was ghost pale. The old man stared at the ground. The lieutenant's face could have been carved from one of the stones behind me. Loathing covered the señora's broad face.

"I should have you all shot."

Wilson coughed damply. From beyond the first line of hills a cow bellowed. Tears formed and I blinked them away. I swore to all the unseen gods that I would be good forever if they let me live.

"I have thought much about having that done."

A bee settled on my forehead. I wanted to close my eyes but I couldn't force myself to look away from Ramirez's face.

"However, reflection reveals that such a fate would be more akin to mercy than punishment for derelicts like you, and if there is one certainty in this insane world it is that each must be punished according to his crime."

The bee buzzed off and I swung my eyes to the land flowing flat and hard beyond the old barn.

"Now, who will step forward and tell me which man sold the whiskey and which man bought it? It will go easier on you if you confess. This decision is yours. If you do not make it correctly I will make the next one."

The ground seemed to be shaking and I pressed my trembling legs against the stone wall. Glancing to my left, I could see Wilson still had his head down. One side of the old man's face was highlighted by the sun. Stubble looked like snow shards and one faded blue eye was squinched almost closed. Beyond the old man there were only shadows and sacks of clothes that resembled men.

"One last chance." Ramirez paused, and looked back toward the house as if he had forgotten something. Then he curled his neck and his finely-boned face swung around and he ran his eyes up and down the line of men with their backs against the stone wall.

"All right. Do not say I did not ask. Take them away, Lieutenant. Fifty lashes for each man and no food for twenty-four hours. And chain up the three gringos." His eyes seemed to burn a path across my face. "Without them this would not have happened." His body trembled with rage and he wiped a snail's trail of saliva from his chin.

"If there is a next time you will all die as painfully as possible. That is a promise I will keep."

The bird fell silent. All I could hear was the wind whining in the trees.

Ramirez chopped his hatchet face at the lieutenant. The lieutenant saluted. A gun barrel jammed into my ribs. Ramirez was studying the orchard. The lieutenant gave me a look I couldn't read. Señora Ramirez parted her broad lips and spat a fat warm glob against my right cheek. "Bastard," she whispered. "Worthless drunk American bastard."

A crimson tide of anger boiled through me. Unthinking, I stepped forward. My right hand was moving forward when Wilson grabbed it.

"Hold on, man," he whispered. "It's not worth it. Look around."

Through an angry red haze—it was like looking through a blood smeared camera lens—everything looked still and distant, posed for action, but frozen in time.

Then one of the guards sneezed and I felt myself going back down a long tunnel and I knew I was not going to die, at least not in that crimson moment.

Fifteen

"We're lucky, you know," the old man said. He was lying on his stomach and the words were muffled.

"What do you mean, Pops?"

He giggled high in his throat like a girl. "We only got twenty-five."

"Twenty-five?"

"Twenty-five lashes."

"How in the hell?"

"Money can accomplish much," the old man answered.

Easing over on one side, I tried to ignore what felt like electrified barbed wire striping my back. "Did you hear that, Wilson? We only got twenty-five lashes yesterday."

"Still hurts like hell," Wilson mumbled out of one corner of his mouth. His eyes were shut. Trickles of dried blood networked his back. His skin was sallow and the outline of ribs showed distinctly.

"Yeah," I said, "and today we still get beer. Courtesy of old Pops. Tell me, old man, how do you manage to procure alcohol on a daily basis?"

"Hampton, you ask too damn many questions. One of these days you'll ask the wrong man and he'll cut your nuts off for you. But I ain't that man, at least not anymore, so I'll answer your question for you. Answer it in one word. Gratitude."

"Gratitude?"

"Yeah, gratitude. Couple of guards around here are grateful to me. One of them because I was able once to loan him some pesos when he had a life-threatening need. The other because I was able to secure employment north of the border for his mother and sister on a no green card basis. The family is large and poor and desperately dependent on the cash that flows south. He knows that with a single phone call they are back in Mexico. He is very grateful every day I don't have that phone call made. Now, no more questions about the booze. Surely even you can appreciate the need for a code of silence."

"All right, no more questions." I arched my back and let a stream of beer slide down my throat. The beer was warm and the position made my back hurt. Sacrifices, however, must be made.

I twisted my head and glanced at Wilson. He was quiet, not drinking much and seemed to be lost in thought. On the other hand, I was trying to avoid thinking. I found it depressing. Still, thoughts crept in unexpectedly, like stray coyotes. Lately, I'd been thinking about how to get out of here and trying to live up to my promise to be good. I wanted to be good, but then again, I didn't. I wanted to stay sober at the same time I wanted to get drunk. Goodness versus the glow. Contradictions were splitting me right down the middle. I wanted to scream. Instead, I took another drink and drug my legs closer to my chest.

"Damn these chains are heavy."

"Fuckers eat into your skin," Wilson said.

"That's what they are designed to do," the old man said, and sipped from his bottle.

Wilson shifted his body, trying to find a more comfortable position. "Wonder how long they'll leave them on?" Spider webs of discomfort sketched his face and circles under his eyes were the dark purple of overripe plums.

"Maybe not all that long," the old man said.

Wilson propped himself up on one elbow. Straw dangled from his hair. "What do you know, Cisneros?"

"Nothing much, only I hear that Ramirez is heading out again soon. Going away on business. Since the señora doesn't usually come down to the barns we should be able to induce someone to take these impediments off." The old man lifted the bottle to his thin lips.

"Praise Mary, the beer is still good." He took another drink. "I'll hear when he's gone and speak to my *amigos*. It was only bad luck that we're in this mess anyway. Some damn tenor cancelled a concert because he caught cold. Otherwise the Ramirezes are still in Vera Cruz."

Wilson closed his eyes. "Shit happens," he said.

"Yeah," the old man said, "and sometimes the world craps all over you."

Wilson snorted like a winded horse. "Ain't that a pretty picture."

"Shut up and drink your beer. I'm going to take a nap. Make this long day go faster." The old man farted loudly, and let his empty slide onto the straw.

Sipping slowly on my last bottle of beer, I stared at the faded black wooden slats of the old barn. Quiet gathered haphazardly around us. Judging by the sweat forming on my skin it was the middle of the day. In the heat the birds had gone still. A honeybee buzzed faintly, but incessantly, from the far corner of the barn, and now and then a cow mooed from the hills that rose steadily to the north. The still air was permeated by the sour smell of animal dung, old hay, human sweat, beer going flat, and the old man's flatulence. I tried not to think about tomorrow coming with a chain still around my leg, or the beer still standing in Wilson's bottle.

Sixteen

I kept my back off the ground and my eyes open. Wounds healed and I discovered something important.

By the end of the week Ramirez and his beloved were gone. No one knew where, or they weren't saying. At roll call the next morning I told a young guard with a soft mustache I had the stomach flu. He nodded and pointed toward the barn. I walked toward it slowly, pretending I was a hippopotamus with a kink in his lower bowel.

I spent the morning thumbing through old magazines the guards had cast our way. The slick-backed publications were written in Spanish, a language I hadn't seriously read since high school, but most were laced with enough photographs to help the hours slip by. As noon approached, my stomach, which had missed breakfast, began to rumble. Tossing aside *Mexico by Night*, I went in search of nourishment.

The old barn was virtually an empty larder. All I found to eat were two half-melted peppermints and a deadly looking slice of beef-jerky under Wilson's jacket. Promising myself to keep them in mind, I decided to reenter the outside world.

Pausing at the door, I put my ear up to a crack that looked like the peninsula of Florida. Quiet, broken irregularly by the humming of bumblebees working a small patch of clover, ruled the barnyard. Easing the door open just enough for me to slide out, I stepped into the sunlight.

Moving in the shadows as much as possible, I angled toward the stone fence.

Just beyond that fence, dangling from scrawny branches, were a few apples. In the fractured light they were a dull red. I duck-walked across the dusty ground and boosted myself over the stones.

The apples were wrinkled and going soft on the ends, but they tasted like Sunday brunch at the Waldorf. Juice ran down my lips and chin and dripped onto my shirt. Slivers of peel escaped my tongue and hid in the grooves between my teeth. Sitting with my back against the stones, I savored apples and life and let the wind blow unchecked across my face.

I was finishing the third apple, ruminating on how fine a brandy Alexander would taste, when I heard voices. At first they were only voices, carried on the wind along with dust and birdcalls. Gradually the sounds formed syllables, then words.

"The usual?" I'd heard that voice before.

"*Sí*, the beer, but also, if it can be arranged, a half-pint or two. I hear they are moving us to the cattle pens for a couple of days and I need to procure my supplies in advance. You are staying here, or so I understand." The old man was walking; I could hear the hiccupping rhythm of his footsteps. For a moment the steps paused and I thought he'd seen me, but the rhythm resumed.

"Who is staying here?"

"For certain all the house staff, probably the sergeant and the Gomez brothers."

"Of the prisoners?"

"Hampton I figure, because he has the flu," said the old man, "and probably the tall man with the bad foot. Don't know his name."

"Nor do I, but I believe you are right. That man cannot move fast and he would be in the way with the cattle."

"I can count on you then? Tonight at the well?"

"*Sí, sí*, but now we had better move. That lieutenant is everywhere these days."

"I see your point, Jimenez. As usual, you are astute in your observations."

I sat very still and listened to their footsteps fade into the earth and wind. A smile spread across my face. I had discovered a name, and in the name was the knowing.

Seventeen

I had the grace to wait until the following afternoon. The old man had been correct. At dawn the day after I learned the name, we'd been awakened by the throbbing of a large engine. Wilson crawled across the still dark floor and put an eye to a crack.

"It's the truck."

The old man propped himself up on one elbow. "The old blue one?"

"Yeah, faded worse than ever."

Someone was tugging on the latch and Wilson was double-timing it across the floor, racing the beam of light sliding through the darkness.

Closing my eyes, I kept my mouth shut, and when they poked me in the ribs with the sharp end of something I moaned. Wilson told them I was sick and after that they let me alone. I listened to the call of the guards and the grumbling of men who were not free and the clank of a huge tailgate going down and the metallic groan as it went back up. After the truck left, I lay with my eyes fixed on the ceiling and watched the light, filigreed by dust, slowly consume the room. A feeble shame filled me, but I'd told so many lies another was no more than one more pebble on a great stone pyramid. The barn grew so quiet I could hear the zombies taunting me.

~ * ~

Jimenez came on duty at noon, with his long, drooping nose and wet brown eyes. The tall man with the bad foot and I were sitting quietly in the soft sunshine at the north end of the barn. His name was Helmut

Brandt and he had been born in Berlin. Helmut told me he was wanted in three countries, but he neglected to say which three countries wanted him, or what they wanted him for.

We talked away the afternoon, chatting in a desultory fashion about the weather, our fathers, the last girl we had kissed. Jimenez sat with a rifle across his lap on the bed of an old wagon with two bad wheels, smoked dark cigarettes, and rubbed his paunch. Twice, he blew his nose softly into a nasty gray handkerchief.

About four o'clock Helmut asked to go take a dump. Jimenez gave him the Juarez head jerk and the most wanted man I knew limped off for the communal outhouse. He walked like both his feet had been permanently broken, his shirttail flapping behind him like a pennant in the breeze. When the door closed behind him I stood and walked slowly toward Jimenez, making sure my hands were palms up to the man with the long ugly gun.

His Labrador retriever's eyes never left my face, even as the angle of the rifle changed. Ten yards away I stopped.

"The usual tonight, Jimenez?"

It was humorous to watch the patterns in his face change.

"What are you talking about, asshole?"

"I'm talking about the beers and whiskey you bring the old man every night."

His eyes were only brown slits now. "*Gringo*, you are *loco*."

"Perhaps, but do you want me to talk to *Señor* Ramirez when he returns, or sooner to the lieutenant."

"I could shoot you."

"You won't," I said with more conviction than I possessed. "Dead men always create more questions than they are worth. Besides, that outhouse door could open at any minute."

The rifle barrel rose.

"I could shoot you both."

Sweat trickled down the back of my neck and slid under the collar of my shirt. I ignored it.

"Yeah, you could shoot us, and how would you explain why you had to shoot a sick man and a cripple?"

"I could think of something."

"You had better think of it fast. Maria is coming over the hill."

Jimenez twisted his neck and flashed a glance at the plump young woman carrying a basket of clothes toward us. Her long black braids swung in rhythm.

"Fuck you," Jimenez hissed, his words rattling in his throat like a sore-tailed snake.

"And the horse you rode in on."

"Shut up." He raised the butt of the rifle.

"Oh, I'll be silent. I can be very silent. Just don't forget the beer, and maybe a half-pint of your finest whiskey." Turning away from Jimenez, I watched Maria's breasts rise and fall under a faded red blouse.

"Beer, no whiskey."

"Both."

"Impossible."

"Nonsense," I said. "You have done it before."

"For the old man." Jimenez shook his head from side to side. His long nose seemed to wobble in the air. "Not for you."

"As for the father, so for the son."

"He is not your father."

"We are all sons of the Father. If you do not believe me we can ask *Señor* Ramirez when he returns." I grinned at my new Mexican friend.

I hoped he couldn't see the sweat soaking the back of my shirt. His fingers trembled faintly. Just when I thought he might be considering shooting, he turned and stared at Maria.

I smiled at Maria as though she were my old Sunday school teacher at First Methodist.

~ * ~

The first night was fine, the second even better. The third night, however, was a different story. It was a single beer night, and bad beer at that. Although I suppose there is no such thing as a truly bad beer.

Jimenez slipped me the single bottle after lunch, and merely shrugged. I tried not to let it bother me. Misfortune happens. It had happened to the old man. One day he'd only brought a single beer back to the barn. Wilson had nicknamed it the Lone Ranger.

Now and then I thought about Wilson. He'd treated me like a human being, the first to do that in so long I couldn't remember. In a silly sort of way, I missed him. Wilson's cough had sounded nasty before he left and I wondered how sleeping out in the open was agreeing with him. Neither of us was a youngster anymore.

The more I thought about Wilson and how good he had treated me, the more I became ashamed at my subterfuge. Being here and healthy while Wilson coughed his guts out wrestling cattle seemed immoral. Still, it was every man for himself. In the daylight, I almost believed that.

Sipping slowly made the single beer last until almost midnight. One only made me desire more. After a few minutes the zombies and the memories hooked up to torment me. I told them to go to hell, but none of them paid any attention to me.

Focusing on childhood friends and books I'd read back when I aspired, briefly, to a literary life got me through an hour. There had been nights I'd talked myself into holding on until morning. This wasn't one of them.

If Wilson had been there he might have been able to talk me through it. But he was herding cattle and the old man had been sent to Nogales to work on some books and I was stuck in an old barn that creaked in the wind with a bad-legged German who snored like a wounded buffalo. When I could no longer control the shakes, I stuffed the empty bottle under the hay, pried apart a couple of rotting planks, squeezed my body through the gap, and stepped into the night.

Starlight sprinkled silver across the corral. Standing with my back against the barn, letting my eyes adjust, I listened to the wind working against the old barn and, once, far away, a high-pitched howl.

I slipped away from the barn, crossing the barnyard with a low loping stride. Sliding under the bottom rail of the wooden pole fencing, I worked my way toward the dark elongated smudge that was the hacienda.

Dangers lay ahead. I didn't know where the guard was. I didn't know how many people were in the house. Yellow bug-lights glowed above the kitchen door. Fear made me tremble, but the memory of the liquor cabinet was stronger.

I picked my way through the cholla and brittlebrush, then hovered just outside the bug light. No one challenged me while I stood listening, a shadow within a shadow. Only the wind, moaning fitfully to itself, came to my ears.

Taking a deep breath, I stepped into the light. The night was warm and the big wooden door was open. Only a screen door barred my entry. Holding my breath, I crossed the open ground and gently pulled on the door. The night answered me with silence and I stepped inside.

A nightlight was burning in the hallway and I crossed the tile floor on tiptoe with the hair on the back of my neck standing up. I had no idea if the maid and cook slept in, but, given the isolation of the ranch, I was guessing they did. Wilson had told me the guards slept in a bunkhouse on the other side of the garage, but there was always the possibility that one was stationed inside the hacienda at night. My sphincter was squeezing tighter by the second.

Sconces, pictures, and tapestries hung on the walls, so I stayed in the middle of the hall. The floors were hardwood and I was afraid of squeaks. With exaggerated slowness, I placed my feet with care.

The hall was longer than I remembered and the lighting was poor. I kept worrying I'd taken a wrong turn. Finally I caught a glimpse of light glittering off glass and I remembered the crystal goblets.

I knelt before the liquor cabinet, and slid my fingers over the smooth wood, searching for the handle. Locating it seemed to take an inordinately long time. Nerves did calisthenics in my arm. Finally, eager fingers gripped the handle and pulled it down. With the faintest of clicks the door slid open.

Illumination in the hallway was too feeble to allow me to read the labels but I made out shelves containing various sized and shaped bottles and decanters. In the poor light they gleamed dully, but they looked like pure gold to me. Wrapping my fingers around what looked like a whiskey bottle I lifted it gently from the shelf and hugged it to my chest. I reached again and again and again until I couldn't hold any more. It was as though I was a very sick man and the bottles held a precious life-saving elixir.

With my arms full, I stood. My plan had been to slip back to the barn with my contraband. Now a sip to fortify my nerves seemed like a good idea. Another darker hallway branched off to the right. Quiet filled the house. Promising myself just a couple of shots, I started down the corridor.

At the far end of the passageway I could see light. Slipping past darkened rooms, I headed for the glow. Near the end of the hall light was drifting in through windows above a king-sized bed. Lacy, ruffled curtains were pulled back and tied with sashes. Starlight spilled across the bed, turning the comforter silver. I turned in and sat down on the bed like I owned the place. The bottles were heavy and anticipation was rising. As the song goes, I'd been too long in the wind.

Taking great care not to let them clink together, I laid the bottles on the bed, arranging them like soldiers on parade. I liked the way they stood at attention.

I sat listening to the quiet, trying to decide what to do next. Choices kaleidoscoped across my mind. Something ticked inside my brain like the countdown to the end of time. Eventually, I realized it was the ticking coming from an alarm clock across the room. A ceiling fan hummed in the distance. I got up and closed the door.

I made myself wait. Forbearance was exquisite torture. In that moment of waiting I felt young again, as though I had traveled back to before Jolene, to before the drinking, to before the great boredom, when the world seemed exciting, full of promises.

The bottles stood at attention beside me on the bed. They were lovely and naked and they called out to me with promises I could not resist. Stretching out one trembling arm, I opened the first one and pulled it to my lips.

Eighteen

I was floating on a great sea. Waves rose and fell beneath me, gentle, silent swells. I drifted through an all-encompassing darkness. With almost infinitesimal changes the darkness began to give way to the light. The swells began to grow. The sea was no longer a calm evolutionary tidal pool. Fear replaced peace and an infantile sense of well-being gave way to nausea.

I tried to open my eyes but their lids were extraordinarily heavy. There was something I wanted to say but the words were stones in my throat. Without warning the nausea rose in a tsunami and spewed hot, sticky, chunky liquid. Bile was violently bitter in my throat.

The world faded to black and the sea began to calm and in my mind there was only a vague, dark uneasiness. Again, I was drifting in a timeless sea with no port of call. I drifted into sleep, dreaming of pale horses running in a March wind.

~ * ~

Voices now, angry buzzing waspish voices, intruding on my sea of dreams. The voices irritated me immensely and I waved my arms to drive them away. I tried to tell the voices what I thought of them, but the words got all mixed up and came out garbled, fragmented, disjointed.

Steel vises encircled my arms, gripping deep into my flesh. A slap of pain stung my face and I tried to raise my arms, but the steel vises held them down. Pain begat pain and then there was light, growing exponentially as my eyes fluttered open.

A blurry figure towed above me, waving its arms and screaming words I couldn't understand. I blinked my eyes and kept on blinking until the world came into focus.

I was on my back on a bed, and men, not steel vises, held my arms. The figure towering above me was Señora Ramirez and her words were obscenities strung together with a few choice adverbs and adjectives.

"Bastard," she screamed. "You goddamn drunken son-of-a bitch. I am going to kill your worthless ass. You are nothing. You are not a man. You are only a drunken asshole."

"But—"

"Shut up! Shut the fuck up. Shut the fuck up, now." Spittle glistened in the corners of her mouth.

"I warned my husband not to leave you here, but he would not listen. Oh no, he knows it all. Well, he is not here now, so I will make the decisions."

"Hey, listen—"

Her right hand exploded against my left cheek. She was a big woman with powerful arms and the slap stung.

"No, you drunken bastard, you listen to me. What could you say anyway? I come home and find you passed out on my bed, my bed, lying in your own vomit. You have drunk our whiskey and wrecked my bedroom, and God only knows what else. Probably raped our women and stolen our jewels.

"I warned my husband you were a drunk. Perhaps you would prefer to call yourself an alcoholic, but you are nothing more than a drunk with delusions. A rich American drunk who thinks he can come into my country and my home and do exactly what he pleases. Well I have news for you, you slimy prick, that is not the way life works in the home of Anita Louisa Maria Ramirez. I have had to endure much to get what I have and I am not letting some drunken pretense of a man come into my life and destroy it."

She paused for breath, her breasts rising and falling like undulating hills while I searched for calming words. My stomach wasn't right and I was still hung-over in a major way. Two empty bottles stood empty on the bed beside me and a third was half empty. If she would leave me alone I would probably die anyway. If she didn't quit slapping me around and rocking the bed I was going to throw up again. All my befuddled brain could think to say was, "I'm sorry."

My words only enraged her more. She ripped back the soiled covers and sank to her knees on the bed, straddling me, and began to slap and punch my face. Blows fell indiscriminately, like a hot, violent rain. I struggled to get my arms free, but I was weak and the hands that held me were strong. Between the blows I could see the faces of the guards staring down at me. They were void of expression and could have passed for statues.

Blood was on my tongue and I choked back rising bile. Señora Ramirez was heavy on my chest and sweat stood out on her forehead and ran down her hawk's nose. Large teeth bit at her upper lip as her fists smashed against my face. A warm worm of blood trickled from my left nostril and my right eye was going shut. I wanted to lift my legs and kick her, but there were guards and they had guns and I had enough sense left to know I really only thought I wanted to die. All I could do was try and hold on.

Eventually, the blows began to slacken. Finally, they ceased. Anita Louisa Maria Ramirez looked at her hands as if they were small wild animals then slowly descended from the bed. She bent down until her face was inches from my face, cheekbones poking at her skin like mountains forming.

Thick lips parted and warm breath blew against bruised flesh. "You are a bastard, Hampton, a goddamn drunken rich, egotistical, selfish, greedy, whore-hopping American bastard. And I know how to treat bastards. Nobody messes with Anita Louisa Maria Ramirez. That you will see for yourself before you die."

She hawked and spat hot saliva against my face. Then she smiled and fired off a barrage of orders in Spanish. Strong arms dragged me from the bed. Her spit slid down my face like warm snail tracks. I tried to walk but my legs were gone and they had to drag me, feet scraping across the hardwood floor. I wanted to beg for mercy, but there was no priest to give me absolution.

Nineteen

The chain was roughly ten feet long, heavy iron links forged together. One end curled around the ancient cottonwood that stood sentinel on the first rise behind the hacienda. The other end was a wide, flat steel cuff that encircled my left ankle. A large padlock secured the chain to the cottonwood. My entire world consisted of the circumference of the circle created by stretching the chain.

Sunshine woke me early in the cool mornings, pouring through cracks in the rounded hills that encircled the ranch to the east like half-baked loaves of dark-grained bread. In the evenings, threads of fading sunlight gave me a parting benediction, a final touch of light before the uncertain dark. Between dawn and dusk the sun scorched my world.

I lived in the shadow of the cottonwood. Its ever changing shade patterns darkened the dry ground and provided the only succor from a violent sun. Throughout the day I followed its trajectory, moving often to avoid being baked. Above, the desert sky was clear and hard and uncompromisingly blue. To doze anywhere but against the trunk of the cottonwood was to risk sunburn.

Three times a day someone brought me a tin pan of food and a plastic Coke bottle full of lukewarm water. Usually one of the guards brought my meals, but occasionally the fattish cook, Rosita, or the young girl, Elena, made the trip on foot up the hill. No matter who brought it they didn't talk to me. They simply placed the fresh food and water where I could reach them, picked up the dirty tin and empty bottle, turned and walked away.

They never looked back. The few times I tried to make conversation they ignored me.

I ate with my fingers and drank sparingly, making it last, never confident they would bring me more. The pan usually contained beans and tortillas, and sometimes a piece of fruit or stringy beef. Once there was a piece of angel food cake. It had no icing and tasted like used foam rubber. There was no way to wash my hands except with the water they brought which was too precious to waste. I had to conduct my bodily functions in the open. Once I sobered up I could smell myself. I never got used to the stench.

Mornings weren't too bad. Usually, there was a breeze blowing from the west. In the heat of the afternoons I dozed, often waking to find my body exposed to full sunlight, the sun having moved on while I slept. Exposed flesh turned red, then a burnished shade of bronze.

Nights seemed to stretch endlessly. Coyotes howled from the darkness and there were strange nocturnal rustlings in the sagebrush. Night sleep was full of troubled dreams that left me drenched in cold sweat, trying to remember what had frightened me.

Above my corner of Mexico, the night sky was filled with stars. The moon rose huge and melon colored, growing smaller and silver as it climbed. It was far more pleasant to stare at the lights glittering against a vault of ebony than to face the nightmares.

With no one to talk to and nothing to read, I spent the day watching the shadows change as they curled across the landscape, thinking about the way I had truly fucked up my life. It was painful to remember my parents and old friends and lovers. The only gratitude I could feel was that none of them could see me now. It occurred to me that perhaps none of them would ever see me again.

Hours were spent trying to figure out when and where the long slide had begun. Eventually I decided that, like so many bad choices, it must have begun in an unguarded moment, one so unremarkable that no image remains. I swore that if I ever got out of Mexico, I would never forget the old sycamore and the smooth iron chain, and what had led me there.

The first day I'd been hung-over, sick with the lingering taste of vomit. Throughout that day I only drank a little water. Toward evening, I ate a package of stale crackers I found in a pocket.

On the second day the zombies found me. As they began arriving I started wanting a real drink.

By the third day I needed one.

On the fourth day I was shaking like the last aspen leaf before the first Colorado snowstorm of the season.

The fifth day I saw visions.

I woke myself up screaming on the sixth.

By the seventh, time no longer had meaning. I couldn't make myself eat and the world swam in sticky vapors that smelled of scorched oranges and left the aftertaste of hell in my mouth. I told myself to be strong and brave, but that was only cheap talk. Tears rolled silently down the furrows in my checks. I'd often wondered how far I could sink. Now I knew. I made myself sick at my stomach.

And it was the heebie-jeebies that visited throughout the day, and the hurdy-gurdys that danced all night. All I could think of was a drink: whiskey, vodka, tequila, wine, beer, home-brew, aftershave, it didn't matter. My body, my mind, my soul all craved alcohol, alcohol in any way, shape or form.

Nothing else mattered anymore, not the bloody orange sun burning a hole in the baby-blue sky, nor the wind whispering through the sagebrush, or the soft smile of the fat woman who brought my lunch, or the hard-edged memories of a childhood that never was and the adulthood that had never happened. All that was in me was the desire for one, tall, cool, forever lasting, one hundred percent proof drink that I could consume, and then would consume me. That desire drove my mind into crevices so dark there was no light at all.

There were moments, usually just before dawn broke crystal on the mountain peaks, when the zombies left me and the fever receded and my brain was cool and clear and hollow all the way to the essence of my being.

In those eclipses of insanity I saw my true self and wept. Morning sun dried my tears and the first wind of day forgave me. I promised myself a new beginning. With daylight, however, came desire, and I knew I'd only been lying. Again I wept. This time for all my iniquities.

There was no one to see me and no one to care, only the wind and the gently waving sagebrush. In the way a child will tell himself that Jesus will watch over him, I told myself that the Holy Spirit moved in the wind. And I wanted to believe and I wanted to be good. But the sagebrush was mute and the wind kept drifting away and I could never quite make myself believe in salvation.

Twenty

The harsh cry of an unseen bird woke me. I came awake all at once, with a clear coolness running through my mind. It was the moment before dawn and I looked across the flat plain that ran for a quarter mile to the east before it rose to form hills. Tawny grasses moved in waves before a steady breeze. The world was backlit by the rising sun.

The wind was cool against my face, carrying with it the smells of soured dust, animal dung, smoke, and meat cooking. By far the strongest odor was my own sweat and filth, hanging heavy and foul like a pestilence, making me long for a shower.

Daylight was coming. The tops of the hills looked like fire. Reddish gold flames slid down the slopes like fingers of the sun god. Shadows, the keepers of ancient secrets, still held in the crevices and on the west side of the boulders that rose from the sunbaked earth like smooth brown mastodons.

Even with my ragged clothes, garnished with sweat and urine and vomit, my scraggly, two-toned beard, the grit between my teeth, and the hot, foul breath in my mouth, I felt extraordinarily alive. An indefinable quicksilver element ran through my veins. It was alive and throbbing in my brain, honing my senses and making my flesh quiver.

I sat there with the wind in my face and watched the sun god's golden fingers stretch to the bottom of the slopes and then cross the plain. While the sunlight grass became golden brown, white light sparkled in the mica embedded in scattered stones. The tall grass was alive with birds and more swung on the branches of the brittlebrush.

And I asked for nothing and wanted nothing except the morning being born before me. I felt incredibly young, as if I had been born again that morning in the streaks of sunlight and the rush of the wind and the welcoming call of the birds. Lizards crawled out of the darkness of the land to sun on boulders as ancient as the earth itself.

God was there in that moment. And I knew He existed, although His form was incomprehensible; and I knew I needed Him, needed His strength. And I made myself one final promise.

Conscious of the beat of my own heart, I stared into the golden coming of the morning and chanted silent, unpracticed praises to the unseen God, and He whispered to me on the wind.

Twenty-one

Clouds, dark and heavy, mounded against the peaks. Already there was a freshness to the air, and I watched the sunlight fade from a blue sky turning charcoal.

In the afternoon heat I had slept and dreamed and I came awake with the sense of a vividness to the dream, a feeling that it was offering me a forecast of a coming reality. But the wind blew the dream from my mind and left me with the dull ache of loss.

Yet I was alive in the real world and I sat up, smelling myself and the dust blowing down the hillsides and the rain falling somewhere beyond the hills. In the rising wind, sweat felt cool running down my back.

A long way off, near the hacienda, a lone figure was moving, crossing the barnyard in some hurry, then turning and coming more slowly up the slope toward me. Suddenly I was extraordinarily hungry. My throat felt coated with dust and I couldn't remember the last time I'd taken a drink of water.

The figure became a man and he walked up the slope like his feet were hurting. I recognized the way his short legs shuffled against each other as he walked, but I didn't know his name. Nothing was in his hands but a rifle. It was early for supper and I wondered what he wanted.

The sky was growing darker and the wind was a cool river against my face. The rain smell was stronger and beyond the hills I could see the silvery flicker of lightning.

The walking man was hurrying now. I could see it in the way his shoulders hunched and his head bent forward and his legs rubbed together more quickly. Raising a hand to his mouth he shouted something, but the rising wind snatched the words away and all I could hear was a high-pitched cry. The man shouted again and waved his arms. He looked like a collapsing windmill. I waved back. Shouting against the wind was useless.

He was still forty yards away when the first raindrops splattered fatly against my face. Rain began sweeping the ground in silver curtains. I scooted against the trunk of the cottonwood. You weren't supposed to sit under a tree in a storm, but what difference could it make to a man wearing a solid steel cuff and joined to the tree with an iron chain? Thunder rumbled against the hillsides and lightning imitated strobe lights above the crest.

Rain fell harder, great windblown sheets smashing against my face. Even though he was only twenty yards away it was difficult to see the fat man. Thunder again, closer, and I could smell the burnt cordite of a lightning strike. I prayed the fat man was coming to unlock me.

He was shouting again, but the rain washed away the words. He kept on shouting as he came, an indecipherable mixture of Spanish and broken English. Rainwater streamed off his round face. His mustache was wet and drooping across his upper lip like a drowned caterpillar.

His mouth flopped open and I could see twin rows of broken teeth. His breath came in great heaving gasps that lifted his torso. He bent at the waist.

"We must go," he panted, fumbling with a ring of keys hanging from his belt.

"Hurry."

"I am," he shouted. "I do not like this storm any more than you. It is a very bad one. Very dangerous, the radio says."

He found the key he wanted, a short flat one. It seemed ludicrous that my life might depend on a small piece of metal.

Every second had a life of its own. Thunder smashed against a hilltop and the ground trembled. Then the metal slid from my flesh and I scrambled to my feet with rain pelting my face and the guard shouting at me. Around my feet the chain lay coiled like a wet, metallic snake.

"To the *establo*. Hurry, hurry!"

My legs felt strange and faraway, weak and trembly. I moved awkwardly, but I moved. It seemed bizarre to separate from the cottonwood. For uncounted days I'd lived beneath the shelter of its branches and now the open ground seemed a foreign country. Blood began to flow and I eased into a jog. The guard plodded beside me.

"Where are we going? To the hacienda?"

"No," he panted. "You must go to the *establo*. How do you say it? To the stable?"

"To the barn?"

"*Sí*."

I nodded and picked up the pace. Strength was seeping back into my legs and I could feel the leg muscles working more smoothly. Grass was sparse and where the ground hadn't gone soft the going was good. A dozen strides and the barn and hacienda were clearly visible. With thunder rolling on all sides I put my head down and sprinted. Raindrops stung my face and water ran in rivulets down my neck. My clothes were plastered to my skin. I felt amazingly young. I lifted my head and ran with my face against the rain. I could no longer see the guard nor hear his gasps for air. I wanted to run forever.

For a moment I considered running on by the barn and up the hill and on to Nogales and the border patrol. Then the barn loomed dark and wet before me and I acknowledged reality and turned in.

In the lee of the barn the rain was less intense. The guard ran by me shouting. I waved him on and watched his broad back lumber toward the hacienda. The path had already turned to mud and he sloshed on doggedly through the puddles, slipping now and then, sticking an arm out for balance.

Lights burned in the house, small yellow beacons glowing haphazardly against the gray rain. To the right of the kitchen an unidentifiable face was pressed against the glass of a small round window. Sheets of rain fell between us. The other face looked a world away.

The wind was changing, blowing harder and starting to come from the south. The rain began to slacken. Standing under the overhang of the tin roof, I watched the fat guard make the hacienda and realized I was the last man standing, alone, staring at the rain. Thunder sounded distant, as if it had moved beyond the hills. A feeling that I was the last man in the world ran through me and I wasn't sure if I was glad or frightened.

For a long time I stared at the smattering of yellow lights. Blowing rain made them seem to flicker off and on, as if a message were being sent. If there was a code it was beyond my understanding.

Then the face was gone from the window and a sharp loneliness filled me. My shirt was soaked and plastered to my back and a chill racked my body. I turned and walked close against the barn until I came to the doors. They were unbolted and I tugged one of them open.

It seemed extraordinarily dark inside and I simply stood for several seconds, letting my eyes adjust, giving thanks, listening to the rain striking the tin roof, trying to glimpse the future.

Twenty-two

We were carrying stones to the wagon. Wilson walked in front of me and a short-armed man who went by Gonzales walked behind me. One guard stood in the gully of large flat rocks while another leaned against the wooden wagon positioned at the crest of the hill. Both men cradled guns in the crooks of their arms. The wagon needed three new slats in the floorboard.

Two sway-backed horses were hitched to the wagon, tails flicking at flies, nickering now and then to themselves. One of the horses stamped and blew air out his nostrils. I spoke to Wilson's back.

"I should have gone on."

"Gone where? When?" Wilson spoke without turning around. He was lugging a big rock and there was a strain in his voice. A vertical sweat line two inches wide bisected his back.

"When the storm came and the guard unlocked the chain I should have just gone on, anywhere."

"You wouldn't have made it. This is hard country and you don't know it."

"And you do?"

"Been living south of the border for the last five, six years. Spent some of that time doing business out there." He nodded at the expanse, grunted and adjusted the rock.

The path went steeply uphill for several yards and I waited until it leveled out before I spoke again. "I don't care about the country. I just need to get away. They're never going to let us go and I can't stand it here forever."

"They let the old man go," Wilson said.

"Yeah, but he could make them more money on the outside, cooking the books for one of their companies. Don't know about you, but I don't have that skill."

"I've been here almost two years. Does that answer your question?"

I stepped around a pipe organ cactus. "Don't think I am up for parole either, Wilson. Face it, none of us are. We're too valuable to Ramirez as slaves."

"What are you saying, Hampton?"

"That we need to get the hell out of here."

Wilson paused and eased his rock to the ground. He stared out across the landscape. Lowering my burden, I followed his gaze. As far as I could see there were only hills and arroyos, dust and rocks, and unfiltered sunlight hot enough to kill a man not packing enough water.

He turned and looked at me. Sweat trickled down his thin, lined face. His shirt hung on him like it belonged to an older, larger brother and his eyes were sunk deeply and underlined with dark semi-circles. All color seemed to have washed out of his face. He was only a few years older than I was.

"That's a nasty slice of hell out there, Hampton. Just how do you propose to get across it?

"Been thinking about that. We could travel at night. Carry our water with us."

"A man can't carry enough water to cross. It'd be too heavy. Besides, where are you planning to go? You told me that you've never been in this part of the country. You can't just start walking. That'd be suicide."

"We could go back to Nogales. I know the general direction. Follow the roadway by night, hole up like a snake by day."

"Nogales, hell. That's the first place they'd look." He wiped at the sweat line below his Padres cap with the back of his shirt sleeve. "Besides, what's all this we shit? I don't feel so good these days. Be more of a burden than a help."

"You just need to get out of this hellhole. Anyway, since you know this country, I need you to guide me." A small gray lizard ran out on a ledge of rock jutting from the hillside and stared up at me with golden eyes. I looked at Wilson.

"We could get Gonzales and a couple of others to go with us."

"You don't want too many. Numbers make it easier for them to spot us."

"What if we sent a couple of them in the opposite direction? Make the guards divide their forces."

Wilson licked his lips. His eyes looked flat, as if his vision was reflected inward. "Gonzales is the newest man and the strongest."

"Yeah, he told me he only got out of the army a few weeks ago. Still looks in great shape. Should be a good man to have around in a pinch."

"Deserted, didn't he?"

"We're all deserters from something, Wilson. Anyway, we've got to go with the players we have. Gonzales looks like the strongest."

"Yeah, and I'm probably the weakest." Wilson looked at me out of the corners of his eyes. "I wouldn't be anything but a burden if I went along, Hampton. I can tell you all you need to know."

"No way in hell I could make it without you, Wilson. Way too damn much ground to cover for you to map it for me. I'd never remember."

"Write it down. I've got a pencil and you can snag some paper."

"Things, especially terrain, always look different in real life than on paper. No man," I said, "I need you along."

Wilson shrugged, but before he could say anything the guard up the trail shouted for us to get moving.

Wilson and I picked up our rocks and started up the trail. He coughed as he moved, trying to smother the sound with an arm. Behind us, Gonzales panted faintly. I bulled my rock on up my left shoulder, bent my neck and walked faster. The guard at the top of the hill was a mean-natured prick. He liked to play little tricks on a man, like ramming the butt of his rifle into his kidneys. With the journey in mind, I couldn't afford a bruised kidney.

The sun was directly overhead, the heat almost unbearable. Sweat slipped into my eyes and I blinked against the burning, stumbling on with blurred vision, cursing under my breath, pretending I was a burro crossing the Sierra Madres. Wilson's shadow fell at my feet. Slowing, I kept my eyes on the ground.

"Moon's dark at the start of next week and I hear that the king and queen, plus a third of the guards, are going to Acapulco on Sunday."

"Info reliable?"

"Very."

"The old man said you needed moonlight to cross."

"Starlight's plenty. Trust me."

"Good," I panted as the incline increased. "When do we go?"

"How about midnight Tuesday? Give them time to get gone and the dust to settle. Plus, that's the sergeant's night off."

Sweat dripped onto the dust in front of me. A smile was growing under my tattered sombrero. "Sounds good. I'll let Gonzales know. He can tell the brothers from Redios. Those two can go in the opposite direction. By the way, Wilson, which way are we going?"

Wilson laughed. It was a silly snort of a laugh, one more for himself than anybody else. Stopping in his tracks, he turned and looked back. Washed out eyes half-circled in printer's blue, found mine.

"Hampton, old buddy," he said, "we are going right straight to hell." Then he laughed again, longer and louder. After a couple of seconds I quit listening. I was already staring at midnight Tuesday.

Twenty-three

Midnight Tuesday.

Blue starlight covered the ground. Voices quivered in the darkness. I went flat against the barn. "Hold it," I whispered. "Someone's still out there."

Voices again, easier to hear now. The shift change should have occurred twenty minutes ago. Fat Thomas had made his regular eleven-forty check. I'd heard him rattle the barn doors. The coast was supposed to be clear. I began to ease along the side of the barn, staying in the shadows, breathing shallowly.

Voices still murmured in the darkness, speaking Spanish. I was picking up about every third word, just enough to comprehend that they were talking about women, loose women with long nipples and urgent needs. Trying to blend into the wood, I listened as the blue night bled slowly away.

One of the voices said something about *cerveza*, followed by mutual *buenos noches*. A slender, elongated shadow emerged from the darkness and fell on the ground. A man stepped into the arc of the security light, his silhouette clearly visible. He merged into the shadows thrown by the hacienda and disappeared. I counted to thirty before I started moving back toward the opening in the boards, going more quickly than I'd come. Fat Thomas usually took a smoke and a dump after making his rounds and I could smell the acrid odor of his cigarette.

"Wilson, let's go. Now."

I waited until his shadow fell on the ground before I began to move, going hard in a low crouching duck-walk. Beyond the corral I came erect and began to jog. Cresting the first slope I picked up the pace. Another fifty yards and I was running as hard as the starlight would allow. Two makeshift canteens full of water, a hunk of fried meat, and half a loaf of Indian fry bread liberated from the kitchen banged against my legs.

I ran down the slope and up the next and then full out across the flat stretch of ground that separated the hillocks from the higher ridges. Breathing was harder and the muscles in my thighs were burning, but I pushed on until the curve of the hill began to split, one finger sloping south, the other rising to the west. Bending at the waist to catch my breath, I looked back across the ground I'd covered. A few months ago it wouldn't have been possible.

Grasses were still and silent in the starlight. Four figures swam into view, running across the flat ground. As I watched, the two at the rear of the pack caught and passed the others. One of the men who was passed ran with an awkward hobbling gate as though he were a wagon with one wheel off. In a minute I could see that the man with the bad leg was Wilson. He ran herky-jerky, using his good left leg for drive. Faces grew visible. In the pale starlight all I could see was fear, or maybe that was my own emotion projected onto the faces of other men. We were runaway slaves, and I found myself listening for the barks of dogs and the shouts of guards.

They came two by two, like animals preparing to board the ark. Feeling vaguely like Noah cum Moses lost in the wilderness, I hoped I wouldn't have to wander for another forty years.

Listening to them pant like wild dingoes after the chase, I peered back toward the hacienda. All I could see were the grasses, shimmering in the starlight, and, just at the edge of my vision, the security lights burning white. Only the grasses moved on the plain, and the only night sounds were the gasps for breath of men who had run hard.

I turned to Wilson. In the starlight his face looked ashen. "What happened?"

"Stepped wrong coming down the first slope. Turned my ankle, maybe strained the Achilles." Pain ran through his words like a fine blue highlighter.

"Can you make it?"

He nodded. "I'll make it."

Bending my head toward his, I peered into his eyes. All I saw was reflected starlight.

"Is this the place?"

Wilson glanced at Gonzales. Gonzales nodded twice. "Yeah," Wilson said, "this is where we split."

"Sure?"

"Sure as I can be."

I shifted my gaze to Gonzales, short and thick and dark in the starlight. His eyes were bottomless ebony pools.

"Tell them," I said, "this is where we split. They go south towards Redios." I jerked my head toward the west. "The three of us will go that way. *Comprende?*"

Gonzales stared over my shoulder into the night. His face was as empty and unmoving as a chunk of granite. After a few seconds he turned and directed a fistful of Spanish at the two men. They nodded in unison, then one raised his hand. Gonzales gave them a twisting salute with his right hand and they turned and started jogging south.

In a moment the darkness swallowed them. For some time after I could no longer see them I could hear their footsteps on the hard ground. When there was only silence and starlight, I jerked my head and we started west, moving more slowly than we liked. Gonzales walked on Wilson's left and I on his right, helping him navigate.

Moving as quickly as we could, we tracked starlight along a narrow ridge running high above a gorge. When we paused to catch our breath, I peered down into the blackness. Far down, a shimmering of starlight reflected on a slender band of water curling into oblivion. Time ticked inside my skull like a bomb. I nodded at Gonzales and we pulled Wilson erect. Pain finger-painted his face but he didn't make a sound. We started walking again, following the starlight streaming from the blue-black sky.

Time was our friend and our enemy. Daylight would bring roll call and pursuit. The ground was dry and we would leave few tracks, but it was barren land and moving men would stand out like blood on snow. Wilson needed to rest his ankle, but we couldn't afford the time. We pushed on through the darkness.

The ground began to undulate and curl downward. A soft moan escaped Wilson's lips with every step. Behind us the horizon was rimmed in tangerine. Daylight was coming faster than we could walk. I began looking for shelter.

Fifty yards ahead a dozen rocks had pushed their way through the crust of the earth. Some were as large as small buses.

"We'll go to ground there, in those rocks."

Wilson was staring at the still, dark earth. His head rose slowly, as though it were almost more than his neck could lift.

"You can make that, can't you, Wilson?"

He took a deep breath. "I can make it."

"Good. Let's go," I said, and then we were walking with the ground going light before us and our shadows running on ahead. By now they would know that we were missing. We hadn't gone far enough, but daylight had come and Wilson could go no further. Gonzales was giving me the evil eye, but too damn bad. All we could do was go to ground and wait for night; that, and pray for mercies from an unfathomable God.

Twenty-four

It was the day that would not die; at least it wasn't going without a hell of a fight. We'd been on the defensive throughout the day, staying in the shade, drifting in and out of sleep, sipping water, nibbling bread and meat, watching shadows move and listening for sounds of the posse coming over the ridge. The sun was finally bleeding to death in the west. The heat was still awful, but its life-sucking power was abating. Dabbing with the sleeve of a dirty shirt at the sweat pooling under my eyes, I watched the shadows lengthen.

During the course of the afternoon Wilson's breathing had changed. It was labored now, sounding as if all the water he'd drunk was gathering in his lungs. He lay in the shadow of the rocks, eyes closed, lips parted. Hard to tell if he was asleep or enduring, but now and then a spasm of pain worked its way across his face.

Gonzales sat with his back against a boulder, his legs stretched out before him. There were holes at the ends of his dust-coated tennis shoes. His face pointed west and was as smooth as the surface of the rock behind him. He turned his head in my direction.

"The afternoon, it is getting late. What time do you think it is?"

"Five, maybe later."

"I agree. Soon it will be cool enough and dark enough for us to move again." His eyes flicked to Wilson then back to my face. "We need to move soon. We will blend with the shadows."

"Yes, we can't stay here."

"No, they will find us if we do not put more distance between us and them." He inclined his head toward Wilson. "Can he make it?" he whispered.

"He'll have to," I mouthed.

Gonzales leaned closer. "First he hurt his ankle. Now he has the sickness. I'm not sure he can walk. How can we cover ground with a sick man?"

I glanced at Wilson, a dark bundle deep in the shadows, and said nothing.

"We could leave him here, go on, then send help later." Subterranean emotion was running through Gonzales's voice. I couldn't define the emotion and wondered if it was fear.

I shook my head. "We can't leave him."

Gonzales shrugged. "Then we cannot make it. A sick man makes us too slow. By now Ramirez will have been informed. He will spare nothing to find us. The search will continue until we make it across the border, or they catch us. The latter would not be pleasant."

"True, but we can't leave him."

Gonzales lifted his shoulders slowly, then let them fall. He didn't say anything, but an expression I couldn't identify flickered across his face.

My eyes were burning from the glare and lack of sleep. Rubbing at them, I told myself to think of anything but the heat, the posse, and Wilson. An image of my father formed in my mind. I shook my head and looked at Gonzales. "How far you think it is to Matazora?"

He formed a circle with his mouth and blew air out. "Hard to say." He shrugged "Two days? Maybe three if the luck is bad."

I peered out across the sandy ground. Thirty yards ahead was a thin spire of rock. Remaining sunlight burnished it copper. Its narrow, elongated shadow was halfway to us. When that shadow touches my foot, I told myself, we will move.

Instead of saying anything to Gonzales about the shadow, I asked him the question that had been worrying me all day. "How far to water?"

Using the back of a hand, Gonzales wiped away sweat from the right side of his face. His dark eyes were empty of meaning. "I have never been this way to Matazora so I cannot say for sure, but from what I have been told there should be a small river perhaps half a day's walk away." Looking away, he spoke to the desert, "a half day's walk for a strong man."

Anger rose in my throat. I swallowed it. "Don't worry, we'll make it."

Lights moved in Gonzales's eyes as he turned to look at me and I thought he was going to say more, but he simply stared at me for a long minute, then turned his head and peered into the dying afternoon. After a few minutes he pushed himself off the ground and walked to the edge of the shadows.

I scooted across the shadow-soaked ground and placed a palm on Wilson's forehead. His flesh was warm and my palm came back damp.

Suddenly, without warning, the desire for alcohol swept over me like a rogue wave. My throat contracted until it was difficult to get my breath. I told myself to get real and focused on the stretching shadows.

Long, and growing longer by the minute, they were dark and shapely like women against the light brown dust. As I watched the light began to fail. Dusk, the purple of overripe plums, began to merge with the shadows, kissing and hugging and melding. When the long thin shadow slipped across the toe of my boot I whistled softly through my teeth at Gonzales and put a hand on Wilson's shoulder.

"Time to get up, man. We've got to go now."

Wilson moaned as one eye came slowly open, looking weak and wild at the same time. He sat up and peered into the gathering dusk. Then he shut his open eye and let his head sag, thin hair falling down across his face. His head hung as though he were some gigantic bird whose neck had snapped in mid-flight. All sound seemed to have vanished. I could hear my own breathing.

A wandering shaft of wind blew across the earth and Wilson opened his eyes and slowly got to his feet. For a moment he stood swaying, then started hobbling forward. I got up and walked after him. In a few minutes I could hear Gonzales walking behind us.

Night was falling soft around us. Stars were starting to burn holes in the blue velvet sky.

Twenty-five

The land fell away to a flat, dusty plain, only to rise again as if in defiance. The slope was steep and rock-strewn, although here and there saguaros lifted their arms to the heavens. Daylight was coming fast and we would need to seek shelter soon. We were only halfway up the slope.

"Come on," I said, "we're way too conspicuous out here. We've got to get to the ridgeline." I glanced down at the man sitting at my feet. "Wilson, you can make it to the top, can't you? It's not that far."

He looked up toward the ridgeline. From the expression that blanketed his face I could tell that it looked a long way up to him. "Yeah," he said after a moment. "I can make it." I nodded and he pushed himself up and we started walking.

Climbing became harder, the trail narrowing and curving, filled with loose pebbles that gave way under our feet. Sharp-edged rocks formed a natural wall and cactus and brush hung over the trail, scratching at our flesh and snagging our clothes. Behind us the sun was climbing, gaining strength with altitude.

Gonzales led the way with Wilson in the middle while I brought up the rear and kept lookout. Where the climbing was roughest either Gonzales pulled Wilson along or I gave him a shove. Full daylight and the crest still looked half a mile away.

Suddenly Wilson stopped in front of me. I couldn't stop in time and bumped against him. He gave way easily, and I had to grab him to keep him from falling.

"Look," Gonzales said. "Dust."

There was an edge to his voice and I jerked my head up to look at him. Standing with his back to the mountain he was facing the way we had come. His right arm was extended and his index finger pointed east. I turned to face the rising sun on trembling legs.

No more than two miles away, and moving closer every second, was a cloud of dust. As we watched, the dust fell apart into half a dozen smaller clouds. Out of the clouds trotted horses. In less than a minute I could see men on the animals' backs. The posse was moving quicker across the rocky ground than I had imagined they could.

"Damn," Wilson said.

I tugged on his left arm. "Come on, we've got to move. If we can see them they can see us. We're way too goddamned exposed out here on the side of this mountain. We've got to make the other side."

Wilson looked down at me. Sweat and pain and defeat were swimming across his face. He coughed and dust fluttered out of his hair, hanging for a heartbeat in the clear air like dark punctuation.

"Go on without me. I'll only slow you down."

"Bullshit."

"No, get going. Without me you can make it. Should be more cover on the other side. That side of this mountain gets the rain."

Tightening my grip on his arm I jerked my head at Gonzales. "Quit farting around and let's go. We've come this far together; I'm not leaving you."

"Hampton..."

"Grab his other arm, Gonzales. We've got to get moving."

I bent my knees and started working my way up the slope. Gonzales was on the other side of Wilson, but reluctance to be there was easy to read on his face. The incline was steep and we pulled ourselves up by grabbing boulders that had sprouted like young corn. My shirt was plastered to my back and sweat slid into my eyes.

Pausing to catch our breath beneath the protruding lip of a large boulder, I swiped at my eyes with a shirtsleeve and peered back the way we'd traveled. The horses were coming across the flatlands at almost a full gallop. I counted them, four, five, six. They were maybe fifty yards away from the base of the mountain. All that was between them and us were dust, rocks, and stubby-armed cactus.

"Come on," Gonzales shouted. "They've seen us." His voice broke and he turned and started to run up the slope. Wilson's shirt ripped, but Gonzales only ran on. I shouted at him but the report of a rifle drowned my words. The bullet pinged off a rock twenty yards below.

I tugged on Wilson's arm and he moved with me. Curling around the overhang, we came out the other side running with only the tops of our heads showing. Another bullet smashed into a stack of granite ten yards below us.

Wilson's legs gave way and he pulled me down with him. He lay in the dust coughing and choking, eyes closed and the coughs wet and deep. A sheen of sweat glistened in the morning sunlight.

Another bullet ricocheted off a rock in front of us. Wilson moaned as I crawled back to him, dust rising around me in a fine brown powder. I was too scared to shit.

Shouts were audible below us now, but the wind blew them on to the top of the ridge and beyond. Wilson's eyes fluttered open. Our faces were less than a foot apart.

"Come on, man. We've got to keep moving. You know what'll happen if they catch us."

"Go on, Hampton. I can't make it. You can." His voice was weak and came from deep inside his chest as though the words were trying to go down instead of up.

"No."

"Yes."

Time for talking was gone. I got on my knees and slipped my arms under his shoulders and tugged him toward erect as I worked my torso under his. Taking a deep breath, I pushed hard with my calves and quads. He moaned as we rose, but I ignored him and kept on pushing. He was lighter than I'd guessed and I came stumbling to my feet.

Shouts grew louder and I risked a quick glance down the hill. At the bottom, horses were slipping in the loose gravel and the riders were shouting and kneeing their mount's flanks. I got my feet under me and started moving.

The terrain was leveling off and the outcropping of rock formed a natural battlement. The crest of the ridge was visible and I could see the tops of saguaros on the other side. Gonzales had disappeared.

More rifle shots and I dug deep and went as hard as I could across the ridge top. Wilson's arms flapped against my back and his feet banged my chest. There were more shouts and then I crossed over the ridge and started down the other side.

Scrambling in the loose rock, I stumbled down the slope. Cactus were taller and thicker here and they tore my face and hands and clothes. A rock shifted beneath me and I fell to my knees, Wilson banging heavily against the back of my head. Sucking air, I spent precious seconds studying the terrain.

Straight ahead patches of cactus gave way to open grasslands which ran on to a thicket of scrub pine. Off to my right was a wall of rock. Shouts grew louder. Time to roll the dice. Without looking I hurried left.

Fatigue was setting in fast. Breathing was difficult and my chest ached. Wilson was a dead weight. Even with adrenaline pumping like it was coming straight from a needle, I could feel my legs starting to go. A liquid thicker than sweat snaked down my face and into my eyes. Suddenly it was like moving through a red-filtered universe. Gasping for breath and struggling to keep my footing in the loose shale, I hurried on. Ahead was an overhang and I pushed for it.

Under the overhang it was cooler and quieter, cave-like. Darkness enveloped me as I moved deeper, going slower, trying to catch my breath and think at the same time, wiping with my free arm at the dampness seeping into my eyes.

Wilson was growing heavier and I knew I'd have to rest soon. Just ahead a large stone column split the darkness into two chambers. The light was chancy, but I could make out where the caverns split into a rabbit warren of dark dens. From where I stood it was impossible to determine which ones ran deeper into the bowels of the mountain and which ones died a quick death. One was half hidden by a buttress of smooth, damp looking stone. I chose it.

Rounding a curve, I sank to my knees and lowered Wilson gently to the earthen floor. He hadn't made a sound in some time, at least not one I'd heard over the sound of my running and breathing. Sucking air into my lungs I knelt beside him, letting my eyes adjust to the dimness.

Shapes began to define themselves. I bent closer to Wilson's face.

His eyes were closed and his mouth hung open in a toothy grin. His body was twisted awkwardly on the cavern floor and I reached under his shoulders to reposition him. His back was soaked. I pulled my hand away. A sticky dark substance covered it. I recognized the smell.

"Wilson," I said, slipping a hand under his head, "can you hear me?"

All I could hear was the faint whoosh of wind at the mouth of the cave.

I bent my face to his. No warm breath brushed my face. I let him down gently and felt his wrist for a pulse. There was none.

In the dim light I could see that my arms and chest were smeared with blood, Wilson's blood. Nothing anyone could do now. One of the rifle shots had hit home. Death must have been instantaneous. I couldn't help but wonder if he'd stopped the bullet with my name on it.

My stomach churned and my head began spinning. Pinpricks of golden light danced before me. I was acutely conscious of my own breathing. It was hollow and rapid like an old dog's after a hard run.

I couldn't stand it, being there with a dead man lying in his own sticky blood, so I pushed away and crawled back down the corridor. It wasn't just any dead man I was leaving. I'd known the man when he had breathed and hoed beans and built fences, and when we drank whiskey from the same bottle, and when he had saved my life. There was no way I could stand being there with his eyes closed forever and his mouth open and his body oozing blood, simply because someone thought he owed them something.

I didn't say goodbye. Goodbyes are for the living.

For the dead there is only death. Death, and a strange half-life that exists in the memories of those who have known or seen or heard of the dead, and after they too are gone, only in the memories of those to whom they have told the tales, and on and on until the dead are no longer spoken of, or remembered, even as ghosts. It is as if they never walked this earth. And so it is with all of us, I told myself as I moved toward the light.

~ * ~

Sunlight was strong on the hillside that fell away before me. Standing in the shadows of the overhang, my sweat starting to cool, still smelling blood on my hands, I let my eyes adjust to the light and tried to think only of the living.

I could see a long way in all directions. Glancing to the right, I searched for a break in the wall of stone, but it was solid and massive. Directly ahead of me, beyond the open grassland, was the pine thicket. There trees grew dark and thick, too close to each other to permit a horse to pass. The pine thicket held promise.

Sounds filtered in from the left and I turned to face them. Puffs of dust rose on the horizon, drifted higher and dissipated in the clear thin air. Because of the distance and the terrain it was difficult to get an exact count on the dust clouds. I figured it for a half a dozen. I figured it for horses. I figured I ought not to go left.

Taking a final look at the dust clouds, I plunged down the slope toward the pine thicket. Once there, I worked my way along the edge, putting distance between me and the dust.

By noon I was hungry and ate all the bread that wasn't soaked with blood and drank the last of my water. If the water had been whiskey I would have drunk it. Throughout the afternoon I kept moving, watching the day unfold its promise, thinking about my sins, and sinners I had known, and sinners I hoped to know again. When twilight smeared purple across the tops of the pines I said a final prayer for the soul of a man known as Wilson.

Twenty-six

The crest of the bluff curled in twin ridges that met on the far horizon, creating a vast, living bowl. At the bottom of the bowl, houses and barns and shops floated on a sea of grass like so many letters in alphabet soup. Dirty, tired, and hungry, I didn't have the faintest idea of the name of the town. Over my shoulder, I took a final look at the flat, hard miles stretching as far as I could see, knowing I'd come even further. Sunlight was edging over the narrow band of clouds that crowded the bottom rim of the eastern sky and the diffused light was gentle on my face. I started down the slope toward the nameless town that held my future in its dark and silent streets.

Houses and barns and shops grew larger as I worked my way down the hill. Grass grew tall on the sloping ground and wildflowers bloomed yellow and white. I followed a narrow winding cattle path. Now and then I saw evidence of their passing and once the footprint of a man's boot made when the ground was damp.

Halfway down the hill a narrow stand of trees grew in a jagged arc. Pausing in their patchy shade, I drank the last of the water I'd collected at dusk the day before from a rocky stream. The water had been clear and cool, sparkling in the final slanting rays of sunlight as it ran. I'd no means of purification, but I had to drink.

The air was noticeably warmer when I stepped from the tree line. During the night the air had been cool enough to make me long for a coat. Now I relished sunlight's warmth.

It was easy walking down the hill with nothing to carry except myself. Three days had passed since I'd left Wilson and all I'd eaten were some dark purple berries that grew in great profusion along the banks of shallow streams. I was hungry, but it was a good hunger, one that made me feel slender, young, and vibrant. It felt fine to walk down the slope with the morning sun on my back and the good hunger in my belly.

Gradually, buildings began to take shape and people and animals formed thin moving lines beside them. As I walked, the lines thickened into stick figures and then real people with arms, legs, and faces. The faces did not smile. They only stared at me with question mark eyes.

The trail wandered across a broad meadow, edging away from the town, drifting toward a low, stone barn. I left the trail and cut across the meadow. The grass was soft and wildflowers nodded as I passed. I walked like I owned the world, and in a way I did. I owed no one. Here no one knew me or anything about me. I was as free as the wind that blew across my face and the mountains that rimmed the horizon and in that moment I was a king.

~ * ~

Buildings rose on both sides of the road, one-story adobe, with doors painted turquoise and wavy glass in the windows that stared like square eyes.

But they were only glass windows and I was only a hungry man walking down a dirt road without a cent in my pockets into a one-street town I'd never heard of.

I tried to read the street signs but they were in Spanish. I kept walking, past a barbershop and a store that sold shirts, blankets, and cooking pots. Heavy wooden doors stood open at the next building. I could smell stale beer and strong cigarettes and hear zombies slow dancing in the corners. The memory taste of whiskey was on my tongue, while old-time zombie songs reverberated inside my head. I made myself take one step at a time until I could no longer smell the beer or the cigarettes and the songs of the zombies were only a gentle murmur.

At the end of the second block a brick building rose higher than the rest. A wooden porch with a lodge-pole railing ran across its face. A dozen chairs stood in a wavering line behind the rail. A small colony of men and women sat in them. Through the open door I could see a wooden-bladed ceiling fan turning above a circle of cracked leather armchairs fronted by end tables. Brightly colored magazines spotted the tables.

Beyond the chairs was a tall wooden counter with a cash register on one end and two men in white shirts and ties standing behind it. Affixed to the wall behind the men were twin rows of narrow wooden boxes. Some held flat metal keys, some held mail, and some were as empty as my stomach. Boards creaked beneath me as I crossed the porch. I could feel the eyes following.

A dry, hollow odor permeated the old hotel lobby, as if it had stood still while time moved on. Even the white shirts of the men behind the counter looked dingy. Only their ebony hair and black ties were shiny. No one sat in the cracked leather seats or read the garishly colored magazines. The only life in the lobby was a bent, silver-haired man sweeping the wooden floor with a short-handled broom. I walked around his dust and stood before the counter.

The older of the two men behind the counter came and stood in front of me with his hands flattened on the polished wood. He studied my face as if he wanted to remember me.

"*Señor*, how can I help?"

I had to swallow a couple of times to get my throat working. "I'm new in town and need some work. Do you have any suggestions?"

The man turned without answering and spoke in Spanish to the younger man who was writing in a ledger. The younger man looked up and shrugged, then turned back to his ledger. The older man turned to face me.

"*Señor*, Goeteza is a small town, and a poor one. Jobs are not many here. Do you have special skills?"

I thought for a moment. "I can speak English and know how American businesses operate. Does that help?"

The man smiled at me, his long brown face cracking into a spider web of wrinkles until it took on the look of distressed leather. "Sorry, in Goeteza we do not do much business with the Norte Americanos." He shrugged away his uncomfortable smile. "Perhaps one of the ranchers could use some help, or one of the restaurants. It is my understanding that both have people who leave from time to time. Are you a cowboy?"

"More of a city man. But I can wash dishes. Where are the restaurants?"

Smiling again, he told me where they were. I thanked him and walked across the ancient lobby tucking in my shirttail and brushing at the dirt on my clothes. The old man leaned on his broom and watched me pass.

Stepping out into the sunlight, I looked at the people lined up on the porch. Faces turned and stared at me without expression. I smiled at them. One woman, fat in a yellow dress, smiled back. I crossed the porch with the boards talking to me and stepped into the brown street.

Going back the way I'd come, I entered the bar, looking for the door with a man's face painted on it. When I found it, I crossed the poorly lighted room and pushed the door open.

It was a small square room, lighted with a single naked bulb dangling from the ceiling on a thick black wire. It was furnished with a urinal, a stained commode, a cracked porcelain sink, and a grimy mirror decorated with water spots.

A dirty-faced white man with a scraggly beard stared back at me from the mirror. The man's clothes were torn and stained and his hair was unkempt. His eyes had a haunted look. If he was a king, he was the king of nothing.

I smiled at myself, but that only made me look demented. I took off my shirt and laid it on the back of the commode. I washed my face, hands, arms, and chest as best I could, drying off with the dirty towel hanging from a tarnished brass rod. Then I worked on my hair with water and fingers.

When I finished washing I took another look in the mirror. The best you could say was that I was cleaner. Putting my shirt on, I walked back into the smoky darkness of the bar.

I was hungry, thirsty, and wanted a drink in the worst sort of way. Who knows, if I'd been more fluent in Spanish I might have listened to the zombies and tried to cage a drink. Instead, I crossed the dark, oil-stained wood quickly, looking only at the door and the sunlit street beyond, sensing eyes staring at me, expecting to be accosted.

After the bar, the sunlight felt good and strong and clean and for a moment I stood with my naked face turned up to the sky and let the sun and wind caress it. Feeling foolish, I lowered my eyes and started walking over the packed earth toward the block where the desk clerk said I might find work. Stomach growling, I kept my eyes open for a potential handout. Pride was no longer a viable option.

~ * ~

It was the third restaurant I'd tried. It was the last restaurant I could see. Tired, hungry, and frustrated, I didn't want to face another rejection. I didn't see where I had much choice. A short man wearing a serape opened the door and I followed him in.

The interior was small and crowded. Eight or nine tables, each surrounded by at least four chairs filled most of the room. A row of stools lined the front of the counter. All the chairs and stools were full and everyone seemed to be speaking at once. Rapid fire Spanish mingled with the aromas of frying meat and onions, burning tobacco, perfume and aftershave, and sweat. The heat in the restaurant was sweltering.

Overwhelmed, I stood just inside the door with my back against the doorframe and watched the well-orchestrated madness. Three young, dark-haired waitresses hurried back and forth between the counter and the tables. They were pretty and their arms were full with trays covered with food and drink or empty dishes. Steam rose from the food in misty wisps that mingled with the thick cigarette smoke clouding the room. I could feel tremblings in my stomach. All of the waitresses were hurrying. Just watching them move made me tired.

Behind the counter an attractive woman, who looked to be in her early forties, handled the people sitting on the stools. She joked and laughed with the customers and called them by name. Pouring coffee with a practiced ease, she kept the plates moving and the counter wiped. A smile rested easily on her face as she casually flipped the waterfall of hair out of her round brown face.

Stomach growling, I began to head toward the counter. I was too damn hungry to smell all that food and watch a hundred hungry people eat and drink. I was so hungry that I was tempted to grab a double handful of food off a plate and run for the door. Instead, I worked my way through the flow of people who had eaten and paid and were headed back to work. I felt like a salmon swimming upstream against a tide of humanity.

By the time I made the counter, the woman with the free-falling hair was serving beans and rice to a man with a Frank Zappa mustache. I could see directly into the kitchen. Through the steam and smoke I could see a man in a blue shirt, blue jeans, and long apron stirring something in a large copper pot. His arms were muscular. In a previous life the apron had been white.

Two small boys stood beside the man. The man turned and said something to the taller boy. The boy picked up a large, metal shaker and handed it to the man. The man smiled and patted the boy on the head. The boy smiled back.

"*Por favor?*" The voice was mellow, fully female, but without sexual pretense. I turned and looked into brown eyes set widely apart. Below the eyes was a heavy, loose-lipped mouth. The mouth was smiling. I smiled back.

"Sorry, I thought you were at the other end of the counter."

"Pardon, *señor*, can I help you?" She spoke slowly, as if she had to see the words form in her head before she could say them. I nodded to show that I understood.

"I've just gotten into town and I need a job. The desk clerk at the hotel thought you might need some help." I widened my smile.

There was a sadness in her smile. "I'm sorry, but we are only a small family restaurant. We do not hire people to do the work. We do the work ourselves, my husband and I. Our children and nieces help." Rotating her gaze, she looked around the room as if all the people in the restaurant were her family. I wished I were part of her family. So did my family.

"Well, thanks anyway." I hesitated, then spoke again, the hunger driving me. "What about just one day's work, even just enough for a meal. Maybe I could work enough to get a meal." Even to my own ears I sounded pitiful.

"What's this? What is happening?" A deep voice, rough around the edges. I turned and stared into the face of the man with the stained apron. He had a large head, smooth brown skin, and jet-black hair cut short, angled as though it had been sliced by a knife.

"I was asking the señora here if there were any jobs I could do in exchange for a meal."

"And what did the señora say?" He passed me a signal that let me know the señora was his wife. I did the caterpillar with my eyebrows and curled up the ends of my mouth to let him know I understood.

"She didn't."

He studied my face. I grew conscious of voices behind me. One shrill voice rose above the tide, calling for a *cerveza*. He called for it over and over. He sounded like he had already downed several.

The man studied my face like he was going to have to draw it for the art exam final. He glanced at his wife. A look passed between them. For lack of anything else to do I watched the man's face. A tiredness was etched there.

"You are a *Norte Americano*?"

"Yes."

"Why are you here? Goeteza is a long way from the border."

"A very long way." Over the sea of sound behind me I could hear my stomach growling. I smiled at him to cover the embarrassment. "You might say I lost my way. Fell in among evil companions."

"You think all Mexicans are evil?"

I was watching his face closely. His expression did not change. I could sense a depth to him; it seemed genuine.

"Of course not. Just like Americans, though, some are."

"Am I evil?"

"No way." I waved a careless hand at the crowd behind me. "You're way too busy to get into much trouble."

He grinned. "You are most correct, *señor*. Perhaps only a little trouble. Can you wash dishes?"

"Like a Whirlpool."

"What?"

"Never mind, I'm half brain-dead. Sure, I can wash dishes with the best of 'em. Where do I start?"

His brown face twisted and pointed over his left shoulder toward twin sinks. The one on the left was overflowing with dirty dishes pyramided like an Aztec temple sliding into the jungle. I started around the counter.

A hand gripped my arms. "*Uno momento, señor.* First you must eat. You will need your full strength to do so many dishes."

"*Gracias.*" I felt like crying.

"*De nada.*"

Rotating his head, he looked across the top of the crowd. His heavy lips smiled as he saw what he was looking for. "Evita, Evita, come here."

One of the waitresses hurried between tables and stood beside me. Tall and slender, she was about twenty years old with a beauty mark low on her left cheek. "Yes, Uncle?"

"Fix señor..." he paused. "Pardon me. But what is your name, *señor*?"

"Hampton, Paul Hampton."

"So, Evita, fix Señor Hampton a plate of beans and rice. Give him many tortillas. He will need much energy. He can eat at the cutting table. Go girl, can you not see that Señor Hampton is very hungry? Is that not so, *señor*?"

I nodded. "Thank you very much. May I ask your name?"

"My name is Gomez. And we will see how thankful you are after you finish with the dishes." His laughter followed me as I followed the girl.

We walked across a tile floor spotted with grease. Standing on tiptoe, the boys had taken over the cooking. Out of the corners of their eyes they watched me as if I might be an evil spirit. I smiled at them as I followed Evita into a pantry. They smiled back, but shyly.

Just inside the pantry a thin mirror hung by a thick black cord. I glanced at the mirror. It was easy to understand why the boys had been staring at me.

I washed my face and hands in a small metal sink. The warm water felt good and I could not recall a more pleasant scent than the thick yellow cake of soap emitted. I dried on a clean towel and went to a small table in the back where Evita was standing beside a plate full of rice the color of ripe wheat and a pile of refried beans that looked like a lump of fresh dog shit. Beside the plate a red plastic basket was filled with tortillas. It was a small mercy that Evita did not watch me eat.

I forgot to pray until I'd finished eating. Walking toward the pile of dishes I felt grateful, and only a little guilty. Inside I was smiling. Then I remembered Wilson.

Twenty-seven

"Do you like to wash dishes, *Señor* Hampton?"

I looked over a lopsided mountain of dishes waiting for me in the sink, then another I'd already washed. "Not exactly."

"Then why have you done them for three weeks without a complaint? You have not said a word."

"I like to eat."

"Don't you want to do something else with your life?"

I jammed my hands into the warm soapy water and sought a submerged plate. "Sure I do, *Señora* Gomez, but your husband is feeding me because I wash dishes."

She leaned closer, her black hair swinging above the clean dishes stacked on faded blue towels. I could smell her sweet musky smell, full of warm flower petals and smoky summer evenings; it was the smell of my Mexico, the Mexico I treasured.

"Tell me about your ramblings," she said.

"They're not worth telling." I scrubbed the plate and held it up to the light.

Her shoulder nudged against mine. "Oh come on, tell me. It is so boring around here. Nothing ever happens. I bet you have led an exciting life."

"Not really. Let me put it this way—I was lost, but now I'm found."

She laughed. She had a nice laugh, full of yellow sunshine and tubular bells. "I see now; you wandered in the wilderness for forty years."

"Forty days would be closer to the truth, although it felt like forty years at the time."

"And you don't want to talk about it."

"Right."

"You're the strong silent type, like the American movie star from the old days. What was his name?"

My hands started swiping at another dirty plate. "John Wayne?"

"No."

"Jimmy Stewart?"

"No, not him either. I know these men and I like their movies, but I am thinking of someone else."

I finished the plate and started on a bowl that had recently held beans, thinking about old westerns I'd seen as a kid. "Gary Cooper?"

"*Sí.*"

"No, I'm not the Gary Cooper type. He was too clean living for me. Humphrey Bogart was more my man."

"*The Treasure of the Sierra Madre?*"

"That's right. Haven't seen that one in a long time. You must be a big movie fan."

She reached over and picked up a plate to dry. As she moved, her hand inadvertently brushed against the side of my face. It was soft and smooth against my flesh. I thought of Jolene.

"I've been there, you know?"

"To the Sierra Madre?"

"*Sí*, my father took me as a child." She shook her head and her hair fluttered against my face. "He and his brother used to go to the mountains to hunt."

"What did they hunt?"

She was silent for a moment, as if she were traveling again to the mountains. Chatter from the noonday crowd drifted back, a soft, pleasant rumble. "You know, I don't remember." Señora Gomez spoke the words softly, almost to herself, and with a flavoring of surprise, as if she hadn't thought of the hunting trips for a long time and hadn't considered the possibility that she wouldn't remember the details.

She seemed lost in the mountains, so I listened to the murmur of the crowd and the sounds my own hands made in the soapy water and the soft fall of thoughts inside my skull. Deciding to act like Gary Cooper, I listened and waited for her to speak. While I pretended, I tried to decide who I was inside, but dark thoughts swirled in my mind and made my head hurt. So I thought about my job and listened to the kitchen sounds while I smelled Señora Gomez's hair.

The past came alive for her again and words slid between her lips like water tumbling through an open sluice gate. "I do remember much, though. I remember campfires at night and the stars so full of light against the sky I thought they would burst any minute and the smell of wood smoke and my father's aftershave and my uncle's cigars. I remember birds calling to each other and strange animal sounds in the brush and my sisters screaming in the dark when my brothers pretended to be bears. Also I remember lying awake at night and staring at the campfire after it had burnt down low with only the embers glowing, and all the crazy wild young girl thoughts I had. Or maybe those were dreams."

"What did you dream?"

She went silent, her entire body still, tensed into a statue adorned with a dishcloth. Then she expelled her breath and her hair moved like a dark mist lifting. "You must not ask that. It would not be right to tell you."

"And why not?" I added a plate to the pile. It was chipped along the rim, but very clean.

"If I told you, you would know."

"Know what?"

"Too much."

"Okay, don't tell me then."

"Thank you, *señor*."

"You're welcome. Is the crowd gone?"

She turned and looked toward the front. "Almost. My husband is taking the money of the mayor."

"Which one is he?"

"The fat man with the white shirt and black string tie." She pointed with the hand that did not hold a dishcloth. "There, just beyond Maria."

"Beside the man in leather with the mustache?"

"Yes, that is him."

"He looks American," I said.

"Who, the mayor?"

"No, silly, the Leather Man with the Zappa 'stache."

Señora Gomez laughed. "You are the silly one, *Señor* Hampton. Yes, I think the Leather Man is American like you. He eats here almost every day. So does the mayor."

Nodding, I turned back to my dishes. "Your food must be very good."

"No, nothing special. But there are only three restaurants in Goeteza. We are clean and cheap. One of the others it is not so clean, and the other is not so cheap. So we do all right."

"Make lots of money?"

"I wish. But we make only a little, barely enough to feed ourselves."

I washed a blue plate and then a brown one. "Why don't you move on? Go to America. There are good jobs there. Well, perhaps they're not really good jobs. Actually, they're ones that none of the people who already live there want, but they still pay better than most jobs in Mexico."

"My husband, he has lived here all his life. He will not leave. One of his brothers went to Texas, and there he was killed in a car wreck. My husband will not cross the Rio Grande. He believes that north of the river the land is cursed. His mind is made up."

"I see," I said, although I didn't.

She leaned close again, making me wish I'd shaved. "Tell me about America, *Señor* Hampton. From time to time we have customers from America and my cousin went to America and I heard much about your country from her. Also, I have seen many American movies, but I will never get to go there, so tell me about, oh what do they call it? Ah, yes, the land of golden dreams."

There were lights in the depths of her brown eyes, foolish lights to my mind. Such foolish lights made me sad.

"Dreams," I said, "are not the word I would use. Nightmares would be better, *Señora*. America is full of nightmares."

"Nightmares? What sort of nightmares?"

One of the waitresses came in bearing gifts. She smiled as she stacked dirty dishes a foot high. I smiled back. I didn't mean it. Sticking my hands back in the soapy water I started washing an aluminum loaf pan that Gomez used to bake bread. The water needed changing.

"You ask what kind of nightmares the great United States of America has to offer, well let me tell you. There are as many nightmares north of the border as there are people. Everybody has their own personalized, solid steel, chrome plated, unique nightmare. For some it's whiskey, for others cocaine, and then there are heroin, paint fumes, the stock market, gambling, sex, loneliness and depression, abuse, work and poverty, and religion and no religion, and that doesn't even begin to get at the fears. Fear of the dark and heights and the unknown and the known, and everybody has them but no one does anything about them, and I could go on forever. But what's the use?" Turning my head, I looked into her face, brown and smooth and expectant. "And, *Señora*, you know what the funny thing is?"

She shook her head.

"Well, the funny thing is that all these nightmares are inside all these different people and they all try to keep them bottled up, so they end up walking around like so many robots until the buildup of those nightmares is too much to handle. Then the people explode and do something totally horrendous, like murdering their mother, or sticking their child in scalding water, or burning down their church full of worshipers, or stepping their damned self in front of a rolling train. Next some other poor lost soul writes about it in the papers and the rest of us just talk about it for a week.

"But don't delude yourself, nobody does anything about it and in a little while the whole monstrous moment is forgotten and everybody goes back to being a robot. Funny thing though, the whole time this moment of madness is occurring all the people are walking around with the appropriate expression on their faces, but possessed by their own private hoodoo demon, and all the doctors and all the money and all the prayers don't do a damn bit of good. Now, don't you find that hilarious, *Señora* Gomez?"

She shook her long black hair at me. "No, *Señor* Hampton, I do not find it funny at all. I find it sad, very sad." Putting down the plate she had been drying, she rearranged her face. "I think that if you will tell yourself the truth, *señor*, you will admit that you are sad."

"So I'm sad."

"Were you always sad?"

That question made me think. I didn't like my thoughts, so I said words that were true, but not the truth. "That's a good question."

She smiled at my answer, smiled the way a good teacher will humor an unsure student. "So, *señor*, answer it."

"I did."

"Not really."

Placing the loaf pan on top of the rinse stack, I grabbed a dirty plate. "One of my philosophies is never to tell anyone everything."

She leaned closer. "Then you keep secrets?" she whispered.

"We all do," I whispered back.

She laughed. "True," she said. "Tell me all your secrets."

"No," I said, and bent my head over the dishwater.

"Then just one. Tell me one."

"First tell me how you speak English so well."

"My cousin taught me some and for a few years a, what do you call it, oh yes, an artist lived here. He was from California and he liked to paint our mountains. He ate many meals in our restaurant."

"Okay. So what do you want to know?"

"Anything, just something about you and America. I have never really known a real American before. Only the artist and he did not talk much about himself."

"I'm real all right, as real as they get, as real as dog shit." I looked up from the dishes. Her lips were still smiling, but her eyes were going damp.

"Sorry. Forgive my language. You really want to know something about America?"

"Please." She blinked rapidly and kept smiling. I felt lower than a Gila monster's gut. I'd seen plenty of those creatures back at the ranch, sunning on the rocks while Wilson and I worked on the fence. Suddenly I missed that long-faced, sick, ornery son-of-a-bitch so bad it made my head hurt. Not being able to bury him still bothered me. Not that religious formulas were my cup of coffee, but it seemed uncaring to simply abandon the body. I hoped Ramirez was in hell, or dying of thirst somewhere in the Mexican desert.

I drug myself back to the kitchen, and the moment. "Okay, let's see, what can I tell you that might be of even the least bit of interest? Actually, I'm basically a pretty boring guy."

"Anything, just tell me anything." She leaned closer, her breath was soft and warm against my cheek. If she was that interested in my life she must be lonely as hell or damn near bored out of her mind. Or maybe she was just a nice lady being polite.

"Well, let's see. How about I do a mini-biography, the *Reader's Digest* condensed version." Leaning back, I watched her nod while I collected my thoughts. Not that there was much to tell, but she would never believe the paucity of my existence, and she and her husband had been good to me. Hurting her feelings was not on my agenda.

"Born and raised in Kentucky. You've heard of Kentucky? Horse races? Basketball? Good. Well I grew up there. Our family had a number of successful dry cleaning establishments. Folks moved to California when I was about thirteen. My dad had landed a job with an internet company near San Francisco. Guess he'd gotten bored with cleaning other people's clothes. Anyway, he made a lot of money with the new firm, then one hell of a lot in the stock market. Then he died of a heart attack and a few weeks later my mother killed herself and a good percentage of those lovely dollars were mine.

"Wait, it gets better. I was twenty-two and didn't have a clue what to do with that money. So, I hired a financial director. Beginner's luck. He was just a guy I knew from the gym where I worked out. Man made all the right moves and suddenly I seemed to have more money than I can ever spend."

"So what did you do?" She was staring into my eyes. I felt as though I had become an *objet d'art*. No one had ever looked at me quite that way.

Just to break the spell, I laughed and looked down at the dishes. "Wasted a lot of years married. Married the wrong woman for the wrong reason. We moved to Vegas and took up gambling, drinking, and whatever other forms of entertainment seemed interesting. For a while we were serious about our new passions. Then I got tired of the life and she started making lots of new friends, all of whom loved spending money, my money. A few months ago my wife and I, along with one of her eminently likeable new friends, came to Mexico. At that time I was pretty much a drunk and things got very nasty and I don't remember much after we crossed at Nogales." My skin puckered at the remembering.

"Nasty?"

"Yeah, nasty. And speaking of nasty, I really have to get serious about these dishes. Besides, they seem to need you in the other room. Isn't that your husband calling?"

She didn't speak. Instead, she lifted her smooth dark head and listened. Then she laughed, sounding like the mission bells at sunrise.

"Yes, I must go, Mr. Rich American who likes to drink and can't remember Mexico. Get busy now on your dishes. My husband needs me."

"Go on and go," I said to her back. "I like my dirty dishes just fine. They are very honest."

But I was only talking to the walls, and they weren't interested. I shut up and went back to washing dishes and thinking about my dead parents, my meandering life, my unfaithful wife, and all that beautiful money I used to have.

After a few minutes it occurred to me that maybe I needed to leave the dirty dishes to Mexico and cross the border and check on all my money. I washed dishes and thought about my money north of the border until the light outside began to change.

Twenty-eight

Every afternoon the clouds mounted each other beyond the hills, thickening and darkening, threatening rains that never came. After I finished washing the luncheon dishes I drank strong coffee and shared lies and philosophies with Gomez. When he departed for his daily siesta I grabbed one more cup of coffee and slipped out the back door that had been painted turquoise within living memory. Standing in the shadow of the old building, watching clouds cloaking the mountain tops and wondering what lay beyond, I wondered about my wife, my money, the land beyond the Rio Grande, and how I could get there again. Some days I wondered if I truly wanted to. There was a certain relief in not seeing Jolene's face. Wasn't sure what I would do when I did. One minute I preached forgiveness, the next revenge. In any case, staying sober seemed easier in Mexico.

You could feel the atmosphere thickening and sense the pressure building inside the dark clouds. As if in sympathy, an intensity gathered inside me. My body felt restless, ready to move or strike out at something. It was impossible to bring a stillness to my mind.

The promise of rain was always there, hanging in the lining of the clouds, waiting for the bottoms to rip open. Afternoons drug on, thick and hot and humid. If you moved at all, sweat broke out. If you sat quietly it still came, a slow moistening in the curves and hollows of the flesh. People moved slowly, walking on the shady side of the street, wiping away sweat. Mostly they sat in wooden chairs, fanning with folded sections of newspaper, talking about the heat that had come and the rain that needed to.

All the while the pressure was building up inside me, too, as though I were one of the dark clouds draping the mountain peaks, thick and swollen, ready to burst. Wants rose inside me as well: desire for money, a change of clothes, even a small place to call my own. I'd grown weary of rice and beans, poverty, unrelenting heat, dirt and flies that buzzed even in my dreams. One day evolved into the next with an unexciting and depressing regularity. In the shade of the old building I realized I wanted more out of life than I'd tasted. I'd only been going through the motions of living. Buried in the bowels of Mexico, I wanted another chance. How to achieve it gnawed at me like an afflicted rat.

The same people came to the restaurant day after day until I could recognize their faces and learned their names. There was the fat woman with the wart on her cheek. She always wore blue and the wart sprouted long, black hairs. There was the man who wore a suit and smoked thick greenish cigars and always ate steak. The señora told me he was a banker. There was a hard-faced man who spoke little, but smoked many cigarettes. He wore leather and Gomez told me he was an American. There was a young woman with a fat happy baby. She was pretty and wore a wide gold wedding band. There was an old lady, bent nearly double, who walked leaning on a silver-headed cane. The cane was intricately carved with vines and flowers and wide-winged birds. The old lady only sipped coffee and talked in a clear, alto voice about social life in Mexico City in the '70s.

I knew them all, and a dozen others who came to the restaurant every day for the same lunch or supper, then drifted away to their secret lives. They floated in a holding pattern, existing only in brief intimacies at the restaurant of Gomez. I wonder what the people were waiting for. I wondered what I was waiting for.

~ * ~

At first I did not recognize the sound. It was late in the afternoon, only an hour away from supper. I was sweeping the floor.

The sound came again, out of the northwest, low, deep, and rumbling, muffled as though it were on the far side of the mountains that rimmed the valley. The sound was that of a train coupling. Then I remembered there were no train tracks in Goeteza. Out in the street people were shouting and I leaned my broom against a whitewashed wall. I stepped over the dirt pile on my way out.

By the time I reached the back door, thunder was rolling again. The sons of Gomez were standing in the alley that ran behind the house with their faces turned up to the darkening sky. Dark clouds had come down from the mountains, covering Goeteza like a charcoal blanket. A silver flash lit up the sky and the faces of the boys.

Their mother was calling for them to come in, but they ignored her, running in circles, shouting excitedly in Spanish and pointing to the sinking sky. Cloud bellies seemed to touch the bell tower of the church across the alley and the thunder was a steady rumble, like potatoes rolling down the wooden sides of an upturned barrel. Lightning etched jagged silhouettes in a blackening sky and I could feel the adrenaline rising. I looked around for Gomez.

The church bell began to toll. The wind was sharply cooler and rising, carrying with it the smell of rain.

At every door someone stood staring up at the sky with a bright expectancy caressing their face. People congregated on corners, peering at the lowering clouds. I saw only one man who wasn't looking up.

The Leather Man was leaning against the red bricks of the bank with his bearded face pointing down the alley that ran behind the restaurant. A brown cigarette dangled from the corner of his mouth. Just for the hell of it, I waved at him. Casually he lifted a hand in response as he kept on smoking.

The first fat drops splattered against the baked earth, against the smooth adobe walls, against the upturned faces of the sons of Gomez. Then they stopped. Water streamed off the still-upturned faces of the boys and the sides of the buildings. A monumental clap of thunder exploded over the church and the rains came again, in sheets this time, so silver and solid that they might have been metal, washing streets, houses, animals, baptizing the people.

Above the noise of the silver rain, I could hear the bellowing of cattle, the barking of dogs, and the cries of the boys as they ran in eccentric orbits.

Water cascaded off roofs and trees and parked trucks and cars, channeling its way down the street like a stream being born. The alleyway behind the restaurant sloped downhill and rainwater ran off hard and fast, turning brown as earth softened and yielded.

As other streamlets flowed into it, the stream deepened and widened until sidewalks were submerged and water lapped brown against buildings. Moving water was above the boys' ankles, rising faster than seemed possible until it almost to their knees. No longer able to run, they walked slowly and with great effort through the rising water.

The sky was tinged with purple and the rains came so hard they obscured the world and drowned out all other sounds. There was rain, nothing more. The wind begun to moan to itself, carrying cool, silver rain against my face. Standing in the doorway, I felt the front of my clothes dampen and cling to my body.

Slowly, as if it were an evolutionary process, the rain began to slacken. It was the changing sounds I noticed first. I could hear the animals crying out and Gomez calling against the rain to his sons.

Beyond the back of the restaurant only the huge cottonwood was visible. After a moment, I could see where the street had been and then across to the buildings on the far side. Brown, roiling water ran deep and fast, submerging the street and coming up above the wheel wells on an ancient pickup that had not moved since I hit town. Blurry faces peered out of windows across the confluence, but I could not see Gomez's sons.

Rain still came down, but no longer in blinding sheets. You could hear it peppering against adobe walls, and cars and trucks, and cottonwood leaves, but you could clearly hear sounds other than rain. People were calling out to each other from their doorways and a dog barked in staccato bursts. Gomez kept calling to Tico and Manuel. Urgency had infiltrated his voice and I looked where I'd last seen the boys.

Brown swirling water covered the street like a river in flood. Across the water I could see buildings and vehicles parked at the curb, but no boys. Off to my left there was splashing and shouting. I let my eyes track the sounds. Gomez was knee-deep in water and moving deeper.

"Tico, Manuel, answer me. This is your father...do not play games with me." His head was swinging from side to side, his dark eyes sweeping the inundated street. His eyes swept across my face like a lighthouse beacon.

Gomez shouted from across the street. "My sons, have you seen my sons?"

"Only when the rain started. They were over there, by the truck." I pointed at the rusting Ford. Water was almost up to Gomez's waist and he moved as if the water was thick and grudgingly yielding.

"Good, good. I will go there now. Can you see how deep it is?"

"No, but it looks deep."

Gomez nodded and plowed on. He was less than a quarter of the way across the street. Water was above his waist and he moved with agonizingly slowness. Muscles in his neck stood out in sharp relief against his brown skin and he moved his arms with a visible urgency. I wondered why he was trying to walk through the water.

"Gomez, can't you swim?"

He turned his head. The muscles in his neck curled slowly. Every move seemed to be made in slow motion. Gomez was a strong man, but the force of the water was stronger. He mutely shook his head.

Pulling off my shoes, I stepped into the water. It was cooler than I'd expected and a shiver ran through me. In two steps it was above my knees. The current pushed me, making me go where it wanted me to go. I forged deeper into the brown water until it was above my knees. Its strength was greater than I'd imagined. It rose above my waist and I let it carry me away.

I started swimming with the current, not trying to go directly across, but rather angling with the flow. I floated by Gomez like he was a tree stump. He stared at me with glazed eyes. Before I could give him any sign of comfort, the current had swept me away.

In the middle of the new river the current was even stronger, pulling me along as though I were nothing more than a broken branch. Stroking harder, I kicked my feet, but the current was too strong. My arms were starting to tire and my legs felt heavy. My clothes were waterlogged.

Water was in my eyes and mouth as I struggled to keep my head out of the rising water. My body felt inordinately heavy and there was a growing tiredness deep inside my arms. For a moment, strange serenity engulfed me and I drifted with the brown waters, moving down the river to nowhere.

Cold began to seep through my body. Like an electrical current, adrenalin raced through me in response and I kicked hard for the far side of the street.

One second I was caught helplessly in the main current, the next I was on the other side and swimming strongly. I got my head out of the water in time to see the last building as I floated by. Unencumbered by stone and adobe, the water spread out, flowing across the flat landscape. Above the sound of the moving water, there were shouts, actually screams, shrill and lined with fear.

I quit swimming and started drifting, listening. I could hear the screams more clearly, off to my left. I looked that way. A row of trees stood with their upper branches showing above the muddy waterline. I started swimming toward them, listening to the high shrill cries that came from their branches. The cries didn't come from birds.

The current was with me and I swam in smooth easy strokes. Nearly to the line of trees, I heard my name and looked up. Among the green leaves and brown limbs, just above the rising water and twenty yards to my left, were arms and hands. Faces emerged from the network of leaves as I swam closer.

Tico and Manuel were clinging to a tree limb inches above the water. Their legs were already in the water and it was lapping at their waists. They called to me in high thin voices. All the words were in Spanish, too high and rapid for me to understand. I didn't need to understand the words to comprehend their meaning.

"Don't let go." I shouted, trying to make myself heard above the water swirling angrily at the trunks of the trees. "I'm almost there!"

"Hurry, *señor*, hurry. My brother cannot hold on much longer."

"Tell him to be strong a little longer." I put my head down and swam.

One of the boys shouted something, but I wasn't listening. I grabbed a tree limb. It was smooth and wet and slick and my fingers slid away into the brown water. I swam back and curled around the tree, angling so that I floated into the trunk. It was big around as a telephone pole and I wrapped my arms around it and let swirling waters pin me there.

The bark was rough and pitted and I found a grip above the waterline and worked my way up. When I was high enough, I stretched out my right hand, clinging to the tree with my left. My fingers wrapped around the limb, slipped, then hung on, and I swung a leg up, hauling myself aboard, then monkey-crawled along the limb.

Huge, dark eyes were devouring their thin faces. Hurrying, I worked until I was straddling the limb inches away from the boys.

Their mouths were open, but they were mute. I took a deep breath and a quick glance around. There was only brown water, dotted with floating animals, brush and boxes, the tops of trees. Surely it had to be receding soon.

Bending at the waist, I got one arm around each boy. For a moment the water seemed determined to keep them from me but they came free with a plop and wrapped their arms around my neck. Their wet hair was in my face and their high voices were sweet in my ears.

I felt the water tugging at my legs and the rain peppering down onto my head and the boys wet and warm and alive against me. My mind began to play games with me. I wanted a drink very badly. I wanted to see Wilson again. I wanted another chance at life.

I wanted a lot, I told myself and wasn't likely to get any of it. I made myself think only of the boys, pushed away from the tree, and started kicking like hell for Gomez.

Twenty-nine

Moon and stars hid behind the clouds and darkness enveloped the earth. I sat on a low stone bench behind the restaurant under an old cottonwood that had grown for longer than I had lived and listened to the sounds of the night.

Close to midnight, the air was still warm and sticky. The rains had moved on but the humidity remained thick enough so that you wanted to slash at it with a knife. My shirt was molded to my back.

The darkness had a lush tropical quality to it, as if it were another vibrant element of the jungle undergrowth. Inside the restaurant a single bulb burned and tiny pools of yellow light glowed where there were houses. Goeteza had no streetlights and, except for the saloon, businesses were shuttered for the night.

Light and sound splashed out the saloon's open doors, scooting the darkness back a few feet until they were absorbed by the silence. Patrons' voices came to me as a single sound, rising and falling, muffled and confused in the darkness.

I was tired, but not sleepy. For the first time in so long that I couldn't remember the last time, my mind was whirling at full tilt. It was as if the rain had washed away the Vaseline that had been coating my brain and now thoughts were sparking off into the night, returning recharged and full of portent.

The zombies were out in force. I could hear them calling my name and whispering whiskey prophecies in the shadows. The back door of the restaurant creaked open and a small red dot began to glow in the darkness. As it advanced through the heavy air, night birds called to each other.

Footsteps accompanied the glow and I could make out Gomez coming toward me, his bulk darker and heavier than the night. The pungent, faintly sweet aroma of his cigar seemed natural in the darkness. Sucking on his cigar, Gomez leaned against the cottonwood. The red tip of his cigar glowed like a flock of fireflies fattened on nuclear waste.

Gomez puffed on his cigar as the birds fluttered in the cottonwood. The night drifted on, thick, heavy, dark as forever. The glow moved and Gomez cleared his throat.

"I want to say again my thanks, *Señor* Hampton." His feet shuffled in the dark. Cigar aroma grew stronger. "You saved the lives of my sons. I am forever in your debt."

I didn't want his thanks. I couldn't afford the responsibility. "*De nada*. It was nothing."

"No, no, *señor*. Excuse me, but I know better. My sons told me how you swam through the snakes to them."

"Snakes?"

"Yes, snakes. Tico and Manuel say that around their tree the water was full of long, dark snakes. The big rain undoubtedly drove them from their dens and they were swimming for their lives, like the rest of us. Except for me. I cannot swim. That is why I am so grateful. Without you..." Gomez let the sentence dangle in the dark. I didn't pick it up.

"I didn't see any snakes in the water," I said.

Gomez laughed low in his throat. "Perhaps your mind was on other things."

There didn't seem to be much I could say. So I kept my mouth shut, just like Gary Cooper would have. Gomez put a hand on my shoulder. "You're a quiet man, *señor*."

"Guess I am." I didn't mention the Gary Cooper syndrome. He might not understand me movie-talking to his wife.

Silence grew between us, curling and braiding itself. Gomez lifted his hand from my shoulder. I could hear him sucking on the cigar and smell tobacco burning. High above, clouds were moving, beginning to break apart. For a moment stars sparkled. Then they disappeared.

Gomez tossed his cigar on the ground. I could hear him grinding it into the earth. The moon popped free and I saw his silhouette. Moonlight ran off his dark face like silvered water.

"May I ask you a question?"

I stared at the moonlight writing my sins across my hands and nodded.

"*Bueno*. Are you happy in Goeteza?"

"It's a place to be. Better than the one I came from."

"The reason I ask, *Señor* Hampton, is that you have been with us for some weeks. I was wondering if you ever thought about going back to your United States."

"Are you asking if crossing the border would be a problem for me?" I didn't follow Gomez's drift. "No, it wouldn't be. I'm not wanted for anything there, except stupidity." Cupping my hands, I gazed at the moonlight slow dancing in the cottonwood. "Sure, there are times I think about going back. Right now my problem is no money. Can't get to the border without it."

"You do not have friends or family you could call?"

I stared into the alive darkness. "That's a very good question." I didn't tell him it was one I'd been asking myself. Somewhere in the night someone was playing a radio full of sad songs. We listened to them as the night grew older. I could feel it aging in my bones.

"Would you be interested if I knew a way?"

"Depends on what it is."

"Do not misunderstand me. I do not want you to go. My family does not want you to go. Indeed, you have become like family to us. You and I have had many conversations, told each other many secrets, many dreams. But there are days I see the sadness in your face and nights I hear the loneliness in your voice."

"We've all got issues. Tell me about this way you know."

"It is dangerous."

"So's life. Especially in Mexico."

"That is true. Mexico is dangerous, but she is also very beautiful."

"Sure, snakes, deserts, and ranches that are prisons. Mexico is beautiful as hell. Just ask Wilson."

"Pardon?"

"Never mind. Sometimes the nights get to me, Gomez, and I ramble. Don't pay any attention to me. I'm just another *loco* gringo jousting with zombies."

He moved until the moonlight was behind him and he was backlit in its silvery wash. There was a breeze and it tugged at his hair and shirt. He raised his arms like he was surrendering to Pancho Villa. His palms were facing me. "Okay, but remember I warned you. Since you gave me the most wonderful gift, I will make you a present of this small, dangerous one. That does not seem fair, *señor*."

"Life's not fair." Whiskey zombies crawled across my shoulders and my insides bubbled like a pot of bad chili. "Tell me."

Gomez shrugged. "You know the man in leather who eats every day at the restaurant?"

"What about him?"

"I hear he needs someone to cross the border for him."

"Why doesn't he go himself?"

"I do not know. Perhaps he has more important business here. Perhaps there are other reasons. I only know what I overhear. You understand? I do not even know his real name."

"But you hear he wants someone to go north for him?"

"Someone to cross the border. I hear that he will pay good money."

"This is a poor town. There are few jobs here. Why don't some of the young men go?"

"I cannot say. Perhaps they do not want to leave their families."

"Perhaps they are afraid?"

"Perhaps."

"That shouldn't stop them. Every man is afraid of something. What are you afraid of, Gomez?"

174

"Of many things, *señor*. And you?"

The wind whispered to the cottonwood leaves and a bird called out against the night. I thought about Wilson dead in a dark mountain cave, and Jolene and Stan, and Ramirez and his pleasant little Rancho Detention, and his wife who used her fists, and the snakes swimming black and thick in the roiling brown water.

"Only one thing," I said.

I didn't tell Gomez about the zombies. Instead, I told him to introduce me to the Leather Man.

Thirty

"It's not a fucking picnic, you know."

"Didn't figure it was."

He leaned the straight-backed chair against the adobe wall and plopped his feet on the porch rail. One of the chair's front legs was missing and half the slats were broken, but the man fished a pack of Mexican cigarettes out of the pocket of his leather vest and eyed me over the pack as he sucked a cigarette out of the red and white box.

"Ever been in this business before?"

"No, but I work cheap."

He laughed at that, but the laugh turned into a cough and Leather Man didn't think that was funny. After he got the coughing under control, he glared at me as if he suspected me of tricking him into coughing. He scratched the match head across the side of a boot and lit the cigarette.

"Actually," he said, "you work for free, except for your expenses. I cover those and provide you with transportation, which is what you are looking for. Right? A way back to the States?"

"You got it."

"What you've got, Hampton, is an attitude. I advise you to lose it, and quick. Before I beat it out of you. Gomez gave me the good word on you. Don't want to make him out a liar, do you?"

"Sorry, didn't mean to hack you off. Was just answering your question."

He puffed on his cigarette and blew smoke through his nostrils. He studied the smoke as if it contained a message. "Forget it. I'm behind on a shipment and we've got work to do. Gomez gave you the general outline, I presume."

I stepped up on the porch and leaned against the railing. It sagged beneath my weight, but I could feel the trembling in my legs and didn't trust them without support. Leather Man made me nervous; I didn't want him to know how nervous.

"He said you might need somebody to transport something special across the border."

"That's right. I'm strictly *persona non grata* in the good old U.S. of A. at the moment. And that is a major pain insofar as my business interests are concerned. So I need someone to carry a little something across the border for me. You know what that little something is?" He blew smoke at me.

"I can guess."

"Good for you, Hampton. You know, you look like an over-the-hill choirboy. No one should suspect you of a damn thing."

"Hope not."

"For your sake they'd better not."

His eyes were Seven-Up bottle green. "What about for your sake?"

He snorted through pinched nostrils. "Don't worry about my sake. I'm deep in the wilds of Mexico and you don't know my name and the bastard rat drug enforcement honchos sure as hell ain't going to be able to extradite me from this godforsaken hole." He grinned. His teeth were a dull ivory. I looked out across the dirt road at nothing in particular.

"Word on the street is your name is Jones."

"Fuck-off, asshole. Even somebody as dumb as you has to know better than to use their real name if they're in this business."

I turned and faced him. "I don't care what your name is. Do you want me to do the job or not?" I was still scared, but I was also tired of his mouth. He might be one bad hombre, but so far he was all talk.

The Leather Man sighed as though he had too many burdens to bear and I was the worst of the lot.

"Guess you're about as good as I'm likely to get down here. Damn Mexicans would smoke my dope, or sell it, before they get halfway to the border. Then I'd have to go after the bastards and when I caught up to them I'd have to kill them. Be one hell of a lot of work, with no fucking profit."

He shared his nasty smile with me again and dug in a pants pocket and pulled out a black-handled switchblade. He flicked it open. The blade was six inches long, yet no wider than a lizard's tongue. He began to gouge at dirt under his fingernails. Jonesy's fingernails were cracked and the tips of his fingers were discolored with nicotine. After a minute he looked up. Green eyes glittered in the morning sun like ground glass.

"Wouldn't try to cross me would you, Hampton?"

"No."

"Good, 'cause I know your name and, after I finished with Gomez and his family, I'd find you anywhere in the world. No way someone like you could disappear on me. And I wouldn't want to be in your shorts when I did find you."

Tired of staring at his pockmarked face, I looked over his shoulders into shadows that lay fallow along the western side of the porch.

"Don't worry, I won't cross you. Now give me the details."

Leather Man let the chair thump down on the porch and stood. He studied the end of his knife, wiped it on his jeans, folded it and stuck it in his back pocket. He walked across the porch and leaned on the railing beside me. His breath was bad and he had a peculiar body odor, a too sweet smell that made me half sick. I wanted to walk away and breathe fresh, cool morning air, but I didn't want to piss off my ticket to the Promised Land. So I stood still and tried to breathe shallowly as I stared at the shadows.

"Lots of ways to carry the load," he said. "Depending on the size and how you cross, you can stick it in a condom and swallow it, or stick it up your ass, or your pussy if you was a woman, or just carry it in some sort of case, purse, or money belt. I've heard of people who had it implanted in their legs, even in their scalp."

I looked at him to see if he was joking and he made a face to show me that he wasn't. The facial contortions made him look like a degenerate troll.

"We, however, ain't going to no scientific extremes. You'll just cross the Rio Grande with a pack of wetbacks I run and carry it in a money belt I had specially made. I'll show you how to camouflage it. Okay?"

I nodded. Just thinking about crossing carrying his dope made me nauseous.

Leather Man grinned at me with all his ivory teeth. My stomach rolled.

"All you have to do is remember to keep your pants up in public. Think you can handle that, Hampton?"

I grinned as nastily as I could, while silently telling him to go fuck himself. I hoped he got the message.

For a few seconds we stood there grinning at each other like two over-aged, mentally retarded tomcats. Then he jerked his head toward the door and we walked across the porch with the boards creaking and my nerves doing double time.

The room beyond the door was dark and smelled of urine, old smoke, and stale sex. I didn't want to go inside, but I told myself to quit whining and followed Jonesy's snake hips. I couldn't see where I had a lot of choice. The Leather Man whistled softly between his teeth as he walked. I'd never heard the tune before. I doubted I'd forget it.

Thirty-one

Murmuring to herself, the Rio Grande flowed quietly twenty yards away. We lay still in grass that grew as high as a man's chest, waiting for night to fall. She ran shallowly here, churning into little ripples where the channel narrowed and bubbling white where the water passed over rocks. Birds waded at the water's edge, jerking their sleek heads at sounds I couldn't hear, then lowering them to the water again.

There were twenty of us and we'd been in the tall grass since noon, chatting, thinking, maybe praying a little, but always watching the flat point of land that jutted like a discarded arrowhead across the shallow waters that separated us from the Promised Land.

About an hour before, a jeep carrying two men in brown shirts and baseball caps had worked its way slowly along the northern bank, sunlight glinting off their binoculars as they stared into Mexico. We had been as still as the earth, while the grasses waved gently above us, nodding in the freshening breeze, glittering green and golden in the sunlight.

The light was changing. On the western horizon the sun was an orange blur, while above us the heavy air hung purple. I was lying next to an older man with a rawhide face and silver streaks dancing through his hair. Torres was his name, and the Leather Man had told me that he knew where and when to cross.

They had spoken briefly in Spanish, Torres had nodded, and they'd shaken hands without smiling. Then the Leather Man had turned to me and told me again where to go if I made it, and what would happen to me if I didn't. We both understood his words were a righteous promise.

Torres was staring across the river into the gathering dusk. Dying sunlight splashed against the grass while shadows fell across his face like prison bars. Brown eyes were as still as stones.

"Torres?"

"*Sí.*" In the fading light his lips didn't appear to move. His expressionless eyes still focused across the river.

"Will we cross before dark?"

"After."

"There's no moon tonight. How will we see?"

Torres spoke without turning his head. "If we can see the far side of the river then those on the far side can see us."

"Will there be someone there?"

"Sooner or later." A smile played at his lips. "They're over there somewhere. Who can say exactly where? An hour ago they were there. In another hour they may be back, or they may not return for days. When it's dark we'll take our chances." He lifted his shoulders and let them fall. "Who can say what will happen?"

I watched the shadow lines thicken and merge on his face. Dusk was coming in a rush and the breeze was fading. Still, heavy air turned from purple to charcoal.

"How many times have you crossed?"

"Dozens."

"Ever been caught?"

"A few times," he said. I could hear him breathing softly as the last pinprick of light faded to oblivion. All the land was dark and only the sound of birds settling down for the night intruded on the silence. I felt myself merging into the night. Torres spoke and the sound of his voice jarred the quiet.

"Twice I have crossed and stayed for a year and come back on my own. I cannot remember the number of times I have helped others cross." The grasses rustled again and I knew he'd turned toward me.

"It is easy to cross, *amigo*. The trick is staying free. It is good to be both careful and lucky, but if you can only be one—be lucky."

"The Leather Man said you'd get me across and someone would meet me."

"That is the plan," he said. "*Señor* Jones always plans well, but sometimes plans don't work. I will cross with you and take you to the back trail to Tucson. A man named Hendley is to meet us there.

"You stay with me. If we get separated and you do not make the rendezvous just keep the morning sun on your right and keep moving, going always to the north and west. It will not be a short walk. You must cross New Mexico. Count on two weeks. We are well to the east of Tucson, but here the Border Patrol is not so bad and Jones has many friends. These men will be on the lookout for you. They will help you. Jones has seen to that. Understand?"

"Yes."

I waited for him to say more, but he fell silent. I rolled over onto my back. Stars were hanging like diamonds pinned against black velvet. Along the riverbank an owl hooted. A small animal rustled through the grasses off to my right. The river murmured to the sky.

I listened to the river, stared at the sky, and wondered how the night would end. I wished Wilson were with me. I pulled my pack up onto my chest and checked the special belt that hugged my waist. My burden to bear. The smell of my own sweat was in my nostrils and my stomach gurgled. With hunger or fear I couldn't say. But I could taste the promise of the land across the murmuring, sparkling river, and it was sweet.

~ * ~

The evening was full of indecipherable whispers, like a coalescing dream. I could hear grass rustling and see simian shadows rising up from the earth. "It is time, *amigo*," Torres said.

Rolling over, I pushed myself off the ground and repositioned the special belt. Metal snaps were cool against my flesh.

"Let's go," Torres whispered as he moved down the creek bank. Following in his footsteps, I could see the ghostly shapes of men moving toward the Rio Grande in a starlit wedge, with Torres at the point. Starlight shimmered off the water as we pushed through the tall grass. I could hear water rippling over rocks. Beyond the water the land rose. Without the moon it was difficult to see much, but as far as I could tell there was no one waiting for us on the far bank.

We were moving across the mud flats, the ground going softer and my feet sticking now and then, coming loose with a sharp, sucking sounds. Torres whispered something, but the sounds of the river filled my ears. Puddles evolved into pools and I was surprised at the coolness of the water. I wondered how deep it was, and if there were snakes in the water. It had rained recently and I didn't relish another swim.

I rechecked Jonesy's belt. Crossing without it would sign my own death warrant. The water was moving more quickly than I'd expected. It rose to my ankles and kept rising, cresting at my knees. Torres's bulk moved before me and I followed him.

Wet pants clung to my legs but the walking was not difficult. I kept waiting for someone to shout at us, or for the sound of a rifle shot. All I could hear was my own splashing.

Halfway across there was a loud splash off to my left, followed by a soft barrage of curse words. I scanned the northern bank for movement. Not a shadow wavered.

Before I was expecting it, the water gave way to mud and the ground began to rise. I slipped, got a grip on an exposed cottonwood root and pulled myself up the bank. My hands were muddy and I was chilly in the night air but I was back on American soil, strangely pleased in the way that you are when you have been gone from a certain country for a long time and when you return it was the same as you remembered.

The man who called himself Jones and wore leather and smoked dark Mexican cigarettes seemed a thousand miles away. I saw Torres silhouetted against the northern sky and I knew the back road to Tucson awaited me. I was no hero coming home, only a lost soul dodging my personal zombies and trying to slip in the side door to paradise.

Torres watched me clamber up the bank and waited until I had adjusted my belt before he jerked his head and started walking across a stretch of open, flat ground. As I followed, I could hear the others moving off to their own destinations.

North of the river the breeze was stronger and meadow grasses and wildflowers nodded before us in the faint light. Away from the tree line the light was better and the earth not as flat as it had appeared. Rather, it gently undulated like an ocean between storms. The ground was firm and the going easy. We walked in silence beneath a sky so full of stars it looked alive. Grasses swished against our jeans and the wind was cool against the stubble that had sprouted like young wheat along my jaw line. Muscles in my legs moved smoothly as they warmed and it was pleasant to walk with the promise of Tucson glowing in my mind.

After an hour we stopped to rest in a line of trees. Their low-slung branches formed a natural canopy. Torres sat with his back against a tree and dug into his canvas backpack. He pulled out two sandwiches wrapped in wax paper and handed me one. A stray thought that it might be my last meal flashed across my mind. I had a bad feeling about the deal that was going down. I didn't know Hendley from Saint Paul or Satan, and I was in unfamiliar territory. I didn't like the odds.

Starlight couldn't penetrate the leaves and the blackness reminded me of the cave and Wilson. I wanted a drink more than I had in months. I held the sandwich without unwrapping it.

"You'd better eat. We've got a long walk ahead of us."

I started unfolding the wax paper. "How long to the rendezvous?"

Torres took a bite of his sandwich before he answered. "If we walk hard and don't run into trouble we should be there shortly after daybreak."

The bread was homemade, thick-sliced and going dry. The soft substance between the slices smelled like cheese. "You mentioned trouble. What sort of trouble?"

"Who can say? The Border Patrol might be out, or we may run across bushwhackers or snakes. Who knows, *señor*, you might wander off in the dark and fall off the edge of a mesa." Torres laughed like he thought that idea was hilarious.

"Don't worry. I'll stay close."

Torres was chewing with his mouth opened. I nibbled at my sandwich. It tasted like it smelled. I took another bite. It was no better than the first. I sincerely hoped this would not be my last meal.

"Tell me, Torres, how will we know who's meeting us?"

He was fooling with the water bottle he had tied to his waist. Water gurgled. He stood up, walked over and handed me the bottle.

"Jones said the man would know us and he would say 'they're getting good prices for tomatoes in California this year.' His name is Hendley. When he says that, you give him the package and I go back to Mexico."

The water was cool against my throat. "You don't want to stay?"

"I'm too damn old to be dodging the Border Patrol and sleeping on hard ground. No, my worrying friend, I will get you to the meeting place and then go back to Mexico to collect the rest of my pay."

I wondered what would happen to me when Torres headed south. The prospects worried me. To occupy myself I ate the rest of my sandwich and washed it down.

Torres stretched and peered into the darkness. After a minute, he snorted like a weary mule. "Get up. We need to be moving."

As we hiked out of the trees the land opened before us. Hills rose on either side, but Torres kept us in the valley. Judging by the stars, we were headed almost due north.

So slowly I thought at first I was imagining it the land began to slope upward. Boulders, smooth and rounded like discarded molars of a race of giants, began to dot the landscape. For an old man Torres moved well. I struggled to keep up.

Air grew cooler as we went higher. Rock-strewn, the trail twisted up the side of the mountain like a lost snake. Even in the chilling air I could feel a sweat line forming under my hair. I wiped at it with my sleeve. Stars shone directly overhead with cool ethereal beauty, silver tattoos on an ebony sky. The trail grew so narrow boulders brushed against both shoulders as I passed. It wound steadily upwards. I felt all I had to do was reach an arm skyward and I would touch a star.

Torres was waiting for me at the crest, sitting on the decapitated top of a boulder, massive and charcoal-colored in the starlight. My legs were trembling and the muscles in my thighs burned. I sat down on Torres's rock. He looked at me but didn't say anything.

To the north and east there were more mountains, dark and jagged against the sky, dwarfing the one we'd just climbed. The mountain we were on fell away to the west, dissolving into a broad flat plain, bisected by winding arroyos. Under the pale stars, it looked like lonely country.

Looking back the way we'd come, all I could see was darkness. Mexico and the Rio Grande and Wilson and Gomez and the Leather Man were only memories.

I bent to tie a boot and the gouge of the pouch against my underbelly reminded me that until I completed the delivery I'd better keep the Leather Man very much on my mind. I felt sure I was on his.

Thirty-two

The sky was changing as we curled out of a thicket of sagebrush and low-hanging mesquite. Stars were fading and a pencil line of coral outlined the eastern horizon. All around us the air was metamorphosing from ebony to smoke and wisps of spider web fog floated above the open ground. Birds were stirring in the mesquite and our footsteps seem unnaturally loud in the pre-dawn.

Torres was moving smoothly and easily as if night hikes were a common occurrence. Maybe they were for him, but I was sleepy and hungry and thirsty. Exhaustion was settling into my bones. I could smell the odor of my own body. Last night's cheese sandwich seemed like last week's news.

Daylight was coming fast and I could see the grass waving and parting as we marched through it. In the distance I could hear water flowing over rocks. Torres's long white hair moved like a banner through the morning air.

"How much farther?"

Torres extended an arm. My eyes followed along the line of sight. We were crossing a meadow. At the far end the land rose into a line of trees, still blurry in the tentative light. A dirt road curved through the trees and a Chevy Tahoe stood square-topped and black in the sunlight striking the higher ground.

"Hendley?"

"Better be," Torres said over his shoulder. He kept walking.

I picked up the pace and came alongside. The night before had left its marks. Fresh lines were etched on his face and his skin looked dry and drawn, like poorly tanned leather.

"What am I supposed to do, just hand him the stuff?"

Half-turning his head, Torres gave me an indecipherable look. "Just keep your mouth shut and follow my lead."

"What happens after we do the deal?"

"Like I told you before, I go back to Mexico."

"What about me?"

Torres stopped and peered into my face. I don't know what he saw there; he only shrugged and resumed walking. "You'd better hope Hendley gives you a ride back to civilization," was all he said.

The ground rose gradually toward the north and sunlight was golden in the treetops. The sound of running water was stronger. As we came up the rise I could see a tall, slender man in a long black duster and wide-brimmed hat leaning against the front of the Tahoe. His face was hatchet-shaped, thin and hard looking, with a sharply angled jawline. The brim of his hat shaded his eyes and both his hands were in the pockets of the duster. What I could see of his face looked grainy and unhealthy, the Marlboro Man in the final stages of lung cancer.

A second man, shorter and thicker, stood in the shadows, while a third sat behind the wheel of the Chevy. Sunlight reflected so fiercely off the windshield that all I could see was the outline of his face. Torres walked up the slope as calmly as if we were going to six o'clock Mass.

We were thirty feet away when the thin man took his hands out of his pockets and adjusted his hat as he stepped away from the Tahoe. Torres stopped so abruptly I almost bumped into him.

"Torres?"

"*Si.*"

"I'm Hendley," the thin man said.

"Good," Torres said.

In that moment I wanted a drink. I was glad there wasn't any alcohol in sight. I was weak and didn't need any temptations.

Hendley took a step closer. Out of the corner of my left eye I could see the man in the shadows move. My hands started shaking and I put them in my pockets. A film of nervous sweat covered my body.

"Word is they're getting good prices for tomatoes in California this year."

"*Bueno.*" The old man flicked a quick glance at me and nodded his head.

Hendley reached up and tipped the brim of his hat up. Sunlight splashed across his eyes. They were small and green, like fresh peas. His eyebrows were pale. His tongue took a lap around his lips.

"You got something for me?"

I shifted my weight, trying to disguise the trembling in my legs.

"Maybe, if you've got something for me."

Hendley jerked his head and the passenger window on the Tahoe slid down with an automatic swoosh. Seconds later an envelope emerged. Hendley reached behind and grabbed it, then swung it around toward Torres.

Torres ran a finger under the flap and peered inside. Satisfied, he turned toward me and moved his head in a long slow arc toward Hendley.

I pulled my hands out of my pockets and slid them down my shirt. The snaps stuck and every second seemed like a minute. Then the snaps clicked and I pulled the belt free and extended it toward Torres. He nodded toward Hendley. I walked across the open ground on legs feeling like freshly cooked spaghetti.

Hendley's eyes never left Torres's face. When I got close he held out a hand, palm open, and I laid the belt across it. The veins at his wrist were thick and twisting over and through each other like a family of incestuous worms.

There were noises behind me and to my left, inside the tree line, but I kept by eyes on Hendley. Morning seemed to be evolving into a staring contest.

Hendley fumbled with the belt for a moment, then got the inside pouch open and stared at it. My whole body was shaking as though it were honeycombed with minor earthquakes. He folded the belt and stuck it through the open window. Leaning against the Tahoe, he pulled his hat down.

I glanced at Torres. He was standing at parade rest with the morning sun burnishing his bronze flesh. Tiredness was visible in his face, but not fear.

The man inside the Tahoe said something, but I was concentrating on Torres and missed the words. Hendley caught them. I saw him nod. His lips curled in what his mother might have considered a smile.

"All right, Torres, you can head south now. Tell Jones it was a pleasure doing business with him again."

Torres flipped him the Mexican salute and started backing down the hill. Hendley eyeballed him for a few seconds, then reached behind his back and opened the door. The motor coughed and caught as Hendley climbed on board. The Tahoe backed up turning into a clearing. The third man jogged out of the trees, opened the back door and climbed inside, shotgun first. Gears changed and the motor revved. In less than a minute the Tahoe was out of sight.

I turned and looked for Torres, but he'd vanished into the morning sun. I walked toward the sound of the moving water. On the far side of the clearing the land sloped down to a stream. I drank cool, clear water until my brain ached, then doused my head and came up shaking like a retriever. After a few minutes of deliberation, I climbed back up the slope and started walking west down a dirt road that ran between twin lines of trees. Sunlight filtered through the canopy and patches of light splattered on the road like phosphorescent markings left by aliens.

Thirty-three

At the end of the second day I hit the highway. Afternoon was dying behind a bank of crimson-bottomed clouds huddling together low in the western sky. Nearly exhausted and hungry as hell, I came around yet another bend in the road, wiping at sweat, suddenly realizing the trees were gone. Black asphalt ran to the horizon.

Only yards away the little stream was still talking to itself and I slid down the shallow bank and washed my face and hands and combed my hair with my fingers. The rank odor of my own sweat was in my nostrils and my empty stomach gurgled, but I tucked my shirttail into my pants, smoothed out the wrinkles, and strolled back up the bank to the edge of the asphalt. Putting a smile on my face, I waited for the world to drive by.

It took its own sweet time but the world came. Three cars and a cargo van before darkness fell. None of them even slowed. Night came suddenly, a dark curtain falling. One minute I'd been staring into shimmering twilight, the next I was enveloped in blackness, broken only by a handful of fireflies who seemed to represent the last light on earth.

Staring at the empty road and praying, I'd never felt more alone. Every ten or fifteen minutes headlights would pierce the blackness and I would stick up my thumb, squinch my eyes against the alien light, then curse as the cars sped on.

Just as I was trying to convince myself to go lie down in the ditch line, the driver of an ancient station wagon headed north flicked on a right turn signal and eased onto the gravel. Swallowing the fear lumping my throat together, I forced my legs into a jog.

It was an old station wagon, probably a Buick, light in color; faded yellow was my guess. Its taillights burned red against the blackness of the night. Over my own breathing I could hear the irregular heartbeat of the wagon through an obviously well-ventilated muffler and I wondered what awaited me in this chariot of the night. Jogging around to the passenger side of the car, I pulled the door open cautiously. The dome light glowed dimly, as though it was tired.

The driver was alone in the car, an over-aged hippie in faded jeans and a stained peasant shirt. Scents of smoke, road dust, moldy time, and fading dreams rose to meet me. He gave me a watermelon grin and the earring dangling from his left ear sparkled as it twirled.

"Need a lift?"

"Sure," I said, sliding my backside across the cracked vinyl.

Giving me the once over, he shifted into drive. The station wagon eased onto the asphalt and slowly picked up speed. Twin headlights stabbed the night. The man behind the wheel turned and glanced at me, then swung his eyes back on the road.

"Where you going?"

"Wherever you're going suits me."

"How does Tucson sound to you?"

"Like a winner."

His long hair kept falling down his face and he kept pushing it back as though the motion was a religious act. His window was down and the rushing air played with his beard. Grinning, he said, "Sorry man, no air conditioning."

"Not a problem." Gratitude came a lot easier these days.

"Been on the road long?"

"Feels like forever."

"Know what you mean. I've been headed to the coast for a week. I'm from Memphis. Damn fan belt went in Oklahoma. Took me two days to find another one and get it on. Parts are hard to get for a car this old."

"At least it runs."

"Yeah, she runs pretty good most of the time. Got over two-hundred and fifty thousand miles on her. Everything works, too, except for the air, the left turn signal, the horn, and the right wiper blade."

We both laughed and I said, "Guess we've all seen better days."

My stomach started to rumble again and he took his eyes off the road long enough to eyeball me. His eyes drifted back to the road as we took a sweeping turn in what seemed like slow motion. We rumbled across a patched place in the road and the car rose and fell like a ship on a rising tide.

"Shocks ain't so damn hot either." He jerked his head toward the back seat. "If you're hungry, there's snacks in those two Piggly-Wiggly sacks."

"Thanks."

I tried not to be greedy, but I ate a sleeve of saltine crackers, an apple, a banana, and a Butterfinger. He had a pair of gallon milk jugs filled with water and I drank almost half of one. Neither of us spoke until I'd finished.

"Hadn't eaten in a while, had you?"

"No, I hadn't. Thanks for the food. Sorry I ate so much."

"Don't worry about it. Brought a ton with me. Sometimes I get the munchies. You ever get the munchies?"

"Sure."

Nodding his head, he twisted the radio on. Blues came faintly through a cracked speaker head. "Sorry," he said. "That's all I've been able to pick up since midnight, 'cept of course for some Mexican."

"It's cool."

He nodded again and refocused on his driving. Penetrated by the headlights, the night rushed by in a whooshing, whitish blur. Heaviness was building in my eyes and I closed them, easing my head back against the vinyl.

"What's your name?" he asked.

"Paul Hampton." I answered with my eyes still shut, the sound of my own name strangely foreign on my lips.

"Mine's Daniel," he said over the moaning of a sax, "Daniel Winston. You can call me Dogs 'cause that's my nickname."

"How'd you ever pick that up? Would have thought Dan or Danny."

"Got it from my fat Uncle Frank. My mother's brother. Always had a smart mouth on him. Never did like him, and wasn't crazy about the name. But it stuck. He didn't."

"What happened to your uncle?"

"Don't know for sure," he said, voice softening. "Guess he went a little crazy. Just walked away from his wife, his job, and a damn near new Cadillac Eldorado. Only had twenty-one thousand miles on it."

"Where'd he go?"

"All I know is he went to Mexico. Heard from him once. He sent me a postcard with a donkey, a cactus, a pretty señorita, and one of them big Mexican hats on it. What do you call 'em?"

"Sombreros?"

"Yeah, sombreros. Anyway, I only got the one card from him and nobody else got anything. Wanted me to come down and join him. Said the living was cheap, the women was pretty, and the beer was good." Dogs sighed. "Never did go. Sort of wish I had. Guess it's too late now. Frank's probably moved on by now, or he's dead. Anyway, nobody ever heard from him again."

My eyes grew very heavy. I didn't want to be rude. The man had been kind enough to give me a ride when I looked like yesterday's garbage and it seemed I could at least chat away the long, asphalt night.

"Don't suppose you remember what town the postcard came from?"

He went quiet for so long I thought he was ignoring me, or I had only imagined I'd asked the question. "Nogales," he said finally, in a pleased-with-himself voice. "Nogales, Mexico. Always liked the sound of that town. Frank called it Noproblem." He laughed at the memory.

I truly wanted to talk some more, keep my benefactor company, and I told myself I would, after a short nap. Tires hummed against the asphalt

while the blues crackled cool and slow from radioland and the wind blew
warm and dry against my face. The world started to slip away from me.
Just before everything went black, Dogs said, "Frank, Frank Wilson of
Memphis, Nogales, and who-the-hell-knows where else."

~ * ~

I woke with the sun in my eyes and Dogs smiling like the promise of
a thousand wild tomorrows. Purplish circles underscored his eyes and
lines I hadn't seen the night before etched his face, but a certain mellow
aura clung to him. Smoking a hand-rolled, buff-colored cigarette, he
looked young and old, happy and sad, and totally open without revealing
anything. An innocent smile was spread across his face. Young boy
dreams danced in eyes that had seen it all. Propped between his legs was
an open can of Bud. Yesterday's memories crackled on the radio.

Dogs extracted the cigarette from his lips and waved it vaguely in my
direction. "Wanna a hit?"

"No thanks," I said, and rubbed at my eyes. An ocean of desert was
baking under the morning sun. Broken only by sagebrush, scattered
cactus, and outcroppings of black rock, the sand ran in all directions as far
as I could see. No houses, no people, no animals; only desert and sunlight,
and far away to the east, at the very edge of vision, a thin blue line of
mountains poking the lining of the sky. I had the sensation of cruising in
an intergalactic chariot, drifting under a prideful sun.

"Where are we?"

"Coming up on Continental." He pointed a finger at the blue-rimmed
mountains. "See those?"

"Yeah."

"Those are the Santa Rita's. We came through them after
Greaterville. That's where I gassed up. Man, you slept through it all."

"Sorry. Meant to stay awake to talk to you. Guess I was more tired
than I realized." My words sounded lame.

He took another drag off the cigarette, followed by a hit of beer. His
eyes never left the road and the smile never left his lips. "Not a problem. I
like New Mexico in the night. It's Arizona by daylight that gets to me.

Glad you're back in this universe. Anyway, won't be long to Tucson. We'll pick up I-19 just the other side of Continental. Then it's just a straight shot north. You got family there?"

I shook my head. "Contacts." At least I hoped to make some there.

Dogs puffed on his cigarette and nodded. "Contacts, that's a good word, good thing to have, too." His head swung in my direction, moving as though it was very heavy, almost more than his neck was able to maneuver. "Been to Tucson before?"

"First time."

There was a rhythm to his nodding, as though he were responding to an internal pulse. His head swung back toward the road.

"Not me. Believe it or not, Hampton, but I went to school there once." A smile worked its way across his eyes. "However, as they say, that was in another lifetime."

Smoke was thick inside the vehicle, and now and then Dogs' eyes closed, only to flutter open. Mine were starting to burn. I lowered my window more. Incoming air was hot and dry but it dissipated the smoke. In the rearview mirror the mountains were a blue smudge.

The cigarette between Dogs' lips grew steadily shorter. The station wagon weaved gently across the center line, then drifted back. I was grateful traffic was virtually nonexistent.

The song on the radio changed into a slow, smooth tune. We began to cut across the asphalt in great swirls, curving from one edge of the road to the other as if we were the only vehicle in the world. Dogs nodded to himself over the steering wheel, out of time with the radio, hearing his own rhythm from a place in the universe I couldn't fathom.

"Did you graduate from Arizona?" I asked the question to keep him awake. After all I'd been through, to die in a car wreck caused by a stoned, over-aged hippie seemed asinine.

"What?"

I repeated the question with a straight face.

"Hell no. I just attended. Like I attended Arizona State and Berkley and Utah State and Wyoming and Memphis State and another school I forget the name of right now. *Amigo*, I was a great attender. Not much of a graduater, though. How 'bout you?"

"Went to Vanderbilt for a while. Later on, I went to Louisville."

"Didn't like 'em?"

"No, I liked them all right. Flunked out of the first; got kicked out of the second."

Dogs nodded slowly and carefully, as though I had just laid bare a cool bright truth. He looked as high as the mountains we'd crossed. The old car continued to weave majestically across the shimmering asphalt. When we drifted too close to the edge, tires sang in the sand. Being crippled or killed in the middle of an Arizona desert had no appeal. I decided to try and talk him down.

"Hey man, you with me?"

"Yeah, I'm here." His words were slurred, difficult to understand.

"Can I ask you a favor?"

"Sure."

"What about pulling over and letting me drive for a while? Haven't driven in a long time and I've really got the urge."

Turning his shaggy head, Dogs started at me with great seriousness from eyes underlined faintly by bluish flesh. "You wanna drive?"

"Sure."

Swinging his eyes back to the road he nodded some more. He kept nodding, just like one of the little bobbing dogs you used to see in the back windows of cars. The station wagon swerved, tires spun sand, then found the pavement again.

"You want to drive my car?"

"Sounds like a good idea."

Dogs began to steer the station wagon to the side of the road. We eased to a stop on a windswept patch of sunbaked ground. Stepping out of the car, I let warm air take me in its arms. We walked around the car together and I got in behind the wheel. Dogs was already in my old corner with his head against the doorframe. The cigarette stub still smoldered between his lips. Smiling and nodding to himself, he was a happy child.

Slipping the transmission back into drive, I steered the wagon back on the dark ribbon that ran straight and hard across unending sands. The road was sun soaked and empty in the rearview mirror. Even the mountains were gone. We were as alone as if we'd been on Uranus.

Rolling across the quiet desert bathed in the bright hollow light of forever, I could feel a smile crawling across my face. Tucson seemed only a few miles away. The Eagles were singing about the Hotel California and I leaned over and cranked the radio. Dogs nodded his approval. I put my foot to the floor and we went like a bat out of hell down the highway with no name. The sunlight was very bright.

Thirty-four

Sand and silence slowly gave way to gas stations and road noise. Eventually, we encountered gridlock in South Tucson. A thousand people seemed to have instantly exited from a military base with the fervent desire to occupy the same lane at the same intersection at the same time. Jamming on the brakes, I worried the behemoth to a stop six inches behind a Cadillac that had once been green. Dogs lurched forward then sank back against the vinyl with his eyes open.

"Whoa," he said. "Whoa, whoa, whoa. Man, that was some incredibly fine vision." He rolled his head toward me. His pupils were solid steel BBs set in cracked mosaic eyes. "Let me tell you, Hampton, that was one dream ride." Lifting his hands in front of his face he spread them apart and then back together as if he were parting spider webs.

"See, I was floating on the Intercostal. Forget whether I was going north or south. Anyway, it doesn't matter, 'cause see I was on this big old sailboat with this big-tittied blonde and she was sure crazy for me. But, see, there was this manatee following us, and the manatee was wearing sunglasses, 'cause he was really Buddha or the Christ Child or some great person, and he didn't want anybody to know who he was. So, naturally, I had to like protect him, you know, and the blonde she was shaking her boobies at me and getting real mad 'cause I was paying more attention to Jesus in sunglasses. Then the wind started blowing hard and the sailboat started flying just above the water. Everything was whirling by in this mystical blur and the blonde started screaming and the manatee started screaming, too, 'cause he thought the blonde was screaming at him and he was trying to talk her language. And I was like ready to scream my own damn self. Only then, I woke up. Hey, why are we sitting still? Or actually, where in the world are we?"

Biting my lip to keep from laughing at his dream-talk jag, I said, "We're stuck in traffic in South Tucson."

Dogs sat up straighter and looked around like he was newborn and this was his first out-of-the-womb sighting.

"Oh yeah, I see now. We're here." Dogs let his head fall back against the vinyl as if the effort had been entirely too taxing.

As we inched forward I kept glancing back and forth between Dogs and the road. We were here, according to my man Dogs, but I didn't have a clue where we needed to go next. When Dogs continued his comatose yoga for five consecutive blocks, I reached and gave him a nudge.

"Hey, man, where do we go from here?"

He blinked at the sunlight pouring in through the glass, then looked around with a dilatory air.

"Uh, what street are we on?"

It took me a second to recall the last street sign I'd seen. "Believe we're on Henderson."

"Whoa, we're way too far south. A bend east and we are in the barrio." He massaged his forehead with the palm of his left hand, moving it rhythmically across the faded red and blue bandana.

"Let me think. What's the name of that street? Way the hell north of here, more up toward the university, only some east of there." He rolled BB eyes at me. "Don't rush me. The name will come." He twisted his head toward the window as if moving air might energize his memory. I hoped he had more than a manatee in the memory banks.

Drifting with the herd, dodging Volvos, listening to Van Morrison, we angled north, moving with painful slowness toward nowhere in particular. We passed Hall, Richardson, Pfeiffer, and Gelhorn. Dogs moaned when we got to Welsh. Still staring out at a smoldering Tucson, he mumbled something I couldn't understand.

"What was that?"

"We still on Henderson?"

"Yeah."

"Cool. Keep going and let me know when we get to Speedway. The street we want is between Speedway and Grant. Remember that much. Once we get in familiar territory, I'll recognize the house. How we doing on gas?"

"Just dropped below a quarter of a tank."

"Good deal, we'll make it easy. Where we're going the folks have real cash money. They'll help old Dogs out." He rotated his head in my direction. His eyes were slits.

"You cool man? Can you handle the drive?"

"Sure. Just go back to sleep. I'll wake you when we get to Speedway."

Dogs closed his eyes. "Wake me at Speedway."

"Will do," I said. Before we made the end of the block he was snoring. I drove on through the migration of the homeward bound, half wishing I was going home myself.

Sunlight poured hot against my face and a tortured wind blew in off the desert. Sweat pooled under my arms and trickled down the back of my neck. Flies buzzed against the windshield and old dogs slept in the shade of bus-stop benches. People hurried out of buildings; people hurried into buildings. All the people and all the buildings began to look the same. Traffic crawled north in fits. A longing for the simplicity of Goeteza sprang up. Dianna Ross came on the radio and I turned it off.

Idling in traffic, I passed the time looking at the men lounging against the walls of buildings. The walls were stained, smeared with dirt, dust, and sand. The men were short and tall, dark and light, and forty-seven shades and sizes in between. Some were smiling and some looked ready to fold their cards. Some stared back at me and some were only dreaming with their eyes open.

The jam finally broke and we drifted north. Dogs snored gently, a monstrous, benevolent baby on the cracked vinyl of the ancient yellow

Buick. A red light caught me at Adriana, and Dogs came awake, coughing and blinking. He ran his tongue around his lips and made a face. His eyes whirled like balls on a roulette wheel. "Fuck, I'm getting too old for this shit."

The light changed and I let the Buick roll. "Why don't you give it up?"

Leaning his head back against the cracked vinyl, Dogs grinned. "Like it way too much. Besides, old hippies never die, they just smoke their life away, one joint at a time."

We rolled on in our rusty metal chariot, two lost souls going nowhere fast under a brutal sun. To our right, I could see swing sets and a basketball court with one iron rim still clinging to a backboard. A sawdust walking trial bisected an expanse of earth.

"Hey, I recognize this place. Turn left, turn left. No, no, at the next block. Yeah, man, take a left on Stein."

I twisted the wheel and the lost boys of summer motored down Stein, past bungalows and bougainvillea, trees with sidewalk-cracking roots, old men leaning on canes, and children running and screaming, by old cars abandoned at the curb, their wheels up on concrete blocks, their bodies splattered with rust spots that looked like bullet holes. People sat on shadowy porches, staring at the strangers.

Dogs stuck his face out his window, the wind blowing his hair back from his face, his eyes studying the houses. In the side mirror his face appeared to be pushing out against the air, his nostrils quivering, as if he really was a dog sniffing for old scents of memory.

"Not much farther now. Should be in the next block or so," he said. "I'm recognizing more and more. There, see the white frame house, the one with the saggy roof. That's where that old fart lives who called the cops on us on account of our music. Claimed it was too loud and interfered with his sleep. As if sleep would do him any good. Hell, the old bastard's hide was so damn wrinkled it looked like a rhino's. Wasn't no amount of beauty sleep going to help him."

Dogs gestured toward a brown house with peeling paint and the gutter swinging loose at one end. "Man, there it is. Pull in here. Yeah, right in front of the Pontiac. That two-story is the one we want. Hell, that gutter was hanging last time I was here and that's been at least six months. Damn lazy bastards. Hope they at least have some good dope."

I maneuvered the behemoth against the curb in front of a forest green Grand Am missing the rear fender and the left taillight. Dogs had his door swinging open before I cut the engine. Hopping out of the Buick like a rabbit on uppers, he strode across the weedy lawn.

Getting out more slowly, I followed him like Cortez traversing the southwest. In the yard there were more weeds than grass, and not a lot of those. Dust billowed with every step. Except for a yellow and brown hound who sprawled under a decrepit elm, the yard was empty. Music drifted out from the house—heavy metal with the bass cranked. I trailed Dogs around to the back. Before I rounded the corner I heard a screen door slam.

The back yard was small and square, contained by a tall wooden fence that looked like it hadn't been painted since the first Clinton administration. Scraggly grass dotted the landscape. Between clumps were children's toys, used motorcycle parts, sagging lawn furniture, the skeleton of a '67 Volkswagen Beetle, and a battered assortment of metal trashcans, only one of which had a lid. On the far side of the Volkswagen was a vinyl-coated shed that might have served as a garage in an earlier era. Now the roof sagged and three of the four panes of glass in the solitary window were missing.

I turned, climbed two concrete steps, and pulled the screen door open. No one said anything, so I stuck my head through the opening and said, "Hello."

Only the stillness of a junk-filled back porch greeted me. After the sunshine of the backyard, the porch was dark and I worked my way carefully between an abandoned washing machine and a pyramid of cardboard boxes. With each step the odors of cooking meat, onions, tomatoes, and grease grew stronger. I crossed the porch with the dusty floorboards creaking, then stepped into the kitchen.

A huge pot, full of something dark and thick, gurgled on the stove. Bubbles popped steadily on the surface, creating the illusion of life. A woman with stringy brown hair and a wooden spoon in one hand sat on a stool next to the stove. A cigarette dangled from one corner of her mouth. Ashes had fallen across her blue sweat pants making her look as though she'd been too close to an erupting volcano. Her white tube top needed washing and her feet were bare.

She gripped the rungs of the stool with her toes and nodded. I nodded back and smiled. She kept nodding. I left her nodding to herself and went looking for Dogs.

I found him in a living room nearly bare of furniture. Pillows were scattered about the room and a trio of striped Indian blankets lay on the dusty wood floor. From one corner a huge stereo blasted away. Across the room little men on motorcycles chased each other silently around a dirt track on a thirty-five inch Sony.

At least a dozen people were lounging about the room. They all seemed to be talking. Dogs had a hand-rolled cigarette in one hand and was jabbering to a tall man who sported a Van Dyke and a celestial blue patch over his left eye. Patch stared at me over Dogs' shoulder with his good eye. It was precisely the same shade of blue as his patch. I was suitably impressed.

Dogs turned around. It took a couple of seconds for the synapses to connect. I watched recognition dawn in his eyes. He rolled them toward the man with the patch.

"Hey, Sean, this is the guy I was telling you about. The hitchhiker I picked up on the road." He turned back to me.

"Tell me your name again." He grinned with his upper lip. "Sorry, man, it's just that I've always been real bad with names."

"It's Paul," I said. "Don't worry about it. I just need to use a phone. Long distance, but I'll call collect."

Sean indicated the other side of the room with the can of Budweiser he held in his right hand. A yellow phone sat on a three-legged table at the mouth of a hall that ran toward the other end of the house.

"Thanks."

Sean took a sip of his beer. His blue eye stayed fixed on me until it disappeared behind rising aluminum.

Cutting through hazy, fragrant smoke, ignoring all the people who were ignoring me, I crossed the room, dodging a snotty-nosed girl of five or six who ran down the long hallway and disappeared into the dusk at the end of the corridor.

Smoke and babbling conversations rose and fell behind me. I picked up the receiver. First, I called my attorney and spoke at length with his secretary. Then I called my accountant. He sounded very surprised to hear from me. He seemed to have been under the impression that I wasn't going to return from Mexico. Then I called a number I knew by heart.

All I heard before the operator cut in was my own voice. It sounded thick and distorted, as though I had recorded the message through a mohair sweater. After the operator disconnected the call I stared at the receiver. There wasn't anybody else to call. I cradled the receiver and opened the phone book that sat on the table beside the telephone. Turning to the Yellow Pages, I studied one of them. Then I turned and traipsed back through the smoke.

The plan had been to say good-bye to Dogs, but he was coiled around a dishwater blonde in running shorts and a Charles Manson tee-shirt. He arched his eyebrows at me and I waved at him and mouthed thanks. He winked and smiled and we nodded to each other. I let my gaze sweep the room. Nothing else here for me. I walked out the way I'd come in.

In the kitchen the woman still sat on the stool with the spoon in her hand. Her head still bobbed up and down as if she planned to do that for eternity. Something was beginning to scorch on the bottom of the bubbling cauldron. Drifting over, I peered into the bubbles. The mysterious affair smelled like chili. My stomach was tempted, but I didn't trust the chef. I kept walking. There was an open, nearly full half-pint of

Jack Daniels on the counter next to a rather squashed loaf of Wonder Bread. I picked the whiskey bottle up. The glass was cool and smooth against my palm. Saliva was already gathering in my mouth.

I capped the bottle and slipped it into the front pocket of my pants and walked out. On the porch I pulled the bottle out of my pocket. The smooth, cool bottle was halfway to my lips when Mexico drifted across the back of my mind like a high cloud above the canyon floor. For a stretchy moment I stared into the dark moving shadows. Then I went down the steps, crossed the yard and placed the bottle on the hood of the Volkswagen.

Cursing softly to myself, I strolled around the house and across the dusty yard to the sidewalk. The old hound opened one amber eye, stared at me, decided I wasn't important, and closed it.

Sunlight was smooth and warm on my back. I started stepping toward the Western Union man. My legs moved beneath me and a fine sheen of sweat formed in the small of my back, under my arms, and across my forehead. It was sweet to walk in the youthful sunlight of Tucson with money waiting and revenge on my mind.

Thirty-five

Five hundred dollars sounds like a lot of money. But see how far it gets you. By the time I bought new clothes, a razor, the essential toiletries, rented a motel room, and had myself one fine supper I didn't have the price of a plane ticket to Vegas.

I considered a bus ticket. Over warm pecan pie smothered in whipped cream, I decided to think about it during my one night stand at the ever delightful, and cheap, Ketchum Inn.

My waitress was a redhead with blue eyes, minimal breasts, and abundant freckles. Smiling profusely, she called me sir and didn't stare at my shoulder-length hair. I left her a five, paid the bill, and hotfooted it back across Grand to the motel.

I took another shower, brushed my teeth for the third time that day, and watched television gibberish until it began to make sense.

Diffused light filtered in through the gap in the heavy drapes, casting a placid luminosity across the worn carpet. Reflected neon flashed without mercy in the mirror on top of the laminated dresser. After Mexico, it was strange to see any other lights at night except the stars, the moon, and long-tailed comets. Lying on the sagging mattress, I stared at the flickering man-made lighting until it etched imprints on the fabric of my mind.

Even with my eyes closed, I could see the neon dancing in the dark. I'd been too long in the wind to instantly succumb to civilization and the messages embedded in the silently flashing neon were incomprehensible.

Thinking about Wilson, the Leather Man, and Jolene and Stan pushed sleep aside. I began to long for the wind in my face, the moonlight in my eyes and the silence that fell like a shroud at dusk.

Gradually, as though it were a timed-release capsule, the neon blurred and faded. My breathing slowed while the rhythms of my mind smoothed out. Traffic began to die off on Grand. Silence slipped into the room.

I thought about the simple wonders of a belly full of good food and a soft bed, and how exquisite it felt to be clean and safe in a room that was my own, at least for the night, with money in my pockets and clean clothes hanging in the closest. Part of me was ashamed of the man I had been, but the promise of tomorrow glowed like a nebula on the horizon.

Memories came unbidden from the quiet darkness. I thought of my father and men who had been my friends in another life, then Jolene, Stan, Señora Ramirez, Wilson, Gomez, Leather Man, Torres, Dogs, and the woman with the wooden spoon who only nodded. I wondered where they were tonight and what they might be doing and if they ever thought of me. Just for kicks, I said a prayer for each of them.

Sleep came and I dreamed of Mexico by moonlight bisected by a river of whiskey flowing deep, dark, and everlasting. In my dream Wilson was alive, and he and I crossed a broad desert to lie in the whiskey river where we drank until we sank to the bottom. Lying on our backs at the bottom of the river, holding hands and staring at the lights flickering above whiskey running deep and fast, we knew with a certainty beyond denial all secrets of all men of all the ages. Wilson smiled at me through the whiskey waters and I smiled at him. Neon lighting flashed in our brains and we saw God.

Thirty-six

I opened my eyes. The room was filled with sunshine and I blinked against the light. Watermarks and aging stains made a modernistic statement on the walls while spider webs enhanced the corners. I wanted a drink.

Instead, I rolled out of bed and went and urinated into a toilet bowl that looked cleaner than some of the bowls I'd eaten out of over the last, lost year. In the mirror that hung over the sink, I could see myself quite clearly. I washed my hands and face, prayed silently for a blessing, and called my lawyer. Two collect calls inside of twenty-four hours might be pushing my luck, so I billed this one to the room.

His secretary, whom I'd long suspected of being a direct descendant of Pontius Pilot, answered on the third ring. She recognized my voice. I could hear the disgust in hers. "One moment, please," she said through her nose.

It was a long moment. I listened to the line hum, occasionally picking up voices lost in the void. Finally, the call went through.

"The prodigal son, *déjà vu*."

"More like the Lone Ranger rides again."

"Now, don't be bitter."

"Easy for you to say, Perry Mason. You're not stuck in Lodi again."

"Thought you were in Tucson. Hadn't you better make up your mind?"

"Fuck you, you're fired."

Laughter ran down the line like a live current. "Fired from what?"

"From being my attorney."

"You can't fire me," he said. "I'm a volunteer. I quit."

"After all I've paid you?"

He laughed again. "I can't remember the last time you paid me."

"Don't tell me you have been billing the estate, Gerald. I'm not as dumb as some people think I am."

Quiet filled the line. I wondered what he was thinking and why he had to think it for so long.

"Paul, are you sober?"

"Yes."

"Sitting down?"

"I can be. Why?"

"Trust me," Gerald said, "just do it."

"Okay, I'm sitting down. Now what?" I didn't like the direction this conversation was going. Some of my dislike must have seeped along the wire, because when Gerald spoke again he spoke softly and sincerely, two qualities I'd long ago learned to fear in a lawyer.

"I hadn't heard from either of you in over six months, so it was a surprise when Jolene popped up in the office one day just before closing time." He paused, sighed. "Let me give her the benefit of the doubt, Paul, and say that perhaps it was the end of a long, rough day for her."

"Why do you say that?"

"Suppose I want to sugarcoat this a bit."

"Gerald, just tell me what happened."

"You're right, Paul. Just want you to get the total picture."

"So give it to me." His evasiveness was getting on my nerves. I didn't like long distance conversation. Face-to-face chats were more my preference. That way I could see Gerald's eyes, or strangle him.

"All right, here goes." He sighed again. I gnawed my lower lip as I waited.

"Jolene showed up here just before five one afternoon. One of those hot-as-hell days and she had sweated through her blouse, which, by the way, was none too clean. Her hair was longer than I'd seen it, darker too. It needed a good shampooing and was all tangles, curls falling out and limp bangs. It was all I could do to keep from asking what had happened."

"Anybody with her?" I interrupted.

"Yes," Gerald said carefully, "one person and one document." He paused again. He was getting good at the pauses.

"Come on man, give. I'm your client, not the police."

"Hang on, I'm getting there."

Yeah, I thought, at two hundred an hour this is costing me a fortune. I didn't say anything though. Just sighed loudly.

"As I was saying, Jolene shows up, looking like she's been on a binge for a month, with a piece of paper and this guy. He was tall and slim. Guess you could call him attractive, even if he did need a shave."

"Let me guess, his name was Stan."

"You know him?"

"I knew him when. Actually, he was our new, best friend in Vegas. Thought we were really swell, fun people. I'm fuzzy on how we met, but, yeah, I remember old Stan."

"Actually, he didn't say much. Seemed pleasant, but let Jolene do most of the talking."

"She always was a good talker," I said, and stretched out on the bed, staring up at the stains on the ceiling, looking for hidden messages.

"She certainly did a lot of talking that afternoon. A long imbroglio about a trip the three of you took to Mexico. I didn't understand half of it that day, even after questions, and I won't pretend to remember all the details now. It's been four, five months. Know I'm rambling, Paul, but that was one strange conversation."

"I get the picture, Gerald. Remember, I've been married to this woman for years. Get to the point."

"Sorry. Well, in addition to the aforementioned Stan, Jolene had this document with her, a most interesting document. It was written in Spanish, and I read that language poorly and slowly, but it was full of official seals and signatures and I finally figured it out. Know what it was, Paul?"

"No, Gerald, I don't." I could hear the sarcasm running through my voice and shut up. Silence filled the line.

"Sorry. Now tell me what this official seals document was all about."

Gerald cleared his throat. "Sorry, Paul, but this isn't easy to tell to you. The document was a Mexican legal document that officially classified you as a missing person and gave Jolene power-of-attorney over all your affairs."

My mind and my fingertips felt like ice. No wonder Gerald had sounded so surprised to hear from me. Coins were starting to fall down the right slots.

"You checked this out?"

"Thoroughly. I called an attorney I know who is fluent in Spanish and has solid legal contacts south of the border. I also touched base with our embassy in Mexico. Everything checked out. The document carried weight even in this country. As far as the world knew, you had vanished off the face of the earth. There was a good deal of semi-official speculation that you were dead."

"As you can hear, I'm very much alive."

"I know that, now."

"But then?"

"But then I didn't know and she had the document, and the document was legit, and she was also my client, and her name was on all the accounts, and..." He let the sentence die.

I was doing some fast thinking. I didn't like the answers.

"How much has she gotten?"

That pause again. I was getting to hate those pauses. Before Gerald Perkins spoke I knew I wasn't going to like the answer.

"All of it." He said it short and sweet and flat as a smashed armadillo.

"All of it?"

"Every cent."

"All those millions?"

"Gone."

Anger swelled in my throat, hot and bitter. I tried to swallow it. It kept sticking and I kept swallowing. "Gone on what?" I finally spit out.

"I don't know it all. For sure I know she went through it like it was water, or should I say whiskey. She and Stan, they went through it like they were in one big hurry."

"Goddamn it, you can't drink away that much, Gerald. Not even if you tried. Believe me, I know."

He sighed again, another sad, meaningful, expensive, lawyer's sigh. "It wasn't only drinking and partying, Paul. Although, God knows there was enough of that. No, the big problem was the gambling. She gambled and he gambled. She gambled at the tables and he gambled on the stock market. She lost big and he lost bigger. Went in the top of a tech boom and rode it all the way down, day trading like mad, guessing wrong nine times out of ten. It happened unbelievably fast. At the end he couldn't get even ten cents on the dollar and she had markers scattered all over the strip. Nobody lets them near the tables now."

"Speaking of now, where are they?"

"Haven't heard from them or of them in over a month. Last time I knew for sure, they were at the Club Madrid."

"That dive? Is it still around?"

"It was six weeks ago."

I listened to the hum of the wires and Gerald's faint breathing. He sounded a universe away. I wished I were.

"Paul, you still there?"

I took a conscious breath. "Yeah, I'm here."

"I'm sorry."

"Don't be. You couldn't help it. After all, the documents were legit, weren't they?"

"Good as gold. Oh, we had to go through a few procedural matters here in the U.S. courts, but those were mainly formalities. No one came forward to challenge anything."

"Don't sweat it. I'll make it. Only you ought to say the documents were as good as thirty pieces of silver, the betraying bitch."

"Paul..."

"Everything's cool," I interrupted. "I'll make it."

Another long pause, as if we were both dying and the first to speak would be the first to die. Gerald swallowed the cyanide capsule.

"When you're in town, stop by."

"Sure."

"Paul?"

"Yeah."

"You okay?"

"I'm fine."

"Call me anytime."

I looked at the phone in my hand and then at my face in the mirror. I learned nothing from either one. "Gerald?"

"Yes."

"One more question for you."

"Sure."

"The five hundred you sent yesterday, where did it come from?"

I could hear him swallow. "That was from me, Paul."

"Why?"

"Let's just say it was for old times' sake."

I glanced at the phone again. It didn't have any more answers than I did. My turn to swallow. "Thanks."

"You're welcome. Remember, call me if you need me."

"Happy trails, Gerald."

I cradled the receiver and stared at the four walls until the shadows started to fall the other way. Then I got up and walked across the room and out the door. Sunlight filled my eyes and a hot wind was blowing in off the desert. I started walking west.

Thirty-seven

By noon on the third day I was damn near out of money, and patience. The only jobs I'd been able to locate were fast food. After Gomez's, I didn't think I could stand that. However, if I didn't find work this afternoon I'd have to sleep on the streets, then head to Taco City in the morning.

I was somewhere way the hell north on Henderson, near the far northeastern axis of Tucson. Development this far north was scattered. Sand, mesquite, and prickly pear cactus still lined the asphalt between the strip malls and the tract-housing developments. Blue-black mountains rose against the sky, close enough to throw afternoon shadows across the north end of town. Two streets east the country was still wild, long sections of low-slung scrub interspersed with sand, cactus, and sagebrush.

Traffic was sporadic, but I kept to the soft sand along the side of the road, trying to stay in the meager shade thrown by the mesquite. The weatherman had promised ninety-five degrees by mid-afternoon. Sweat soaked my shirt and ran down from my hairline to pool beneath my eyes. Every twenty steps, I wiped at it with my fingers, knowing it was a lost cause. One leg of my pants rubbed against a creosote bush, and a rabbit jumped out the other side and hopped lethargically across a strip of sand to the next bush. I knew how he felt.

I crossed a side street with a Spanish name, then walked on under a broiling sun past a Quick Cuts Hair Stylist, an Albertson's supermarket with the asphalt parking lot turning to mush, a place that sold swimming pools and spas, an empty real estate office, and a Chicken-To-Go with three cars out front and two around back. Two of the cars in front were police cruisers.

Blue mountains loomed closer with each step. Trails winding their way up the incline puckered the earth like old scars. Little vegetation grew on the mountainsides and the tops were bald like the heads of old men. I walked around a resort complex ringed with chain link fencing topped with barbed wire. Through the fence, I could see three asphalt tennis courts, a basketball court in the shade of a large cottonwood, a fountain ringed with blue and purple flowers, and the shadowy entrance of the main building. Off to the right of the building was a swimming pool. Water in the pool was so blue it hurt my eyes. I kept walking.

Closer to the mountains, a mile north of the barbed wire fence, a ring of two story buildings orbited a flat-roofed building fronted by a small courtyard that featured a swimming pool and a hot tub. This pool was about a third the size of the one up the road and the water was a less intense blue. Still, it looked cool and inviting. A scripted sign on the front of the flat-face building said MOUNTAIN EDGE APARTMENTS.

A four-plank wooden fence ran around the property. The narrow entrance was guarded by a lift gate that opened when people drove up and inserted a plastic card in the metal arm extending from a small concrete tower in the center of the drive. The fence was painted white. There was no barbed wire on top. However, there was a cardboard sign taped to the concrete tower. Deep blue lettering said: HELP WANTED: MAINTENANCE/ SECURITY. GOOD WAGES, BENEFITS. APPLY WITHIN.

Tucking my shirttail in, I ran my fingers through my hair and wiped the sweat off my face. Then I turned and walked down the black asphalt drive toward the cardboard sign.

I strolled around the mechanical arm and cut across a flowerbed full of weeds and gravel. A couple of plants in the middle might have been flowers before they had succumbed to the rigors of a Tucson summer. Dead leaves hung from sagging stalks like limp penises. The rabbit and I understood.

Half a dozen cars were parked in front of the main building. Several more, along with pickups and a couple of motorcycles, were scattered around the parking lot that encircled the building. Most were in parking spaces covered by metal awnings. Along the perimeter of the lot, next to the wooden fence that separated asphalt from sagebrush, people had parked a speedboat, an old aluminum trailer missing its tires, and a golf cart. The golf cart had tires but no steering wheel.

The flat building had three narrow windows and a glass door shaded by a large green and blue awning. All the glass was darkly tinted. Someone had painted: MOUNTAIN EDGE APTS: *DAILY, WEEKLY, MONTHLY RATES* on the glass in neat script.

The tint was too dark to allow me to see through the glass, so I worked my way between a recent model Corvette and a Jeep with cracked leather, stepped into the shade of the awning, then pushed the door open.

It was dark and cool inside and my mind shifted back to Mexico. For a heartbeat, I was back in the cave with Wilson.

"Can I help you?" The woman's voice was warm and tinged with concern, as if she wasn't sure about me, or sure if she could help me.

My hands were fluttering like trapped birds against my thighs. I put them in my pockets and arranged a smile on my face. Except for Goeteza and Taco City, I'd never had to ask for a job.

"I came about the job." My voice sounded high and hollow.

"Oh, good." The woman stood and came around from behind her desk. She'd been in shadows before and I hadn't really seen her.

She was a big woman—our eyes were level—and broad through the shoulders. Plenty of flesh covered the bones. Her hair was thick and brown, flecked with gold and silver, hanging in a loose shag to her shoulders. Prominent bones poked at her cheeks and a determined nose jutted above narrow lips. Her brown eyes were her best feature, soft and warm, like a friendly dog's. I guessed her age at forty.

She stuck out a hand and the flesh above the elbow jiggled. I pulled my right hand from my pocket and shook hers. She had a firm grip and gave you all her hand, like a man.

"My name is Karen." She let her eyes traverse my face. "I'm the manager here at Mountain Edge. And you are?"

"Paul Hampton. Was walking by and saw the sign. I'm between jobs right now, so I thought I'd come in and see what sort of job it was."

She lifted her round chin and looked down her nose. Her nostrils were curved and dark and deep. I was still seeing caves.

"Well, Mr. Hampton, what we have to offer here is a lot of work, and not a great deal of pay. However, there are compensations. Have you ever worked with the public before?"

"I was in the restaurant business for a while. South of here."

"Good. All our jobs deal with the public, even the one you are applying for."

"Can you give me some specifics about the job?" I tried to ask the question like I had other opportunities.

"Sure. Now, because it covers a lot of territory it's one of those hard to define jobs. Mountain Edge rents apartments, by the month, by the week, even by the day. Some people who stay with us don't take care of their place. Probably because they are only staying a short while. When they leave we often have to do touch-up painting, even some light plumbing or carpentry, plus basic cleaning. As you may have seen, we have a swimming pool that needs daily maintenance, and we haven't had anybody to tend to the grounds for a couple of weeks."

"Saw the flowerbed on the way in."

Karen smiled. Behind the thin lips her teeth were large and crowded, but clean. "Yes, despite the brochures, Tucson is still desert country. Except for cacti and a few other native species, plants here need care and water, especially water." She shrugged her broad shoulders and I watched her breasts rise and fall under her blouse. "Since the last man left, I've had to do most of the work. Afraid the flowers have suffered.

"Anyway, Mr. Hampton, the job description includes everything in the general maintenance line. With ninety-six units, the pool, the grounds, and the laundry room there is always plenty to do." She let the smile vacation in her eyes. "Are you interested?"

"What's the pay?"

The smile slipped back to her lips. "As I said, the pay's not that great, but there are some benefits."

"Such as?"

"Let me explain. The actual pay is one hundred a week, but there is a sleeping room in the back of the laundry area." Tilting her head, she tucked her chin and pointed her curved nose at me. "Now it's small, but private. Plus, it has a hot plate, a microwave, and a small refrigerator, so you can do your own cooking and save quite a bit of money. Often our short-term guests overestimate how much food they'll need during their stay and leave behind lots of canned goods and untouched bananas, apples, grapes, not to mention those little individual boxes of cereal and bags of chips. Sometimes they leave unopened two-liters of soda. All that goes with the job."

She stretched her thin lips, trying to broaden the smile. "Plus, you get to use the pool after hours and some of the staff have supplemented their income by doing odd jobs for the guests, cleaning their cars, running errands, even babysitting. Of course, that would be up to you."

She lifted her face and peered into my eyes. I could sense her probing. I wasn't sure if I wanted the job. It didn't sound like a career. On the other hand...

"Are you interested, Mr. Hampton?"

I took a deep breath and made the leap. "When can I start?"

"Right now." She began walking back around the desk. "Just come over here and sign some papers. I'll need to make a copy of your social security card and driver's license."

"Uh, actually, I lost my wallet recently."

She stopped walking and showed me her nostrils again. I was getting tired of the view and was tempted to walk. I'd made up my mind; begging was out. Finally the chin came down.

"That's okay. I'll take a chance on you. You can get me copies later. Come along, Mr. Hampton. There's lots of work that needs doing."

She turned and high-heeled it around the desk. I followed, with misgivings. She had a large, soft rear end that wobbled when she walked, but her legs were nice and her ankles were trim. I was back doing manual labor. Smiling a little, I wondered what Wilson and Gomez would think. I could hear the zombies laughing.

Thirty-eight

"You like cleaning the pool, mister?"

Turning around, I eyeballed a tow-headed boy who looked to be about nine years old. I'd seen him before. His family had moved into 612 earlier in the week.

"It's okay," I said, leaning on what I called the dip net. I was sure it had a more professional name. So far I'd captured leaves, sticks, abandoned toys, a bikini top, and a dead bird.

"You do it every day?" He smiled at me. He was missing at least two front teeth and sporting a sunburn.

"Part of my job," I said, wiggling the aluminum stick, hoping the boy would get the message I needed to get back to work.

He didn't. "What else do you do?"

I shrugged. "Oh, some yard work and painting and cleaning up after people leave. Whatever needs doing."

"Are you going to clean up after we leave?"

"Maybe. Depends on how long you stay."

"Why?"

"You ask a lot of questions, boy. Now it's my turn to ask some, okay?"

"Sure." He lifted his chin and stared into my face. His eyes were aquamarine and they glistened in the sunlight.

Suddenly conscious of towering over him, I squatted until our heads were parallel. He smelled fresh, clean, and faintly coconutty.

"Let's start with your name," I said, smiling to show I meant no harm.

He didn't look particularly worried. "My name's David. What's yours?"

"Paul. Where are you from, David?"

"We're from Ohio. Westerville, Ohio. That's near Columbus," he added for my edification.

"You here with your folks?"

"My mom and sister." His mouth made quirky movements. "My dad's dead. He got shot. He was a policeman. Mom said he was trying to stop a bank robber." David shrugged like none of what he said mattered.

"I'm sorry." The words sounded hollow.

"That's okay. Mom says he's gone to Heaven and we'll all get to see him someday." He paused and looked at the pool as if there were an answer floating in the clear water at the four-foot mark. "Anyway, that was about two years ago. Right now, Mom's trying to find a job. She didn't want to live in Ohio anymore."

I smiled at him. I wanted to tell him it was all right. But we both knew it wasn't, and never would be.

"Why did you guys come all the way out to Tucson?"

"My mom heard about some jobs out here, and Aunt Barbara lives in Arizona. I don't know exactly where, just that it ain't too far away."

A woman began to call for David. She had a clear, youthful sounding voice. The boy cocked his head and listened.

"That's my mom. I'd better go."

"Yeah. You'd better scoot."

"Will I see you tomorrow, mister, I mean, Paul?"

"I wouldn't be surprised. Now you run along."

"Okay," he said, and turned and started jogging toward Building 6. "See you tomorrow," he yelled over a shoulder.

Shading my eyes, I watched him round the corner and disappear from sight. Then I turned back to the pool and started dipping. The water was clear and the surface sparkled in the sunlight like it was encrusted with diamonds. The water was precisely the same shade of blue as David's eyes.

I shifted my gaze to the mountains, blue and hazy against an all-encompassing sky. Cleaning sticks and dead birds out of a swimming pool didn't seem to have a great deal of meaning when you stacked it against the loss of a little boy's father. A man who had given his life in the line of duty.

Without warning, chunks of my life exploded in my mind. There was a sudden, penetrating clarity to my vision. I could see through all the whiskey, all the women, all the wandering, all the lost days and squandered nights, all the way down to the bottom. With exquisite clarity I could see that, up to now, I'd been of no more consequence in the universe than the dead, blackened aloe vera leaf floating in the shallow end of the pool.

Turning away from the water, I hung the dipper on the chain-link fence and walked across the concrete toward the office. I needed to find out when the new shipment of plants was due from the nursery. Heat radiated from the concrete through the bottoms of my tennis shoes and the sun was a branding iron against the back of my neck.

Thirty-nine

Stars were mysterious ingots looming so close it seemed I could stretch out a hand and touch them.

I lay on my back in one of the plastic lounge chairs beside the pool and dangled my fingers in the water while I stared at the stars. My brain was crowded with thoughts of Las Vegas, Jolene and Stan, Mexico, Wilson and Gomez, Arizona, Dogs, and David. I wanted a drink more than I had in a long time.

I could hear the zombies whispering in the darkness beyond the fence. I closed my eyes and bit my upper lip and breathed hard through my nose until the urge to drink began to subside. Opening my eyes, I looked at my trembling hands, grateful for the shadows.

Water was cool against my fingers and the stars looked a million miles away.

Deep in the night the wind began to blow in off the desert and the stars began to swing on their fixed points until they merged and melded, fusing into a solid light that filled the blackness. The wind was warm and soft against my body as my eyes closed against the light.

Forty

Sunlight silhouetted her body. Breasts hung low, sagging against her stomach like overripe pears. Shoulders slumped as though the day had become too heavy a burden. Her head was tilted to one side and her eyes were open, staring beyond the dusky room, looking into a world I couldn't see. Lights moved in them, but her brow was smooth and she appeared calm.

I'd slipped in the back door. Perhaps I should have cleared my throat or rapped knuckles on the wall, but in the serenity of late afternoon I was content to study her quiet beauty.

That beauty had surprised me, coming into focus suddenly, the way an object does occasionally when it has been there all along only you have been overlooking it, leaving you to marvel how you'd managed to miss it. Other than the fading sunlight, the only light in the room came from a small florescent lamp on her desk. Its meager light glazed the avalanche of paperwork spread across the dark wood.

Papers overflowed the In and Out baskets on her desk and a dozen pink to-do slips decorated a cork bulletin board on the wall behind her. Her trash can needed emptying and there were two baskets full of towels that needed folding. Adding machine tape cascaded in a paper waterfall off one side of the desk. Dust motes drifted in shafts of mellow light. The scent of roses was faint, yet persistent.

I should have said her name. Instead, I watched her stare into another dimension. Her breathing was slow and deep, breasts rising and falling as though riding an unseen tide.

The phone rang, loud and harsh in the dusky silence, and we both jerked and she turned. Lights changed in her eyes as she noticed me and her lips made quirky little movements. Turning her back to me, she picked up the phone and said, "Hello, Mountain Edge Apartments."

I stepped out of the shadows, crossed the room and began studying the pictures and plaques on the wall.

There was a plaque from the Arizona Hoteliers Association, and one from the North Tucson Club acknowledging the generous support of the Mountain Edge Apartments. There was a pair of licenses and two framed pictures.

The larger was of ancient, gnarled bristlecone pines growing stubbornly at the edge of the Grand Canyon, with the far rim purple and coral, back-dropped by a soft blue sky with white clouds smearing the far horizon.

The smaller featured a man in a serape and loose fitting trousers and one of the old, wide-brimmed sombreros no one wears anymore, except to impress the tourists. His sandaled feet dangled the flanks of the small gray donkey he was riding down the street of a small village. A load of brush was tied on behind him and one of his hands held a switch. In the painting, it was late afternoon, and most of the adobe houses were closed and shuttered against the coming night. Lamplight spilled yellow from one of them and an old brown and black dog lay in front of another. The impression created was of a man hurrying home against the darkness, perhaps to be with his family. Something about the village put me in mind of Goeteza, and a family I had known there.

I heard the click as the receiver settled on the cradle, pushed Goeteza to a benign corner of my mind, fixed a smile on my face, and turned to face her.

"Pay day, Mr. Hampton," she said, smiling lightly and pushing an envelope in my direction.

"Thanks."

"Bet you were ready for it."

"It's been a while."

Karen nodded, then bent her neck. Her hands were busy with a pyramid of paper on her desk. Light from the desk lamp struck the crown of her head, bringing out gold and silver highlights. Her entire body swayed as her hands felt blindly for the arms of her chair. A soft sigh escaped her lips. I wanted to comfort her, touch her hands, caress her hair. I kept my hands to myself.

After a moment she looked up. Lamplight splashed softly against her face and reflected in her eyes and her mouth went loose, and she was lovely.

"Still here, Mr. Hampton? Was there something else? Oh yes, you need to check on six-twelve tomorrow, the folks from Ohio. What is their name? Damn, I'm getting forgetful. Samuels, that's it. Check on the Samuels family in six-twelve tomorrow, won't you, Mr. Hampton?" She rearranged her slightly dilapidated mouth into a serviceable smile.

I allowed my eyes to make contact with hers. She held the gaze almost belligerently, as though daring me to make something happen. Then she broke contact and focused on the papers.

"Sorry to be short, but, as you can see, I've still got a ton of paperwork to do. Trust me, Mr. Hampton," she said with her head still down, "there is always paperwork to do in the apartment business."

I liked the way the light softened the top of her head. Traffic had died off and I could hear one bird calling to another in the dusk. The tip of her tongue slipped out, licked her lips and went back in.

Longing was a sudden hard lump in my throat. Swallowing it, I turned and walked out of the room. The evening spread out so clear and blue before me that I half-convinced myself I could see all the way to Mexico.

Forty-one

The door swung open after the second knock. A cute blue-eyed blonde made a face at me. She had jelly on her face. She was also no more than four years old. I made a face back at her and she turned and ran, yelling for her mommy. I stood just outside the door with the morning sun warm on my back and waited.

Before I had time to get restless, I could hear footsteps and another blonde stuck her head around the door. This blonde was significantly older. Like her predecessor, she had large blue eyes wedged in a thin face. Her cheekbones were set high and her lips were full. She was the loveliest thing I'd seen since Vegas, a lifetime ago.

"Yes," she said, making the word a three-syllable question.

"Karen, from the office, said you needed to see me. I'm Paul Hampton, the maintenance man."

"Oh yes, I am glad to see you. Come on in." Her smile was quite nice.

I followed her slender hips across a toy-strewn landscape. "Please excuse the mess," she said without turning around. "I was out job hunting yesterday and didn't have the time or the energy to pick up last night."

A television set blared from one corner of the living room. The boy from the swimming pool sat in front of it, transfixed by the antics of small furry animals with human faces. The little creatures rode skateboards and stunt bikes over hills and up concrete ramps. Beside him, a few soggy

Cheerios floated in a bowl of dirty-looking milk. As our shadows fell across his face, he glanced up.

"Hey, I know you. You're the swimming pool man."

I drug his name out of the cobwebs. "That's right, David."

A frown drifted across his face like the vanguard of a frontal system. "I forget your name."

I gave it to him along with a smile.

He smiled back, then the crash of something on the television caught his attention and he was gone.

"You'll have to excuse David, Paul." She said my name as if it tasted funny in her mouth. "He's easily distracted."

"Just an excitable boy, Mrs. Samuels. What sort of problems are we having today?"

She stopped so suddenly I almost bumped into her. Turning her face toward mine she smiled enough to let me see how pretty she could be. Her features were finely drawn. She opened her eyes wider and let me gaze into blue eyes that looked as big as quarters. It was like looking into twin reflecting pools. She tilted her head and I could see my reflection move.

"I have several problems, Paul. However, the one I think you can help me with this morning concerns my old VCR. I can't get it to take the videos. It's like there's something jammed inside. Or maybe it's just worn out. I've had it for years. Oh, and please call me Mona."

"Okay. Where is the problem unit?"

"It's in my bedroom. I don't understand it. It worked fine yesterday before I left for the interview at Albertson's." She smiled a helpless-little-woman smile for me. "It wouldn't work at all when I got back. Wasn't even gone an hour. Albertson's is just up the street."

"Yeah," I said, "I know where Albertson's is. Let's go look at that VCR. I'm no expert, but maybe I can figure it out."

She led the way into the bedroom, turned and pointed at the offending machine sitting atop a twenty-one inch RCA. The pose emphasized her flat stomach and sharply pointed breasts. It was straight out of the senior play.

"Thanks." I took a quick look around the bedroom as I walked toward the VCR. The bed was neatly made and all the clothes put away, except for a frilly peach negligee hanging from one of the posts at the foot of the bed. The closet door was closed, as was the one to the bathroom.

I pushed open the tape slot on the VCR and peered into the darkness. I dug a flashlight out of the hip pocket of my slacks. It had already come in handy in dealing with recalcitrant washing machines. I shone the light down the dark passage.

It wasn't hard to locate the problem. Something thick and white was where it wasn't supposed to be. I pulled a screwdriver out of my tool belt and dug out a sock, just the right size for a boy David's age.

Mrs. Samuels smiled at me. "Ah-ha, now I see. Sorry to have drug you all the way up here for that, Paul."

She still couldn't say my name easily. I wanted to tell her not to bother, but the guests aren't supposed to be wrong. So I said, "Not a problem. That's what I'm here for."

Well, thank you so much." Mona turned her finely chiseled head toward the living room. "I'll certainly have a talk with a certain young man."

"Don't be too hard on the boy. At his age, he's curious and full of energy."

Turning her head again, she took a step closer to me. Her breath was warm against my face. It smelled minty and sweet. Acutely conscious of the queen-sized bed behind us, I put my flashlight away.

"I made a cinnamon coffee-cake just this morning," she said. "Would you like a piece and a cup of coffee?" She let me see all her fine white teeth. They looked too white and even to be real. Suddenly the bedroom was quite warm, and much too cozy.

"Thanks, but I'd better pass. Mr. Pellegrino in three-oh-nine is having bathroom problems. Promised him I'd get by as soon as I had a chance."

The smile stayed on her lips, but the lights changed in her eyes. They were hypnotically blue. They looked hungry to me.

"Maybe another time?"

"Sounds good." I told myself Gary Cooper would have been proud.

Mrs. Samuels didn't say anything else, and she didn't move. I had to brush against her as I maneuvered past. Her breasts were firm. All the way up the hall I sensed blue eyes following me.

The little girl was sitting with David. She had put on a baseball cap. Enthralled with the cartoon universe, they never looked up as I passed. I let myself out.

As I stepped into the sunlight I glanced at my hands. They were trembling. I told myself it was only because I needed a drink. Feeling faintly foolish, and slightly juvenile, I started walking toward 309.

Forty-two

Water was cool against my skin, cooler when the evening breeze curled around the corner of the laundry room. Security lights had arced on and their glow danced on the surface of the water. The bottom of the pool was a dark blur. Leaning back, I curled my fingers through the water. Glancing at the big clock in the laundry room, I could see it was after ten. Now the pool was mine; I smiled to myself in the darkness.

A nasty little thought that it would be fine to sip on a short glass of Jefferson Reserve kept trickling through my mind. I could almost taste the bourbon, smooth and mellow against my tongue. It had been months, but there were still moments when, despite all my good intentions, the urge rose from its hiding place and rippled the surface. For another moment I savored the taste of my imagination, then silently cursed both the zombies and my weakness and pushed myself face first into the water.

I swam until my breath came in ragged gasps and my shoulder muscles burned. Grabbing the edge of the pool, I hung on with my eyes closed and mouth open, greedily sucking air.

As my breathing returned to normal I could again hear the night sounds. Even this far north of the city, cars, trucks and motorcycles rolled all night in a never-ending cacophony of tires moving against pavement, glass-packs popping, brakes squealing, and horns blowing. Closer in, I could hear birds settling down in the squatty trees that grew in the watered courtyard. On the far side of the chain-link fence, small animals scurried about in the underbrush in search of food or to avoid becoming dinner.

Faint sounds of televisions that lived behind closed doors and radios that played south of the border songs drifted to me. When the traffic eased, I could hear the soft splash of waves against the side of the pool, the suicide sounds of insects as they flung themselves against the bug zapper, and my own breathing. Small silences began to fill the pauses.

A harsh screech shattered the night, metal rasping on metal. I jerked my head around in time to see the gate to the pool separate itself from the six-foot high metal fencing and swing open.

A shadow slid into the night. At first I thought it was a child, but as the shadow became flesh it grew too tall for a child. Flesh took form. Mona Samuels stepped into the light.

She was barefoot, and for a moment I thought she was naked. She took another step and I saw that a bikini the color of ripe wheat rode high on her hips and low on her chest.

She walked quietly across the smooth concrete, still warm from the remembered sun. Judging by her walk, she knew I was watching her. Her stiletto body sliced through the night. She held her head high and kept her eyes on the pool.

When she reached the edge, she dipped one toe into the water. Pulling it out, she daintily shook off an offending drop of water. Security lights played across her thin face, creating shadows under prominent cheekbones. Without warning, her teeth flashed white against the darkness of her tan.

"I read the sign, Mr. Hampton," she said in her seventh grade English class voice. "No swimming after ten p.m. for guests. But don't you think you could make an exception just this one time? I've been so hot all day."

"I don't make the rules, Mrs. Samuels." My voice sounded high and strange, like a rogue wind in Jamaica.

She stuck the toe back in the water. "You just enforce them."

"Nope, just obey them."

"What about everybody else? Do they have to obey the rules?"

"That's up to them."

She sat down on the edge of the pool, extending slender legs into the water. They barely dimpled the surface. I watched them disappear and tried to control my breathing.

"I'm coming in, Mr. Hampton. You gonna try and stop me?"

"No."

"Make a citizen's arrest?"

"Don't think those are legal in swimming pools."

"Lots of things aren't, Mr. Hampton."

She laughed and water splashed against my chest as her body penetrated the water. She floated away and swam back slowly.

Drops of water cascaded against my face, then her fingertips brushed against my chest. Her arms slid around my neck and she pressed her body against mine. It was firm and soft at the same time, and a tide of longing rose in me.

She brought her face so close to mine I could see water droplets on her nose and the reflection of security lights in her eyes. Her breath smelled of peppermints and Maker's Mark.

"I've been watching you, you know?"

"You have?"

"Watching and wondering."

"Oh."

"My name is Mona." Her voice was scarcely a whisper.

"Mine's Paul."

"I know."

Memories of a clogged VCR and soggy Cheerios floated by. "That's right, you already knew."

"I already know lots of things about you."

"Such as what?"

"Such as you want to kiss me."

Her lips were too close to resist. They were soft and moving.

Water and wind were cool against my back, but her body was warm against my chest. Our fingers were suddenly active below the waterline.

She murmured my name as I entered her. My mouth was busy against her throat.

Her arms tightened around me. Her body seemed to dissolve into mine. She was so warm and alive that the zombies were momentarily stilled. I figured she must have been lonely for a long time. Maybe as long as I'd been.

Over on Henderson someone had their car stereo cranked. Cool alto sax jazzed across the desert and my mind began to separate at the seams. I closed my eyes and we were one with the night.

Forty-three

I was eating breakfast in 612.

A few minutes before, I'd been rearranging the stone border of the flowerbed. Mona had called out to me from the balcony to join her. Said she'd baked homemade banana-walnut muffins. She'd been wearing a white terrycloth robe and it didn't look like she had anything else on. In the fresh sunlight her faced had looked clean and sharp and fine. Leaving the stones hadn't been difficult.

The muffins were still warm enough so the butter melted and ran down the sides. Pushing the last bite of the second one in my mouth, I chewed slowly, then washed it down with coffee that was strong, black, and hot enough to scald my tongue.

Mona's first muffin sat untouched on her plate. Now and then she sipped orange juice from a cut-glass tumbler. She said she didn't like coffee and had made it just for me. Hunched over in her chair, she was reading the morning paper. She seemed especially interested in the classifieds.

"I've really got to get a job soon. The insurance money won't last forever, and I'm going to have to have a car. The bus system out here is too unreliable."

She spoke without looking up from the paper. It had been a full week since we first made love. Since then we'd made love every night. Sipping on my coffee, I watched her reading the paper and felt like an old married man. It was a peculiar feeling, but not an unpleasant one. Then I remembered I *was* an old married man.

"What work do you want to do?"

Beyond the wall of newspaper I could see her shoulders rise and fall. "I'm not sure."

"What sort of experience do you have?"

"That's just it. I don't have any."

"None?" I was surprised. There weren't a lot of stay-at-home moms these days.

"None, except for fast food when I was in high school. I know I don't want to do that again, or dig ditches, or climb telephone poles, or sell vacuum cleaners door to door. Trouble is I don't know what I really want to do." Mona looked up from the paper. Her eyes were exceptionally bright this morning, the blue more intense, like the sky after the passage of a storm.

"Anyway, jobs are hard to come by out here with all the illegal aliens willing to work for below minimum wage, and more of them are coming in every day. Just read an article in the paper about that. They caught seven of them south of town yesterday and, thankfully, are going to send them back across the border. The article said for every one we send back five stay, and ten more cross the next day." She tossed the paper down and stood up. The robe gapped in interesting places. "Sometimes I wonder why I ever came out here."

I put my coffee cup down. "Why did you come?"

"I don't know, not for sure." Her eyes turned darker as her thoughts crossed the miles.

"Guess I wanted someplace warm," she said. "And with Alan gone, Westerville didn't seem like home anymore, just cold and lonely, full of memories I couldn't handle."

She took a deep breath and slowly let it out. I watched her breasts rise and fall. Nipples poked at the terrycloth. She saw me watching, smiled, and did it again. After the exhibition, I sneaked a peak at the kids.

They were eating Cheerios and watching cartoons. Mona was talking again and I struggled to catch up.

"My sister Amy used to live here in Tucson and she was always writing and telling me what a great place it was and how nice the climate was, especially in the winter, and how there were so many jobs. All that sounded good, and I thought I had this really good job lined up with this cell phone company I stumbled across on the internet. Only they went under the week I got here. Been scrambling ever since. I could start tomorrow, only it would be McDonald's, and this lady has done enough fast food to last a lifetime."

I stood up and walked over and put my arm around her shoulders. I could feel bones beneath the terrycloth.

"They've got some nice malls here. What about a sales job? Maybe at a nice boutique?"

"Been there and talked to the stuck-up bitches. Only part-time, and only at night. I've got to work full time just to cover daycare, rent, and groceries. And I've got to be home at night."

She put her head on my shoulder and made humming sounds against my chest. "Thought I had a nice receptionist slot yesterday, but they gave it to this young girl. She said she was from Texas, but I swear, Paul, she looked like a Mexican to me."

I couldn't quit staring into her eyes. While I was looking into them they changed and I sensed her mind moving away from Tucson. To bring her back I kissed the curling lips.

When she was with me again I told her to eat her muffin. She patted me on one cheek and went to change clothes.

When she came out of the bedroom she had on a navy suit that featured a deep frontal cut and wicked pin stripes. Her feet were jammed into pointed-toed shoes with three-inch heels. She wore almost no makeup, only light rouge to highlight her cheekbones, eye shadow one shade lighter than her eyes, and just enough lipstick to turn her mouth into a crimson slash. I would have given her whatever job she wanted.

"Be back in an hour, two at most. Can you watch the kids?"

"Sure."

"I'd kiss you only I don't want to smear my lipstick. Wish me luck."

"Luck."

She smiled and pressed a soft hand against my left cheek. Her cool blue eyes looked empty, like a swimming pool with a blue painted bottom but no water. Mona rearranged her lips, turned, and walked across the room without looking back. Inside the tight blue skirt, her backside swished. The door closed behind her with a snick.

I wandered over to the window and watched her until she crossed the street and turned north toward the bus stop. For a few seconds I could see her shadow in the sand along the road. Then it disappeared.

Forty-four

Tuesday afternoon, a few minutes after four, and I was trying to doze on Mona's couch. David had the Rugrats cranked on Channel 5 and his little sister, Linda, was babbling gobbedly-gook to her baby dolls. In the laundry room the dryer was chugging away. A couple of times I actually nodded off, but a stray thought always jerked me back to reality.

Closing my eyes tighter, I tried to remember the infield the one time I'd gone to the Kentucky Derby. All I could remember was losing two hundred dollars and drinking too much beer.

Something warm and sticky began moving on my forehead. I wasn't sure that I really wanted to know what it was, but figured I'd better check. I eased my eyes open.

David had one hand on my forehead. The other was descending, covered with a black substance that looked sticky. I grabbed his wrist.

"Whoa there, cowpoke. What in the world do you have all over your hand?"

"Chocolate syrup," he said, sounding like he was stating a scientific fact.

"David, why do you have chocolate syrup on your hand?"

"I'm hungry."

I struggled into a sitting position. "We just ate lunch."

"Uh-huh. Lunch was a long time ago."

"Just two o'clock."

David gave me the evil eye. "Don't care; I'm hungry now."

"What happened to your Cheerios?"

He curled his upper lip so that it almost touched his nose. "Linda fed 'em to her baby dolls."

My eyes followed his pointing finger. Sure enough, Cheerios in various stages of decomposition were scattered across the floor. Some had returned to the dust from whence they came.

"All right, what do you want to eat?" I had reached the stage where it was easier to go along.

"Peanut butter sandwich," David said, smiling broadly enough so I could see his missing molars.

"And what about you, Miss Linda?"

Miss Linda was interested only in playing with her doll babies. That was fine with me. I pushed myself off the couch and dodged Barbie dolls and G.I. Joes all the way to the kitchen. I had the lid off the Peter Pan and the butter knife in my hand when the telephone rang.

Picking up the receiver, I breathed into it lightly. I didn't want to speak first. I was supposed to be working. I needed the job, at least until the dust settled and I located my wife, or recovered some of my money. At the moment my life was a balancing act, like walking across a tightrope in the dark. The rope stretched out before me leading me to a destination I couldn't even imagine.

"Hello, hello?"

"Hey, Mona."

"Why didn't you answer, Paul? Is everything all right?"

"Everything's fine. Just up to my elbows in peanut butter."

Her laugh rippled down the line. "David must be hungry."

"Again."

"Honey, I'm sorry, but this is taking longer than I anticipated."

"You still haven't had the interview?" The interview had been scheduled for one-thirty.

"Well," Mona drawled, "yes and no. I mean we have had the formal interview, but Mr. Turner wants to take me out for a drink. He says we'll have to entertain clients, and he needs to see how I react in a non-traditional office setting."

"Sounds like nirvana to me."

"What?"

"Never mind," I told her, keeping the bullshit to myself. For the first time in twenty-four hours I wanted a drink. To get my mind off alcohol I started talking.

"When do you think you might make it home? I need to clean the pool and pick up around the fence. Some trash has blown in there, and Karen mentioned it to me this morning."

"Oh, I don't think this will take long. Bob, Mr. Turner, said it would only be a quick drink. He just wants to get a sense of how I handle myself in public." Mona spoke as though she had to catch a plane.

"You know, Paul, you could take the kids with you when you go to clean the pool. They could sit at one of the tables and read. I unpacked their books yesterday. They're in their room, on the dresser."

"Don't think they're in the mood to read. I'll just wait on you to get here."

She made a squeaky sound. "It may be a while."

"Thought you said it was only going to be a quick drink."

"It will be, only Bob has to wait on a call from Seattle first. A business call." She sighed as though I were a sweet child who was just a little slow. Slow I was willing to admit.

"What sort of business is our friend Bob in?"

"He's a financial advisor."

"A broker?"

"I guess so."

Quiet drifted down the line. I could hear the line humming to itself. Now and then it popped just to break the monotony.

"Well, hurry home."

"Oh, I will. Kiddos okay?"

"They're fine. David's hungry and Linda's in baby-doll land."

"Here comes Bob," she whispered. "I've got to go."

"Got to run myself. There's a peanut butter sandwich getting antsy on the counter."

The line clicked in my ear so I hung up and started knifing peanut butter onto white bread. David gave me another big smile. He was a good kid. However, I wished I were somewhere else at the moment. Alone, say, with a tall cool one and all the time in the world. On the far side of the counter the zombies were chanting. A stray thought worried the back of my brain. Before I could locate it, David and Linda started fussing and I went to head off the brewing fight at the pass.

Forty-five

"Damn. More wetbacks. Look at this article. No wonder jobs are hard to come by in this town. Bastard Mexicans are coming across the border, then heading straight to Tucson like they've got radar stuck up their butts."

Mona tossed the newspaper down by her half-eaten grapefruit and curled her nostrils. She pushed her chair away from the table, picked up her bowl, and stomped off toward the kitchen.

I watched her backside twitch beneath her nightie. The bottom of her panties were cornflower blue. Back in the kids' bedroom the television was talking to itself. I sipped coffee.

Mona dumped the grapefruit in the trash can, then rinsed the bowl. Her jaws separated in a huge yawn. She arched her back and the top half of her breasts lifted into view, twin moons rising.

"Sleepy?"

She shut down the yawn and gave me a quick smile. "A little."

I hit the coffee again. "Didn't hear you come in last night. I was up till midnight."

Pirouetting, she turned away, stepped to the refrigerator and opened the door. Behind the door she made noise and came out with a glass of orange juice. She peered at me over the brim of the glass.

"It was later than I figured it would be. You were asleep on the couch and I didn't have the heart to wake you." From the far side of the juice, she smiled at me. "You looked so peaceful. Just like a little boy."

The kitchen lighting was behind her, drifting through the filmy negligee and highlighting her figure. Her breasts were firm, with dark nipples and shadows below the curves. Determined not to stare, I made myself take a bite of bagel.

"Did you get the job?"

She sipped at the juice and made a face, as if it were sour. "Think so. I'll find out for sure tonight."

"You're going back tonight?"

Mona gave me a quick look from under her eyebrows. Something in the look made me think of a wild creature. Then she smiled as she walked over to the sink and poured out the juice.

"Got to. Bob's partner wants to meet me, and he had this dinner for some clients already set up, so he included me in the invitation." She smiled at me with her lips, but her eyes had gone unfocused and I couldn't read them.

"Bob says if all goes well tonight I'm sure to get the job."

"Thought your trial by food was last night."

"What?"

"Never mind. Tell me again, Mona, what sort of job is this you're trying to get?"

"Like I told you before, it's a receptionist position."

"I never heard of a receptionist going to dinner with clients on a regular basis."

"This is a small firm, Paul. Every person has to perform lots of different tasks. One of mine, if I get the job, will be entertaining."

"I'm sure you will make a very entertaining receptionist."

"I've never heard you complain about my entertainment skills."

Not trusting my mouth, I stared at my coffee. It was starting to cool and a miniature oil slick was forming on the surface. A nerve had started jumping in my right eye.

"I'm not complaining."

"You sound like you are."

"Just stating facts."

Twisting her head to one side, she gave me something more than smile but less than smirk.

"Let me give you a fact, mister. We can't live on your salary. Not out here. Not four people. Not even close. I have to get a real job."

"And I can't?"

"You haven't. Actions speak louder than words." She spoke slowly and distinctly, as though I were a challenged child. Her voice was loud in the apartment.

"Maybe I like my job."

"So keep it. I'm not going to live like this." Her arms made a sweeping motion that encompassed more than the room.

"You never said you were unhappy."

Lifting her head, she thrust her breasts at me. "Didn't think I had to. Thought you were more perceptive. Anyone can see this apartment is not exactly my style."

After I counted to ten, I blew the oil slick aside and sucked up a mouthful of coffee. It tasted bitter, acidic. I swallowed it anyway.

I could sense her looking at me, but the zombies were starting to whisper so I kept staring at the coffee, trying to hold the truce together. I heard her sigh. Then there were footsteps going the other way.

I don't know how long I sat at the table remembering things I should have forgotten. Old urges were coming on strong, the coffee was cold, and my will was shot to hell. Life had a way of turning around and slapping you in the face. I felt like screaming.

There were more footsteps. I looked up. David was standing just inside the kitchen staring at me. His eyes were big and bright and his lips quivered as though he were on the verge of saying something.

We stared at each other. I slowly shook my head at him and he turned and walked back into his room, shutting the door behind him.

The coffee was so nasty I gave up on it and studied the walls. There were no hidden messages, so I pushed myself out of the chair, picked up my cup, and carried it to the sink. The coffee swirled down the drain like a black whirlpool.

Mona walked out of her bedroom, wearing a blue dress I hadn't seen before. It was cut low and high and made her eyes looked as blue as the middle of Lake Huron.

She started to walk toward me, then stopped abruptly. We stared at each other. Seconds tick-tocked inside my head.

"I'm going now. Be back as soon as I can."

"I'll watch the kids till you get back."

"Thank you."

In her wake, the scent of her perfume lingered. I didn't allow myself to go over to the window. After a few minutes I poured myself another cup of coffee and carried it back to the table. I picked up the newspaper Mona had tossed down earlier. I could detect her scent in the folds.

A black and white photograph of a pickup truck full of people caught my eye. Faces peered out of darkness. The eyes reminded me of those of jack-lighted deer. Something about one of the faces looked vaguely familiar. Pulling the paper closer, I studied the faces.

Identification took a while. Seven or eight faces stared out from the paper. They all looked Hispanic, and all but one were male. Some of the faces looked very young. I studied them more closely. Something about them nagged at me.

The third time around I found it. Two of the faces belonged to the sons of Gomez. They were in the back of the photo, near the cab, faces half averted. Just to make sure I looked again.

The last time I'd seen the boys was in Goeteza. They were the boys I'd pulled out of a cottonwood tree, with the water running high and hard and brown below them. I had held them close, as their thin arms had tightened around my neck. On more than one occasion Gomez had told me emphatically he would never cross the border. I studied the photograph more carefully. Gomez was not in the picture. I wondered why his sons were.

The caption read "ILLEGALS NABBED BY THE TRUCKFUL." The article was below the fold. I flipped the paper and started reading.

I didn't learn a lot. The writer, somebody with the distinctly unlikely name of Heidi Golden, had written the story like she had covered it before. There was not much more human interest than if she had been covering a fire ant convention. The photo was the best part of the article.

I read the article twice and made a mental note about where the illegal immigrants were being held, and when and where and how they would be returned. I put the paper down, got up, and cleaned off the table. I carried the dirty dishes over to the sink and washed them. After I finished, the kids came out of their room and said they were hungry. They were tired of Cheerios and I was bored with pouring cereal and milk into a bowl. I gave them a choice of scrambled eggs or French toast.

After French toast, I ruled out television and we went outside. It was still early and a cool freshness lingered in the air. Two blocks over, on Jackson, was a small park I'd come across running my errands. There was a swing set, a slide, and a seesaw in the park, each strategically placed among trees, plus soccer goals and water fountains. I maneuvered into the middle of our gang of three. We held hands as we walked.

We stayed on the sidewalks and looked both ways when we had to cross a street. The sun was shining and the breeze was in our faces. Children of various hues were playing in the park. I sat in the shade of the picnic shelter and watched the kids run in the sunshine. David got into a pickup soccer game, while his little sister played in the sandbox. I stayed out of the way. I had considerable thinking to do. When the sun was overhead, I corralled the kids and we walked back to Mountain Edge.

We ate lunch, watched television, and waited for Mona. It was an afternoon full of cartoons and cookie crumbs. It was a long afternoon. I tried to read to pass the time, but my mind wandered south of Faulkner all afternoon.

When shadows fell across the yellow line that ran down the middle of Henderson, I put my book down and fixed myself a cup of strong coffee. Then I started supper. I fixed the never nutritious fish sticks and French fries. After supper, we cleaned the pool and had a swim before we worked on cleaning up the laundry room. I hoped the child labor people weren't pulling any surprise inspections.

It all made for a long day and the kids went to sleep watching their *Mary Poppins* video. I washed the dishes then dozed off on the couch reading Hemingway. I was too tired for Faulkner or Wolfe. I was grateful for the Tucson Public Library. I wanted another world this night. I couldn't stand my own.

I woke in the middle of the night not knowing where I was. The door creaked and a shaft of light spilled across the floor. Mona came in on tiptoe. I closed my eyes as she drifted toward the couch. Hair brushed against my face and I could smell her perfume and the whiskey on her breath. She whispered something, but her words were slurred and I had one ear mashed into the couch.

When I didn't respond, she sighed and clip-clopped away on her three-inch heels. When I heard the water running in the bathroom, I opened my eyes. I watched the lights in her room until they went out. I lay on the couch, watching the car lights moving through the darkness on Henderson, listening to the night growing old. About two o'clock I got up and let myself out, taking Hemingway with me. I figured Ernie was always ready for a little night action.

My mind was restless as I lay on my narrow rollaway bed and stared at nothing in the night, wondering about more than I knew how to handle. Visions rolled through my mind like marbles dumped without warning, shining and smooth, moving inexorably. I kept smelling Mona's scent and hearing Wilson's cough and seeing Jolene's face swimming in an alcoholic haze. I could sense the zombies lurking in the shadows. Shivering, I pulled the sheet up. The last thing I remember was daylight beginning to infiltrate in the Venetian blinds.

Forty-six

I looked in the back window. She was bent over the desk, intent in the paperwork before her. Incoming light was kind, spreading softly across her face, highlighting the curves and painting ladylike shadows in the hollows.

Her forehead was wrinkled and her lips sagged in the corners. Holding a pencil in one hand, she rubbed the back of her neck with the other. She was leaning forward, as if getting closer to the numbers would make them compute, and her breasts hung down until they brushed the table top.

Content to be the watcher, I studied her through the window until the numbers became too much for her and she pushed the pile of papers aside, crossed her arms on the desk and let her head settle on them. Hair spilled down, covering her face like dark camouflage. Sunlight was hot against my back and sweat trickled down the back of my neck. My mind was fuzzy from the night before and my legs felt like concrete setting up as I walked around to the front of the office.

Karen raised her head as the door swung open. For a second I might just as well have been the man who invented the Martian Hop. Her eyes changed as recognition arrived. Neither of us spoke.

I could smell coffee warming in the back office and I went and helped myself. The coffee was hot and slightly bitter—exactly what I needed.

"Working hard?"

Her eyes remained on the papers before her. "Always."

I took another sip. The coffee was still hot enough to scald the tip of my tongue.

"Ever think about getting some help?"

Her pencil checked off one number in a long column. "I can't afford good help, and the rest is often worse than no help at all."

"You own this place?"

Lifting her eyes, she gave me a look too layered for me to decipher, then flicked them back to her work. "No, I'm the manager."

I leaned against a beige filing cabinet. "Why not ask the owner for help?"

"He's already given me two increases in the budget this year."

I watched her eyes rove across the ledger sheets and greenbar. Some of the papers had columns and some didn't. All were filled with numbers, reminding me of all the money I used to have.

"He's got to be cognizant of inflation."

"What he's cognizant of is the bottom line. And I don't blame him. He's a businessman and his goal has to be to make a profit. As much as possible, too, because who in hell knows about tomorrow."

Pushing my body off the file cabinet, I walked around behind her desk. Her back stiffened, but she didn't say anything. Keeping my coffee cup in my right hand, I put my left one on the back of her chair. In the sunlight her hair looked like dark silk.

"You don't want to kill yourself, though, Karen, not for his profit."

Her neck went rigid and she smoothed out a wrinkle I couldn't see in one of the greenbar pages.

"Not that it's really any business of yours, Mr. Hampton, but I like my job, and I like to eat. To continue doing both I have to make sure the Mountain Edge makes a profit."

"And are we?"

"You're asking a lot of questions this morning."

I glanced at the white face of the clock hanging on the wall to her left. It was expressionless.

"It's afternoon, and I seem to have a lot of questions these days."

"Why so many questions?"

"Guess because I need so many answers." I could smell her perfume as I studied the swell of her breasts.

"Mr. Hampton, as you can see, if you will simply look, I have work to do. A great deal of work. So please take your lame sense of humor somewhere else." Her head swung heavy and loose at the top of her long neck and her brown hair swirled like a dark beaded curtain blowing in a strong wind.

"Speaking of work, don't you have things that need doing, Mr. Hampton? You seem to have fallen behind the past few days."

I took another sip of coffee. It was going cold. "Yeah, I need to paint the kitchen in four-oh-four, but first I've got an errand to run." I rubbed my free hand along the smooth worn leather of her chair. "Can I ask you one more question?"

She straightened the papers before her. "Okay."

"How do I get to the Tucson Detention Center?"

Her head came up. Her dark eyes were full of questions. "Going to visit someone?"

"Just someone I used to know."

She told me what bus to catch and roughly when it ran. Her eyes were still dark with questions and I kept waiting for her to ask more. However, she bit her lip with her prominent front teeth, while, for one elastic moment, something passed between us.

There was a message there, but Old Paul wasn't smart enough to decipher it, so I strolled to the back office and poured the rest of my coffee down the sink. I stood there reliving events in my mind, deciding nothing. Finally, I put the empty cup in the dishpan and headed for the front door.

Out of the corner of my left eye I saw Karen open her mouth. She didn't say anything. Just sat there with her pink tongue showing. There were words I wanted to say and they surely lay heavy on my mind. I didn't stop though. I had a bus to catch.

Forty-seven

Karen's directions put me off the bus one stop too soon. I didn't mind. It wasn't as hot as it was going to be and a breeze stirred the air. One side of the street was still in shadows thrown by the buildings that lined the asphalt and it was pleasant to walk with the shade on my face, the sidewalk warm beneath my feet, and listen to the world whirling by.

Besides, I hadn't quite worked out exactly what I was going to say. Scenarios ran through my mind as I strolled, trying to formulate thoughts while dodging stray memories. I was still debating with myself when I walked through the door of the detention center.

Ten minutes, and a lot of verbal fertilizer later, I got past the front desk and into the visiting area. For over an hour I sat in a small waiting room crowded with well-worn furniture and well-worn people. After a while the people began to look as if they had been used harder than the furniture.

Every few minutes a uniformed man opened a door on the right side of the room and called one of the waiting to come inside. I hadn't brought a book and conversation was non-existent, so I thumbed through a two-year old issue of *National Geographic* and learned more than I wanted to about crocodiles and the people of the Mongolian Steppes. When I got tired of *National Geographic,* I studied the back of my hands and watched a long-haired white man sporting a gold stud in his right ear chain smoke Marlboros while I half-listened to the mumblings of an overstuffed middle-aged couple seated to my left. I gathered they were from Denver and their son had done something so shameful they would never be able to hold their heads high again in Colorado. I wanted to tell them that everyone made mistakes. However, their folded arms and silent downward glances discouraged conversation and my courage and conviction were both in short supply, so I thought about mistakes I'd made and kept my mouth shut. About two o'clock the Marlboro Man got his call, and twenty minutes later the profoundly embarrassed couple was allowed into the inner sanctum.

A young girl with a pinched face, dirty clothes, and a woebegone expression came down the hall and sat across the waiting room from me. We were alone, except for a dark-skinned man in the corner who'd been asleep since I arrived. His mouth hung open like the hinges were sprung and a peaceful expression covered his face. In the quiet afternoon I could hear his gentle snores. In his rumpled clothes he looked like a gigantic abandoned baby.

The girl took a panoramic look around the room and the realization of where she was dawned in her pale green eyes. Tears formed, then, accompanied by sobs, began to slide down narrow, elongated cheeks. Soft at first, the sobs steadily intensified. Shoulders jerked and she hung her head and let her dirty-blonde hair fall over her face.

After a couple of minutes I couldn't keep my mouth shut. "Want to talk about it?"

She whipped her head from side to side so violently that at the apex of movement her hair stood straight out from her head.

"You sure?"

She nodded, less violently.

To keep from boring myself to death I got up and walked around the room. The place smelled faintly of smoke and sweat and perfume. There was also a scent of something indefinable, an abandoned emotion perhaps, or maybe the aroma of the inexorable passage of time. There were no windows and no artwork on the concrete block walls and I felt as though I were the one in a cell. Only I wasn't sure if it was a prison cell or a group discovery room at a mental institution.

I was studying the back of the blonde's head when I heard my name. I turned and followed a slim-hipped officer down a long, brightly lighted hall. He had a clipboard in one hand and a fine polish on his black shoes. Halfway down the hall, he stopped and opened a door on the right with a key from the ring on his belt. He held the door open and motioned for me to go inside.

There was a small round table in the center of the room, encircled by four plastic chairs. I sat on one and the officer sat across the table from me. He laid the clipboard on the table and consulted it. I read his brass name badge. It gleamed dully in the fluorescent lighting. His name was Anderson, D.

Lifting his face, he appraised me with bright eyes. They were brown and his carefully groomed hair was black. Handsome, in a slim-faced, clean-cut way, he looked quite young to me.

"Says here your name is Paul Hampton. Is that correct?"

"Yes."

"And you're here to see two of the illegals the sheriff's office picked up yesterday?"

"That's right, Officer."

He scooted the clipboard away and put his hands on the tabletop, fingers interlacing. I wondered if the pose signified anything. Anderson, D. caught me staring at his hands and pulled them apart, spreading the palms down on the table. There were no rings on his fingers and no dirt under his nails.

"Mind telling me why you want to see..." he glanced at the clipboard, "Tico and Manuel Gomez?"

I shrugged to imply that my mission was not particularly important. "I was in Mexico a while back and think I know the boys slightly. At least in the newspaper photo they looked like the same boys."

"What were you doing in Mexico, Mr. Hampton?"

"Traveling."

"Business or pleasure?"

"Vacation."

"Why Mexico?"

"Why not?"

He stared at me. I said, "Hadn't been there before and I'd heard a lot about it. Thought I'd see for myself."

Anderson leaned forward. The crown of his black hair glistened.

"See what?"

I shrugged again. My shoulders were getting tired. "Just to see if all I'd heard was true."

"And what had you heard, Mr. Hampton?"

"You know, how nice the climate is, and how beautiful the scenery is, and how friendly the people are."

"And were the people friendly?"

Anderson's questions were beginning to get tiresome, but I smiled and answered him. "Some were, some weren't. Just like everywhere."

He cocked his head to the right and looked at me casually out of the corner of his left eye. "Where all did you go in Mexico?"

"Oh, lots of places. Started out in Nogales and worked my way out from there." A funny feeling I was evolving into a prisoner spread across my mind. I did my best to ignore it.

"What were some of the towns you visited?" A smile just short of a smirk had settled on Anderson's lips. Part of me wanted to knock it off. Instead, I tried to look innocent and a touch embarrassed.

"Afraid I'm not too good with foreign names. One of the towns was Goeteza."

Anderson shifted in his seat. His body leaned in my direction. "That where you met the Gomez boys?"

"Yeah. Actually, I knew their father better. He runs a restaurant down there." As I talked I watched Anderson's eyes. Movements were occurring in the depths, but I couldn't decipher them.

"Do any gambling down there?"

"No."

"Run across any illegal activity?"

"Such as?"

"Prostitution, counterfeit CDs, drugs?"

I could feel his eyes on my face. My skin felt hot where his looks landed. "Nothing like that," I said. I wasn't under oath and he was getting on my nerves.

Anderson looked at me without speaking. The silence grew uncomfortable before he pushed his chair back and picked up his clipboard.

"Please empty your pockets, Mr. Hampton, then I'll take you in to see your friends." He let the official police department smile sit on his lips. It never made it to his eyes.

Emptying my pockets didn't take long. All I had were a few one dollar bills, forty-seven cents in change, a brass key to the laundry room, and a black plastic comb guaranteed to be unbreakable. Remembering all the money I used to have I had to suppress a sudden urge to laugh. Anderson, D. might not understand. I wasn't sure I did.

We went back into the hall and down the corridor until it intersected with another. We turned right and Anderson stopped at the second door on the left and unlocked it. Pushing the metal door open, he flipped on the light switch and motioned me inside.

"Ten minutes." The door clicked shut behind him.

The narrow room was furnished with a single wooden table and four ladder-backed wooden chairs. No mirrors or pictures hung on the concrete walls. There were no windows. High on one wall, set in a corner, was a small surveillance camera. It was a card room for naughty monks.

Murmurings from the hallway were muted. Slowly the room seemed to void itself of all sound. All that quiet gave me the creeps as I sat in a chair facing the door.

Time seemed to have disappeared within the silence. There was no sense of it moving, or even existing. There was no clock and I no longer owned a wristwatch. The room was an encapsulated, soundless vacuum. Although I couldn't name its origin, fear wormed through me. I wanted a drink, wanted it so badly I rapped my knuckles on the table until they hurt. Just to give my mind something else to think about. I'd started to sweat.

I sat there long enough for the sweat to soak through the back of my shirt. Police psychology impressed me more by the minute. I was nearly ready to confess; they just needed to give me a list of unsolved crimes.

My nerves were singing like I was waiting on a first date and they jumped when the door swung open.

Tico and Manuel came in first. Behind them was a woman in a tan uniform and a darker brown baseball cap. She was petite, with soft brown eyes and full, puffy lips. The gun on her right hip was large, black and ugly. She cast a short, hard look my way. "Ten minutes," was all she said. Ten minutes seemed to be the favorite unit of time around there.

The boys crossed the floor without speaking and sat on two of the wooden chairs. Both wore dirty jeans and tee-shirts, and fearful expressions. I smiled at them. "Remember me?"

They nodded.

I kept on smiling. "It's okay, you can talk to me. I'm your friend. Your friend from Mexico."

The boys looked at each other across the table. "*Si*," said Tico. "We remember you." He was the older boy, and seemed to have elected himself spokesman. Manuel nodded.

Fear was still smeared across their brown faces. Leaning my elbows on the table, I put my chin in my palms. "You can talk to me. I'm the man who pulled you from the river."

Manuel glanced at Tico. Tico nodded. I wondered how much the boys were understanding.

"Yes, we know you. We remember you, *señor*."

I nodded. "Before I left Goeteza I talked often with your father. He did not want to cross the river. Why would he let you?"

Tico shrugged.

"If I am to help you, you must talk to me."

"We are very confused, *señor*."

"I know, but if you don't talk to me I can't help you. May not be able to help you much anyway. But for sure I won't be able to do anything if you don't tell me what's going on."

The boys exchanged glances that meant something to them. Tico twisted in his chair to face me. "Manuel and I, we have no choice. We know if we do not get help from someone we will be sent back." He lifted his eyebrows. "Of course, we can come back, but we may only be caught again. It is important that we stay, very important."

"Why is it so important? Hundreds cross every day and many are sent back. They just cross again."

Manuel lowered his head to the table. He looked very young. Tico watched him for a moment, then turned back to face me. I waited for him to speak. Time beat a syncopated rhythm inside my skull.

Tico blinked his eyes and expelled his breath. It made a soft, sibilant sound. "You do not understand, *señor*. Much has changed since you were in Goeteza." He peered into my eyes to see if I was following him.

"Our village is not the same. Do you remember the one they called the Leather Man?"

"I remember him."

Tico nodded as if I were a promising pupil. "He is now the most powerful man in Goeteza, more powerful than the mayor or the police chief, more powerful even than the priest."

Confusion rose in my mind. The Leather Man had been a curiosity in Goeteza, nothing more. I wondered if the boy was confused. "How did this happen?"

Tico rolled his eyes and raised his shoulders. "Who can say for sure? I only know that people came across the mountains, rich people, very rich and powerful people. A man with silver hair, a beautiful woman and others. They came with money and men and guns. Worst of all they came with their drugs. They sell those drugs to men and women in all the neighboring towns and make much money."

The boy glanced down at the table and back up at me. An idea was crawling across my mind like a diseased rattlesnake.

"With every day they grow richer and more powerful. As the days passed my father became very afraid for his friends and his family. My father said Goeteza was no longer a safe town. He said it was no longer a fit place to live. He could not go and leave his father and mother. They are old and sick. So he made us cross the border." The boy shrugged as if nothing in the world really mattered. He looked away. A teardrop dangled from the corner of his left eye.

There was a knock on the door and the woman in brown came for the boys. Patting their shoulders, I made promises I had no idea how to keep. If that nasty little notion that was squirming around inside my head was correct, Goeteza, Gomez, and I were all in deep shit. One thing I knew for sure: I was scared enough to need a drink. Was I never to be free from that response?

New lights were in their eyes when they left the room. I hated to see them dim. It looked like Old Paul had miles to go and many promises to keep.

A different guard escorted me down the hall. Tall and broad through the shoulders, he looked like he might start to shave next week. I tried to make conversation while he gave me back my money, keys, and comb. He wasn't interested. He walked me to the front door and stood outside as I walked down the sidewalk.

The bus was late. I amused myself by pretending I was Kerouac researching the next installment of *On the Road*. I read the brightly colored newspaper ads taped to the windows of the grocery store next to the bus stop and, when I got tired of that, I watched the people going into and out of the grocery store. They were poor looking people from the rainbow coalition. Most wore jeans and tennis shoes and carried all they bought in a plastic sack or two. Many smoked and more than one smelled of liquor.

When my legs started to ache, I sat on the faded wooden bench by the bus stop sign. Across the street an old man walked a little dog in front of a Rite-Aid drugstore. The old man's white-haired head was bent, and even in the throbbing heat he wore a long-sleeved white shirt. He moved with slow shuffling steps, making so little progress that he seemed to be on a treadmill rather than a sidewalk. Every few steps the little dog lifted his head and gazed up at the man. It took them a long time to negotiate the block and shuffle out of sight around the corner. When they had disappeared into the shadows I got up and crossed the street and went into the drugstore. I bought a Butterfinger and a coffee to go.

No shade fell on the side of the street where the bus stopped and I felt foolish drinking hot coffee in a broiling sun, but I needed the kick. I ate half the candy bar before it started to melt. I tossed the empty cup and the rest of the Butterfinger in a green metal trash can then licked chocolate off my fingers while I thought about what I'd promised.

It wasn't that I wanted to do it. Bravery had never been a quality I readily manufactured. Probably that had always been part of my fascination with alcohol. It had a way of making a man feel brave. That first drink had been so long ago I no longer remembered it with certainty. In the dying afternoon it occurred to me that perhaps the search for personal courage had taken me to the bottle.

An old Mexican woman in a red rebozo and a full-skirted blue and silver dress gazed at me from her end of the bench without speaking. I kept my revelations to myself.

By the time the bus arrived, a small congregation had gathered and I'd figured out my next move. The bus pulled to the curb with hissing brakes. I got in line behind a young man with a blue tattoo of a hangman's noose on his left arm. From my angle it looked like an elongated penis. Below the penis the words *Fuck 'Em High* were tattooed in red. An old man with long, black hair and coppery Indian features was behind me. More people were behind him and in front of the Tattoo Kid. We all followed the Mexican lady onto the bus.

The afternoon was wearing on and wearing people down. Nobody was talking much. In the seat in front of me two elderly ladies, both with white hair piled high in identical buns, chatted sporadically about someone named Mabel. Mabel was their cousin who had married a preacher who'd run off with a young girl who ended up robbing a bank in Utah. I heard enough about Mabel to last two lifetimes. I was relieved when the old ladies got off at Japonica.

Leaning my head back against the brown vinyl, I listened to the traffic talking to itself and tried to figure how I was going to pull everything off. From the other side of the aisle a tow-headed boy about seven made faces at me all the way to Mirage. A twenty-five-cents-a-minute pay phone stood on the corner of Mirage and Gladstone and I got off and spent my last seven quarters calling my attorney. His snooty secretary acted like I'd pissed in her Christmas eggnog, but Gerald had two good ideas how he might be able to keep the boys north of the border. It was a most satisfactory conversation.

By the time I hung up, the sun was slipping on the Pacific side of the mountains. I walked the last two miles to the Mountain Edge with a smile on my face. Karen was locking the door as I crossed the squishy asphalt. She gave me a tired smile and waved with her right hand. A stack of papers was tucked under her left arm. Smiling back, I gave her a casual salute and kept walking.

Back in my room, I changed to shorts and sneakers before I walked Mrs. Hemphill's poodle, then picked up trash from the parking lot. After policing the grounds, I was hot and the blue water in the pool looked cool. I did a belly-buster at the five-foot marker and came up shaking the water out of my eyes. A cab was pulling up at the southern end of the office. Treading water, I watched Mona slide out the back door. She was wearing heels and a green dress I hadn't seen before. It wrapped around her body, going in at the dips and out at the curves. Behind her sunglasses she stared at me. Then she turned, paid the cabbie, and walked to her apartment without looking back. I put my head down and started swimming.

Forty-eight

"I'm going south for a while."

Karen peered around the side of her computer. I didn't want to answer the questions her face was asking. Instead I said, "Hope you can hold my job for me."

"How long will you be gone?" She used her business voice. Her eyes mirrored the image of the computer screen.

"I'm not sure."

Out in the parking lot someone started their car. A dog barked from the subdivision behind the complex. I rubbed my hands together. There were calluses on the palms. The city was paving a new side street across the road from the office and I could smell the hot asphalt. A memory of my father and summer vacations surfaced without warning. But that had been another life and I had been a different person.

"Why are you going?" Her voice was softer, different in pitch or timbre or some more intrinsic element, as it came from a separate personality.

"I've got business down there."

"Business business, or personal business, Mr. Hampton?"

Tired of looking around a computer monitor into eyes filled with artificial light, I walked around the desk. In the sunlight sifting in through the back window, she looked tired and there was gray in her hair I hadn't noticed before.

"Personal business." I spoke as gently as I could.

Her head rose slowly, as though it were unsure of its way. "By south, do you mean Mexico?" I could hear concern in her voice, or maybe I just wanted to hear it.

"Yes. I'm doing a reverse crossing."

Her eyes were like deep waters. "But why? Why go back to Mexico? When you first came here you led me to believe you had it rough over there."

I gave her my version of the Sonoran shrug. "Don't know if I can explain it, Karen. Guess I'm not totally clear in my own mind why I have to go. Just know I have to." Scooting a pile of papers over, I propped a hindquarter on the corner of the desk.

"Let me see if I can make it a little less confusing."

Karen rolled her chair closer. She smelled faintly of tropical flowers. The computer hummed like a small, satisfied god. I felt sixty and sixteen at the same time.

"When I was down there I had some bad times, some very bad times. About as bad as they get. Some of it was my own fault, maybe most of it, especially at first. But never all of it, certainly not near the end. Understand?"

She smiled up at me with her eyes and nodded.

"Good. Now, I also had some good times. Some people were very good to me, especially a family named Gomez. The father was a good man and extra helpful to me. When I was down there he explained why he would never leave his town. He loved it very much, and some members of his family who had crossed the border had experienced bad luck."

I shifted until I was directly in front of Karen. I had to ask her a big favor and I wanted to do it in a personal way, hoping she was more than a tired businesswoman.

"Remember when I asked you how to get to the Detention Center?"

"Yes."

"Well, the people I was going to see were the two sons of this Gomez who was so good to me."

"How did you know they were there?"

"Saw their photographs in the paper."

"In Mrs. Sampson's apartment?"

I bent my head toward her face. "You notice a lot, don't you?"

A faint smile transformed her lips. "I notice a lot, about things and people I care about." I watched her lips as they moved. They looked as soft as whipped cream.

"Yeah, not that it matters, but I saw the photos there."

Her eyes seemed locked onto mine. They exhibited unexpected depths, like pools of water in a small stream. "You two are close, aren't you?"

I shrugged. "Sometimes. Maybe. Who knows? Who cares?"

"You might be surprised."

"Really."

Nodding, she rearranged her eyes. I told myself to be careful, that they looked like drowning pools.

Afraid, but in an excited sort of way, I made myself look out the window at the sunlight that covered the earth. Keeping my eyes on the white-hot sunlight, I started talking.

"Anyway, I went down to where they're keeping the boys and, after some wrangling, I got to talk to them. Things have definitely changed in my little slice of Mexico. The town where Gomez lives is being run by people who belong behind bars. One of them I know, and he's a rattlesnake on two legs. Could be I know some of the others. If I'm guessing right, they're worse. Karen, I have to go. Gomez and his family were good to me, better than anybody has ever been, and you want to know the real kicker? Well, here it is, they never asked for one damn thing. I'd never feel right about myself if I didn't at least try to help."

I quit talking and started listening. I could hear the faint hum of traffic, the hiss of the air conditioner, and the zombies chanting in the darker caverns of my mind.

"I understand." Her voice was faint, as though she had moved far away. The thick sweetness of her perfume was potent. Not trusting myself, I kept my eyes on the sunlight. It looked fresh, pure, and oblivious to men, good or bad, north or south of the border.

"I'm not sure how just yet, but I'm going to keep those boys north of the border. They're too young to resist, much less understand, what's going on in Goeteza. I've got to cross myself, though. So I need somebody to help me, watch over them until I get back."

"If you get back." Her voice was closer.

Taking a pen out of my pocket, I wrote my attorney's name and telephone number on a yellow sticky-pad. Unsure of what awaited, I turned my head and looked at her. Karen had risen from her chair and was leaning forward. Lights I hadn't noticed danced in her eyes.

"You make it sound very dangerous, Paul. In Goeteza, I mean. Is that how you say it?"

"Yes, you say it like that, and yes, it will be dangerous. Here's a phone number to call if you don't hear from me in three weeks."

Her face moved again, closer. So close I could hear her breathing, slow and rhythmic. I wanted to say something, but the words that would convey what I was feeling escaped me. Her breath was warm and soft and moist against my face. Desire rose until my throat ached. I watched her face move once more.

Her lips found mine and I closed my eyes and pulled her to me. Her breasts were soft and heavy against my chest, while her lips were as soft as I'd imagined. Her breath was warm and sweet in my mouth. I curled an arm around her until I could feel her heart beating and I no longer thought of Mexico, or zombies, or all my past inequities.

Forty-nine

I was walking up Henderson Road, heading toward Albertson's. There were no sidewalks, and whenever a car or truck buzzed toward me I had to step off the asphalt onto the sand. Actually, it wasn't pure sand; there was enough dirt mixed in, or lying underneath, for cacti and yucca to take root. Further from the road the plants grew taller and thicker, and diminutive, twisted trees thrust narrow branches skyward, throwing skeletal shadows on the desert floor. Birds flittered among the thin greenness and small mammals scurried about in the shadows that shifted in the hot dry wind.

The sun was high in hard blue sky and sweat was plastering my shirt to my back by the time I started across Albertson's parking lot. Heat waves shimmered above the asphalt and two disjointed rows of shopping carts shimmered outside the store. Beyond the carts, in the shade cast by the building, there was a single wooden bench. Three people sat on the bench, their faces white blurs. Just to the right was a pay phone you could use to call anywhere in the United States for only a quarter a minute.

Asphalt was squishy beneath my feet, sucking and grabbing at my shoes. It felt like I was walking across a giant tar pit and I was grateful to step into the cool shadows. The people sitting on the bench turned their heads in unison. It was like being stared at by a three-headed creature. I smiled at them and all three faces smiled back. I dug quarters out of my front left pocket and started feeding them into the phone. On the third ring Perkins answered.

"Well, well, well, if it isn't the man himself; imagine a lawyer answering his own phone. What's the matter? Is the beast off?"

"Everybody gets a day off, Hampton, even people you don't like."

"Why do you keep her on? She can't be good for business."

"Everybody has to be somewhere. Consider it my contribution to society. Besides, she's been with me for years."

"Knowing you, she must work cheap."

"I'm going to choose to ignore that. Anyway, enough small talk, Paul. I'm busy and you didn't call to inquire about the state of my health."

"No," I said, "I called to see how you were coming on the boys."

A long sigh, like the fading whistle of a distant train, came down the line. "I've called in the favors I had with INS. Those are tough boys to deal with, but—"

"But what?"

"But I've engineered a ninety-day extension for your two young amigos. You'll have to damn near sign your life away when you pick them up, Paul. It's one hell of a hassle. The boys have to report in weekly and you have to file reports on time, or else. Plus, the INS agents can pull a surprise inspection at any time. Legally, they can even put surveillance on you. The penalty for screwing up is severe. Sure you want to go through with this, big boy?"

I'd already done all the thinking I needed to. After a while a man gets tired of only making promises. "Yeah, I'm sure. Give me the details."

As I listened to Gerald giving me all the legal mumbo-jumbo, I let my eyes drift to the three souls on the bench. They were all staring at me with a quiet intensity. We eyeballed each other across the shimmering air. I wondered what they were seeing.

I came back to the sound of Gerald repeating my name.

"What?"

"Where the hell did you go?"

"Just drifted off. Sorry. What were you saying?"

"I was saying I talked to a buddy of mine who just got back from old Mexico earlier this week. He spent some time in one of your favorite places down there."

"Nogales?"

"That's right. Your old stomping grounds."

"And?"

"And he had a very interesting story. Thought you might like to hear it."

I made myself speak calmly. "So tell it."

"Well, old friend, it seems as if an American couple we both know crossed the border a few weeks ago and have really involved themselves deeply down there."

"What do you mean, involved?"

"Rumor has it, this is all rumor, you understand? I can't substantiate any of it."

I looked back at the three amigos on the bench. Their eyes were still fixed on me. I looked away, across the parking lot, out across the desert scrub. "I understand."

"Well, Mr. Paul Hampton, rumor has it that this fine, upstanding couple from north of the border has gotten themselves entwined in a number of rather nasty underground activities with some most undesirable characters."

A pinprick of light flickered to life in the darkness of my mind. "What sort of activities?"

"No one knows for sure, but the rumor mill says drugs, kinky sex and blackmail—for starters."

"In Nogales?" I knew the town was not overly puritanical, but it sounded like risky business to do too much there so quickly. But then, what little time I'd spent in that town was enveloped in an alcoholic haze.

"Nogales is supposed to be only where the contacts are made."

I waited for him to go on. He didn't. Lawyers think they are so goddamn cute sometimes. I watched a blue Chevy pull into the parking lot. A woman with a mass of blonde hair got out and started walking vigorously. "And where does the action go after Nogales?" I prompted him. I couldn't afford the anger anymore.

"Ever hear of a little town called Goeteza?"

I could hear the smile in his voice. The light at the back of my brain was burning brighter. I wanted to hang up. I had to swallow before I could speak. "Yeah, smartass, I've heard of Goeteza. Matter of fact, I've been there. Plan on seeing it again, soon."

Warm air carrying the scent of sagebrush, hot tar, and perfume swept across my face. The blonde hustled by, the automatic door swishing open for her. The three people on the bench watched her enter the store. Their faces could have been death masks. I had to ask one more question, just to make sure.

"These people got names?"

The bastard actually snickered into the phone. "Do the names Jolene and Stan strike a familiar note?"

"Fuck you," I said, and jammed the receiver onto the cradle. So much for promises to myself. The people on the bench opened their mouths in unison, then looked away. One of them made a whimpering sound.

Fifty

I tucked my shirttail inside my pants and stepped across the border into Nogales.

It was early in the day and the light was still merciful. A breeze curled around the corner of the concrete wall that rose higher than my head. It felt cool against my face.

Vendors were setting up on the sidewalk. Only a few people were crossing and they were headed north, walking with their heads down with their hands in their pockets. No one was talking. It felt as though there was a quiet glaze to the morning that a spoken word would crack. I kept my mouth shut and my nose pointed south.

Standing at the end of the walkway, where the world turned into Mexico, were two policemen, lounging against the concrete wall, large in their tan uniforms. One of the men smoked a cigarette, while the other stared into a Styrofoam cup. Steam rose from the cup, visible for a moment before the morning swallowed it. As I walked by, one of them coughed and cigarette smoke assaulted my nostrils, but no one spoke. The thin shell that encased the morning held.

I turned right and stepped into the sunlight. At the far end of a small piazza a man was on his knees, spreading out porcelain figures before him with a reverent air. He looked up as my shadow fell across his statuary. Something in the lines of his face seemed familiar. He smiled. Smiling back, I asked in my poor Spanish if he knew the way to the bus station. He pointed toward the Pacific and I started walking.

After three blocks, I saw a sign and turned left onto a street with a name that started with a Z. The landscape began to change. Dark warehouses replaced small houses. Knots of men stood in front of what looked like factories. Vacant lots separated the buildings and scrubby grass grew in the sidewalk cracks.

The bus station was at the end of the third block of Z Street. The door was standing open as if to welcome the morning. Just inside the door I paused, letting my eyes adjust to the abrupt change in lighting.

There was a long wooden counter opposite the door and a man with a droopy mustache stood behind it. He was selling tickets for the buses. All the bus schedules were written in white chalk on a blackboard affixed to the wall behind him. I watched him sell five tickets to a man with a wife and three small children. They were going to Juarez. I strolled across the well-oiled floor and asked for one ticket to Goeteza. I gave the mustache man some pesos and he gave me a yellow bus ticket.

Wooden benches ran along the walls. Most were full with people waiting for their bus, but I found an empty spot and sat while I studied the blackboard. My Spanish was weak, but I knew my numbers and Goeteza, and I soon figured out I had an hour and forty minutes before my bus pulled out. I wished I'd brought a book. I tried to kill time by studying the people, but they soon started to look alike.

After a few minutes, I noted a sign on the wall. Red letters read: RESTAURANTE. Below, a blue arrow pointed right. I got up and walked down a short hall. The café was on the right. Restrooms were across the hall.

I pushed open a wooden door with a silhouette of a man on it and went in and washed my hands. There was plenty of soap, but no hot water. I passed on the roll-towel that looked like it hadn't been changed since Pancho Villa rode and dried my hands on the front of my jeans.

Five or six tables were arranged haphazardly across the dining area and a row of ten stools fronted a counter. I sat on the stool at the far left end of the row.

A dark-haired woman, with tired eyes and a hint of a mustache, came over. She had bad teeth, but a pleasant smile. I tried to order coffee, a cheese sandwich, and a banana. She didn't speak English, so I resorted to pointing and drawing pictures in the air with my hands.

The coffee was hot and strong, the cheese sandwich was edible. It would have been better if the cook had toasted the bread and had a go at warming the cheese. I didn't complain. Simply ate my sandwich and drank two cups of coffee while I wondered what I'd find in Goeteza. I wondered how Gomez and his wife were doing, and if they'd heard from the boys. When I began to want a drink, I picked up my uneaten banana and stepped over to the cash register.

I picked up a can of orange soda to take on the bus and gave the woman a handful of coins I'd picked up at the Exchange Office north of the border. She counted them carefully then gave several back. She gave me another smile and a brown paper bag to carry my soda and banana. When she turned to pick up an order, I quietly placed a couple of coins on the counter and hustled to catch the big silver bus to Goeteza.

Fifty-one

It had once been silver and you could still see a trio of blue stripes racing down the side. Years of Mexican sunlight had faded the colors to little more than memories. Rust spots decorated one side and a dent personalized the right rear. Shimmering in the morning light, my chariot shook itself. The windows were open, which meant the air conditioning had died. The scent of diesel fumes, stale sweat, and garbage accompanied me across the parking lot. The combination smelled like dying dreams to me.

I was lucky and got a window seat. An old man plopped down beside me and pulled a book out of a ragged satchel. The words were in Spanish, but it looked like a Bible.

A young couple occupied the seat in front of me. Their hair was long and black, glistening with oil. She cradled a sleeping baby in her arms, while he studied colored drawings of the human body from an anatomy text book. Bones were silver, muscles blue, veins green, and the arteries red. Looking over his shoulder at the pictures made it seem like all those colors were sparkling inside of me—as though I were the original Illustrated Man and everyone on the bus could see everything inside of me.

I turned away and looked out the window at the sunlight playing on the street, the tops of people's heads, and the façade of the building across the street.

The driver jammed the bus into gear and we jerked away, trailing fantails of dark smoke. The motor rumbled and the seats sagged as the old bus rolled across pitted asphalt. Midway down the aisle, I became surrounded by the odors of beer and onions, burning tobacco, perfume so sweet it made my stomach roll, and cologne so strong it made me sneeze. Running through it all was the sad, sweet odor of humanity.

Stained concrete and crumbling brick soon gave way to dark-leaved trees and long-horned cattle. Beyond the window there was a clearness to the air that seemed holy and I could see, across the fields—just at the edge of the horizon—indigo mountain tips that pricked the bottom of the sky.

Gradually the landscape changed, until miles of arid, flattened earth flowed toward the mountains like a great dun sea. The sun was higher and sunlight poured hot through the open window. As the shadows of Nogales faded, the miles grew between the small towns and the land, sun-splattered, empty, seemingly without end, whirled by under a cloudless sky. There was only wind and sun and the endless hum of rubber against asphalt—the lullaby of the road. Soporific conversations, murmurings, filled the bus. In a drowsy haze, I thought about Karen, then Jolene, and then Karen again. I refused to think about Mona. My eyelids felt coated with sand blown in from the great dry sea. Blue mountain tips rising at the edge of the world were only smudges.

Fifty-two

My eyes fluttered open as the bus sputtered to a stop. White houses spread out before me, deep in shadows. I could see all the way to the edge of town. Quiet consumed the late afternoon.

People were getting off the bus while others were getting on—as if they were exchanging lives. One of those who hustled on board wore a sweat-stained Giants baseball cap. A metal cooler hung from his shoulders on a broad fabric strap. His torso bent under its weight. The first passenger put a hand on the man's arm and they chatted in Spanish for a minute. The man in the baseball cap opened the cooler and handed the passenger a sandwich. He sold three more before he got to me. He eyeballed me from under the bill of his cap.

"American?"

"Yes."

He smiled at me, letting me see all his teeth. They were large, yellow, irregular. "All my sandwiches are good. I make them fresh every day. I have cheese sandwiches and meat sandwiches." He nodded at me, a nod for every other word. I found myself wanting to nod back.

"Ah, *señor*, I know you must be hungry. This is the Nogales bus and you have been riding most of the day. Ahead of you," he paused, shrugged, "truly, I cannot say much for the food."

He was right. I was hungry—it had been a long time since the bus station. However, I was afraid of the meat. "All right, give me a cheese sandwich. How much?"

He told me as he rummaged through his cooler. He gave me the sandwich. I had the correct change.

"How far to Goeteza?" I asked. Sleep had deprived me of my bearings. I felt lost, isolated, alone, in a universe vaster than I'd dreamed.

He paused stuffing pesos in his pocket and gave me a rabbit-quick look from under the stained cap bill. "You are going to Goeteza, *señor*?"

I nodded. "You don't seem to approve."

He lifted his shoulders up around his ears. "It is not that. Only I have recently heard disturbing things about Goeteza. You, of course, can go wherever your ticket takes you."

"What have you heard?"

"Many stories, but who can say if they are true." He shrugged again. "I, myself, have not been there for many years. Still, I meet the buses daily, going both ways, and the passengers, they tell me many things." His eyes probed my face like nut-brown searchlights. "*Señor*, many sad stories come from Goeteza these days."

The faces of the sons of Gomez rose before me. "What do you hear?"

He bent closer. His breath smelt of tobacco and beer. His voice was no more than a whisper. "I hear of drugs and robberies and rapes and murders." He crossed himself with quick stabbing motions. "I myself would not go to Goeteza. Perhaps you would like to change your ticket at the station. There is still time."

"*Gracias*," I said, "but I have friends there."

There was a solemn cast to his eyes. "I understand. A man must do what needs doing." He shifted the cooler so the straps rode more evenly across his shoulders, nodded again. He started down the aisle toward the back of the bus.

My legs were stiff and I was tempted to get off and stroll around the town that looked like a postcard picture. But the bus had pulled away from earlier stops unannounced and I was afraid of being left. The old man had taken his Bible and departed, so I stretched my legs across his empty seat, unwrapped my sandwich, and listened to the young mother in the seat in front of me coo to her baby.

I nibbled, listening to the baby-talk, thinking about what lay ahead, washing it all down with orange soda. My banana I saved for later. The mother fell silent and I gazed out the window. Above the peaks, the sky was turning to red and gold. Mountain shadows fell long and blue across the plain.

The bus driver came hustling out of the station and people began to settle in their seats. Only a dozen were left on board. The sandwich vendor patted me on the shoulder as he walked to the front of the bus. When the vendor stepped off the bus, the driver shifted gears and we rolled away into the dying afternoon.

Fifty-three

The sun was a snake, dying in a curling red smear on the western horizon. Twilight was falling hard and fast, sweeping down from the mountains, purple shadows spilling across the valley, covering the mesquite, the cactus, and the sagebrush.

I leaned back against the cracked brown vinyl and stared into the coming night, alone with my thoughts, my fears, my desires. For the first time in days I not only wanted a drink, I needed one. My insides were churning like one of those rock tumblers lapidary shops use to polish stones. Hundreds of zombies had lined up on the rim of canyon in my brain, waving spears as they danced in front of a flickering fire. They were screaming words I couldn't understand, but the message came through with a frightening clarity. They wanted me, lusted for my soul, hungered for my madness.

My hands were trembling. I felt exposed. I looked to see if anyone was watching me. Less than a dozen passengers remained and they all appeared occupied with their own visions. Stuffing my hands into the pockets of my jeans, I stared out the window until the blue-tipped mountains merged with the deepening blue of the sky and the dying red snake was no wider than a single strand of a spider's web.

I dug in my bag and found the banana—going soft and flecked with brown—and ate it. Night had taken over the land and only red exit signs and the glow of a cigar lit the interior of the bus. I could have been floating through the ebony of deep space. Lights from a passing car flickered against the window at the front of the bus. Then they were gone, nothing more than stars whirling through the night.

Sometime in that long night I slept, jolted from one surreal dream to the next. Just before dawn I woke in a cold sweat, dreaming of my mother. She had been dead so long the dream was more real than my memories. Perhaps, I thought, dreams were closer to the truth than memories, or the fulfillment of them.

Fifty-four

The bus was quiet as I watched the sun come over the top of the mountains and splash gold down furrowed slopes. The driver and I seemed to be the only ones awake to see the morning in. Daylight chased the wisps of voodoo dreams still lingering in the corners of my mind. The bus rounded a sharp turn and Goeteza spread out before me like fragments of my broken dream.

I blinked and Goeteza was a quiet, whitewashed town bathed in morning light. It looked so peaceful I wondered if the stories I'd been told were true. I looked around for a face I knew, but the streets were deserted except for an old dog stretched out in front of the *farmacia*. He pointed his baleful face at me, one brown eye glinting in the early light of day.

Airbrakes hissing, the bus slowed and pulled to the side of the road. The driver maneuvered the lever and the door whooshed open. I pushed myself off the cracked vinyl and stretched. A young boy, five or six, stared at me from the protective curve of his mother's arms. I smiled at him, but he kept his lips pressed together. Everyone else seemed to be asleep. As I walked down the steps the driver wished me good fortune in Spanish.

A putrid odor greeted me. The air was fetid and the stench made my stomach roll. It was easy to determine where the stench originated. Uncollected garbage pyramided in side streets and alleys. It spilled out of trashcans and boxes and in places it looked as if it were growing out of the dusty soil.

I strolled over to the *farmacia* and leaned against the building until the bus pulled out of Goeteza. No one was waiting to board and the driver eased the clutch in and pulled away, trailing a black rope of smoke. I watched until the bus was a blurred silver bullet. Then I turned and began to walk down the familiar street.

Half a block away I could see the lights in Gomez's restaurant. I paused and tried to clear my mind. Standing in the middle of the empty street I could smell bacon frying, strong coffee brewing, and the first cigar of morning. As I started walking again, Spanish voices flowed like a spring rain against my ears and I felt as if I had come home after a long journey in a strange land.

No one paid any attention to a solitary man walking quietly into the room. Conversations babbled on and men stared at their plates with a just-past-dawn glaze. Gomez was bent over, his head hanging below the counter. I walked toward him.

Before I was halfway there his head came up and I watched his eyes focus on me. A smile started to spread across his face, but he rubbed one hand across his mouth and jerked his head toward an empty stool at the far end of the counter. I crossed the floor and eased onto the stool.

Gomez fussed below the counter for a couple of minutes before he walked over. He carried a glass coffee carafe and a ceramic coffee mug and stopped several times to warm up cups for bleary eyed customers. When he reached my stool he placed the white cup down with a flourish.

"Coffee, *señor*?"

"Yes, black."

While Gomez poured, I swiped my eyes along the line of men at the counter, then across the room. There were no women, but there were many more light-skinned men than had frequented the restaurant during my previous tour of duty. From the snippets of conversation I could catch, a pair sounded German, one man was probably Italian, but the majority sounded like Americans. Most were younger than I was and wore their hair down over their collars. Several had beards. Earrings and tattoos were prevalent.

Gomez cleared his throat and I turned around. "Would you like some breakfast, *señor*?"

It was obvious my presence made him uncomfortable. I thought I knew why and decided to play along. "No thanks, I ate on the bus."

Gomez nodded and I watched his eyes. He couldn't keep them still. He started to say something, but just then someone called to him from the far end of the counter and he gave me an apologetic shrug and turned away, moving quickly, coffee sloshing in the carafe.

Sipping on coffee, I listened to the desultory conversations behind me. I could understand about half the Spanish and most of the rest. It didn't amount to much—a few complaints about the weather, the lack of money, and the cold-heartedness of women. The conversations were subdued, with none of the boisterous discussions, verbal bantering, and punch-on-the-shoulder joshing I remembered. In fact, about half the men looked hungover or stoned; the rest looked like they didn't give a damn.

The man on the stool beside me had finished playing with his eggs and was smoking a cigarette. He was a thin-faced, scraggly-bearded man who kept his thoughts to himself. His skin was sunburned and he wore an orange and white Tennessee Volunteers baseball cap. The grayish ash of his cigarette matched the color of his beard. Our eyes met and I nodded. He turned and looked the other way.

I nursed the coffee and watched Tennessee smoke. He was a slow smoker. When he finally finished, he ground the stub out against the rim of his plate, turned his head, and gave me a hard-eyed stare. He tossed a few pesos on the counter, turned and walked across the room without speaking.

Gomez and the man helping him stayed busy busing tables and collecting pesos. When the pace slowed, Gomez strolled over with his coffee carafe and poured me half a cup. As he picked up Tennessee's dirty plate, he spoke quietly out of the side of his mouth. "Meet me around back in twenty minutes."

When my cup was empty I paid the other man. He was new to me. There was an abrasion on one side of his face and he wouldn't look me in the eye.

Outside, the sun was higher in the sky, the heat starting to build. However, the stench was no better, so I turned away from the streets and started walking toward the river.

The rains had not come and the raging current I remembered had been reduced to a trickle. Only the deepest pools still held water. Stones lay smooth and dry in the riverbed, while dust cloaked the curling leaves on the trees.

I walked along the bank for a hundred yards, turned and came back without seeing anyone. When I'd lived in Goeteza before, the riverbank had been a popular strolling ground for young couples, old friends, and energetic boys with time on their hands. Now, I could hear the rustle of a small animal in the underbrush. From the limb of a cottonwood that overhung the riverbed, a pair of black-winged birds regarded me with hot yellow eyes.

By the time I climbed the path back to Goeteza, sweat was popping out on my face and trickling down the center of my back. There was no wind and muggy heat cloaked the town. Far away, pinned against the southwestern horizon, a few gray clouds hung low, almost kissing the mountain peaks. If they held rain it wouldn't be much.

I was anxious to see Gomez and picked up the pace in spite of the heat, stepping quickly through the shade of the huge cottonwood that stood behind the restaurant, crossing the yard in a few strides. I made myself small against the wall and scratched on the door like a wounded cat. It swung open and I stepped inside, nudging the door closed with a foot.

Gomez gave me a huge grin and enveloped me in a bear hug. His arms were strong around my back and I could feel his sweat through his clothes.

"*Amigo*, it is good to see you. Never did I expect to see you in Goeteza again." Releasing me, he stepped back and nodded. "You survived the crossing."

I nodded, "And so did your sons."

His eyes widened and his lips rearranged themselves. "You have news of my sons?"

"I have seen them."

Gomez took a step back, then a step forward. For a moment he stood still, his thick body swaying as though buffeted by a wind I couldn't feel. His arms quivered and his eyes searched my face. They looked greedy to me.

"How are they, *amigo*? Are they well?"

I smiled in an effort to reassure him. He looked like a man in great need of reassurance.

"They're fine now. Their group was picked up by a local version of the border patrol and they had to spend the night in jail. They're out now and staying with their American uncle."

His face underwent contortions before settling on confusion. "Their American uncle? But they have no uncle in America." I watched his eyes wash across my face. "Ah, I think now that I see. Could you be their American uncle, *Señor* Hampton?"

"I signed a few papers to that effect. My lawyer tells me we have bought a little time."

"You are certain my sons are all right?"

"Absolutely. While I am down here, they are staying with the woman I work for. She's a good person. They're in good hands." I tried to anticipate his next question. "I came here because of what they told me."

Gomez grabbed my right hand in his and began to pump vigorously. "Oh, *Señor* Hampton, I am so grateful. My wife and I, we have been so worried about our sons. I did not want them to go, but Goeteza is not the town it was when you were here. Do I understand that Tico and Manuel told you of the changes that have taken place?"

"They said that since I left many bad things have happened here."

Gomez shook his head. He looked like a puzzled bear. "You would not believe it. I would not believe it if I had not been here and seen them for myself."

Frustrated over the generalities, I wished, not for the first time, that my Spanish was better. Perhaps Gomez would have found it easier to relate the events in his native tongue.

"What has happened here?" I asked.

"Come," Gomez said, "sit down so that we can talk. It has been a busy morning and my legs are tired." Gomez smiled at me. The smile struck me as sad. "I am getting to be an old man, *amigo*." I smiled back. Feeling old I understood.

I followed him across the kitchen and we sat at the small table that had three good legs. Gomez's eyes canvassed the room. He sat with his head cocked to one side, listening to the morning. After a moment, he turned to face me.

"One must be careful in Goeteza these days. Lately, there are many hidden eyes and the walls often have ears."

"What is going on in this town, Gomez?"

"Coffee, *señor*?" He nodded toward a pot on the warming plate. "It is good. I made this pot myself."

Gomez was not a man to be rushed. I knew that, but I didn't like it. I didn't like anything about the current setup. Gomez was too nervous, the streets too deserted.

He poured with a steady hand, eased the pot back on the warmer and sat. In the light pouring in through the window, I studied his face. Lines I didn't remember etched his brow and his eyes were sunk deep in his skull. Dark and bottomless, they gave away nothing.

Steam rose like a hot, moist fog over his coffee. Gomez's eyes were focused on a place I couldn't see. I sipped coffee, waited. The coffee was strong.

"It began with the visitors," Gomez murmured, his voice uncertain, or perhaps puzzled, as though he knew his destination but was not sure which path would take him there. "A man and a woman. He is a distinguished looking man, slender, with silver hair and the manners of a gentleman. She is a big woman, not fat, you understand, but taller than many men and her body..." Gomez silhouetted air sculptures with his hands. "She has long dark hair, and her face, it is full of large bones."

The descriptions aroused memories. I could feel them stirring in the underbrush along the edges of my mind. "How did they arrive?"

"In a big black car."

"A Mercedes?"

"You have heard of them?"

Aromas of meat frying and beans baking, mingled with the scents of coffee, cigarette smoke, and sweat and filled the kitchen. Part of me wished I was back across the border with Karen. The rest of me knew I couldn't go there right now. "Believe I do know them," I said. "If I'm right, *amigo*, I know them very well. What have they done since they arrived?"

Gomez glanced down at his coffee, studied the dark surface for a moment, then lifted his eyes to my face. "They have nearly destroyed Goeteza, *Señor* Hampton. They have brought bad people here and run off many good ones."

"What sort of bad people?"

Gomez sipped his coffee. His eyes turned inward. What he was seeing was not in this room. I waited. After a moment his eyes lifted. They were unreadable.

"People who buy and sell drugs. All kinds of drugs flow into Goeteza now—marijuana, cocaine, heroin, and others I do not even know the names of. The people who handle these drugs are bad people. They have much money, though, and do what they want. If they want your donkey, or your car, or your house, or even your wife or your daughter they will offer to buy them from you. If you will not sell, they will take them from you." Gomez leaned closer. I could smell his sweat and the coffee on his breath. I thought I could smell his fear, but maybe that was only my imagination.

"If you try to stop them, they will kill you. Several who tried are now missing or dead." His head swung from side to side, a bell tolling for the dead and missing of Goeteza.

"Have the villagers not banded together and tried to stop them?" Goeteza was not a large town, but neither was it a few adobe huts at a crossroads. Surely, together, the citizens could have done something.

Gomez looked away and shrugged. "When they first came we did not understand them. We tried to be hospitable, but they deceived us. In only a few days many more of their kind came. These men had guns and knives. They were not afraid to use them. They are very dangerous men. The people of Goeteza are basically peaceful. We were not prepared for men such as these. We thought they existed only in books or movies."

"If they're who I think they are, you're right, they are very dangerous. Did they come from the east? From over the mountains?"

"They came from that direction, at least the first ones. In the last few weeks it seems as if they come from everywhere."

"Wonder why they chose to come to Goeteza?"

Gomez shook his head. "Who can say? I know they went first to see the man you call the Leather Man."

"That makes sense," I said. "He runs drugs. When I was here before he did it on a small-time basis. Sounds as if he's expanded."

"Now he has much more money than when you were here before."

"Stands to reason. Tell me, are there many Americans here?"

"*Sí.*"

"American women?"

"Only a few."

The table was jiggling. The coffee in my cup roiled like a lake surface in a rising wind. I looked down. My leg was bouncing up and down, brushing against the bottom of the table. I eased back in my seat and made myself take a deep breath.

"Is one of them blonde, with a long, thin face and green eyes? About my age?"

Gomez rubbed his chin. Stubble rustled under his palm. It sounded like a strong wind blowing through a Kansas wheat field. Then the lights changed in his eyes and he nodded. "I remember now. I have seen one who looks like that, but only a few times, from a distance."

Bitter thoughts tumbled over in my mind. All the pieces of the puzzle were starting to come together. "Have you seen her in the cantina?"

Gomez nodded, his dark eyes searching my face. I wondered what he was seeing.

"Was she with a younger man, one who is tall and slim and wears a gold chain around his neck?"

Gomez's eyes were full of questions he didn't ask. "I have seen just such a man with her."

I pushed my chair away from the table, stood up and walked to the window. Standing with my face in the sunlight pouring through the glass, I stared at the dusty white street.

Sweat dotted my forehead. A question formed in my mind. I didn't feel like facing Gomez at the moment, so I asked it without turning around. "What about the police in Goeteza? Why haven't they put a stop to the mess?"

Gomez was roaming around, rattling pans, opening and closing drawers. I kept staring at the street. My battered psyche found a comfort in its indifference.

"Two days after the first man and the woman came, the police chief was killed. His home caught fire in the night and he was burned to ashes. It was ruled an accident. The other two policemen, they are not strong like Chief Oliveries, and after what happened to him they do not do anything to try and stop the strangers."

"What about the army or the federal police forces?"

"Goeteza is a small town and very poor. We are on the wrong side of the mountain and difficult to get to. Goeteza is of no great value to Mexico. Eventually, the army patrol will come. However, they stay only a day or two. The evil ones simply stay in the shadows until the army leaves. They do not fear them much.

"We have sent requests for the army to come, but have received no response. Most people in Goeteza are too scared to leave their houses after dark, let alone testify against these banditos."

I turned away from the window. Gomez was scraping food off plates. He looked tired, and sad.

"You sent your sons away. Why have you stayed here?"

Gomez looked up from the dirty plates. His eyes were like brown stones set deep in his face. "My father and mother are still here. They are old and feeble. They could not survive a difficult journey. Also, they are very stubborn. Even if I had a way for them to go, they would not go. I know they will not leave this village. They will not leave their home. They gave me life. I owe them more than I can ever repay. I cannot abandon them, *señor*. You can see that."

There wasn't anything to say. To talk of his sons would only have created more sadness. There was plenty of that already. I walked over to the sink and started washing the dirty dishes.

Fifty-five

Midnight was dancing in the shadows as we walked out of the restaurant. You could hear the cool wind whining softly to itself in the alleys. The moon was full, but the sky was splattered with dark clouds and moonlight fell in broken silver ingots.

Above the wind, I could hear laughter and singing, mingling with shouts from the bars. Men and women wandered the streets. Sometimes they were arm-in-arm, and sometimes they were alone, except for a bottle. Men on raised porches leaned against railings, watching the streets, cradling a gun in their arms.

We kept to the darker side of the street, moving from one pool of shadows to another. For the first two blocks we didn't talk. Then we only whispered.

"There is where the Leather Man lives," Gomez murmured. His mouth was so close to my ear I could feel his breath.

"Your sons told me he practically runs the town."

"The dirty stuff, anyway. I think he works for the man and the woman you know, the ones with the Mercedes. In Goeteza his word is law. No one is brave enough to cross him. He is *uno* mean *bastardo.*"

Just hearing about him made me nervous. I changed the subject. "Where do the people with the Mercedes live?"

Gomez paused at the edge of a narrow street. "They stay at the Hotel Liberation. They have the entire third floor to themselves, and only their friends stay on the other two floors."

I waited until we had crossed the narrow street before I whispered my next question. "Do you see these people much?"

"Not much. Most of the time they are in their rooms. When they leave them they usually go out of town."

"Where do they go?"

"No one knows."

"When they are in Goeteza, how do they act?"

Gomez didn't answer. In the blackness thrown by a two-story hacienda, I saw the red glow of a cigarette and, as the clouds rearranged themselves, the glint of moonlight off metal. We walked without speaking until we were out of hearing range.

Gomez cleared his throat. "When these people go out in Goeteza the man does not say much. He never seems to get excited."

"And the woman?"

"One hears many stories. I cannot say for certain, as I have seen her only from a distance. However, people who have met her say that at times she is nice and even talks to the people of the village. Other times though, they say, she becomes angry for no apparent reason. People say that she can curse like a gaucho and that she has slapped some of the women and even one or two men. Manuel, the barber, swears she has had some of the men of Goeteza taken out at night and horsewhipped because they did not treat her with the respect she judged proper. I know for a fact she had some of her men shave the head of Angelique, the daughter of *Señor* Morales who runs the feed store, because the girl talked back to her."

I didn't doubt the stories. I knew Señora Ramirez well enough to believe anything anyone said about her. I could have told a few tales myself. Tales I never intended to tell.

We turned down a dusty side street, then angled across a small park. I could make out a swing set, a seesaw, and a soccer goal standing empty in the hollow dark. As we picked our way across the open ground, the moon slid out from behind a cloud and moonlight glittered off metal like a spell being cast.

Gomez was quiet, living inside himself, and we walked side by side across the park without speaking. Moving through the patchy moonlight, I thought about Señora Ramirez and Jolene and Karen and a woman named Mona whom I had once known for a few days that felt like a year. Many women were on my mind. All of them made me want a drink. I concentrated on walking.

Fifty-six

The promise of morning fell across my face and woke me. I rolled over and tried to go back to sleep, but the floor beneath my sleeping bag was hard and I couldn't recover my half-finished dreams. Thinking about what loomed before me, I sat up, put on my clothes, and rose to face the morning.

A quiet so deep it seemed profound enveloped the earth. It was as if the whole world were asleep except for one little lost alcoholic piss-ant. I let myself out the back door. Daylight was a blush on the mountain crests. I walked toward town, still asleep in the shadows of the night, with the cool air pressing against my face and my legs moving smoothly.

I crossed the park just as the first thin lines of sunlight striped the ground. Swings hung empty and dark still lingered in the street beyond. Wisps of fog clung to the treetops.

There was no traffic. Not even an old dog trotting home. No birds were singing. No morning radios blared. The morning silence was holy.

Daylight was winning the battle for the town square by the time I arrived. Darkness had backed into the corners and was trying to hang on. Leaning against the darkest wall of the post office, I waited for the world to wake up.

A door squeaked open down the street. A man with dirty-blond hair stepped onto a wooden porch. Even at a distance, he looked familiar. The man stretched as he walked across the rough boards. He dug a cigarette out of a shirt pocket and lit it with a kitchen match. Cupping the match in his hands, he turned his face toward mine. The Leather Man was alive and well and smokin'em in Goeteza. Edging back into the shadows, I studied the man who had helped change my life.

Smoke curled lazily from the business end of his cigarette. His head turned as if a sound I couldn't hear had caught his attention. I eased right, stepping into the edge of the shadows. I had to watch the changing light carefully. Exposure was a careless moment away.

Maybe that wouldn't matter so much. He was bound to have seen hundreds of Americans over the years and couldn't be expected to remember them all. If he did recall my face, so what? I'd just drifted back into town. Surely he wouldn't see me as a threat. Still, a small voice persistently told me to stay in the shadows.

The door squeaked again and a second man joined the Leather Man. One glance at his tall, lean-hipped body, topped by his wavy, dark hair, and I knew it was my old friend, Stan. From across the square, he looked suave and handsome in his open-necked polo shirt, cream-colored slacks, and tasseled loafers. Sunlight splashed across the upper half of his body and the gold chain he wore tight around his neck glittered like Inca treasure.

They were talking too low for me to understand the words. The hum of their voices was enticing and I moved deeper into the shadows, curled around the corner of the building and jogged down the side street. I made a wide loop and came up the street that ran behind the building where the two men were talking. I eased along the side of the building, watching where I placed my feet, staying close to the building, grateful for the thin, lingering shadows.

I could hear voices, two men and a woman. The woman's voice I knew instantly. Throaty and deep, I'd heard it make love to me and I'd heard it tell me lies. All those years came back to me with a blinding intensity. I hadn't realized how much I had cared. Once I'd thought it was the sexiest voice on earth. Of course, I'd been blitzed for much of our marriage. In the blue shadows I was stone cold sober. There are fools, I told myself, and there are damn fools. I inched my head around the corner.

Squinting against the light, I could make out the figures on the porch. Three of my favorite people in the world were lounging under the awning, sipping from coffee cups, smoking cigarettes, and chatting about the next shipment from Tucola, wherever the hell that was. Too far away to catch every word, I began easing closer.

Ten steps later I could see their faces clearly. They were staring at the sunlit street in front of them. A black Ford pickup was parked at the end of the alleyway. It was a chancy thing to do, maybe a stupid one, but I duck-walked across the packed bare earth and got my back up against the front wheel well, shaking and starting to sweat.

"I'm telling you, Jolene, we'd better get out while the getting's good. We've got enough to live like royalty in Vegas for six months. No need to press our luck."

"Oh shit, Stan, you get more nervous all the time. You're worse than some old woman. What's happened to you? Ramirez told us before we left Nogales this wouldn't be a picnic. Besides, this next shipment is the big one. Isn't it, Daryl?"

"Yeah," the Leather Man said. "It's a damn big one and it's due in tomorrow, day after for sure. I've got most of the mules lined up already, and I'll get the rest tonight. Once we deliver this load we'll all be set for years. Just be cool, dude."

"What about Ramirez?" Stan's voice rose and broke on the name.

"Don't worry about Ramirez." The Leather Man's voice was cold. I could picture the contempt on his face. I'd seen it before.

"To hell with Ramirez," he said. "I'm not afraid of him. After this shipment we don't need him. Not him, or his big-assed wife, or Mexico. We get the shipment and move the shit then blow this town. For two years I've been laying low and I don't aim to do that much longer. Nothing here for me, and I've been hankering for some down-home Cajun cooking, not to mention a certain Cajun woman. Once I get the payoff I'm to Baton Rouge."

"How long will it take to move the merchandise?" Jolene was already spending the money. I could hear it in her voice. That particular tone I'd heard before.

"Day or two at most. I'm going to deliver a shipment to Nogales myself and tie up a few loose ends. Then I'll head west. Got to collect from Brewster in Tijuana. I'll cross there. You two make the deliveries in Mexico City then fly to San Diego. We'll meet at the Marriott just north of Sea World and do the split. Then you can go to Vegas. Old Daryl is headed home."

"What sort of loose ends?"

"Shut up, Stan. It's obvious the man has some private business. Don't you have any sensitivity for a situation at all?"

"And you do? Lately all you seem to have any sensitivity for is the narrow end of a whiskey bottle. You're damn near as bad an alcoholic as that loser husband of yours. Wonder what ever happened to old Paul?"

A sharp retort of flesh on flesh cracked the morning open. Stan moaned, "What'd you do that for?"

"Don't you ever compare me to that worthless piece of whale shit. I took him for over three million, which we have somehow managed to blow, and next time I'll take someone even richer. I've just got to get a stake so I can finesse the part. Besides, why are you complaining about my drinking? You never minded before."

"You never went this wild before. Now when you drink you can't keep your hands off the flesh, any age, any size, any color." There was a whine in Stan's voice. I could have told him it was going to get him exactly nowhere.

"Understand this," Jolene said. "I'll drink what I want, when I want, and where I want. And, I'll goddamn well fuck who I want. Your nine inches are fine, but don't kid yourself, there are other big boys out there."

"Boys is right," Stan mumbled.

"What was that? Never mind, I need a real drink. This lousy coffee is killing me. Can't a lady get a drink around here before noon, Daryl?"

"Sure, if there was a lady around here." The Leather Man laughed. His laugh always sounded wet and nasty to me and my feelings weren't hurt when it turned into a coughing jag.

"Cut the crap, Daryl, and get me a drink. All this waiting makes me nervous. I thought Ramirez was coming this morning."

"On a good day it's a two-hour drive from his place. He'll be here."

Floorboards moaned. A door squeaked. It was like being blind and trying to follow a movie plot solely from the dialogue and sound effects. I was tempted to sneak a quick peek, but fear was a stronger emotion.

"Ramon," the Leather Man shouted, "Ramon, bring me a bottle. Whiskey. The good stuff."

"Maybe Stan would like a Coke, Daryl. Would the fearful gentleman like a Coke?"

"Shut up, Jolene. I'll only take so much, even from you."

"No, you shut up, Stan. You'll take it and you'll like it. You know where your next snatch is coming from and your next whiskey and your next wad of cash, not to mention your goddamn airline ticket to San Diego. You mess with me and I'll cut your dick off and stuff it down your throat."

Stan didn't respond. Maybe he was biding his time; maybe he knew the truth when he heard it. In the silence I could hear birds stirring in the mesquite trees and the sound of an acoustic guitar playing on a radio.

"Damn, why doesn't Ramirez come? And where is that man with my drink?" Jolene's voice was thick with impatience. I thought I could also detect a trace of nervousness.

"Ramon," bellowed the Leather Man. "Ramon, where the hell are you? Hurry up, you Mexican bastard."

The door squeaked open. "Ah, here's my drink," Jolene said. "You're a good man, Ramon."

Stan mumbled too low for me to hear. There was the clink of glass and the sound of liquid pouring. The morning fell quiet again. I tried to think, but the silence was too loud.

I was glad when a motorcycle engine revved to life a couple of blocks away. My legs were beginning to cramp and I stretched them out in the dust. The silence stretched, too, feeding on itself and growing until it seemed to cover Goeteza. At the back of my brain a plan began to take form.

Stan's voice, high-pitched and querulous, broke the stillness. "That's two already."

"So," Jolene said.

"So, don't you think you need to slow down? Ramirez will be here any minute, and you know how your mouth runs when you've been drinking. We don't want to screw this deal up."

"I can hold my liquor and my mouth. Don't you worry. In fact, you're the one who had better shut his mouth before it gets shut for you."

"I just don't want something going wrong. Ramirez is no fool. If he thinks we can't handle our end he won't take the chance."

"Don't worry," said the Leather Man. "Ramirez will never know what hit him."

"You sure you've got the right men for the job?" Jolene's voice was sharp and clear, as if she had moved to the side of the porch closest to me.

"Reuben and the Jose with three fingers. Manuel will be there for backup."

Jolene laughed, throaty in the morning air. "They'll take care of it, all right. Those first two even I wouldn't want to cross." She fell silent for a moment, then added in a darker voice. "Don't forget the woman is mine. I hate that bitch and her big fat ass and her superior attitude. Before I'm done she'll be looking at the world one hell of a lot differently."

I could hear the sound of a car motor in the distance. As it grew louder I rolled over and scooted under the truck. Dust tickled my face. Looking out from the cool darkness into the sunlit square, I felt like a lost spaceman staring into a newborn sun.

The Mercedes rolled to a smooth stop. From grasshopper level I watched my former host and hostess step out of the car, walk across the dirt, step onto the porch. Fear crawled on its belly through my intestines. I shivered while sweat ran down my back in a thin cold stream. I lay with one side of my face in the dirt, moving only my eyes. I tried to breathe shallowly, but my breath rasped in my ears. I said a silent prayer.

When I got my breath under control and the jackhammer in my chest slowed, I tried to do some thinking. I couldn't concentrate, so I gave it up and rolled back over, scooting closer to the porch.

I didn't like doing it. My body was awash in sweat and my left eye had developed a tic, but this was one conversation I couldn't afford to miss.

The preliminaries were winding up. They had the weather and the car ride out of the way. The three men stood in the middle of the porch, drinks in hand, towering above me like giants. The women had gone to neutral corners. I could see the left side of the Leather Man's face and all of Stan's. He looked scared enough to cry, but he wasn't. He sipped on a short glass full of dark liquid. Ramirez was turned away from me; he was talking. His soft voice filled with hard words. The other two men appeared to be hanging onto every one of those hard words.

"The shipment comes tonight. I have received assurances. We must be ready. My men have heard rumors that the army plans to come this way soon."

"But they were here just last month." The whine in Stan's voice grated on my nerves.

I couldn't see the look Ramirez gave him, but Stan's face withered, the lines deepening. He was aging by the minute. If I'd been charitable I'd have felt sorry for him. However, I hadn't mastered forgiveness yet.

"Shut up, Stan," the Leather Man said. Ramirez made quieting sounds in his throat.

"I understand your point," he said. "However, not all of the officers are as cooperative as we wish they were, nor are all of them amenable to bribery. Frankly, some of them cannot be bought or scared off." Ramirez's voice sounded like the voice of experience.

"You sure of the info?"

"My employees have friends and family in the army. They hear things you would never dream of. Trust me, we must move quickly."

"We're ready," said the Leather Man. Stan swallowed, then nodded.

"Good, the shipment will be here by dark. Juan will be the driver. You know him?"

Stan nodded. He was getting good at that. His head bobbed like it was on a tight spring.

"You must be ready to unload and move the merchandise into the distribution pipeline. You may not have long. Understand?"

"We'll be ready. Haven't we always been?" The Leather Man was selling. I wondered if Ramirez was buying.

"You have always handled your end. However, this is the biggest shipment we have ever had. Much money is involved. I run a big operation, much bigger than you realize. Of late the cash flow has been poor." Ramirez shifted position and half of Stan's face disappeared. The remaining half looked like it wished it could.

"I need major cash from this operation," Ramirez said. "I owe people money. Not the sort of people who will wait long."

"Speaking of waiting," Jolene interrupted from the far side of the porch, "I'm tired of waiting for another drink."

"You always want another drink," *Señora* Ramirez said.

Jolene pushed herself off the rail and started for the other woman. "You bitch," she snorted.

Stan grabbed her arms and the Leather Man started talking loud and fast. A smile curled the thick lips of Señora Ramirez as she lifted her broad bottom off the rail. I watched it sashay inside. Stan hustled Jolene off the porch and around the far side of the building. The Leather Man was trying to sell Ramirez on staying for some party he'd set up. Ramirez turned and started for the door. His face looked like brown stone. His eyes chunks of dark, frozen ice. Just before he went through the door he turned and looked in my direction. Blood seemed to solidify in my veins. The second he turned his head I started scooting backwards through the dust.

Out from under the truck, I crawled through the dirt until I could get my back up against the shadowed wall of the building. Praying Stan and Jolene stayed on their side of the building, I sucked in a lungful of air and started running, grateful to be alive.

Fifty-seven

Darkness was falling in the valley. Sheets of purple had collapsed on the streets of Goeteza. Sunlight still glittered off the mountain peaks, while coral and tangerine smears were finger-painted on the western sky.

Gomez and I worked our way toward the center of town. Streets were nearly vacant; only the stray motorcycle or dilapidated car chugged home against the coming night. We traveled side streets and alleys, cutting across vacant lots where we could, sticking to the shadows when we couldn't.

Earlier in the day we'd borrowed a Chevy Vega with a rusty floorboard and a spider-webbed rear windshield and moved Gomez's mother and father and his wife to a cousin's farm eleven miles south of town. We'd helped his cousin with a few chores and spent time practicing with a pair of pistols Gomez had borrowed. Rising wind drove clouds across the face of the cratered moon and tugged at my hair. Gomez's shirttail flapped behind him.

"You think they will come tonight, the army men?"

Even though our shoulders were almost touching, I could barely hear him over the wind. "Don't know about them," I said, "but Ramirez's men will come, the ones with the shipment. He was sure of that."

"This is the man you thought you knew?"

"I know him. Don't let his silver hair and fine clothes fool you. He is one dangerous hombre."

Gomez led us down a winding dirt alley I'd never seen. "Will there be trouble tonight?"

"Maybe. For sure if the shipment and the army arrive at the same time. You know, Gomez, I've been wondering all afternoon about something."

"What?"

"If Ramirez had informers inside the army, isn't it possible the army has informers inside his outfit?"

"*Si.*"

"I agree. Something's brewing. It's alive and growing and it's going to explode soon. My hunch is it will happen tonight."

Two blocks from downtown I glanced at Gomez, wondering if he thought I was going loco. If I hadn't overheard the conversation on the porch I'd have wondered myself.

"One thing for sure, *amigo.*"

"What's that?"

"I'm going to settle accounts with a certain American couple."

We turned north toward Gomez's restaurant and jogged across a narrow slice of sand and prickly pear. The blackened skeleton of a house leaned into indigo shadows. It was easy to imagine ghosts lounging on the charred furniture.

We worked our way around the back of the feed store and up Zapata Street. Night was coming in a furious hurry. Lights burned in the haciendas and far away, at the apogee of the mountains, the last sunlight shimmered against white stone peaks like the final light of a dying world. Beyond the pinpoint of light the sky was so black it had taken on a burnished hue, as though it were evolving into a new color.

Gomez touched my arm. "These people, Stan and Jolene—"

"Yes."

"I know them. They are the sort of people who give gringos a bad name."

"That's one of the reasons why I have a score to settle with them."

"One?"

"The other's personal."

We sidled around the corner and stood in the blackness with our backs against a still warm adobe wall of the barbershop. My heart was pounding and the Colt was heavy in the waistband of my jeans. In the thick darkness, my nerves pulsed like quicksilver.

A single low-watt bulb was burning in the back of the barbershop. Gomez's upturned face reflected the light. "How is it, *Señor* Hampton, that you know such bad people?"

"I'm married to one of them."

A low rumble reached us. It sounded like it was coming from the bar at the far end of the street. The Leather Man's house was only a few yards to the east. I was interested in both places. I studied the block. Nothing was moving. I tapped Gomez on the shoulder and we started walking toward the outskirts of Goeteza.

We were no more than a quarter of a mile away and the noise increased with every step. Halfway there, the lights of a car stabbed at the darkness and we pressed against the nearest building. The car kept rolling. Its taillights swung into the curve and disappeared.

The wind was whining like a wounded animal and the Leather Man's house was as dark as the mountains behind it. "Nobody home," I whispered in Gomez's ear. "Let's check out the bar."

"Okay, but perhaps it would be good to go beyond the curve and curl behind the building, then work our way back. Perhaps that way we could see the people in the bar before they see us."

His logic was sound. Much better for me to see the old gang first. At some point our paths would cross. However, I wanted to determine where and when.

"No time like the present," I said, and we started moving. Metal pressed against my stomach like an anchor, a comfort, a promise. Wind howled through the underbrush and blew grit against our faces. I walked on into a dark, noisy world I didn't know.

A truck lumbered up the grade, its lights glowing like gigantic tiger eyes. We crouched in the brush and watched it pass, black and ominous, its motor growling above the wind. When the truck's taillights disappeared around the curve we started moving deeper into the underbrush, making a wide circle behind the bar, trying to come in on the blind side.

Wind was whipping at our faces and pushing the clouds around so that for a few seconds the moon broke through and bled silver across the face of the earth. We followed the curl of the hillside, moving up a rock-strewn embankment, then down again, before crossing an almost barren flat that lay directly behind the bar.

Above the wind we could hear laughter and the blare of music. With all that noise, Pancho Villa's army could have ridden right up to the front door without being challenged. However, I didn't trust Ramirez and the Leather Man not to have sentries posted, so I moved cautiously. Didn't want to stumble across a doped-up fucker with an AK-47.

Twenty yards later the cover gave out and we crossed the open ground on hands and knees, trying to time the movement of the moonlight. I couldn't hear Gomez, but I sensed him moving beside me. Blood sang in my ears and my heart pounded. I kept expecting to hear shouts or gunshots, but there was only the wind and the laughter and the music and my own ragged breathing.

When we reached the flickering edges of the light that spilled from the windows, we got off our hands and knees, crossing the final few yards in a low crouch, praying no one could see us.

Music pulsed and I could feel the walls vibrating faintly. Blasts of laughter and Spanish rose above the music. For a few seconds, the ocean of sound ebbed and I could hear the wind moaning. A woman shrieked with pain, or pleasure—I couldn't tell which. My legs had started trembling, so I leaned against the walls and tried to gather myself.

There were no windows along the back of the bar, only a loose fitting door that allowed a thin band of light to seep out. I needed to see who was inside. Keeping tight against the wall, we worked our way toward the front of the bar.

As we edged down the side of the building, I began to crawl. A car door slammed and sporadic bursts of conversation in Spanish came to me on the wind. At the first window I turned and whispered to Gomez. "Stay here. No sense in both of us taking the risk. Don't plan to be long. Just catch a glimpse of what's going on inside. Understand?"

"*Si.*"

"If anything happens, don't wait around, just hightail it back the way we came. Work your way back to town, sticking to the shadows, but don't act like you're sneaking. If anybody asks, you're just out for a stroll. You're a native so that should play."

"I understand. But what do you think will happen?"

"Who knows? With all the guns and drugs and belligerent women around, World War Three might break out." I fumbled in the darkness and found his hand. "Later."

"Later," he whispered. He spoke again, but I was already moving and the wind whipped his words away.

I snuck a glance through the first window, but all I could see was the back of a man wearing a ZZ Top tee-shirt. I ducked and kept moving.

~ * ~

The ground beside the building was worn smooth and enough light spilled through the windows to give me a good idea of what lay ahead. The wind was loud enough to cover my footfalls. Nobody could hear me coming. The downside to that was, of course, that I couldn't hear them either. So I kept pausing and peering to see if anyone was there. All I saw was darkness.

Shadows moved in the headlights of a large truck at the front of the building. Above the wind and the low rumble of the truck's motor I could hear a burgoo of bracero Spanish and broken English. Light glinted off metal and I hit the ground.

Guards had been posted at the front corners of the bar. Two of them had stepped out of the shadows. The guns cradled in their arms made my guts churn. Fortunately, they were looking toward the truck. I scooted to the middle window and peered in through the glass. The ground was higher here and I only had to stand on tiptoes to see clearly.

The joint was one long room, erratically lighted, with a high wooden bar running in front of the wall opposite from me. A dozen stools, all occupied, stood in front of the bar. Small round tables were slung haphazardly around the room. Each was ringed by five or six straight-backed wooden chairs. Somebody sat in almost every one. From one corner a jukebox blared and there was a small dance floor at the back. Eighty percent of the people in the room were men.

It took my eyes a couple of minutes to adjust to the light. It took them a couple of more to find what I was looking for.

They were in the back, at separate tables. Ramirez was wearing a white suit and an open-neck shirt the color of cornflowers. Every silver hair was in place and his face was placid. He might have been listening to the Mexico City Philharmonic.

His wife sat across the table from him with her back to me. Her hair hung like polished jet across shoulders as broad as a man's. She sat stiffly in her chair, chin up, hands spread on the table.

Stan, Jolene, and the Leather Man sat at an adjacent table with my old buddy from Tennessee and a short dark man I'd never seen. I wondered if the Leather Man's posse was inside the bar, or waiting in the shadows. The stranger and the Leather Man seemed to be carrying the conversation. Amidst the animated twistings of their faces I could make out their lips moving. Stan had both hands wrapped around a beer bottle. Jolene downed her drink in successive swallows and signaled for another. She turned her head and for a moment stared straight at my window. I felt a chill in my bowels before she slowly rotated her head in the direction of Señora Ramirez. Hatred, disgust, and envy spread across Jolene's face.

The short man made a dramatic point, screwing up his face and slapping a hand on the table. The Leather Man nodded. The short man extended his right arm and a flat package wrapped in grocery paper exchanged hands. Tennessee was as still as a cigar store Indian.

The Leather Man slid a finger along the folds and tore the wrapping. He studied the contents briefly, then passed the package to Stan, who did the old finger taste test. Stan nodded and the Leather Man turned and gave Ramirez the eye. They exchanged inconspicuous nods. The Leather Man slid a thin briefcase I hadn't noticed from under the table.

Dark Man picked up the briefcase and laid it in his lap. He cracked it open and surreptitiously eyeballed the contents. He nodded at Ramirez and the Leather Man as he snapped the briefcase shut. I watched him take a deep breath, glance around the room, stand and walk out without looking back. Ten feet from the door, he jerked his head at three greasy looking men holding up the wall. They pushed themselves off and followed him out of the building. I watched them disappear then turned my eyes back to the tables.

Ramirez and his wife were talking. He said something that made her lift her hands from the table and lean forward. I couldn't see her face but something in her response transformed his face to stone. He mouthed a few choice words and stood. She didn't try to stop him. Instead, she slugged down her drink and turned around in her chair, her eyes settling on Jolene.

Ramirez walked across the dingy room like he owned it. His expression never changed and his carefully sculpted cap of silver hair never moved. Alone, he walked into the night.

As if in response, the wind began to shift and the night took on a cooler edge. I decided that was a cue to follow Ramirez. Sliding under the light sloshing over the windowsills, I swung out into the darkness, circling the guards.

I needn't have worried about them. People were entering and leaving the roadhouse in erratic streams that flowed by the guards and were swallowed by either the windswept night or the lighted barroom. The guards stood like so many security cameras, observing and recording the human migration. The difference between the guards and security cameras was that the guards were armed.

Ramirez's silver hair was as easy to follow in the darkness as a lantern. I curled around the perimeter of the graveled parking lot, bisected the incoming flow of humanity, then hustled after Ramirez. He was walking rapidly toward his black Mercedes. The murmur of its motor was barely discernible in a momentary respite of the wind.

I jogged across the gravel, cutting the angle. Ramirez had one hand on the open rear passenger door. Somehow he heard me above the clamoring wind, or maybe his animal instincts sensed my presence, and he turned his head.

We stared at each other across the roof of the Mercedes, our faces lit only by the dome light of his car. His eyes glittered like a wild animal's. Wind whipped at his silver hair as his expression changed from annoyance to recognition, and then to something more than surprise but less than fear.

We stood without speaking, the wind howling in our ears and my heart pounding against the wall of my chest. His head moved and I thought he was going to get into the car without speaking. But he was only focusing on me from another angle. I became vaguely conscious of the blurry face of the driver and the bulk of another body in the front seat. The pulse in my left temple had started pounding and my right eye had developed a tic.

Ramirez moved his head again and caught a stray shaft of moonlight. His face looked older than I remembered. He watched me absorb his face. Something changed in his eyes and his lips rearranged themselves.

"I know you from somewhere, don't I?"

"Probably do," I said.

"Now I remember you for sure. You have a distinctive voice, even for a *Norte Americano*. I don't recall your name, but it will come to me."

"Don't worry about it…you won't be using it again."

"You sound very certain, *señor*."

"I am. I don't plan to ever see you again."

"Perhaps that is for the best."

"Trust me, it is. You know, Ramirez, I have this funny feeling your world is about to come to an abrupt end."

"Because of you?"

"In part."

"You sound very sure." His face was settled again; it could have been carved from cool marble.

"I am. However, I think you've already been thinking along the same lines."

Something twisted in his face, but he smoothed the lines out with a visible effort. His face had changed though, subtly, in indefinable ways that looked permanent.

"You read minds, *señor*?"

"I plan to do lots of things; some of them aren't nice. Trust me, Ramirez, you don't want me in your life."

"Then perhaps I should have you eliminated." His voice was calm. He might have been discussing calling the roach exterminator.

"You've got enough trouble already with your companions and that private prison you call a farm. No telling how many deaths are on your hands. I know of one, a man named Wilson. He was a good man who shouldn't be dead. Remember him, Ramirez?"

He shook his head. He was looking older by the minute.

"Probably you don't. There have been so many, and they were all unworthy of your attention, nothing but animals who had messed on your property. Now it's all going to come back to haunt you. Your best choice is to get the hell out of Mexico. Even it's not big enough to hide in forever."

I was talking fast, trying to sell him. I knew my limits. I had no army, only Gomez armed with one old pistol that wouldn't hit Ramirez's Mercedes at forty yards. Stan and Jolene were plenty for me to deal with. My guess was that if Ramirez left, most of the guns went with him. Now that I knew the lay of the land better, I could always make a few phone calls later. I owed Wilson more than that, but I had to deal with reality. Superman had been missing a long time.

"You talk like a brave man," Ramirez said, "but talk is cheap. You did not always talk this way. When I knew you, you were a man of no consequence. Why should I listen to you now? I am a man of power and influence. Many men will do what I say, when I say it, and they will ask no questions."

"You didn't get so powerful by acting stupidly. Use your brain, Ramirez, and listen to me. Would I be here if I didn't have backup? This part of the world is changing and you're scraping the bottom of the barrel to find your business partners. For sure one is a coward and another is a lush. None of your compadres can be trusted. Surely your spies have told you the army will come to Goeteza soon. If not tonight, tomorrow or next week. If I were you, I wouldn't want to be here when that happens. Also, as you said, I'm not the man I was. Know what I have been doing these past few months, Ramirez?"

"No," he said over the wind. "I don't know. How could I? What have you been doing, *Señor* Hampton?" He showed me his fine white teeth. "I told you I would remember your name. I remember everything."

"Just forget my name. You won't be needing it. What I've been doing lately is kicking some zombie ass, as my old drinking compadre Pedro Romero would say, and you are one of the zombies, Ramirez."

Ramirez chuckled into a dip in the wind. "I am not afraid of you, *señor*, not even if you are loco, not even with all your backup." He looked around the parking lot. "Where are they? Where are all your soldiers?"

"Don't worry about them. Worry about me if you stay here. Some of your friends have a surprise coming and, believe me, you don't want to get caught in the crossfire." I lifted the gun from the waistband of my pants. The barrel glittered in the moonlight. I was careful to point it away from Ramirez. I hadn't forgotten the occupants of the Mercedes. I didn't have a death wish.

Fear crawled across his face, making it to his eyes before he beat it back down. I had to hand it to Ramirez, he was one cool bastard.

"Friends? Crossfire?"

"Yeah, some of the people you were just visiting with. Specifically, the man and the woman who are with the Leather Man."

"The Leather Man? Oh yes, I know who you mean. And I know the couple you mentioned." He shrugged his shoulders. "They are not friends of mine."

"Mine either, but they know me, and they'll soon know me even better. They won't like it."

Ramirez asked a question with his face.

I answered it by lifting the gun. His eyes followed it like it was a snake. "I'm not waiting on the army to repay my debts." I stared into his eyes. "You don't want to be around."

Ramirez stared back. His eyes were dark. Looking into them was like peering into a bottomless well.

"My wife is still in there."

I couldn't let him go back in. It was too chancy. The Leather Man hadn't survived by being unobservant and Stan was looking for an excuse to bolt.

"You don't want to be there when I go in. There are many beautiful women. With your money you can pick and choose. Ask yourself, is she worth it?"

Ramirez stared at me, keeping his thoughts private. Time seemed elastic. I grew conscious of my breathing, and the fear crawling around inside me. Then he smiled. His lips looked like miniature ice sculptures.

"Perhaps you are correct. All day I have had, what do you call them, bad vibes. In my youth I learned to trust my instincts. I will trust them now. Perhaps I should have you killed, but I will not. I understand about a man and his business." He leaned one arm on the roof of the Mercedes. I couldn't read his expression. "May I say, at the risk of offending you, that I hope we never meet again, *Señor* Hampton?"

"We won't if I have anything to say about it."

He nodded as if to punctuate the exchange, ducked his head and disappeared into the Mercedes. The driver slid the transmission into gear and the big car began rolling smoothly across the gravel. For an instant, Ramirez's face was ghostly behind the glass then he was gone. I watched the Mercedes until it merged with the night. I started walking toward a knot of people drifting in the direction of the bar.

Fifty-eight

Inside, the party had gone to hell. The noise level had risen precipitously and much of the crowd had spilled out onto the porch and the dark grounds beyond.

Between parked pickups, two men gestured wildly, arguing about a soccer game or a woman or both; they seemed to be talking at cross purposes. My Spanish was too poor to follow the argument. A circle of onlookers jeered the men.

Closer to the bar, small knots of men stood drinking, talking softly, watching the shadows move. In the backseat of a nearly new Ford a couple embraced. Their lips were pressed together and one of the man's hands was busy below the woman's waist.

The music had changed to a pulsing jungle rhythm, cranked so loudly that the air in the parking lot seemed to vibrate. Glass smashed and a man cursed. Out in the dark a woman sobbed.

Only one of the guards was still on duty, and he wasn't seeing anything short of someone attempting to murder him. I stepped over a shirtless man passed out face down in the gravel and up onto the porch. Ignoring the guard, I took a deep breath and went inside.

In seconds my ears were ringing. Men were shouting orders at waitresses, who shouted them at the bartenders, who only returned dull looks and poured whatever was at hand. I felt like having a good shot myself. Old habits never die—they just reappear at the most inopportune moments.

People were so thick in front of the bar there were no aisles. A writhing mass of humanity obscured the tables. Lowering my shoulder, I bulled through a snarl of drunks. They shoved at me, but those were only reflex actions. They so were drunk I could have been a bull in a pink bikini and they wouldn't have noticed. I sidestepped two men arm wrestling and eased through a seam in the crowd. I could hear women screaming.

A circle had formed around two tables in the back. Bodies were packed so tightly I couldn't see what was happening. I could hear the screaming though, high and shrill, rising above the shouts of the spectators. Climbing on an abandoned chair, I peered over the crowd.

My ex-wife and my former warden were screaming at each other from the middle of the circle. Jolene's blouse was already ripped and drooping like a flag in becalmed seas. One white shoulder glistened. She waved a broken beer bottle in her right hand, the jagged edge slicing the air. Señora Ramirez circled her warily. Black hair had fallen around her face like an ebony curtain. Blood seeped from a small cut on her left arm.

"You bitch!" Jolene screamed. "I hate your condescending guts. You think you're so damn special. Whatever you want you get, all the money, all the men. Well tonight I'm going to fix you. I'm going to cut your tits off." Glass glittered as the bottle arched through the air.

Señora Ramirez sidestepped the clumsy thrust and shoved Jolene in the back as her momentum carried her by. Jolene stumbled into a table and staggered sideways. As she started to fall, one of the spectators grabbed her and spun her back around. She was thick-footed and slow and the señora was ready for her. Mrs. Ramirez slid to one side and hooked her left fist into Jolene's face. Jolene moaned and the bottle slid from her hand.

For a moment Jolene's hands explored her face. Suddenly she screamed with rage and rushed at the señora with slapping hands. One or two slaps grazed the señora, but most were wild and ineffective. Arm weary and drunk, Jolene's fury was soon spent. Her hands dropped and hung loosely by her side as she swayed unsteadily. The señora quickly stepped in and slapped Jolene hard across the face.

Jolene screamed and staggered back. The señora slapped her again and blood curled in a thin red line from her nose. Jolene tried to cover up, but she was too drunk, nothing but an easy target. The señora balled up her right hand and drove it against Jolene's left cheekbone, sending her stumbling across the floor. Dazed and confused, virtually out on her feet from the combination of alcohol and fists, Jolene swayed gently. She looked ready to topple at any moment. The crowd screamed for the kill.

A smile spread across the señora's thick lips. In the light of the bar her lipstick was the color of blood. The crowd shouted for her to finish the *gringo*, beat her senseless, teach her a lesson. The lights in her eyes changed and the señora gathered herself, squared her shoulders, lowered her head, and charged across the floor like an enraged bull.

I don't know if Jolene saw her coming, or if her legs fortuitously gave way. But just as the señora was closing in, Jolene stumbled to her right. It wasn't much, just a few inches, but it was enough.

Señora Ramirez smashed full speed, head first, into the concrete block wall. The crowd fell silent. Pirouetting slowly, she stumbled over a fallen chair and let out a low moan. Her eyes rolled up, her legs turned rubbery then gave way. The back of her skull cracked sharply against the concrete floor. One more long, low moan escaped her lips, a shiver raced through her body and she went still as marble.

It took Jolene a few seconds to realize what had happened. She swayed slowly, woozily, seemingly oblivious to the woman at her feet. Her eyes began to clear and she sank to her knees with a guttural moan of satisfaction.

Straddling the helpless *Señora* Ramirez, Jolene began to punch her in the face. She bloodied the señora's nose and split her lips. Then she began to slap the unconscious woman, striking her again and again until the woman's head began to loll like a loose-necked doll's. An angry murmur ran through the crowd, but the Leather Man pushed aside a Mexican with a bushy mustache and tugged a pistol out of his waistband. The crowd fell silent.

Jolene began to systematically strip Señora Ramirez. Her fingers fumbled with the buttons and snaps, but she kept at it. Many in the crowd gasped when the señora's breasts swung free. A few of the men whistled. One of the women laughed. Jolene grabbed a nipple between each thumb and forefinger and twisted viciously. The señora moaned but didn't open her eyes.

Jolene struggled with the panties, but in the end she got them off and the señora lay naked as the day she was born. I could hear a murmur of Spanish, but it was too low and fast for me to interpret.

After pinching and pulling various body parts, spending extra time on the private ones, Jolene struggled to her feet. She walked unsteadily to a nearby table, lifted a glass half-full of what looked like whiskey and drank it without stopping.

I watched her neck work as she swallowed. When she lowered her head, her eyes were clear—as if the whiskey had been medicine. She stepped across the floor, bent at the waist, and grabbed a double handful of the señora's hair. Cursing steadily, she began to pull the large, inert body across the floor.

She made it halfway to the door before her legs gave out and she sat with a smile plastered on her face. Two waitresses grabbed the señora by the arms and dragged her out of the bar. The señora looked like a fine dead bull being dragged from the ring.

I turned and began to work my way against the tide rushing to see the spectacle. A man bumped into me and started jabbering. His breath reeked of alcohol. I couldn't understand a word. I pushed him away and kept moving. A woman sat at the bar alone, tears rolling down her face like runoff from a tropical rain. I felt a little like crying myself, although I couldn't have told anyone why.

I stepped off the porch into the darkness. The last guard on duty passed me on the steps going the other way.

The wind was up again and cool against my face. I paused in the windswept darkness, letting my eyes adjust, trying to figure out my next move. Around me, the night was falling apart, taking my plans with it. Suddenly, I was sick of mankind in general and myself in particular.

The party from hell was dying a slow death. A few men still wandered around with bottles in their hands, talking quietly, but most of the crowd had departed. Empty spaces glittered in the parking lot. Under the trees, in the deeper shadows, glowing tips of cigarettes were visible. They were widely spaced, as if the men holding them had gone off to enjoy a final smoke before they died alone, like a cat or an elephant.

I hadn't done what I'd promised myself I would do, but it no longer seemed to matter. I glanced at the shadows once more, where the glowing tips of the cigarettes looked like so many wayward fireflies. The men with the bottles had drifted away and there was only the comforting darkness, the murmuring wind, and a growing sense within me that I needed to move on. I was turning to go back to Gomez when the two waitresses who had drug *Señora* Ramirez away emerged from the darkness. They were giggling. I reversed direction and started walking toward where they had emerged from the night.

It didn't take long to find her. She was trussed up like a hog awaiting slaughter, lying face down across a board laid between two piles of cinder blocks, with her hands and feet roped together. Moonlight highlighted her backside. She was moaning softly to the uncaring night.

"Help me, somebody. Help me."

I walked over, cupped her chin in my palm, and lifted her head. Her eyes were open, blinking sporadically but not focusing. I stared at her face, recalling all the promises I'd made myself. Now, in my moment of truth, they seemed hollow. As I watched, her eyes began to clear and come into focus.

"Remember me, *Señora* Ramirez?"

She didn't. I could tell by the eyes. I shifted position so the moonlight struck my face. Then the lights in her eyes rearranged themselves and she said, "Oh."

"Yeah, thought you would remember. Only this time it seems the roles are reversed." The wind was rising, pushing through the trees, singing as it went. I wondered if it had ever serenaded a stranger couple.

"Help me, *señor*."

"Do you remember what happened?"

She closed her eyes and nodded. "Help me."

"Like you helped me?"

Her eyes opened. "Oh, *señor*, I am so sorry for that. I should not have done what I did, but I have a terrible temper and sometimes it takes possession of me."

"Looks like something else took possession of you tonight," I said.

"Oh, that bitch, that American bitch. Did she do this to me?" Tears of frustration began to gather in her eyes.

"Most of it, at least what you didn't do to yourself."

"Oh please, *señor*, my head hurts so bad and it is so uncomfortable in this position. Just cut me loose. At least you can do that."

I didn't answer. I was listening to the sound of powerful engines rumbling in the dark. Headlights stabbed the darkness, and behind the headlights were large trucks. They looked like the kind the Mexican Army used to transport troops. Four trucks turned into the parking lot. As I watched from the darkness, the trucks ground to a halt and men began to pour out of the back of them, light reflecting off their rifles.

Men were shouting and a woman started screaming. People began to run out of the bar and jump out of the windows. The world was dissolving.

I fumbled with the ropes. They were poorly tied, but I was nervous and it took me what seemed like a long time. Señora Ramirez alternated between pleading and sobbing. At last I got the ropes untied. I helped her to her feet, but her legs were trembling and she had to lean against me to keep from falling. As I undid the buttons of my shirt, I could hear a man deeper in the shadows cursing calmly and steadily without repeating himself. After some maneuvering, we got the shirt on her and began to pick our way through the underbrush. Her body was soft and heavy against me and I wondered if Gomez was still waiting for me. Then I wondered what he would say. In the provocative darkness I smiled to my sad self.

Fifty-nine

The night seemed immense. I couldn't see anything further than three feet away. I could hear only the wind. Then the wind blew a hole in the clouds, and moonlight and starlight shot through, splattering on the upwardly sloping ground before me. I'd drifted more east than I wanted and began to work my way west.

When the wind paused, as though catching its breath, I could hear noises off to my left. Barefooted, Señora Ramirez stepped on a rock and moaned. I covered her mouth with a hand and listened, straining to hear above my own labored breathing.

Sounds grew louder and shadows raced across a patch of open ground, angling across our path. I called Gomez's name, but the wind was rising again and it caught the word and carried it away.

At the edge of vision there was a sudden flash of light. Orange flames were dancing across the roof of the bar. Smoke spiraled thickly upward. I could hear the crack and pops of burning timbers, followed by the higher, sharper report of a rifle. Exposed on the top of the slope, I hurried us down the other side. Señora Ramirez stumbled over vines and cursed under her breath whenever she stepped on something sharp.

Halfway down the slope I saw him. He was running hard, long hair flying out behind him. His gun was in his right hand. Head down, he headed straight for us. I drug the Colt out.

Twenty feet away he must have seen my shadow or smelled my fear. Instincts took over and he veered to his right, raising his head as he ran.

Suddenly he stopped and the gun rose in his hand, black, obscene. I stared into the round black eye of his gun and listened to the Leather Man's ragged breathing. The Colt felt like an anvil in my hand, but I kept it still, pointed directly at the Leather Man's chest.

The rise of hard ground was graveyard quiet. The Leather Man crab-walked to his left. His gun stayed pointed at my head and, except for a quick glance at the naked señora, his eyes never left my face.

"I know you, don't I?"

"We've met." I tried to sound tough, but I could detect a quiver in my voice. My knees were shaking. I told myself it was because I was tired.

"Yeah, I remember you. You crossed for me a while back. What are you doing down here again?" He jerked his head at Señora Ramirez, "And what in the hell are you doing with her? She's more trouble than you can handle, at least her husband is."

Shouts rose off to my left and behind me, gathering like angry vultures. Gunfire burst out again and a man screamed. The Leather Man's eyes wavered, flitted in the direction of the gunfire then came back to the gun in my hand.

Sweat trickled down my back and my eyes blinked whether I wanted them to or not. I tried to look unconcerned. "Looks to me as if you are the one who's got more trouble than he can handle," I said. "Ramirez is gone. He hightailed it out of here in his Mercedes five minutes ahead of the cavalry."

"Bastard rat," the Leather Man said. "Yeah, you're right. I'm getting out of here." He took one step back and paused, the gun still high in his hand. "Forget you ever saw me. You ever remember and start talking, I'll kill you. Even if it takes me the rest of my life. Count on that, motherfucker."

"I've never even seen you."

He stared at my face, as though he were memorizing every square inch, then backed into the darkness. The last I saw of him was his long, dirty-blonde hair steaming in the moonlight as he crested a ridge thirty yards away. Only then did I stuff the Colt back in the waistband of my jeans.

The shouts were louder, closer, and the gunfire heavier. Suddenly a scream rose above them. Grabbing the señora by the arm, I pulled us down the slope, going as hard as we could, away from the flames, the gunfire, and the screams.

At the bottom of the hill something was crawling. Three strides later I could see it was a man, half obscured by the underbrush, dragging one leg awkwardly. For a second I thought it was Gomez and my stomach rolled over. Another stride and I could see it was Stan.

He heard us coming and stopped. Flames were finger painting the sky and his face was gold and orange in their reflection. Light flooded across the ground as though Goeteza had transformed into pure fire. Stan looked at Señora Ramirez, then at me. His eyes grew wide with surprise, then dull with pain. They locked onto mine, moving with me as I moved as though he were hypnotized.

"Well, Stanley, looks like your little world is burning down."

"It's not my world," he grunted. "I was never involved, not really."

"Yeah, like you weren't involved with my wife, like you weren't involved in trying to make me disappear in Nogales."

He tried to smile. In the reflected firelight, his lips were grotesque. "We tried to find you. Really we did. We looked for days. Even hired a detective."

"Yeah, right. You two knew where to look for me all along. If I didn't get myself killed in some alley, Ramirez's camp for naughty boys was the perfect place. I saw who you were with tonight, Stan, so don't give me that detective shit. I'm not as fucking dumb as you and Jolene think I am. If you ever see her again, tell her that for old drunk Paul. Then tell her to jump off the highest cliff she can find, without a parachute."

I gave Stan the phoniest smile I could muster. I kept expecting the señora to say something, but she had gone silent and slipped in close behind me. I could feel her breath on the back of my neck.

"See you, Stan."

"Don't go. Please don't go. I'm shot. They got me in the leg."

"So, lie still and wait. You won't die, at least not before the army finds you."

"Don't go. Don't go. Don't leave me. Don't leave me, Paul. Don't leave me, you bastard. I'm hurt. I'm shot. I'll die out here. You bastard—"

His words drifted into the darkness as we started moving away. Soon only the wind and the crackling of the flames were audible. Clouds covered the moon. Gunfire was sporadic and I told myself to be strong a little longer. I got my arms around the señora and hustled us on. In the dark night of Mexico, Gomez was waiting somewhere and I intended to find him.

Señora Ramirez murmured something about her feet hurting, but I ignored her and listened to the wind. After a while she started crying. I tried to hear only the wind, but that small voice that was forever inside me was telling truths that frightened me.

Slowly the screams and shouts ceased and the gunfire died away. When the wind eased, I could hear only the sound of our footsteps on the hard ground, punctuated by the gentle sobs of Señora Ramirez. Once, I paused and looked back, but all I could see was a dull orange glow. The clouds broke apart and silver light flowed like water, highlighting gnarly trees that grew on the high ground.

I was very tired and I wanted a drink, but Gomez was on my mind and I told myself to suck it up. Legs aching, I pushed on through the moonlight, not caring if the señora was following. At times, I could hear her moving through the undergrowth. Other times, I could hear her mumbling softly or crying a little. I was too tired to care. My head hurt and I was worried sick about Gomez and I wanted a big, smooth glass of whiskey so badly my throat ached.

Deep in that special place inside me, I swore again I'd never take another drink. I marched through the night, carrying all my burdens, including those damn zombies who never surrendered, my eyes searching the horizon for the first true light of the new day.

Sixty

On the seventh day we crossed the river at dawn, fording where the trees grew thick and dark in the fertile soil of the Promised Land. No one stepped out of the mists on the far bank to challenge us. There was no border patrol, no Arizona Vigilantes, no men with secret tomato codes.

We stood on the bank in the morning sun, staring back at Mexico. Gomez was silent, a faraway look in his eyes, and I figured he was thinking of his parents. His wife watched him with moist brown eyes. Her bottom lip was quivering and her hands dry-washed themselves in the clear cool light of morning. She looked at me and smiled, and I recalled our Gary Cooper conversations. I gave her my best cowboy grin and a brief salute. Coop would have been proud.

Señora Ramirez only stared at the ground and murmured to herself in Spanish. I hadn't wanted to cross with her, but she'd begged us not to leave her, refusing to eat or change out of the too short, patched dress Señora Gomez had given her. She said she had to perform penance. She pointed out she had no money and no friends, and that her husband had not come for her. By then, we all knew he wouldn't. I had no words to comfort her, but when Gomez had asked me to let her accompany us, I couldn't refuse him.

The sun grew stronger. Sweat formed on my forehead and the birds grew still in the trees. I patted Gomez on his shoulder. "Soon, you can send for them."

He was silent. His eyes were dark and somber, seeing something I could only guess at. He was so still I wondered if he'd even heard me. He turned and smiled. "Yes, that I will do, *Señor* Hampton. That I will do."

"It's a hard day's walk to the meeting place," I said. "Morning is getting some age on her. We'd better start moving."

He nodded, but didn't move. "This woman, this Karen, she will meet us there. You are sure?"

"I telephoned her collect from Treolies and she accepted the charges. She said she would meet us there with your sons. She wouldn't lie to me."

Gomez smiled. "My sons, my sons," he said and then he put his arm around his wife's shoulders and they turned and started walking north. I watched them until Señora Ramirez stepped into my line of sight.

Messages were swimming in her dark eyes, but I wasn't intelligent enough, or sensitive enough, to decipher any of them. For what seemed like a long time, we stood staring at each other, close enough to touch, but as distant as though we had come from separate planets. We were no longer enemies, nor would we ever be friends. We'd passed in a dark Mexican night, shared strange encounters, and now we were parting, traveling separate paths.

Without speaking, she touched my cheek with a large smooth palm. For a single heartbeat, she held it there, then turned and started walking after the others. She never looked back. I sent her one of my unearned blessings.

When Gomez and the women were more shadows than substance, I pivoted and stood on the riverbank with the young sun shining fresh and hot against my face, gazing for a final moment at Mexico, remembering the fat man with the turtles, and the woman who would not lie to me as we danced, and Pedro Romero and his zombies, and the old man who could always get alcohol, and finally Wilson. I saluted them all. Part of each one of them was now part of me.

Smiling to my crazy self, I spun on a heel and started walking toward the line of trees shimmering in the clear, holy morning.

Meet Chris Helvey

Chris Helvey's short stories have been published by numerous reviews and journals since 1997. He is the author of the Wings ePress novel *Yard Man,* as well as the novels *Snapshot* and *Whose Name I Did Not Know,* and the short story collections *One More Round* and *Claw Hammer.* He currently serves as editor in chief of *Trajectory Journal.*

Other Works From The Pen Of Chris Helvey

Yard Man - Judas Cain is just trying to survive the Great Depression—instead he finds a job he doesn't want and a love he never imagined.

Visit Our Website

For The Full Inventory
Of Quality Books:

Wings ePress, Inc

Quality trade paperbacks and downloads
in multiple formats,
in genres ranging from light romantic comedy to general fiction and
horror.
Wings has something for every reader's taste.
Visit the website, then bookmark it.
We add new titles each month!

Wings ePress Inc.
3000 N. Rock Road
Newton, KS 67114